CONFESSIONS
OF AN
ENGLISH MAID

AND OTHER DELIGHTS

CONFESSIONS
OF AN
ENGLISH MAID

AND OTHER DELIGHTS

ANONYMOUS

CARROLL & GRAF PUBLISHERS, INC.
NEW YORK

First Carroll & Graf edition 1995
Second Carroll & Graf edition 1999

Carroll & Graf Publishers, Inc.
19 West 21st Street
New York, NY 10010-6805

ISBN: 0-7867-0642-2

Manufactured in the United States of America

Confessions
of an
English Maid

CHAPTER ONE

During the course of the years in which I have been more or less closely associated with other prostitutes, I have frequently listened to explanations as to just what this one or that owed her degradation; the particular villainy to which she attributed her advent into a life of shame. The usual story is one of seduction by a lover under the inevitable extenuating circumstance of "before I really knew anything," with the occasional variation, "he put something in my drink, and when I came to . . ." or, "he was stronger than I was and I couldn't do anything." In these glib stories, in which none but the inconsequential details vary, the man is always to blame and the girl is never a willing accomplice. She is always, by artifice, force or deception, and subsequent abandonment, the victim of some man's depravity.

I confess that I have listened to these tales and even witnessed a few tears of self-pity, with a certain amount of skepticism. In thinking back over my own life I can find nothing which would serve as a valid excuse to shift upon somebody else the responsibility of my own condition, nor can I in justice accuse any man of having instigated my moral degradation, although the number of those who have taken advantage of my voluntary delinquency is legion. True, were I to hypocritically search for some contributing factor with which to justify myself in my own mind or in the minds of others, I might place some blame upon the environment under which I was raised as a child, yet, a conscientious analysis of my subsequent life leads me to no other conclusion than that had these conditions been entirely normal I would still, just as water seeks its level, have drifted into a life analogous to that in which you find me.

I do not believe that character is made by environment or training. I am something of a fatalist and it is my conviction that the seeds of goodness or badness, kindness or malevolence, virtue or viciousness, are implanted in the soul right from the beginning, and while some slight modifications either for better or for worse may be possible under varying circumstances, the net result will not be greatly changed.

In my childhood days I knew two brothers, sons of affluent parents highly respected in the community. These two boys were raised under the most favorable home and moral environment possible to imagine. The elder, always the personification of honor and circumspection, occupies a position of trust high in the affairs of the nation. The younger child of the same parents, raised under exactly the same conditions and influences, early in life manifested all the characteristics of an irresponsible nature and is today being sought for his participation in a robbery which culminated in murder. I know of other such instances.

I was seduced by no man, but I managed to get rid of my maidenhead before I was twelve years old. By the time I was fourteen I had been fucked by a dozen young fellows and several older men. I wasn't infatuated or deceived or coerced. I let them fuck me because it felt nice, because I liked it, and even the fact that shillings and even larger sums of money could be easily and pleasantly acquired didn't play any very important part in my complacency.

I was eight and Rene, my foster brother, ten when mutual curiosity about each other's little sexual attributes first began to take the form of childish efforts to unravel Nature's mysteries. These efforts, which at first did not pass much beyond the observational stage, with an occasional touching and fingering, were inspired more by curiosity than sexual promptings; nevertheless, we sensed more elements of forbidden fruit and exercised considerable caution in hiding ourselves when the impulse was upon us to gratify our curiosity.

Under the roof of our home was an attic which was used as a sort of storeroom for discarded furniture and other odds and ends. Rene and I converted it into a species of playhouse. Access to this attic was gained by a steep and narrow stairway enclosed between dark walls, and our parents rarely climbed these stairs, and would have given us ample warning by their footsteps had it occurred to them to do so; we felt reasonably secure, and always repaired to this obscure hideaway when the mood to do something naughty was upon us.

Mamma Agnes was not my real mother. My own mother had died when I was four years old. With the practical philosophy of a widower left with a small child on his hands, Papa lost no time in acquiring a new wife, and in less than six months I had a mamma and a stepbrother two years older than myself.

I lay neither censure nor praise at the feet of Mamma Agnes. She was kind to me in an indifferent way and I believe she cared as much for me as she did for her own child, Rene. She was simply not the maternal type, and though she accepted the material obligations which our presence represented uncomplainingly and kept us clean and well fed, there existed an almost complete absence of anything in the nature of moral or spiritual upbringing. We were punished occasionally, but only when our misbehavior constituted an annoyance to others.

For two years Rene and I slept in the same bed. When I was about six I remember hearing Papa tell Mamma Agnes that we were too big to be sleeping together. Mamma Agnes made some protest which I didn't understand, but the next night a bed was arranged for Rene in another room and thereafter we slept apart. I missed feeling Rene's warm little body close to mine in the night and wanted to know why we were not to sleep together anymore. Mamma Agnes made an evasive explanation. "It isn't nice for boys and girls to sleep together," was the tactless reply which only served to kindle the restless fires of curiosity. During the next year or two some light, still of an obscure nature, was thrown on the subject by other children who were not adverse to sharing their knowledge with us.

I was not supposed to see Rene's dickey, and he likewise was not supposed to see my cunny. This was the sum and substance, apparently, of the incomprehensible order of things which had abruptly terminated our bedfellowship. And immediately we both began to feel the itch to see what we were not supposed to see, and to which we had paid but scant attention when the opportunity had been freely at hand and unforbidden.

The juvenile soul thirsts for knowledge—of a certain kind. What was the real basis of all this sly mystery about little boys' dickies and little girls' cunnies? "A boy puts his dickey in a girl's cunny," said one. "That's the way you get babies, only you can't have a baby until you're married." "When you rub your cunny it gives you a nice feeling," said another.

In the security of our attic hideaway Rene and I diligently sought the answer to the mystery. The erstwhile playroom was converted into a juvenile brothel. We dragged an ancient mattress from behind an accumulation of wrecked furniture and laid it out on the floor. I straddled out on this mattress with my legs apart while Rene looked and fingered until his curiosity was temporarily satisfied and I was compensated by being permitted to look at and squeeze his little dickey. It was a source of never-ending wonder to watch it go through its erotic evolutions, expanding, swelling, hardening, until it projected stiffly and rigidly forward. I tried to see whether, by holding it tightly in my fist, I could prevent it from getting big, but in my grasp it seemed to grow even faster, easily displacing my clenched fingers and causing me curious, shivery sensations.

Time and time again we tried to effect actual copulation, but there was something amiss, and the failure puzzled us. The playing, looking and fingering were pleasant, but there was something lacking, something sweet, something elusive which we sensed was close at hand but which still eluded us.

Picture to yourself a group of twenty happy, carefree youngsters of both sexes, ages ranging from eight to twelve, their strident little voices ringing out in careless abandon as they pursue their innocent amusements, converting a refuse-strewn lot into an enchanted fairyland. Even the bloated loafers and derelicts of the street who cast a casual glance at the little innocents must not fail to feel a twinge of sentimentality.

> London Bridge is falling down,
> Falling down, falling down,
> London Bridge is falling down,
> My fair lay-dee.

But, hark! There is more to the song. The shriller masculine voices take the ascendancy, and little girls are heard only in a confusion of laughter and giggling.

> Madge and Jerry are having a suck,
> Having a suck, having a suck,

Madge and Jerry are having a suck,
My fair lay-dee.
After the suck they'll have a fuck,
Oh, what luck, oh, what luck,
After the suck, they'll have a fuck,
My fair lay-dee

Out of a house whose open windows are in close proximity to the merrymakers bursts an old Irish woman, brandishing a broom, her wrinkled face suffused with rage.

"Git out o'here ye narsty little spalpeens or I'll swab yer dirty, stinkin' mouths fer ye, blarsted little imps o'Satan!" she screams as twenty pair of feet fly in twenty different directions under the menace of the broom in the hands of the scandalized old beldame.

When I was about eleven, Pap's earning capacity was so reduced by drunkenness that Mamma Agnes was obliged to take in a boarder. The best room of the house, the one which had formerly served as a parlor, was converted to the purpose and rented to a Mr. Peters.

Mr. Peters, a watchmaker by occupation, was a gentleman of forty-five or thereabouts who radiated jollity and good nature and who professed a great love for children. He took an immediate fancy to me and soon pennies and farthings began coming my way in an abundance I had never before known. Mr. Peters constantly called on me to run trifling errands for him, a package of fags, a penny paper, a bottle of ale, and these small services were invariably rewarded with some fulsome compliment, an affectionate pat on the cheek and a coin of modest denomination.

As our friendship progressed, his amiable affection took the form of playful caresses, squeezings, and pettings. This did not trouble me and I was observant enough to note that the affectionate overtures were more pronounced and subsequently more remunerative when we were alone. So I was soon watching for opportunities to be near him when no one else was around, especially when Mamma Agnes was out with her shopping basket.

On such occasions he took me in his lap and as his hands roved ceaselessly over my body he filled my ears with a running fire of pleasant flattery. My legs seemed to be the principal objects of his admiration and as he pinched and squeezed them playfully to emphasize his words, his good-natured, florid face would become still more florid and little beads of perspiration would appear on his forehead.

One day Mr. Peters surprised me with the following observation:

"Well, bless me, if our little Jessie isn't getting prettier and prettier ever day. Such legs . . . such legs. Do you know," he continued, as he passed his hands appraisingly down over my hips and thighs, "I have a suspicion that you aren't really a girl at all. Girls don't have such fine legs as these. I'll bet you're a boy instead of a girl."

"Boys don't wear dresses or have long hair," I exclaimed.

"A-a-a-h!" he answered, with a knowing look, shaking his finger skeptically in my face, "that could be just to fool people! A boy could wear dresses and let his hair grow long. Yes . . ." he mused abstractedly, "the more I think about it, the more I believe you're really a boy dressed in girl's clothes."

"I am so a girl!" I protested indignantly.

"I've had my suspicions for a long time," he continued, ignoring my protestations. "Tell you what," he added confidentially, "I'll lay you a shilling you're really a boy!"

"Very well!" I exclaimed, excitedly. "You can ask Mamma Agnes!"

"Oh, no!" he objected hastily. "She's not here now and besides she might be on your side and say you're a girl anyway."

"Well, who are you going to ask?"

"Hum-m-m-m-m," he murmured, pausing in thoughtful

meditation. "There ought to be some way we could settle the bet without asking anybody."

I waited expectantly.

"Ha! I've got it!" he exclaimed, as a happy solution of the perplexing problem suddenly occurred to him. "But remember now, if I win you must pay me the next shilling you get! I've got mine right here now to pay you if I lose!" And he fished a shiny new shilling from his pocket and displayed it before my eyes.

"Yes, yes!" I answered eagerly. "I'll pay you if I lose! The very next shilling I get! How are you going to tell?"

"Why, that's easy," he replied. "Funny we didn't think of it at first. Boys have a . . . ah . . . a little sort of dangle between this legs . . . right there . . . and girls haven't any. Now all you have to do is just unfasten your panties and we'll take a peek. And remember, if you've got a dangle, like I think you have, you must pay me the next shilling you get. I'll trust you for it!"

Although I was momentarily confounded by this bizarre but quite obvious method of resolving the question, my eagerness to prove the injustice of his accusation, coupled with the prospect of so easily gaining a shilling, outweighed any small scruples I may have felt about exposing my cunny to him, and without a word I raised my short dress, unfastened my panties and pulled them down low enough to reveal the deciding factor between femininity and masculinity.

Somewhat to my surprise Mr. Peters' doubts were not immediately dispelled. His flushed face took on a deeper hue and he seemed to be having some difficulty in speaking. He suggested that I remove my panties entirely so he could see better and when this was done it was necessary for him to make a most thorough inspection before he was finally convinced that I didn't have a dangle hidden between my thighs.

After quite a lengthy examination, during which he

seemed almost on the point of suffocation as his fingers lingered about my cunny, pressing, feeling, exploring, he sighed deeply and reluctantly conceded his defeat, confessing himself in error. My sex was vindicated, established and proved beyond any reasonable question and his repentant sorrow at having doubted it resulted in an extra shilling in addition to the one originally posted.

When Rene came home I jubilantly displayed the two pieces of silver, explained their origin and told him how Mr. Peters had even thought I might have a dangle tucked up inside my cunny. My account of the incident seemed to make him restive and a few minutes later he suggested that we go up to the attic to play.

The truth was that Mr. Peters' insistent feeling and fingering had left me with an odd sort of itching in my cunny. It felt excessively moist and hot, and I agreed to Rene's suggestion with alacrity. We slipped upstairs and, following our usual routine, I took off my panties and lay down on my back on the old mattress with my knees up and widely apart while Rene nudged and punched at me with his stiff little pintle.

His erratic movements frequently brought the tip against the upper part of my cunny and each time it pressed or rubbed against a certain spot I felt an agreeable tremor. To capture this elusive sweetness I reached down and, taking his dickey in my fingers, I held it against the sensitive spot. There was a little bump of flesh there which swelled and twitched and instinctively I rubbed the end of his dickey against it. The pleasant feeling again permeated the whole lower part of my body, sending such a delicious radiation surging through my nerves that I trembled violently. The sensation culminated with a sudden burst of delight which caused me to moan and gasp in ecstasy. I had experienced my first real orgasm.

I had always loved and admired my foster brother Rene. He was handsomer than most boys. He had beautiful dark brown curly hair and his skin was white and smooth. When he effected my first orgasm something was awakened in me which changed the affection to complete adoration. I do not think I have ever loved anyone more, or even as much as I loved Rene.

I gave him one of the shillings I had won so easily, and as I continued to expiate on Mr. Peters' supreme ignorance, he threw me a pitying look and exclaimed:

"Are you balmy? He knew you were a girl! He just wanted to get to look at your cunny."

The light dawned on me, but the two shillings dimmed any feeling of chagrin, and even a hazy thought of future exploitation half-formed itself in my mind. I had long since sensed the fact that Mr. Peters' interest in me was rather more than casual. If he had given me the two shillings just to look at my cunny, maybe he might want to look at it again sometime.

There was probably something in my eyes which betrayed this expectation to Mr. Peters, for when I again had an opportunity to slip into his room, he arose hastily and snapped the catch on the door. Returning to his chair he drew me between his knees and as I stood there he passed his hands caressingly down over my body from my armpits to my knees, and when they ascended they were under my dress instead of outside. He stroked my bare thighs above the tops of my stockings and all the while a ceaseless flow of words fell from his lips as though with this he sought to distract my attention from the movement of his hands.

"Well, well, well, who's here but pretty little Jessie, come to cheer up poor old lonely Peters. My sweet little cabbage. She's lonely, too. Mamma Agnes is gone and Jessie's all alone in the big house . . . isn't she . . . ?" He paused, waiting for my nodded confirmation. "Well, well, well. We'll have a nice little chat in here all by ourselves."

His hands had worked up inside the loose legs of my

panties and his fingers were squeezing the cheeks of my bottom.

"Such a pretty, clever little girl . . . such legs . . ."

He withdrew his hands after a final affectionate squeeze and raised them to the elastic band which sustained my panties about my waist, and in a moment I felt them being slipped down over my hips.

I waited expectantly.

When the panties were down and hanging loosely about my knees, Mr. Peters put an arm around me, drew me closer, and the next instant his hand was cupped over my cunny. This maneuver surprised me somewhat, for I supposed he intended to look at it again. But no, something different was going to happen. The hand pressed over my cunny began to move with a gentle grinding motion, and almost at once those delicious feelings which the tip of Rene's dickey had previously evoked began again. Involuntarily, I glanced toward Mr. Peters' lap. Along the inside length of his trouser leg was an enormous swelling.

As I fixed my astonished gaze on it I could see the cloth jerking under the spasmodic expansions and contractions underneath. But the rapidly increasing intensity of the pleasurable sensations which were now tingling through my body under Mr. Peters' manipulations soon caused me to forget everything else. As the climax approached my knees began to tremble and when it reached its zenith, releasing those indescribably delicious thrills to go shooting through my body, I swayed dizzily. Mr. Peters was still talking, but I no longer knew what he was saying.

When Rene came home I had another shilling to show him. He listened attentively to my account of just what had happened and wanted me to show him exactly what Mr. Peters had done to me. I took off my panties and placed his hand in the same position in which Mr. Peters had held his. Although the contact of Rene's soft little hand was much more agreeable than Mr. Peters' hard and calloused palm, my sexual orgasm, probably exhausted by the thorough masturbating I had undergone, refused to respond to Rene's efforts.

However, his own emotions were aroused by the pantomime and, yielding to his command, I lay down on the mattress and let him straddle me while he nuzzled and poked at my cunny with his little cock. I took it in my fingers to press it against the spot which was most responsive to its touch and it was while holding it thus that Rene's movements suddenly became more precipitate.

"Squeeze it tight!" he gasped.

I turned my eyes toward his face. It was strained and tense and his breath was short and panting. Something of his emotion infected me and prompted quite by instinct, I clutched his stiff little dickey tighter and began to work it with my fingers. It was no longer even in contact with my cunny but sliding in and out of my clenched fist.

His legs stiffened rigidly and his movements, except for a final convulsive shudder, ceased. At the same instant I sensed the presence of some warm, moist substance in my hand. I looked at it wonderingly and found my palm and fingers sticky with a milky, viscid fluid.

One night, a week or so later, Rene and I were alone in the house. Papa rarely came in before midnight and was generally so tipsy that Mamma Agnes would have to put him to bed. On this occasion she had gone to visit a sick friend and did not expect to return until quite late. Mr. Peters had heard something of this and had whispered to me that I should not go to bed until he returned as he was sure he would want me to go on an errand for him.

He came in about nine o'clock and after confirming Mamma Agnes' absence, sent me to the corner to get a paper with instructions to bring it to his room when I came back. I had already communicated to Rene my suspicion that Mr. Peters would "do something" to me when I took the paper into his room, and Rene was going to peek through the keyhole. It even occurred to me to take off my panties before going in.

My juvenile intuition was quite correct and Mr. Peters masturbated me again while I stood between his knees holding my dress up and my foster brother Rene crouched outside the door watching through the keyhole.

Poor Mr. Peters. He never attempted to do anything except play with me in this fashion and whether it was in his mind to venture further as my sexual instincts unfolded will never be known, for one day, less than three months after his first tentative overture, he was knocked down by an omnibus and carried to a hospital where he died without ever regaining consciousness. I cried heartily when it was known that we would never see him again and his simple effects were packed up for removal. In my estimation he was a kindly and generous soul who had been the fount of many blessings.

A short time after Mr. Peters' departure, a neighborhood scandal was bruited about among the residents of the vicinity. Down the street, in the big house on the corner, lived a retired sea captain and his rather large family. They were rated as well-to-do and employed a maid-servant, a cute little thing whose trim, silk-clad legs, black uniform and lace-edged apron I had always secretly envied.

Among the younger children of his household was a boy named Leonard and a girl named Maisie. Leonard was about the same age as Rene, but was undersized and wore glasses which gave his wizened countenance a peculiarly owlish aspect. Maisie was very pretty. She was two years younger than I. Both these children were precocious. It was said that Maisie would show her cunny to any boy who wanted to see it and Leonard bragged that he fucked the maidservant whenever he felt like it. There was some doubt as to the veracity of this, but the doubt was dispelled abruptly when the maidservant suddenly disappeared and the older children of the household whispered into the ears of their special confidants that she had been summarily dismissed after having been caught in the very act of sucking Leonard's dickey while supposed to be supervising his bath.

"She had it right in her mouth when Mamma caught her!" they whispered impressively.

Rene pressed Leonard for details when the opportunity later presented itself, and listened to an entirely frank exposition of the affair, which he then communicated to me.

The liaison with the maidservant had been started several months previously by the versatile little maid herself. Each night, on tucking him into bed, she had been in the habit of putting her hand under the covers to see whether he had a hard-on. Inasmuch as such was almost invariably the case, and the condition not being favorable in her opinion to sound sleep, her remedy was to reduce the rigidity by means of a hand message to make it "lie down and go to sleep."

One night she told Leonard that her efforts to make him sleepy were having a contrary effect on her and that she couldn't go to sleep for hours after having put him to sleep. There was a way both could have their sleeplessness cured. She would slip into his room later that night after everybody was in bed and explain it to him. She squeezed his dickey to make sure it was in its usual state of erection but refrained from taking the customary measures to make it lie down.

When all was quiet in the household she slipped into his room like a little ghost in her white nightgown, threw the covers back and lay down by him. Taking his dickey in one hand she worked it until it was in its maximum state of rigidity. With the other she guided his fingers between her legs and with various motions and whispered instructions showed him how to reciprocate the massage.

"Her cunny has hair all around it, just like a grown-up person," confided Leonard.

After a while she stopped the rubbing and told him to get on top of her. When he was in the proper position she started his dickey in the right direction and, poppo! It went, inside, just like that.

At this juncture in the recital, Rene interrupted to clear up a confusing point. Had Leonard's dickey gone clear in, or had it just sort of rubbed along her cunny?

Emphatically, it had gone in, entirely and completely, not a bit stayed outside. He was sure and specific on this point. It was dark that time, but they had done it subsequently in the daytime when he could even look down and see it while it was going in and out, and it absolutely went clear in.

The story of Leonard's relation with the maidservant progressed from frigging to fucking and finally to the last act, in which the unexpected entry of his mother into the bathroom while he was enjoying, and not for the first time, the delights of being sucked off by the versatile maid had brought an end to the fun.

Now the maid was gone and he was obliged to massage his dickey for himself at night in order to make it lie down and go to sleep.

The sucking part was rather incomprehensible to Rene and me. We were still rank novices in the arts of love and had much to learn. It was a cause of preoccupation to us that we hadn't been able to approximate anything like the success Leonard and the maidservant had achieved. Rene's dickey simply couldn't find its way in. We knew in theory that it should, and we had both peered and looked and fingered in an effort to find a hole big enough. There didn't seem to be any, or if there was, it was closed up very tightly.

With the candidness of youth Rene confided the difficulty to Leonard and Leonard promptly offered to show

him how to do it. I never objected to anything Rene
proposed, and submitted myself obediently to the demonstration. Leonard knew no more about maidenheads than
Rene but he had the confidence which comes with experience and when I took off my panties and lay down on the
mattress he placed himself between my knees and got his
dickey which, despite his slighter stature, was fully as big
as Rene's, against my cunny. He gave a lunge, and a
shriek escaped my lips which, had there been anyone else
in the house at the time, would have brought an investigation. His dickey had gone in all right, but the sensation I
experienced was far from being conducive to further
experimentation. After the first shriek of pain I began to
cry, the tears rolled down my cheeks and I struggled to
release myself.

Panic-stricken at the unexpected results, Leonard jerked
away from me and his dickey came out stained with a
reddish fluid and a few drops trickled down the inside of
my thighs. Leonard was so frightened that he fled from the
scene, leaving Rene and me alone.

The pain was only momentary and as it died away I
stopped crying, but gazed with fright at the spots of blood
which stained the white flesh between my thighs. Rene
dabbed at them nervously with his handkerchief, and
when no more appeared some of our assurance returned,
but I was aggrieved because of the stab of pain I had
suffered. When I stood up a feeling of soreness in my
sexual parts was very pronounced. Fortunately, Mamma
Agnes made no embarrassing inquiries when she found me
in bed at an hour much earlier than my accustomed one,
and by the following day the soreness had mostly passed
away.

Thus I lost my maidenhead with pleasure neither to
myself nor to my violator.

Having my hymen punched out in so disagreeable a
manner without knowing exactly what had happened ex-

cept that it was something decidedly unpleasant resulted in a reluctance on my part to lend myself to further exploitations which lasted for some weeks and might have endured longer had not my emotions been stimulated anew by a curious incident.

While rummaging through a pile of trash, old newspapers and discarded magazines which had been swept out of a long-vacant house nearby, Rene found a little green-covered book which, on being opened, disclosed to his startled eyes a picture which confirmed the basic theory of love. It was a rather neatly executed sketch showing a beautiful young lady reclining upon a grassy mound under a tree. Her dresses were drawn up, she had no parties on, and above the edge of her disordered and half-open bodice peeped a pair of bubbies of most astonishing proportions.

Between her thighs, half-lying, half-kneeling, with one of her silk clad legs thrown over his hips, was a young boy. From his middle projected a dickey which penetrated and was lost to sight for half its length in her cunny, the protruding lips of which were plainly indicated just below a profusion of curly black hair.

As soon as he recovered from the shock this picture caused him, Rene streaked for home and excitedly signaled for me to follow him to the attic. Breathlessly we gazed at the picture, then turned our attention to the text which accompanied it. As we devoured the printed pages I became aware of that moist, swollen, itchy feeling in my cunny. The desire to experience anew the delicious sensations the tip of Rene's dickey had afforded me began to surge through me and grow more and more insistant as we slowly digested the revelations contained in the booklet and which were phrased quite within our powers of comprehension.

The title which graced the story was: "The Passionate Governess, or Hubert's First Fuck." Before that book finally left our possession we had read it so many times either of us could have recited it word for word by memory.

It was about a beautiful young governess in a wealthy home who entered into amorous adventures with one of her charges, Hubert, a boy of fifteen. After a number of tantalizing episodes, in one of which she catches Hubert peeking through the keyhole and masturbating himself while she is bathing, she decided to gratify his curiosity and save him from the vice of masturbation by letting him have sexual intercourse with her.

The scene chosen for the sweet lesson in love is a beautiful sylvan glade reached by crossing a lake in a rowboat. As the pretty governess sits in the prow of the boat with Hubert at the oars facing her, she carelessly permits her skirts to become so elevated above her knees that Hubert is afforded a delightful opportunity to peek between her legs and get teasing glimpses of the charms only half concealed under the frilly lace of her panties. Under the stimulation of this enticing sight he is in a suitable condition for his initiation in the rites of love.

After exciting preliminaries in which passionate kisses, caresses and fondling of each other's sexual parts are indulged in, and during which Hubert's curiosity regarding the more intimate aspects of feminine anatomy is completely satisfied, the real initiation takes place as shown in the illustration, and Hubert learns that the delights attendant to plunging his dickey into the mossy glen between a pretty girl's legs are far superior to those he had formerly experienced in masturbation.

It was a story with a moral, as you will have observed, intended to discourage young people from practicing self-abuse.

When we had finished the last page I felt moist and sticky and it seemed to me that my panties were wet. Rene's trousers were jutted out in front in a way which showed what effect the story had had on him.

He looked at me, and I looked at him.

"Shall we?" he whispered.

"Yes!" I answered, all recollection of the pain I had suffered the last time this attic had been used for purposes of fornication completely obliterated.

While Rene was unfastening his trousers I kicked off my panties and lay down on the soft mattress. My emotions had been greatly excited by the vivid little story and the first touches of Rene's dickey against the moist flesh of my cunny were indescribably sweet. For a few moments I lay there languidly thrilling to the soft friction and pressure as the tip of his dickey roved about over the sensitive area like a person groping for a door in the dark. But suddenly I stiffened in alarm for I distinctly felt the constriction which accompanied an actual penetration and which brought back to my consciousness what had happened before.

With muscles tensed in readiness to free myself with the first indication of pain I held my breath and waited. But there was no pain. To the contrary, the sensations I felt as Rene's dickey slipped further into the tight little hole were more agreeable than anything I had yet experienced.

I moaned, not with pain this time, but with delight, and the next moment, actuated by those natural instincts which need no previous experience nor teacher to guide, we were both frantically heaving our bottoms up and down in an effort to taste without delay the supreme delight of which the intoxicating thrills now tantalizing us were but the forerunners.

It comes but once in a lifetime, that indescribable, celestial glow which suffuses the souls and blends the bodies of lovers in unforgettable rapture, the first perfect sexual union of two beings who feel toward each other the tender passion of youth unmarred as yet by maturity's grosser complexities, and I affirm that those who have not tasted the fruit of love under these conditions have missed what is probably life's sweetest experience.

Rene and I had finally succeeded in unlocking the door which had hitherto obstructed our progress and with the unlocking, the latent germs of sensuousness, undoubtedly implanted in my very soul, sprang rapidly to full bloom. My ardor exceeded his, and it was I who now suggested and even begged frequent visits to the dusty attic where, with my panties off and my dress up or entirely removed, I writhed and suspired ecstatically in response to his vigorous thrusts. And, after a delicious orgasm had rewarded our efforts, I sighed inwardly with regret at the inevitable transformation his little cock underwent, dropping slowly but surely downward, its virile rigidity degenerating into a flaccid inertia which incapacitated it from further immediate use.

CHAPTER TWO

We now had plenty of time to be alone. There was no tenant for the extra room and Mamma Agnes was working out, with the result that we had several hours at our disposal between the time school was over and the hour at which she returned.

One day while we were standing on the sidewalk in front of the house Leonard appeared. Leonard, being entirely in Rene's confidence, had been appraised of the new state of affairs. He had intimated that he would like to try it again with me, which intimation I had listened to with no great enthusiasm, not through chaste reluctance, but because of the still lingering recollection of what had happened the first time.

I was still in ignorance of the exact physical facts and blamed him for the pain I had suffered. After some desultory conversation the enterprising Leonard suggested that the three of us proceed to the attic and have a hoochy dance. If you are familiar with juvenile parlance you may know that a hoochy dance is a simple but interesting form of entertainment in which the participants take off their clothes or "get naked" as they express it, and either with

21

hands joined or independently, will jump and cavort in a circle in a sort of primitive dance.

The element of attraction in this otherwise inspired diversion being that the boys can look at the girl's cunny and the girl can look at the boys' dickies. "And . . ." continued Leonard, after contributing this suggestion for a pleasant manner in which to pass the afternoon ". . . afterwards, you can fuck Jessie and I'll look, and then I'll fuck her and you can look."

As for me I was entirely agreeable to the first part of the program, and open to acceptance on the latter. It was Rene who interposed the logical objection that three of us weren't enough to properly stage a hoochy dance and we set to speculating as to the possibility of getting additional recruits. A hurried inventory of acceptable prospects only brought to light that this one was not at home, that one was sick, and another being "kept in" as a disciplinary measure, etc. It seemed there was little hope of rounding out the party on short notice and as a last recourse, Leonard rather apologetically suggested that maybe we'd be satisfied with Maisie.

This was a thought. Maisie had never participated in any of our doings because being younger than the rest of us we looked down upon her from the vantage of our maturity and wisdom as being just a kid. Nevertheless, Maisie had earned quite a reputation of her own and Leonard made no secret of the fact that before his ideas had been broadened by the vanished maidservant he had often diddled his little sister. He looked on hopefully while Rene studied the suggestion.

"Can you find her?" queried Rene.

"Sure I can, if you'll wait for me!" responded Leonard.

"Well, all right, then. Hurry up!"

In less than five minutes Leonard was back with Maisie in tow. She was a beautiful little thing and her eyes were shining with elation at the idea of being permitted to participate in older children's secrets.

"Now we're going to have a hoochy dance in our attic," explained Rene, addressing her. "If we let you come, you won't tell, will you?"

"No, no! I won't tell, ever!" she exclaimed vehemently. "I'm not a tattletale, am I, Lenny?" she added, turning to her brother for corroboration.

"No, she won't tell. She knows bloody well we'll knock her block off if she does!" responded Leonard with menacing emphasis.

Up to the attic we trooped and with much giggling and laughter began to undress. True to the usual formula of feminine hypocrisy, Maisie and I both made a great show of being concerned about the boys seeing us before we were "ready" and chided them hysterically for peeking while we were undressing.

This incitation had its natural effect upon the two boys and when we finally faced them, every stitch of clothing removed from our white little bodies, their cocks were standing out in stiff and rigid excitation.

We dragged the mattress to one side and, joining hands, began our hoochy dance, which consisted of nothing more complicated than swinging around in a circle and jumping up and down to the accompaniment of some ribald verses which we repeated over and over while the feminine eyes of the contiguity were fixed on jiggling dickies which bounced up and down with the violent movements of their owners, and the masculine ones on fat-lipped, hairless little cunnies.

When we had finally exhausted our acrobatic and musical repertoire we sat down, breathless, to rest and devise further exploits. Leonard wanted to fuck me while Rene and Maisie looked on, and then have the arrangement reversed with him and me the spectators while Rene fucked Maisie.

I protested that it hurt with him and expressed a preference to do it with Rene. My protest was partly actuated by something akin to jealousy. Somehow, I didn't exactly relish the idea of Rene fucking Maisie. But Rene intervened, and his word was law. It wouldn't hurt me now if I did it with Leonard. I was used to it now.

And so, with Leonard crouched on one side and I on the other, both watching with wide eyes, my foster brother Rene straddled Maisie's naked body, got his cock into a crevice which fitted around it like a tight little ring of flesh and, without a mishap or indication of discomfort on her part, fucked her until he had an orgasm.

Maisie never stirred or made a sound. She just lay there quietly, looking up into his face with her big, wondering eyes until he had finished and then calmly wriggled out from under him, sat up and murmured:

"Now it's our turn to watch!"

"Didn't it make you feel nice, Maisie?" I asked in some astonishment at her placidity. "When Rene and I do it, I just tremble all over, it makes me feel so good!"

"Sure, it makes me feel nice. I like to do it!" affirmed Maisie, but it was apparent that she had not yet experienced a real orgasm, even though Leonard had long since gotten her maidenhead out of the way.

With some inward misgivings I submitted to Leonard's ministrations and, of course, quickly discovered that my fears were groundless, for his dickey was in almost before I knew it, and this time without causing me any pain. Not counting Leonard's previous attempt, this was the first time I had been really fucked by any boy except Rene and, despite my affection for him, the novelty of a new cock had its emotional reaction and very quickly brought my quivering organism to that delicious borderland wherein for a few seconds the senses vibrate in ecstatic anticipation before definitely rendering their delicious offering. Another wiggle or two served to precipitate the ejaculation.

I was about twelve years old when what I have just related occurred. A few days later, on the way home from school, a boy named Bryan sidled up to me and rather timidly asked me if I would do it with him.

Bryan was a boy I would have described as nice. He was fourteen or fifteen, always dressed very neatly, had a pleasing personality and agreeable features. To say that I was not surprised at the overture would be an exaggeration, yet I was not displeased. If I had any doubts as to precisely what he meant by "do it" with him, the doubt was dispelled with one look into his flushed face and averted eyes and the uneasy, furtive glances he cast about as though to assure himself that there was no one else within hearing. Nevertheless, to delay an answer until I could gather my confused thoughts, I murmured innocently:

"Do what with you?"

"Aw, you know what I mean, Jessie!"

"No, I don't!"

"Something nice . . . like you did with Lenny Connors!"

His reference to Leonard caused me a slight chill of apprehension, but did not entirely prejudice me against him. He continued to coax, and I, beginning to enjoy the thrill of being begged for something with such humility, neither definitely denied nor promised my complacency.

"Where could we go to do it?" I asked evasively.

His answer to this revealed the fact that he was well informed regarding my private life and affairs.

"Couldn't we go up to your attic before your mamma comes home?" he suggested hopefully.

This was something Rene would have to be consulted on, so I evaded a direct answer by saying I'd tell him the next day, and with that I skipped off.

"Bryan wants to do it with me. Shall I let him?" I asked Rene.

"Bryan? Bryan who?"

"Bryan Thompson, that boy that lives over on Little Goose Neck Road."

Rene considered the matter for a moment and deciding apparently that it was of insufficient importance to trouble his head over, disclaimed responsibility with an indifferent shrug.

"Oh, I don't know. Do what you want. What do I care?"

"He knows about Leonard and me. I bet Maisie . . ."

"Gee! You better do it with him so he won't tell. I got to go now and see a chap. Goodbye."

And so it came about that Bryan's name was added to my now growing list of youthful paramours. He was bigger than Rene or Leonard, and had something which neither of the other two possessed, a growth of dark, crisp hair on his pubic regions. He hurt me a little, but he was careful and despite the slightly painful distension I soon began to feel the warm, sensuous tremors which precede orgasm. His slow, cautious thrusts brought my organism to a pitch of excitation such as I had not yet experienced, and when the climax came I almost fainted with the intensity of the ecstasy. Afterwards, he showed me where my fingernails had actually cut into his flesh while I was hugging him in the crisis. He was a very gentlemanly little fellow and thanked me in the most courteous and serious manner imaginable for having let him do it to me. In addition, he made me glow happily by telling me that I had the prettiest legs of any girl he had ever seen. Bryan had the makings of a real courtier.

Before long my popularity was spreading and new suitors for my favors were appearing almost magically. Sometimes even boys and young men I did not know accosted me in the streets, some humbly and supplicatingly, and others quite impertinently.

Instead of being alarmed at this situation I took it as a flattering indication of my popularity. And, inevitably, I

discovered that the soft nest between my legs, upon which
a filmy growth of silky hair was beginning to grow, could
be made to hatch financial rewards as well as genetic
pleasures.

That some horrible fate did not overtake me as the result
of my complacency with utter strangers is only proof of
the old, old theory that guardian angels look after the
safety of children and fools, sometimes, at least.

Once I made an appointment with a man to meet him at
a certain corner after dark, expecting to be taken to a
room. He led me into an alley of such sinister and abandoned aspects that I did indeed become alarmed and refused to go any further. For a while he tried to persuade
me with flattering words and promises of generous
compensation, but the more he talked, the more uneasy I
became, and finally, cursing me viciously, he turned away
and quickly disappeared.

One night a young man of genteel but delicate physical
features accosted me in terms so respectful and courteous
that I listened to his insinuations and consented to accom-
pany him to his room which, though far from pretentious,
was neatly and comfortably furnished.

I had long since discovered that men's first thoughts
were to see me naked as quickly as possible; they seemed
literally burning to gorge their eyes with the spectacle of
my nudity, so as soon as I was in the privacy of a room I
always undressed down to my hose and slippers without
waiting to be asked.

No sooner was the door closed behind us in this instance
than I started to take off my clothes. But the young man
stopped me with a gesture.

"No, no!" he exclaimed, "don't undress!"

I paused uncertainly.

"I've got to take off my clothes . . . my panties anyway
. . . don't you want to see me naked?"

"No, no! Don't take off anything! I'll tell you what to

do, don't do anything except just what I tell you. You'll
get your money.''

"But . . . but what do you want me to do?"

"I'll show you. Just sit down and wait. I'll be back in a
minute.''

I sat down in the chair he indicated and he disappeared
into an adjoining room, closing the door behind him. I
heard him moving about, and five minutes later he appeared again, strip, stark naked. He was rather thin, but
his skin was white and clean. His cock, entirely indifferent
to the proximity of a feminine spectator, hung down inert
and listless.

Crossing the room he unlocked a cabinet and took from
it a bundle of thin, pliant switches. Selecting one of these
he extended it toward me and murmured in a voice which
was both low and supplicating:

"Take this switch and whip me as hard as you can."

I gazed at him mute with stupefaction.

"Come!" he urged, putting the switch in my hand.''

"You're joking!" I managed to exclaim. "What do you
want me to whip you for?''

"Oh, don't waste time asking questions! Do as I ask
and you'll get your money!''

I saw that he was in earnest and, thinking that I had to
deal with a crazy man whom it would be best to humor,
dazedly got to my feet clutching the switch which he had
placed in my hand.

"Whip me as hard as you can!" he whispered huskily,
indicating the cheeks of his bottom with a gesture.

Fearfully, I drew back the slender birch and brought it
forward against his flesh with a smart thwack.

"Harder!" he said, "as hard as you can!"

I repeated the blow, with greater force.

"Keep on! Don't stop! Don't be afraid!"

In obedience to this exhortation I struck him several
more blows in succession.

"That's the way . . . only harder!" he exclaimed.

Again I drew the birch back and this time it fairly whistled through the air as it rained stinging cuts over his thighs and buttocks. In its wake livid crisscross lines began to appear on the white flesh. As I saw these marks developing under my blows a curious sensation began creeping up through my own body. A sort of fury took possession of me and instead of feeling sorry for the pain I was inflicting I felt an urge to increase his torment. My face was hot and my heart beat violently. I clenched my teeth and put all the strength I possessed behind the swishing birch.

He stood there rigidly, his eyes glassy, distended, an ecstatic expression on his face. And then I noticed something else. His cock, which had at first been hanging lifelessly down, was coming into a slow erection. It was expanding in size and jerking convulsively at short intervals and with each jerk it lifted itself upward a little higher.

I watched it with fascinated eyes and as it slowly assumed its maximum of rigidity and erection the first shiver of something akin to lewd voluptuousness kindled within me. I comprehended that in some manner there was a relation between the whipping I was inflicting on him and my own obscure, erotic reaction, and I tried to increase the severity of my blows.

"Enough!" he gasped suddenly, and snatching the whip from me he flung it across the room. "Now! Frig me quick!" And he seized my hand and placed it upon his cock.

I was now in a state in which I would have welcomed a reciprocal caress, even masturbation, but I dared not disobey him. Supporting his testicles with one hand I pumped his cock frenziedly with the other and before I had made a dozen passes his seminal fluid was spurting from my fist in copious jets.

For this service, my first experience in the realms of

abnormal sexual practices, the young man presented me with ten shillings and I went home marveling, not only at his curious eccentricity, but at the peculiar sensations I myself had experienced while occupied with the weird business.

My moral status was now pretty well established in the neighborhood in which I had lived since infancy. The echos from shrewish tongues to the effect that "something should be done" had reached my ears on more than one occasion. I had not been able to conceal my occasional financial affluence from Mamma Agnes who had taken note of mysteriously acquired bits of finery and articles of personal adornment which could not be readily accounted for. Her comments, at first veiled, became more cynical as time went on. Her well-founded suspicions were justified when, returning one afternoon at an hour much earlier than the usual one, she opened a door which Rene and I, grown careless with respect to elementary precautions, had left unlocked.

When we first saw her she was swaying tipsily in the open door. Tipsy, yes, but not too tipsy to realize the significance of the picture which confronted her. I, my breasts still heaving under the stimulation of an orgasm just effected, lying on the bed with my panties off and the rest of my clothing in guilty disarray, and Rene, his pants unbuttoned in front and his still rigid cock projecting therefrom as he reached for a towel to wipe it off in the precise moment in which the movement of the door attracted our attention.

There was a dull minute of silence; silence frozen and absolute except for the imperturbable ticking of the small china clock on the dresser. Raising her hands in front of her with the palms outward in a gesture of renunciation, Mamma Agnes murmured thickly:

"I war-r-shh me hands of the pair of ye!"

And she closed the door upon us, leaving Rene and me to stare at each other in blank dismay.

"Gee, Sis! Why didn't you latch the door?" exclaimed Rene when the sound of her footsteps had died away.

"Why didn't you?" I countered weakly.

From this time on Mamma Agnes maintained a stony indifference toward me, speaking only when unavoidable, and then with caustic brevity.

One Saturday evening about a month later, as I was returning to the house after having spent the afternoon with a girl friend, a young man passed me in the street. His glance, as it appraisingly flitted over my face and body, conveyed the message I had learned to recognize and in a brief moment of passing I was able to observe that in addition to a handsome appearance, he was more than commonly well-dressed. The immaculate linen and modish cut of his clothes, together with an expensive topcoat, suggested money, of which at that moment I had none, and I had seen in a store that very day a pair of high-heeled slippers of irresistible appeal.

I slowed my steps and paused before a shop window. I was not mistaken in my anticipations, for he was quickly at my side, murmuring seductive blandishments in my ear.

Up to a certain point my knowledge of what transpired subsequently is quite clear, but beyond that only incoherent and fragmentary recollection remains.

There was a long ride in a cab which took us into a distant section of the city unfamiliar to me, a luxurious residence into which we were received by a uniformed domestic who bowed servilely to each curt order from the young man who accompanied me. I had made a conquest this time which far outshone any previous adventure. All this stands out vividly in my memory, together with the beautiful and costly furnishings of the rooms to which I was conducted, the rich, red wine I drank from a sparkling crystal goblet and which sent the blood coursing through my veins, filling me with a delicious languor as I sat naked on my companion's knees while his hands and lips caressed my body, lips which tugged and sucked at the little nipples of my breasts causing them to puff up excitedly and send delicious radiations vibrating through me, soft, well-kept hands with delicate fingers whose exquisite titillations between my yielding legs evoked other delicious ecstasies.

Another goblet of ruby-red wine, two, maybe three, and the recollection begins to dim, with only an occasional flash reacting upon my memory; a bed, wonderfully soft and warm and yielding, silken covers which caressed my naked body like the touch of feathers, oblivion, and then a return to semiconsciousness and an indifferent realization of the fact that I was being fucked, another period of darkness and again the awareness of a warm, throbbing cock stirring inside my body.

And so on, throughout what seemed interminable hours, I alternated between moments of lucidity and long periods of oblivion. Whether it was one fuck which lasted all night, or a dozen repeated at intervals I do not know. I had never been drunk before, and it was more like some incoherent dream than a reality.

When I awoke I could not at first remember the circumstances which accounted for my presence in such unfamiliar surroundings. I sat up among the disordered coverings and looked about. I was alone. My clothes were draped over a settee where I had placed them on disrobing the previous night. I was entirely naked and had a splitting headache, the explanation of which was apparent in the form of empty bottles and wine-stained goblets on a small taboret near the bed.

As my glance roved about the room it encountered a clock sustained in the uplifted arms of a porcelain shepherdess, and I saw with a start that it was past the hour of eleven. I had never been absent from home all night before.

In this moment there was a rap at the door and hardly had I time to snatch a sheet up over my bubbies than it opened and a servant, the same one who had admitted us the previous evening, entered, bearing a tray with a pot of tea, some buttered toast and marmalade.

"The marster's horders, Miss, to serve you breakfast, and get a cab for you when you're ready."

With the sheet still clutched over my breasts I watched him as he drew up a small table which, pivoting on an iron base, swung directly over my lap as I sat there in bed. After placing the tray on the table he indicated a silver bell.

"You may ring that, Miss, after you're dressed, when you're ready to go."

I sipped the tea and nibbled at the toast after he had gone, immersed in uneasy meditations which the situation naturally inspired. When I had eaten as much as I could with an appetite impaired by a throbbing headache, I slipped out of bed and began to dress.

When I picked up my stocking I felt some lumpy article inside of it. With the thought that a garter had gotten inside I ran my hand down within the silken sheath but instead of a garter I retrieved a crumpled five pound note. I smoothed it out and gazed at it incredulously. I had never possessed that much money at one time in my entire life. And yet, when I picked up the second stocking there was another note of the same denomination in that one also.

Ten pounds! A veritable fortune.

I forgot both my headache and the uneasiness as to what the consequences of my all-night absence might be. I hurried through my dressing, tarried but a moment in the beautiful bathroom, and rang the bell.

The domestic appeared immediately and led me downstairs and out to the street where a cab, already summoned, was waiting. In answer to the driver's query, I mentioned a corner a few blocks from where I lived, and when we reached this destination I got out and walked the rest of the way.

Mamma Agnes listened to my unconvincing story of having spent the night in the home of a girl friend in frigid silence, except for an observation to the effect that she only hoped the girl hadn't given me a dose of clap or perhaps gotten me in a family way.

I was not discreet enough to hide the harvest of this adventure and my sudden acquisition of riches, flaunted in the form of resplendent new dresses, silk hose, modish slippers, a new hat and other articles of adornment, in the face of envious and resentful females of the neighborhood, brought a reprisal.

Upon information gratuitously submitted by a committee of righteous ladies I was taken into custody as a delinquent minor, and as a result of the investigation which transpired, I was first subjected to a physical examination of a most embarrassing nature, and then committed to a reformatory for wayward girls, destined to remain there until I became of age.

CHAPTER THREE

Three drab and dreary years I passed in this institution, submerged in an atmosphere of repression and humiliation which was fairly soul suffocating.

My complete lack of adaptability to the manual work assigned to new arrivals made me the special target of persecution by the female warders. My delicate physique and small hands and tiny, pointed fingers, so patently incapable of performing scullery work, laundering, and floor scrubbing with any degree of efficiency seemed to kindle their resentment.

Quick enough to show fight at first to these manifest injustices, I soon learned that, right or wrong, I was always on the losing end and that the slightest indication of insubordination brought punishment of a heartbreaking nature to say nothing of the loss of certain prerogatives and so called privileges which were greatly prized in this barren place and which were accorded only to those who accepted their fate with the proper show of humility and servility.

The first two or three months were a perfect nightmare of horror. Let me make myself clear, the sufferings were more mental than physical, for there was little or no actual physical brutality. Corporal punishment, though authorized for incorrigibles, was rarely resorted to. I do not think there were more than half a dozen whippings inflicted on girls during the entire period I was in the institution. These whippings though, when they were administered, were something not to be forgotten.

In addition to the humiliation of being forced to lie face down across a massive table with her panties removed, the blows inflicted on the victim's naked bottom were of such severeity as to cause her to shriek with anguish. Five or six or seven times during my incarceration my face blanched at the sound of those shrill cries, intermingled with the dull slap, slap, slap of heavy leather against naked flesh.

However, time reconciles us to any misfortune and we become hardened to the inevitable.

As this institution admitted only minors, many of whom were girls not over fifteen, educational facilities were provided and there were four hours of classes daily, except Saturdays and Sundays. I discovered that in study there was a surcease from the deadly monotony. I had never been very studious; in fact, during the year preceeding my commitment my interest in learning had waned almost to the vanishing point.

Now, however, I found that time devoted to study passed very quickly. It was something like a mental narcotic which kept one's thoughts from useless repining. My application impressed the teachers and matrons favorably, and gradually they became friendly and treated me with greater consideration. And, if it be true that every cloud has its silver lining, the silver lining in this one was that I received an education which I would otherwise never have possessed.

I passed the probation period and was relieved from further scullery work. It would be carried on by new unfortunates, two or three of whom appeared each week.

We slept in dormitories or wards, each ward a long

room with from twenty or thirty narrow iron beds in a row. These wards were locked at night, and a matron slept in each one, locked in with her charges. In addition, there was always a night superintendent on duty, who could be called in any emergency.

At nine o'clock each night all lights excepting a dim one near the ward matron's bed were turned out and no conversation was permitted between girls after that hour. Our movements during the day, except in school or work hours, were fairly unrestricted within the confines of the building and grounds, but at seven o'clock we entered our respective wards and were allowed to talk, read, and attend to our toilet necessities. At nine we had to be in bed and cease all conversation. As it was impossible to fall asleep immediately, the hour which followed was probably the most disagreeable of the deadly routine. By ten o'clock most of us had found peace in slumber.

But there was a variation to this feature to which we always looked forward. The ward matrons were rotated weekly between dormitories. And, as is sometimes the case in correctional institutions, there are occasional kindly hearted individuals who, instead of exercising the last ounce of their authority to make life as miserable as possible for their unfortunate charges, are disposed to mitigate their wretchedness when possible to do so at no great cost.

A certain matron who slept in our ward one week in every five condoned whispered conversations after nine o'clock, even though it was against the rules. Another, also with us one week in every five, was a very sound sleeper and snored so loudly we were never in doubt as to when she was asleep. So, during the weeks when either of these two matrons were on duty we were fairly safe in exchanging whispered conversations as late as we wished. When the snoring matron was on duty we told naughty stories or exchanged venal confidences.

Occupying the bed on my left side, with a space of

about four feet between us, was a girl named Hester. She was but a few months older than I, but much more so in experience. She was taller than I and very pretty. Her hair, which almost reached to her knees when unbound, was that beautiful shade of auburn which just misses being black by the narrowest margin. She had been very nice to me from the start and had given me much kind and useful advice. She was philosophical in her attitude and possessed of an extremely likeable personality. Nearly all the girls in this reformatory owed their commitment to delinquencies of a sexual nature. Hester had been taken out of a house of prostitution.

She questioned me as to how much money I had been accustomed to get for the bestowal of my favors and when I told her, ruefully, that though my last and fatal adventure had brought me ten pounds, I had rarely gotten over ten shillings, frequently far less, and sometimes nothing at all, she exclaimed:

"Why, you little fool! With your form and baby face you could earn fifteen or twenty pounds a week. In the place I was last I got a pound every time I did it beside what the madam got, and lots of times I got more than that! Why, you were just a little charity chippy!"

One night, taking advantage of the snoring matron's somnolence, we whispered stories and experiences until eleven o'clock. The ward lights were out at this hour, but the shaded lamp near the matron's bed gave just enough light to break the darkness. Hester suddenly kicked off the bed coverings and, stretching her legs out lasciviously, exclaimed:

"Oh, Lord! For a good stiff cock!"

I murmured some sympathetic rejoiner as, lying on my side facing her, I observed her pretty round legs dimly visible in the half darkness.

"Gee, don't you ever get that way, Jessie? Sometimes I want to fuck so darn bad I nearly go crazy!"

"Who wouldn't, locked up in this miserable place month after month?" I answered gloomily.

She sighed, and after a moment of silence, whispered:

"Did you ever kiss the baby in the boat, Jessie?"

"Did I ever what?"

"Kiss the baby . . . suck another woman."

"No!"

"I never did, either. But there are girls here that do. I sucked a guy's cock once. I didn't like it much, but if I had one now I could eat it alive." She giggled faintly.

"Well, I don't know what you're going to do. Go hungry, I guess."

"I darned well know what I'm going to do. It's better than nothing!" she exclaimed, and arching her legs she placed a hand over her cunny and began to rub it vigorously.

From around us came the sound of suppressed giggles, sighs, and the movements of other listeners as they stirred uneasily in their own narrow beds.

I watched the rapid movement of her hand, dimly visible in the partial darkness. And when, with a groan of satisfaction, the movements ceased, my own hand edged down between my legs and under discreet cover sought to quench in like form the fires her frank words and franker actions had aroused.

What she had said about girls who did certain things was true. To be caught in another girl's bed or in any other compromising circumstance indicating that something of this kind was going on was one of the things that girls could be whipped for, and two or three of the whippings which took place while I was there were for exactly this cause.

Nevertheless, something of this kind was going on most of the time without the matrons knowing about it. Sometimes the girls would take a chance in the nightime while the ward matron was asleep and get two in a bed, but this was very dangerous because the switch which controlled the lights was right near the matron's hand, and she could flood the room with light instantly should she hear any suspicious sound.

There was a safer way. In each ward there was a linen-room where clean sheets, pillowcases, towels, and extra blankets were kept. It was a very small room, mostly filled with shelves, but there was a little extra space. The doors to these closets were kept locked, but the keys were in the possession of linenroom girls, or trusties, assigned to distribute towels, sheets, pillowcases, etc., as needed in their respective wards.

If satisfactory arrangements could be made with a linen-room girl, the door would be left unlocked, and when two lovers had slipped inside unobserved by matrons, she would lock the door, leaving them inside for half an hour or so, and when the coast was clear, let them out and lock the door again.

Some weeks before my entry in the reformatory, there had been a linen-room rendezvous of this kind in another ward and the lovers had been caught. It came about through a peculiar accident. A matron, coming down the long corridor between wards, saw a girl she wished to speak to entering a certain ward. She followed her, but when she got inside the ward the girl she had seen was not visible, which mystified her, and with good reason. The girl she was following and a companion were already locked inside the linen closet. Seeing the linen-room girl standing nearby, the matron asked her if such and such a girl had not come in a few moments before.

"No, ma'am," was the reply. "She isn't in here. She must be out in the yard, or downstairs."

"But I'm positive I saw her come in here not half a minute ago!"

"It must have been someone else, ma'm!" answered the frightened girl.

"Someone else? There's no one else in here but you!
What's going on here, anyway?"

The puzzled matron glanced around the empty dormitory.
Her eyes fell on the door to the linen room. She went to it
and tried it. The door was locked.

"Give me the key to this door," she requested.

"I . . . ah, I've lost it, ma'm!" stammered the poor
girl.

"Give me that key!"

Inside the linen room two trembling lovebirds were
listening to the ominous conversation. Naturally, when the
matron opened the door and found not only one girl but
two, she grasped the situation and both the lovers and the
linen-room girl were strapped over the table in the
superintendent's office and whipped on their bare bottoms.

For a while after this a watch was kept on the linen
rooms, but the vigilance gradually relaxed and now they
were being used again with considerable frequency.

There was Heloise, whom everyone called Frenchy,
who would suck another girl off for any trifling payment.
And several others who were known or suspected of similar complacencies.

Hester, who had become my special pal and confident,
used to joke with me in her dry, half comical, half serious
way, as we sat on the edges of our beds at night before
lights out.

"Darn you, Jessie, you give me a hard-on every time I
see you undressed. I believe I'll sneak into your bed some
night and give you a good fucking."

"I don't think you've got what's needed!" I replied,
snickering.

"Well, I could gamahuche you, anyway. Do you think
you'd like that?"

"Gosh, I don't know. Two different fellows I went with
did it to me that way. I don't know how it would be with a
girl."

"Must give one a funny sensation to have another girl do that to you. There are women who pay for it that way. And maybe you don't believe it, but there are even some that will pay you just for letting them do that to you, without you doing a thing. Some people have the funniest ideas."

I told her about the fellow who had paid me to whip him.

"That's nothing," she replied, "there are lots of men like that. The ones you have to be careful about are the ones that want to whip *you*. Some of them go crazy and whip you so hard the blood comes. They don't care how much they hurt you."

"Why, I wouldn't let them whip me!" I exclaimed, horrified.

"Well, when you're in a sporting house you have to do everything and pretend to like it. Those fellows who do funny things are generally the best spenders. They're always springing something new on you, too," she continued, "the best paying regular I had was one of the funny kind; you'd never guess what I had to do with him."

"Tell me, Hester!" I begged.

She began to giggle.

"Well, there really wasn't much to it, but it was so . . . so . . . crazy, I nearly went into hysterics the first few times, until I got used to it. He'd lie down on the bed and make me get on my knees, straddling him, right over his face. Then I had to jack myself off with my fingers, and just when I started to cream, put my cunny down on his mouth. And will you believe it, right then he'd start to squirt without my even touching his cock, and the stuff would fly all over my bare back."

"My heavens!" I breathed.

"I couldn't sleep last night," she continued, changing the subject. "I laid awake the longest time, just imagining things, and thinking what I'd like to have the first night after I get out of here.''

"I can guess," I said dryly, "a stiff cock."

"No; five of them, all at the same time."

"Five? At one time?"

"Yes; one in my cunny, one in my mouth, one in my bottom, and . . ." she burst into laughter, ". . . one in each hand!"

"Hester, you're the limit!" I exploded.

"I get so darn tired of jacking myself off I've half a mind to go in the linen-room with Frenchy. She's crazy about that new shoulder scarf I have, and it's no good to me in here, anyway."

"Why, why don't you?" I suggested. "You can tell me all about it afterwards. But be careful! I'd faint if I ever heard you getting the strap."

"Maybe I will. There isn't any danger. They don't watch the linen-rooms much. Besides, I thought of a dandy way to fix things so they couldn't catch us. I saw Amy and that new girl she chums around with sneaking out of the linen room in ward five this afternoon. I had a suspicion that's what Amy was up to when she started being so nice to that little kid."

"Jessie! Jessie!" I heard someone calling softly as I was sitting on a bench in the exercise yard reading the next afternoon. I glanced up, and saw Hester hurrying toward me. "Frenchy and I are going in the linen room. You come up and stand in the corridor where you can watch the stairs! If any of the matrons come, you signal the linen-room girl before they get upstairs, and she'll have time to get us out before they reach the dormitory!"

"All right!" I agreed, rising to follow her.

This was a very practical plan. The ward was far enough from the top of the stairway to allow ample time for them to get out of the linen room should the girl on watch in the doorway receive a signal from me. The only risk they ran was that of being abruptly interrupted in their affair.

I followed Hester up to the corridor and stationed myself where I could watch the stairs and at the same time be seen by the linen-room girl in the doorway of the dormitory who, in the event that I suddenly started to walk toward her, would quickly warn Hester and Frenchy.

But there were no interruptions. I stood there twenty or twenty-five minutes, watching the stairs and picturing in my mind what was taking place within the linen-room. The girl finally disappeared from the entrance and I knew she had gone to unlock the door.

A few moments later Hester and Frenchy appeared in the corridor. There was nothing in Frenchy's calm demeanor to indicate anything unusual, but Hester's face was scarlet and she was holding her handkerchief over it. Frenchy sauntered coolly into another dormitory and Hester went on downstairs with me and out into the yard.

"Well . . . ?" I invited, after waiting for her to say something. "How was it?"

"Oh, Jessie! It . . . I . . . she . . . wait till I get my breath . . ." and she began to laugh hysterically. When she recovered her composure and her face had resumed its natural hue, she said: "I can't talk about it yet; I'll tell you tonight. Look: my hands are still shaking, I'm so nervous!"

"Oh, all right," I answered disgustedly, "but I don't see what you have to be nervous about now."

"It's the reaction. Don't be sore; I'll tell you all about it tonight, honey!"

And, that night, sitting close together on the edge of my bed before lights out, at my insistent urging, Hester told me in whispers what there was to tell.

"Well, we got inside, and as soon as we heard the door lock we turned on the light and took our panties off and hid them under some sheets on a shelf so in case we had to come out quickly we could just leave them there and get them later. Then we put a blanket on the floor and I laid down on it. Frenchy wanted to do 69 but I told her I didn't want to do it that way because I couldn't get my nerve up to do that to a girl. So she said all right, she'd just do it to me. It was the funniest thing, Jessie, all last night and today, while I was thinking about it, I felt hot, but no sooner did I get inside that room with her than my passion all left me. I felt like telling her I had changed my mind and letting her keep the scarf anyway. But then I thought, what a silly thing to do after going to so much bother, and why not let her go through with it. When she pulled my dress up I started to giggle, I couldn't help it, I felt so funny, not passionate, just silly. Well, she squeezed in between my legs, and stuck her tongue right up inside. When I felt it go in I wanted to push her away, but I didn't and after she put it in and out a while, she began to lick me all around down there, and then she started to suck my bottom. I thought I'd go crazy, really. I couldn't stop laughing. It didn't make me feel passionate, but the sensation started to come anyway, and sure enough, she did make me cream something fierce. If she'd have stopped then it wouldn't have been so bad, but she stuck to me like a little leech and it set my nerves on edge so, I felt like scratching her. I almost had to yell at her to make her let go. She wanted to know when I'd let her do it again; I told her 'someday' but I don't think I ever will. It isn't so hot. I don't see how some girls can go batty over that kind of stuff.''

CHAPTER FOUR

The time dragged on. With the exception of such little momentary distractions as those I have described, there was little to break the monotony. During the first year and a half I received occasional visits from Mamma Agnes, and sometimes from Rene. How I would have enjoyed an hour or two with him in privacy, but such was not to be, for visiting was confined to the reception room and there was always a matron present to see that no contraband gifts were passed to inmates. Even the letters written to us were opened and read before being placed in our hands. Often, letters written to girls by male friends were destroyed without being seen by those to whom they were addressed.

Through some artful maneuver, a seventeen-year-old girl in our ward named Georgette succeeded in getting some little pictures of men and women doing everything imaginable. They were not drawings like the one in the little book Rene had found, but real photographs.

Georgette had these pictures about two weeks when apparently some word of their presence, either accidentally or through malicious tattling, reached the ears of the superintendent.

Accompanied by two matrons she entered our ward one night just after lock-up, and proceeded to search it thoroughly. One of the matrons found the little packet of pictures under Georgette's mattress and we knew it was the pictures they were looking for because they stopped searching as soon as they found them.

They took poor little Georgette out, downstairs to the superintendent's office. As soon as they had gone a profound silence fell over the ward. Nobody said anything. We were all waiting with strained nerves to hear certain sounds which would cause some of us to tremble, others to murmur curses, and others to giggle with callow indifference or maybe hysterical nervousness.

Moment by moment we waited but the expected sounds did not materialize. The minutes dragged on, ten, fifteen, twenty, a half an hour. Maybe they were not going to whip Georgette after all. But suddenly the tense silence was broken by a distant but sharply audible thwack. It was followed by another, and another, and with the third blow an agonized scream reached our ears. Four, five, six, seven, eight, nine, ten. Mechanically we counted the strokes as the blood-chilling cadence of strap and shrieks rent the air. With the tenth stroke it stopped, and those of us who were inspired with sentiments of pity and sympathy breathed a sigh of relief.

Five minutes elapsed, and to our surprise, the woeful dirge with its horrid slap, slap, slap accompaniment began again. From one up to ten it again ran its ominous course. This was something unusual; we recalled of no previous instance in which the punishment had been inflicted twice in succession.

At the tenth blow, as before, came silence. Unconsciously I had clenched my hands so tightly that they were numb with the pressure. I glanced at Hester. She was sitting on the edge of her bed, her chin cupped in her hands, gazing morosely downward. After the second whipping there was a long period of silence. Momentarily we expected to see Georgette being brought back into the dormitory, and were fairly paralyzed with horror when the dolorous refrain commenced anew. Even the face of Mrs. Barrows, our ward matron, was pale as she sat at the little desk near her bed, nervously twisting a pencil in her fingers.

"If they whip me like that I'll come back here and kill them if I never do another thing in life!" whispered Hester.

A few minutes after the echos of the tenth and last blow of the triple inquisition had died away we heard the door of the superintendent's office open, and the sound of slow steps on the stairs and in the corridor followed. Finally, there was Georgette, sobbing huskily and supported by the arms of the two matrons. Mrs. Barrows unlocked the door and helped Georgette to her bed.

Kindly hands undressed her and laid her face down on her cot. When her bottom was uncovered we gasped with horror. It was a mass of purple welts, each welt puffed up and swollen terribly. Even Mrs. Barrows expressed surprise as she hastened to get a jar of cold cream with which to allay the inflammation.

"Why did they whip you three times, Georgette?" we whispered in sympathetic wonder.

"They were trying to make me tell how I got the pictures," answered Georgette, her voice broken with intermittent sobs.

"Did you tell them?"

"No!"

All things must end and the time of my release was near at hand. Mamma Agnes was dead. She had passed away during the second year of my imprisonment, and Rene had shortly thereafter come to bid me good-bye. He was going to Canada, and would send me money to join him when I was free, he said. For a while my thoughts were brightened with his hope. But his letters, coming at first with regularity and sometimes containing small sums of money, gradually became less frequent and were less definite in tone with regard to our original plans. They finally ceased altogether and the walls of oblivion closed about my foster brother Rene.

It was destined, seemingly, that the day of my liberation would find me homeless, the last tie which linked me to my former life cut off, and with no provision for the future. It was in this extremity that Hester, whose freedom was due several months in advance of mine, and who had confided to me that a place was arranged for and awaiting her in the atelier of a certain Madame Lafronde, suggested that I also place myself at the disposition of this lady in whom she had the utmost confidence.

She painted a glowing picture of the comfortable life and financial rewards to be enjoyed in the high-class establishment operated by this Madame Lafronde. It catered to a very select clientele recruited among the gentility and nobility. She was certain that Madame Lafronde would welcome me with open arms and so eloquent was she that I did not long hesitate in accepting her offer to intercede for me.

Before Hester passed through the big front doors to freedom it had been arranged that I was to have a visitor, ostensibly an aunt, who would call on me a few days before my own release was due. This aunt would be no other than Madame Lafronde herself, and the purpose of her visit would be to decide whether I was an acceptable candidate for her atelier.

The tight pressure of Hester's hand, and the soft kiss she left on my cheek as she bid me farewell filled my eyes with tears. I had come to regard her with great affection, and her absence would weigh heavily on my heart.

"Don't cry, Jessie darling," she whispered, "we'll soon be together again. I won't forget you. Remember now, when Madame Lafronde comes, call her Aunt Mary, and act as though you knew her or else . . .''

Further conversation was interrupted by a matron, and with a last hug and kiss we separated.

The four months which followed were the longest and dreariest of all the long months I spent in the reformatory. The fact that a new life was close at hand actually seemed to retard the passage of time rather than hurry it.

But there were moments of happiness occasioned by the arrival of little packages containing candies, cakes and other gifts of a nature permitted by the regulations. There were also letters which, despite their discreet wording and the mysterious signature ''your loving cousin, Frances,'' conveyed to me their messages of cheer and the certainty that Hester had indeed not forgotten me. And, true to her promise, a week before my liberty was to be restored, I was called to the reception room to receive a visitor.

As I entered, my surprised gaze fell upon the only occupant, aside from the ever alert and watchful matron on duty, an elderly lady of most respectable, even pious aspect, gowned in somber black silk. So contrary was her appearance to that of the visitor I expected that I hesitated, momentarily forgetting Hester's parting admonition as I gazed on the grandmotherly picture. As I stood hesitantly, she arose from her chair, and coming toward me with outstretched arms, exclaimed:

''Jessie, my darling child!''

The sharp eyes of the matron were on me.

''Hello, Aunt Mary,'' I murmured as I mechanically returned her embrace.

And so, under these curious circumstances, the Madame of a house of prostitution interviewed a prospective inmate. Her eyes roved incessantly over my body as we carried on our aimless conversation, designed to fool the matron who sat idly watching us. I felt from the first that I had found favor with my visitor, and her comments as to how I had changed for the better since she "last saw" me and how nice I looked, and how happy she was sure I would be when she took me to live with her now that my dear, dear mama had passed away, gave me the clue to my future and assured me that for the time being at least, it was assured. "Cousin Francis" was eagerly awaiting my homecoming, she said, and sent me her most affectionate regards.

Before leaving, she advised the superintendent that she would be at the institution the morning of my release to see me safely home. I went back to my ward in a regular daze, my thoughts in a confused whirl. It was very difficult to imagine that nice old lady in the role of mistress of a house of prostitution.

The long awaited day arrived at last.

At nine o'clock I was summoned to the superintendent's office and the usual formalities related to the discharge of inmates were fulfilled.

"Your aunt said that she would call for you at ten o'clock, Jessie. You may go to your dormitory and pack your things," she said kindly, after concluding the customary harangue on the folly of a life of sin and the rewards of virtue.

As I spread my few effects upon the narrow cot in the dormitory, preparatory to wrapping them up in a bundle, a small group of friends and companions gathered around, some to bid me an envious farewell and others to extract promises from me to send them this or that from the outside.

The hour sped by and almost before I realized it I was going down the long stairway which led to the outer offices and freedom.

My benefactress was waiting in the superintendent's office and greeted me with a motherly embrace in keeping with our reserved relationship. The superintendent conducted us to the outer door and as it closed behind us I paused to glance back, hardly able to believe that my freedom was an actual fact. As I did so, Madame Lafronde shook my arm.

"Come on, girl! This damn place gives me the willies!" she exclaimed as she hurried me down the steps to the street. She signaled a taxi and within a few moments the institution which had been my home for nearly three years receded in the distance and became at last only a disagreeable memory.

Within the taxi, Madame Lafronde relaxed, and leaning back against the cushions she extracted a packet of cigarettes from her purse. After proffering me a cigarette which, unaccustomed to their use, I declined, she lit one and puffed away abstractedly.

The taxi, in accordance with her indications, after traveling a dozen blocks, slowed up and came to a stop. But we had not reached our ultimate destination. A few steps away, waiting near the curb, was a large black limousine. As we approached it on foot, a chauffeur sprang out and opened the rear compartment and to my surprise and delight, Hester stepped out and flung her arms about me. She was beautifully gowned and her face was radiant with sincere joy at seeing me. I had always thought Hester pretty, but I was hardly prepared for the change a splendid wardrobe wrought in her appearance.

We did not tarry long and soon, ensconced in the luxurious privacy of the big car, were again winding rapidly through the streets, Hester and I babbling excitedly while Lafronde placidly blew long streamers of smoke through her nostrils, interrupting us occasionally with some questions or observation.

"Let's see your legs, my dear."

I giggled nervously as she coolly raised my skirts and eyed my legs appraisingly.

"Um-m, very good, my dear, very nice legs, indeed. I was afraid Hester might have exaggerated a little . . . and how about your bubbies, let's see what they're like . . ."

and an inquisitive and bejeweled hand passed over my chest and after a brief exploration was withdrawn. "Ah, yes; very nice legs and very nice bubbies. A fortune in them, my dear, if you are wise."

The ride ended before the portals of a large brownstone mansion in a quiet street and shortly thereafter I was ushered into my new home. It was a place of quiet elegance, soft plush carpets and tapestried walls. I gazed about in wonder. There was nothing visible to the eye to mark these circumspectly luxurious premises as an atelier of prostitution, but I was soon to learn that things are not always as they seem, and that within these sedate walls dramas of licentiousness such as I had never seen were of nightly occurrence.

And thus did I cross the threshold of a new life, and the doors of the past closed behind me.

CHAPTER FIVE

A small but furnished alcove with a tiled bath in connection was waiting for me, and after I had examined it Madame Lafronde left Hester and me together, saying that she would have a talk with me later in the afternoon.

A maid appeared with a luncheon tray and as I ate, plying Hester with questions between bites, I learned that Madame Lafronde's "family" comprised eight other girls in addition to Hester and myself. I would meet them later; they did not get up until after twelve, which accounted for the silence and absence of movement I had already noted.

When Madame Lafronde returned, her first request was that I strip myself entirely so that she could examine my body. I did so with some embarrassment, for though I had often enough exposed myself to boys and men, the impersonal, appraising eyes of this strange old lady filled me with a nervous dread that I might be found wanting in some essential.

I was small of stature and feared that the absence of clothing might accentuate the possible defect. However, to my vast relief, she gave every evidence of satisfaction and nodded her head approvingly as I turned around and around in obedience to her indications. When I had replaced my clothing she shot question after question at me, until every phase of my early and subsequent sexual life had been revealed. To her questions I endeavored to give frank and truthful answers, regardless of the embarrassment which some of them evoked.

"Now, my dear," she said, when the interrogating had been concluded, "I want you to know what we're all one big, happy family here. There must be no jealousy or friction or petty animosities between girls. Our gentlemen are very nice, but men are men, and a pretty, new face always distracts their attention from older ones. I have a plan in mind which fits you as though you were made for it. If you handle it rightly you'll be helping the other girls as well as yourself, and instead of being jealous of you they'll all have reason to be grateful. We're all here to make money and as it must come from the gentlemen our aim is to get them to spend it and then come back and spend some more. Never forget that."

And Madame Lafronde explained the unique role I was to play, a role which to a more mature mind than mine would have at once revealed the astuteness and subtlety of the guiding genius behind this lucrative business and which accounted for its success, measured in terms of gold. Madame Lafronde was nobody's fool.

In brief, she proposed to dangle my youthful prettiness before the jaded eyes of the clientele as a sort of visual aperitif, much as water was placed before the thirsting Tantalus, in view, but just beyond reach, the psychological effect of which would be to so whet their passions that they would in the end, perforce, satisfy themselves with such feminine fruit as was within their reach.

I was to tantalize masculine passion while leaving to others the duty of satisying them. This with respect to the regular "parlor" clientele. Exceptions would be made privately with certain special patrons who were always able and disposed to pay well for favoritism.

Things were not as they had been before the war, explained Madame Lafronde. Even this profitable business had suffered from the falling economic barometer, and too many of the gentlemen who dropped in were inclined to pass the evening sociably in the parlor. Of course, between liquors consumed, tips to the girls, and various other sources of minor revenues, their presence was desirable, but the real profits of the business were garnered in the bedrooms, not in the parlor. It was a case of a bird in a bedroom being worth five in the parlor.

As a sort of stimulant designed to inspire blasé gentlemen with an irresistible urge to make use of the bedroom service, I was to be rigged up in an enticingly juvenile fashion and paraded constantly before their eyes in a semi-nude state. Various pretexts and artifices would ostensibly account for my presence and movements. I would carry a tray of cigars and cigarettes, serve drinks, and be available for general services and accommodations with but one single exception. I would joke and chat with patrons, tell a naughty story now and then, even permit them to fondle me within certain limits, but, because of my youth (I was to be only fifteen years old!) my services were not to be expected in a professional capacity.

I gasped at hearing that I was to play the part of a fifteen-year-old, but Madame Lafronde insisted that it would not be difficult in view of my small body and the fact that certain artifices in costume, hairdressing and other details would be employed to help out the illusion.

The first step was to call in a barber who trimmed my hair so that it hung just below my ears. It was naturally wavy, and when the work was finished it was quite apparent that Madame Lafronde had not erred in assuming that short curls would lend a peculiarly childish effect to my face. I gazed in the mirror with genuine surprise at the transfiguration.

When the barber had gone Madame Lafronde ordered

me to undress again, and after taking certain measurements left the room to return later with several garments and a box which on being opened revealed a safety razor, soap and brush.

"We could have let the barber do this, too," she commented dryly, indicating the razor, "but maybe you'd rather do it yourself."

"Do what?" I asked, looking at the razor in perplexity.

"Shave the pretty little curls off your peek-a-boo," she answered, with a gesture toward the dark shadow which was visible through the texture of my single garment.

"What!" I expostulated. "Why . . . even girls fifteen years old have . . . !"

"Shave it off," she interrupted. "If you don't know how, I'll do it for you."

"I can, I can!" I responded hastily. "I've shaved the hair under my arms lots of times . . . only . . ." and I glanced around in confusion for, in addition to Madame Lafronde and Hester, several girls had appeared and were standing in the door watching me curiously.

"Go over by the window with your back to us and stand up, or sit down, whichever you wish, if you're afraid someone will see your love trap. You'll get over that before you've been here long."

Without further protest I took the shaving equipment, turned my back on the smiling assembly and sitting on the edge of a chair with my legs apart I lathered and soaped the hair and shaved it off the best I could. I had to go over the ground several times before the last prickly stubs were finally removed, and when I stood up, much embarrassed, to let Madame Lafronde view the results she expressed her approval and suggested that I dust the denuded flesh with talcum powder.

The absence of the hair from its accustomed place caused me to feel peculiarly naked, and I turned my gaze downward. The two sides of my cunny stood out prominently like fat

little hills, the crease between them tightly closed as I
stood with my legs pressed together.

I was now to don black hose of sheerest silk and a pair
of tiny slippers with exaggerated high Spanish heels. Around
my legs, just above the knees, fitted narrow scarlet garters,
each adorned with a little silk rosette. Next came an
exquisite brocade coat or jacket of black velvet into which
was worked fantastic designs in gold thread.

"What about my bubbies?" I asked, as Madame Lafronde
handed me the garment. "Will I have to cut them off,
too?"

A gust of laughter followed and I slipped on the loose-
fitting coat. It terminated at a point about halfway down
my thighs, leaving a few inches of naked flesh between its
lower edge and the tops of my hose. Fastening just below
the breasts with three braided loops, it covered my stomach all right, but from there down the folds hung loose and
a naked, hairless cunny would be exposed with any careless movement.

The last item of this bizarre costume was a tall, military
style cap of astrakhan, fitted with a small brim of shiny
black leather and a strap which passed under my chin.
Madame Lafronde adjusted the cap on my head at a rakish
angle and stood back to view the effect.

I glanced at my reflection in the wardrobe mirror.
Without undue conceit I realized that I presented a chic
picture, one which undoubtedly fulfilled Madame Lafronde's
expectations, as was attested to by the satisfied gleam in
her shrewd old eyes, by Hester's enthusiastic felicitations,
and by the half-admiring, half-envious looks of the other
girls who were watching silently.

From beneath the edge of the black astrakhan cap my
hair hung loose in short, crisp curls. The low bodice of the
brocade jacket teasingly revealed the upper halves of my
breasts, while its wide and ample sleeves displayed my
arms to good advantage with every movement. The jacket

itself, fitting snugly around my waist, flared out sufficiently to show my hips to good advantage. Further down,
the sheen of glossy silk with the brief variation in color
provided by the scarlet garters gave just the right touch to
my legs, and the high-heeled slippers completed the exotic
ensemble.

The rest of the afternoon and evening Madame Lafronde
devoted to coaching and instructing me. The doors were
open to visitors at nine o'clock, but it was never until after
eleven or twelve that gentlemen returning from their clubs
or other nocturnal entertainment began to drop in in any
considerable number, and from then on patrons came and
went, singly or in small groups, some to linger briefly,
others to pass an hour or two, or to remain all night.

I made my debut at eleven o'clock. With inward nervousness at first, but with growing confidence as I observed the electrical effect my entry made upon the
half-dozen gentlemen who were lounging about the salon
in various attitudes of interest or indifference to the wiles
of the feminine sirens about them. As I crossed the room
with my tray of cigars and cigarettes and matches supported by a strap over my shoulders the hum of conversation ceased as if by magic and every eye was on me.

I approached a tall, well-dressed gentleman who was
sitting on a sofa with a girl on either side of him, and
proffered my wares in a timid voice. His startled gaze took
in the picture before him and lingered a moment on my
legs. Shaking himself free from the arms of his companions,
he sat up.

"My dear, I never smoked a cigar in my life, but I'll
take all you have, if you go with them!"

This was Madame Lafronde's cue. Entering the room
from a side door where she had been waiting, she said:

"Dear gentlemen, I want to present a new member of
our family to you. This is Jessie. Jessie is here under
peculiar circumstances. She is an orphan and, strictly

speaking, not old enough to be here in a professional capacity. Though as you see, she is nicely developed, she is in fact only fifteen years old and I am sheltering her here only because of her orphaned condition. She is to make her living selling you cigars and cigarettes, gentlemen, and serving you in all other possible ways . . . except one."

Madame Lafronde paused.

"In other words," interrupted a tall, thin young man with a tiny moustache who was indifferently stroking the silk-clad legs of a damsel on his lap, "she can be only a sister to us. I knew she was too good to be true the moment she came into this room."

A burst of laughter followed and Madame Lafronde, smiling, answered:

"A sister . . . well . . . maybe just a bit more than a sister, gentlemen, but not too much more!"

From across the room Hester beckoned to me.

"This is my friend Mr. Hayden, Jessie. He wants to know you," she said, indicating her companion.

I acknowledged the introduction.

"Bring us two Scotch and sodas, will you, honey?" added Hester.

Mr. Hayden spoke to me pleasantly and took a packet of cigarettes from my tray, courteously declining the change I tendered him. As I turned to execute Hester's order, the man I had first addressed detained me.

"Wait a moment, Sister. I've decided to take up smoking."

I might add that the nickname "Sister" was unanimously adopted and clung to me during the time I was in Madame Lafronde's house.

The gentleman took a handful of cigars and reached toward his pocket. As he did so, his eyes drifted down below the edge of the tray.

"Hold on! I'm making a tactical error!" he exclaimed, replacing all the cigars but one. "I see right now that cigars should be purchased one by one. You may bring me another when you come back!"

Nothing else was needed to start the ball of my popularity rolling and soon the salon was echoing with hilarity and laughter as all called for cigars and cigarettes at once, each trying to keep me standing in front of him as long as possible.

If this kept up there would be substantial returns on the tobacco concession, for half the profits were to be mine, according to Madame Lafronde's promise, and this in addition to whatever was given to me in the nature of tips or gratuities. Flushed and happy, I ran from one to another, replying to jokes and quips in a half-innocent, half-cynical manner, calculated to fit the role of a fifteen-year-old ingenue.

As the evening wore on new arrivals appeared and I was instantly the first object of their attention. Before long the pockets of my brocade jacket were heavy with silver, I had replenished my tobacco stock several times and received several generous tips for bringing in liquor, and in addition, a gentleman had given me four shillings for being permitted to feel my bubbies, "just in a brotherly way," as he expressed it.

What the effect of my presence was on the regular revenues of the house I could not judge, for though there was a constant movement of couples in and out of bedrooms I had no way to knowing whether this was a normal or an increased activity.

With the advancing hours the movement gradually diminished and by four o'clock the last guest had departed. The door was locked, the girls ate a light luncheon and prepared to retire. It was then that Madame Lafronde informed me that the bedroom service had showed a decided increase, which increase she was fair enough to attribute to my presence.

She was well satisfied and I surely had reason to be, for

when the money was counted up and the tobacco sales checked there remained for me the sum of two pounds and eight shillings, which was duly credited to me and would be at my disposition on request.

I was tired out; I had hardly slept the previous night, yet such was my excitement that I did not feel sleepy and preferred to gossip with Hester for an hour in my room. I had a hundred questions to ask. I wanted to know about the nice-looking, gentlemanly Mr. Hayden, and learned that he was one of Hester's regular and most favored friends.

He had been much interested in me, and Hester had unselfishly confided to him that I might reservedly be at his disposition on some later occasion, to which he had gallantly responded that in such an event he would insist on having the two of us together. How good Hester was, I thought, to be willing to share this nice man with me and maybe risk my supplanting her in his affections. He had appealed to me greatly, and there had been several others whom I would not have been averse to doing something with.

"You made a tremendous sensation, darling," said Hester. "You could have a dozen roomcalls. I heard what every-body said. But Lafronde is right. The other girls would have been ready to scratch your eyes out. There's nothing makes them so mad as to have a new girl take their regulars away from them. Did you notice that fellow who went with me? He comes here every three or four nights. I guess every girl here has had him, but now he always takes me. He's got lots of money and he's kind of nice, but, gee, he never has a hard-on and it takes about half an hour of work to give him a stand. Sometimes I even have to put the buzzer on him, but tonight, oh, baby, it was as stiff as a poker. I jollied him about it and told him I bet it was thinking about you instead of me. 'My word,' he said, 'you're a deucedly clevah mind reader. That little tart did have a most extraordinary effect on me. Wonder what the

chawnces would be to secure her company for an hour or
two? I think that's all bally rot about her virginal estate,
don't you know!' I told him to talk to Madame Lafronde
and maybe it could be arranged. That's two of my regulars
that have fallen for you already, but I'm not jealous. You
can have Bumpy if you want him. It takes too long to
make his cock stand up.''

I laughed.

''What did you mean, putting the buzzer on him?''

''The juice, the electric massage machine.''

''Electric massage machine?''

''Yes, electric massage machine. Don't you know what
an electric massage machine is?''

''Of course I do. They use them for facials. But how
. . . what . . . ?''

''Facials! Oh, baby, you don't know the half. Wait . . .
you're tired out . . . I'll fix your bath water for you and
after you're bathed I'll give you a massage that will make
you sleep like an infant.''

Hester ran into the bathroom and turned on the water.
Then she went to her room and came back with an entrancing little pink silk nightgown, face cream, perfume, and a
large leather-covered box.

While I lay splashing lazily in the tub, soaking in the
pleasant warmth of the foamy, scented water, she laid out
the nightgowns and opened the box to show the apparatus
it contained and which was, in effect, an electric vibratory
massage machine fitted with a long cord for attachment to
an electricity outlet. There were several assorted pieces in
the box and from these Hester selected one fitted with
rubber lips which turned out in the form of a small cup.

When I had gotten out of the tub and dried myself I lay
down naked on the bed. Hester dipped her fingers in the
jar of cream and passed them lightly over my face, neck,
breasts and limbs.

I thought suddenly of the peculiar aspect the shaving

had given me in a certain place and flipped a corner of the sheet over it. Without a word Hester flipped it back and her hands were beween my thighs, softly spreading the cold cream over them and down my legs.

"You're awful good to go to so much trouble for me, Hester," I murmured.

"It's nothing. You can do as much for me sometime," she replied.

When she had finished anointing my body she connected the massage machine. It began to hum and the next instant the rubber cup was buzzing over my forehead, cheeks and neck. My flesh thrilled to the refreshing stimulation and I lay still, enjoying it to the full. Gradually the rubber moved down over my chest, between my breasts, then up over one of them right on the nipple. I came out of my languid rest with a bound. That bubbling, vibrating cup over the nipple of my breast was awakening sensations quite remote to those of mere physical refreshment.

Both my nipples stiffened up, the sensitive area around them puffed out and radiations of sexual excitation began to flow through my body. Laughing hysterically, I sat up and pushed the tantalizing device away.

"Be still, will you? Lie back down!" expostulated Hester, giving me a shove which tumbled me back over the pillow.

"But, Hester! That thing . . . it's positively distracting! Don't put it on my bubbies again . . . I can't stand it!"

Hester smiled.

"You'll think it's distracting before I finish with you. Keep quiet or you'll wake the girls in the next room."

Down over my stomach, in widening circles, around and around, and then back and forth moved the diabolical apparatus guided by Hester's hand. I had a premonition now of what was coming, and as it slowly but surely crept downward until it reached the upper part of the rounded elevation of my cunny, I clenched my fists and held my breath.

No sooner was it close enough to impart its infernal vibration to my clitoris than tremors of sexual agitation began to shake my body. It was simply irresistible; I could not have forestalled its action by any conceivable exercise of willpower.

But I did not try. The fulminating intensity of the sensations which now had me in their grip nullified any will or desire to thwart them. I threw my head back, closed my eyes, and surrendered supinely. My legs parted shamelessly beneath the insinuating pressure of Hester's fingers, and the humming, buzzing cup slid between them. Up and down it moved, three, four, maybe half a dozen times, pressing lightly against the flesh.

My orgasim, wrought up to the final pitch of excitation and unable to withstand the infernal provocation longer, yielded, and in a second I was gasping in the throes of sexual ecstasy.

When I recovered my breath, and in part my composure, I exclaimed:

"Hester! You . . . you . . . I could murder you! Fooling me with that thing!"

"Make you sleep good, honey, and keep you from having naughty dreams," she answered complacently, and she disconnected the device and restored it to its container.

"Does that work on men like that, too?"

"Yes; we use it on them sometimes to give them a stand when they either can't get one or are too slow."

"Well," I commented, "I'll say it gave me a stand I wasn't expecting."

She giggled, tucked the covers around me, kissed me on the cheek, and turned out the lights.

"Sleep tight, honey. I'll wake you in the afternoon."

She departed, leaving me alone to drowsily review the stupendous transition which twenty-four hours had wrought in my life. Last night, a hard, narrow cot in the drab and comfortless ward of a reformatory. Tonight, the soft luxury of a beautiful bed with the seductive caress of silk and fine linen about my body and all around me the material evidences of a life of ease, gaiety, and luxury. Gradually my thoughts became hazy and I drifted off into a pleasant, dreamless slumber from which I did not awaken until nine or ten hours later.

CHAPTER SIX

A week slipped by quickly, each night a pleasant repetition, without any notable variations, of the one I have described. This was time enough to assure Madame Lafronde that the experiment was a success. The continued approval with which my seminude appearance was received by patrons, together with certain other indications, was proof that I really constituted an attraction which was imparting a new popularity to the resort.

But it was not Madame Lafronde's intention to limit my activities to exhibitional purposes. She was already being importuned by gentlemen whose interest in me was not to be resigned to mere optical satisfaction and the subtle old procuress was but biding the time necessary for these gentlemen's inflamed fancies to get the best of their financial perspectives. I was being reserved for the sensual delectation of a half-dozen or so of her most exacting and best-paying customers. To the rest, including the general run of parlor guests, I was to remain only a visual aphrodisiac.

Into the ample pockets of my brocade jacket these more or less credulous victims of my enticements and beguilings poured their silver, eagerly taking advantage of such oppor-

tunities as I permitted them to fondle me tentatively or
superficially, bought my cigars and cigarettes, tipped me
generously for every trifling service, sighed, and generally
visited a bedroom with one of my companions where,
doubtless, evoking visions of my naked legs and other
presumed charms, they ravished me by proxy.

Of the patrons I subsequently served in a more intimate
fashion, five developed into "steadies," that is, became
exclusively mine, and came with more or less regularity.
A sixth, no other than the gentlemanly Mr. Hayden, kept
his promise to Hester and either by virtue of genuine
affection for her or actuated by a kindly sentiment to avoid
wounded feelings, insisted upon having both of us with
him at the same time and maintained an attitude of strict
impartiality.

I think Hester's generous spirit would not have resented
a surrender of her priority to me, but though Mr. Hayden
was one of the nicest men I ever met, I was glad that his
instincts of gallantry saved me from being placed in the
light of having distracted his attention from one who was
beyond doubt my best and sincerest friend. I have never
found another such.

Patrons like Mr. Hayden, unfortunately always in a
minority, were the bright and redeeming features of a life
otherwise vicious and degrading. They were the ones who,
regardless of a girl's lost social status, always treated her
with respectful consideration. Generous in recompensing
the efforts which were made to please them, they never
exacted arduous or debasing services, nor were they addicted to unnatural vices which went beyond the pale of
those sexual practices ordinarily considered acceptable and
legitimate.

To my lot fell the patronage of a Mr. Heeley, a gentleman of this desirable category though with the minor
disadvantage of being much older and less attractive physically than Mr. Hayden. There was a Mr. Thomas, middle-

aged and wealthy, who had garnered his fortune in Ceylon and who always had some interesting story to tell. There was Mr. Castle and Mr. Wainwright, both of whom were addicted to eccentricities of a peculiar and disagreeable nature. At first I protested to Madame Lafronde that these two gentlemen were personages *non grata* with me and insinuated that I would not be loathe to dispense with their attentions. It was unequivocally impressed upon me that my inclinations were quite secondary to those of wealthy patrons. "Do whatever they want within the limits of endurance. Satisfy their whims, fancies, even their aberrations if possible as long as they are willing to pay accordingly. Humor them, please them, get the money and keep them coming back as long as you can!" This was the unwritten law in the world of prostitution.

Mr. Hayden was, I think, about thirty years old. I could easily have become really infatuated with this pleasant-spoken, educated, and cultured gentleman. We never knew exactly who he was with reference to his place in the outside world, nor even indeed that his name was really Hayden, for it was not unusual that gentlemen frequenting such places of entertainment as that provided by Madame Lafronde prudently concealed their identities under fictitious names. Nevertheless, there was no doubt that he was of the real gentility.

I liked him very much and I think the affection was reciprocated to an even greater extent than was ever manifested, but he was of that conscientious, kindhearted type, disposed to go out of the way even at personal inconvenience to avoid causing pain to others and he knew that Hester adored him.

To Mr. Hayden fell the honor, if such it might be styled, of initiating me into the real service of which I was now a recruit. My absence from the salon accounted for the numerous inquiries with the old alibi "a bad time of the month, don't you know." Hester and I and Mr. Hayden enjoyed a little dinner by ourselves and thereafter repaired to Hester's room where we disported ourselves lightheartedly for an hour, romping and tumbling over the bed in good-natured abandon as the wine we had imbibed warmed our blood and attuned our receptive senses to lecherous ideas.

Mr. Hayden was a healthy, vigorous young man, a splendid example of physical perfection. The sight of his clean-cut, well-kept body, and the magnificently rigid and well-formed member which was disclosed when he undressed sent the blood surging through my veins. I did not know by what procedure he intended to make use of two women at the same time, but imagined that he would probably take us in turn, maybe changing from one to the other at intervals.

I waited expectantly for Hester to take the initiative. Inside, I was fairly burning up. Though I had bathed most carefully but a short while before, my cunny was wet with anticipation, my clitoris swollen and pulsing. In excuse of this ardor was the fact that I had not been with a man for three long years and during this sterile period there had been no outlet for my passions except the one provided by my own nimble fingers, an occasional wet dream and, as I have related, the orgasm effected by Hester's so-called massage.

We lay down on the bed on either side of our male companion, Hester and I both naked except for our slips, hose and shoes, which we intended to leave on until done with our play and ready for sleep. Mr. Hayden caressed us impartially for awhile, passing his hands over our breasts, fingering the nipples until they stood up stiffly, and finally a hand drifted down over each of the two cunnies. The contact of his warm hand as it lay over mine with one of the fingers pressed lightly within the cleft produced in me an effect which was almost sufficient to put my orgastic mechanism into immediate action. I literally had to "clench" my nerves and strain my willpower to keep from coming. Had he let his finger linger there a bit longer, or had he imparted the slightest friction, my efforts to restrain orgasm would have failed then and there.

But he removed it after a short interval without apparently having observed my delicate condition, and straightening out on his back he drew Hester across his body where, by urging her forward bit by bit, he eventually got her straddled across his chest with her knees doubled beneath her on either side of him. Her dark auburn curls were right at his chin and it required no great imagination to devine that her cunny was going to be licked French fashion.

"If he does that to her before my eyes I'll cream despite anything I can do to hold it back. I know I shall!" I thought to myself.

In the light of experience throughout subsequent years I confess this: that the sight of another woman being Frenched by a man, or a woman Frenching a man, reacts upon me more violently than any other spectacle of a lewd nature. My senses are excited to a frenzy at the sight of this act, and if I let myself go I can have an orgasm without even touching myself, but simply through the impulse conveyed to the genital system through the trajectory of the eye.

Having accommodated Hester comfortably on his strong chest, Mr. Hayden reached over and took me by the arm, manifesting by his motions that I was to seat myself across his middle, impaled upon the turgid emblem of masculinity, behind Hester. Obeying his wordless indications I crouched over him, passing my arm around Hester and clasping her plump bubbies in my hand. Then, gently, breathlessly, I sank down until I felt the entire length of that glorious member throbbing within the living sheath I was providing for it.

But, alas, to my consternation, barely had I perceived the contact of his crisp hair on my naked cunny than my

emotions, overriding all powers of resistance, as though
deriding my futile efforts to hold them in abeyance, rebel-
ling incontinently, loosed themselves and in a second I
was gasping, writhing and suspiring in a regular paroxysm
of passionate ecstasy.

As the reverberations gradually died away and my
thoughts took on a semblance of coherency, I was filled
with mortification. What would Mr. Hayden think of such
amazing lubricity and precipitation? Hester, surprised at
first, had twisted around, and now burst into laughter.

"What happened?" she gasped.

"I don't know!! I did it . . . I couldn't help it!" I
answered, shamefaced.

Mr. Hayden was also laughing.

"You're a fast worker, Sister," he said, his sides
shaking, and realizing that I was momentarily, at least,
exhausted by the orgasm, he added compassionately: "Better
get off and rest a moment while Hester and I catch up with
you!"

I discharged myself and threw my still trembling body
on the bed beside them. With his hands against Hester's
knees Mr. Hayden pushed her backward to take the place I
had vacated and a moment later his cock slid in between
her legs. Crouching over him, supporting herself on her
hands, Hester worked gently up and down on the glistening shaft, alternating from time to time with a twisting,
rolling movement of her hips as she sank down upon his
member, completely hiding it from view.

As I watched this sensuous play the tide of my own
passions began to gather anew. Yielding to sudden impulse
I inserted my hand between Hester's thigh and got my
fingers around the base of the white column which was
transfixing her. With each of her downward lunges my
hand was compressed between the two bodies, and each
time it was compressed my own clitoris throbbed in
sympathy.

Hester began to moan softly. A delicate color crept into her pretty cheeks, and her movements became more vigorous. As I perceived the more powerful pressure of her moist cunny crushing down upon my fist, and the strong, regular pulsations in the hard flesh about which my fingers were clenched, the fires of reawakened lust again blazed within me. My sexual potency was back in full force.

In this opportune moment Mr. Hayden murmured something to Hester. Instantly she ceded the post of honor, slipped forward, and again crouched over his face. A second later I was on the throne she had vacated, and with my arms embracing her from behind, was quivering in response to the throbbing of the rigid shaft which penetrated me and filled me with its soul-stirring warmth.

To the accompaniment of Hester's low moans as a vigorous and active tongue teased her organism into expression I gasped out my own ecstasy and clung to her, half-fainting, while jet after jet of the hot balsam of life flung itself against my womb.

I was no longer a novice. I had graduated from the chippy stage of harlotry and was a full-fledged practitioner of the oldest profession. I was now a professional prostitute.

Mr. Hayden came regularly, adhering faithfully to his program of impartiality, and his visits were interludes in which both Hester and I forgot the sordid, commercialized circumstances under which we were prostituting our bodies and enjoyed ourselves like healthy, robust young animals.

CHAPTER SEVEN

The next patron to whom my companionship was pledged by the astute Madame Lafronde was Mr. Heely. Mr. Heely had been until now what was termed an occasional parlor visitor. He drank little and had never taken a girl upstairs, but he was very liberal with gratuities and it was suspected that he was more than well-to-do. He was a man somewhat between fifty-five and sixty, very courtly and dignified, a gentleman of the old school.

Until my advent in the bordello he had, on the occasion of his rather infrequent visits, confined himself to sitting quietly in a corner, a silent onlooker as a rule, sipping an occasional peculiar combination of liquor which was mixed in accordance with his own instructions. Sometimes he would engage a girl in conversation and after he had departed the subject of the conversation would be reported with considerable amusement. The nice old gentleman could find nothing more interesting to discuss with a half-naked girl than politics, economics and postwar social problems!

Nevertheless, the rewards which were falling to girls who were alert enough to accord him courteous hearing were sufficiently generous to have attracted Madame

Lafronde's unerring eye, and she had him tabulated for future attention.

Now I had observed a more than casual interest in Mr. Heely's attitude toward me in the course of my ambulations about the salon, and had perceived the covert squeeze he always gave my hand as he pressed a liberal tip into it after selecting the single cigar he invariably tucked away in his pocket. Consequently, it was with no great surprise that on being called downstairs early one evening to the little private room which Madame Lafronde reserved for confidential business, I found Mr. Heely with her and learned that I was the subject of the interview.

"Dear Mr. Heely has taken a fancy to you, child. If it were anyone but him, I would positively not consider the matter for a moment. But Mr. Heely is an honorable gentleman, my child. He knows your . . . ah . . . untarnished condition, my dear, and he will be quite contented to . . . ah . . . enjoy your companionship without encroaching on your . . . ah . . . virginal integrity. In fact, my dear, Mr. Heely doesn't care for the sophisticated type, and it was exactly your . . . ah . . . so apparent maidenly innocence which intrigued his . . . ah . . . admiration. Hereafter, my dear, you will be at liberty to receive Mr. Heely any evening he wishes to call on you. You may let him select one night each week."

Mr. Heely bowed courteously.

"But I hope my attentions will not be distasteful to Miss Jessie," he interposed gently. "Perhaps we should consult her first before coming to any definite understanding. I assure her, and you also, Madame, that I will be most considerate in my demands, and will endeavor to reward each of you in a suitable manner for your kindness. Do you think you could care for me as a good friend?" he added anxiously, turning to me.

Madame Lafronde's peculiar words had filled me with amazement. I did not know what to make of the conversation. Mr. Heely was watching me with an intent, almost supplicating look on his face. I glanced uncertainly at Madame Lafronde. As I did so, the lid of her left eye descended slowly. Her face was solemn, impassive.

"Yes, Sir," I answered, "I'm sure I could care for you. Very much indeed, Sir."

The alliance was pledged over three tiny glasses of wine and it was agreed that the following evening I was to be at Mr. Heely's disposition and thereafter the same night each week.

As soon as the interview was concluded I rushed upstairs to find Hester. Into her attentive ear I poured the details of the mysterious contract. My mystification was so genuine that she nearly burst with laughter.

"But what does he want with me, what does he expect me to do?" I begged.

"The old fool has taken it for gospel truth that you're only fifteen years old and that you've never had a cock in you," she answered finally, wiping her eyes. "He'll be a regular gold mine. I had one like that once. He preached religion to me and sucked me off between sermons. I'll bet all you'll have to do with that man will be to let him go down on you. Those old fellows always want to do that. You'll have to pretend it's the first time, act ashamed, take on, cry about it afterwards a little and, baby, will he fill your stocking with bank notes!"

How different people were in real life to what they seemed, I reflected, as the picture which Hester's words evoked passed before my mind's eye. That dignified, cultured, respectable, elderly gentleman going down on me! It was too bizarre, too preposterous. It didn't seem possible.

Hester broke in on the train of thoughts which were passing through my head.

"Really, darling, you're lucky. Imagine having something like that supposed Italian count wished on you."

"I heard Lafronde tell Rhoda she could chase him if he got too rough with her."

This count, real or alleged, constituted something of a house scandal. He had the whipping mania, and though Rhoda submitted to him voluntarily, the pain he inflicted on her caused her to shriek in a way which alarmed everyone within hearing.

"I think she's half in love with the crazy brute. Do you know what he does to her? He puts her across his knees just like a baby, and whips her on the bare bottom with one of her slippers. He keeps her bottom black and blue."

"What in the world does he do it for? What possible pleasure can he possibly get from hurting her?"

"Oh, what do any of them do funny things for? It gives him a hard-on, I suppose. Imagine having a man whip you like that and then wanting to fuck you afterwards."

Madame Lafronde opened the door and came in.

"You'll have to get up early tomorrow morning and go shopping with me," she said. "Mr. Heely has given some very specific instructions about your wearing apparel. Your present mode of dress is not in keeping with his ideas as to what nice girls should wear. And . . ." she continued dryly, glancing at a penciled list in her hand, "he has provided the funds necessary to renovate your wardrobe."

As a result of the shopping expedition which was duly effected the following day, I found myself in possession of some new clothes which, though of the finest and most expensive material, were so incongruously at variance with the ambience in which they were to be worn that I could only look at them with amazement.

There were three black silk dresses with cream-colored lace cuffs and bodices, all of the same general type, but varying in minor details of style and trimming. They were very beautiful, but of a style suitable for extremely young misses, and reached barely to my knees. Underwear there was in profusion, but instead of the slithery, diaphanous

tinted silk I would have selected, it was of the finest
English linen and cambric; slips, petticoats, and panties
with little bands of lace around their edges, and all snow-
white. There were two pair of little, round-toed, low-
heeled patent leather pumps, and a long narrow box filled
with black silk hose.

As we unpacked the purchases Madame Lafronde said:

"Ah, yes, I nearly forgot to tell you, my dear, that your
new gentleman has a special abhorrence of rouge, lipstick
and face powder. He prefers nature in the raw. So you
may abstain from employing your usual artifices on the
occasion of his visits."

I nodded my head in assent. My mind was still floundering in a maze of contradictory whys and wherefores.

"Can you tell me, please, just what that man expects of
me?"

"My girl, I haven't the slightest idea. But I don't doubt
he'll treat you kindly. Men of his age often have very
curious whims and ideas. My experience is that it's profitable to cater to them. Use your brains; find what pleases
him, and act accordingly. If the screwy old fool thinks he
has found a fifteen-year-old innocent running around naked in a whorehouse don't destroy his illusion. It will pay
dividends. But remember this: he made the proposition
himself that he would respect your alleged purity and right
now he intends to live up to it. But if he runs true to form,
before very long he'll be itching to get his pecker between
your legs. And after he's fucked you two or three times it
will be good-bye Mr. Heely. Now I'm only speaking in
the light of experience. There are exceptions to every rule,
and he might be one of them. So use your brains, girl, use
your brains. This is your chance to show what you can do."

At eight o'clock I bathed preparatory to dressing for the
evening. One of the pretty little black frocks was laid out
on the bed waiting for me, together with the childish
underwear, the silk hose and the patent leather pumps.

Having a little time to spare I decided to get out a jar of depilatory cream I had bought that day with the idea of using it in preference to a razor. To my great satisfaction it removed the hair thoroughly and easily without leaving the suggestion of a stubble which, try as I might, I had not been able to eliminate entirely with a safety razor.

The pubic mound and the sides of my cunny felt as smooth and velvety to the touch as a baby's skin. According to the information which accompanied the preparation, hair would not reappear for some time as it was destroyed clear down to the roots. This would be a great convenience, as the task of shaving frequently was growing irksome.

When Mr. Heely appeared promptly at the specified hour of ten, I was all ready for him, waiting demurely in my room, dressed in a little girl's silk frock which barely reached my knees, my hair neatly combed back and tied with a ribbon, and my face sedately free of any artificial coloring or embellishment. There had been much giggling and laughter when earlier in the evening I had paraded this ensemble before the eyes of my companions. Even Madame Lafronde had laughed.

In one hand Mr. Heely carried a large bouquet of beautiful hothouse flowers, in the other a square package containing a box of delicious candied fruit confections. I thanked him for his gifts, took his hat and coat, and arranged the flowers on my little table.

What should I say to him? What should I do? The thoughts buzzed in my head as I toyed with the flowers to gain time to decide, and ended by doing nothing except sitting down before him to wait for him to begin a conversation.

Considering our previous speculations and Hester's suppositions the visit simmered down to what constituted almost ludicrous simplicity and naïveté. Mr. Heely did absolutely nothing more than sit in my room and talk, for the most part on generalized subjects, departing from these orthodox themes only now and then to pass compliments upon my appearance and conduct in his dignified, courtly way. He manifested pleasure at the good taste with which my wardrobe had been selected, and seemed to feel that I was now dressed in a seemly and befitting manner. He stayed for about two hours.

When he arose to go, he took my hand and pressed a kiss lightly upon the back of it. As he lowered it a folded bank note was resting in my palm. I did not want to look at it in his presence, so did not know until after he had gone the value of it. Before bidding me good-night he said:

"May I have the pleasure of calling upon you again next Friday, my dear?"

"Certainly, Mr. Heely, I'll be very happy to have you," I replied.

Not until the door had closed behind him did I straighten out the folded piece of currency. Before my surprised sight was a five-pound note. I could hardly believe my eyes. Surely the good old man was out of his mind.

Straightway I rushed to find Madame Lafronde, laid the money before her and told her exactly what had transpired. She listened, smiling cynically, and pushed it back toward me.

"It's yours, girl. I've already gotten mine. Take it if you want to spend it. If you don't I'll put it away for you."

"All of it?" I gasped.

"Certainly. Now just use your head, girl, and there'll be plenty more where that comes from. I'll get my share, and you may keep all you get from him. Wait a moment . . ." she called, as I turned to leave after thanking her, "here's some more advice for you. Don't brag about your good fortune to the other girls. Keep it to yourself. That old green-eyed monster is always lurking around, waiting for a chance to make trouble. Don't tell others things that will make them envy you."

How deeply these words struck home could only be guessed by one familiar with the circumstances of my past disgrace which had come about under the very conditions against which she was now warning me. Then and there I resolved to keep such good fortune as might come my way carefully hidden from envious eyes in the future.

As far as Mr. Heely was concerned, I ceased for the moment to bother my head with trying to fathom his purposes. If he was willing to pay me five pounds for dressing up like a doll and listening to him for a couple of hours I had no reason for complaint. Both Hester and Madame Lafronde were of the opinion that he would eventually want to do something besides talk, and in this way they were right in a sense, but his conduct never degenerated into anything of an obnoxious nature.

Indeed, his ingenuousness was almost pathetic, and I often felt a twinge of conscience at the imposition which was being practiced upon him. But I salved it with the thought that it would be more painful to him to be disillusioned than to be deceived. He derived a certain happiness from the strange association, and it doubtless filled some lonely space in his heart.

On his second visit he asked permission to sit on a cushion at my feet, a request which was of course granted, although for the moment I was mystified. A bit later the circumstance of the extremely short dress flashed over me and the suspicion which it engendered was verified when I observed an occasional covert glance being directed between my legs.

From this time on I was more careless as to how I sat, but even in this the kindly old gentleman had frustrated his own wishes by having provided me with panties which were so substantially made as to constitute an effectual barrier to the eye.

Slowly but progressively his familiarities advanced as the visits continued. The sitting on a cushion before my knees reminded me of Hester's predictions. It brought his face conveniently close, and I wondered . . . but nothing came of it. Later, he came to seating me on his lap. This provided me with an opportunity to satisfy my curiosity on another point which I had not been able to determine.

Masculine wearing apparel of present times is deficient in one particular. It is prone to reveal in a rather frank manner a certain physical condition to which men are at times subject, one which does not, on such occasions, escape the observant feminine eye. I had never noticed this condition in Mr. Heely, a circumstance which intrigued my curiosity.

Furthermore, his continued liberality was beginning to inspire me with a desire to show my gratitude in some form. It stood to reason there was something he wanted, some inner wish which perhaps he himself had not fully defined, or else was too timid and reticent to express.

And so, partly to satisfy my own curiosity, and partly actuated by a really unselfish wish to give him something in return for his generosity, I decided to encourage him a little more actively, even though this was contrary to Madame Lafronde's counsel.

It was very difficult to convince myself that he was taking this farcical "make-believe-lady" comedy seriously. How could he possibly think I was chaste and innocent, living as I was in a house of prostitution and associating with harlots? It hardly seemed possible that a man of his age and experience could be so credulous.

Surely he was, like myself, just pretending, and finding in the pretense some peculiar psychic compensation beyond my comprehension. Surely he must know in his heart that it was all sham and fraud.

I had observed that his gaze was frequently on my legs. There are men to whom the feminine leg is almost a fetish.

Also, I had not forgotten the floor-sitting inclinations. The next time he came after I had made my resolution I sat on his lap, and as he talked I worked and fumbled through the texture of my dress at my garter which I had purposely tightened until it compressed my leg unduly.

"Mr. Heely," I murmured plaintively, "I wonder if you could fix my garter for me. The buckle is so stiff I can't loosen it and the garter is almost cutting my leg in two." So saying, I drew my skirt up in the most casual manner, exposing the garter, the top of my hose and a tiny bit of flesh above. "Look," I continued, "it's making a regular ring around my leg!" I pulled the garter toward my knee and turned down the upper part of my hose. There was a purple indentation around the leg.

Mr. Heely was instantly all compassion.

"My dear little girl," he exclaimed, "why didn't you speak of it before? Why, this thing is so tight it's cutting off the blood circulation. We must open the buckle and lengthen the elastic."

As he spoke, his fingers tenderly caressed the puckered flesh. He slipped the garter down over my knee and off my leg. It took him but a moment to pry open the buckle and lengthen the band, whereupon he replaced the garter and smoothed my hose back into place.

"How about the other one? Is it tight? Perhaps we'd better fix it, too."

"I wish you would," I replied. "It hurts my fingers to open those buckles."

My other leg was laid bare above the knee and the second garter received his attention. He spent several minutes rubbing the flesh to restore the impeded circulation, adjusted the garter and put my dress down over my knees.

"You're so kind to me, Mr. Heely, I fear I shall never be able to repay you."

"Why, Jessie, dear," he answered, obviously pleased, "just being near you is quite payment enough. I have lived a very lonely life, my dear, and these are happy hours for me. I only wish they were half as pleasant for you as they are for me.''

What could I do with a man so ingenuous and innocent that he refused to rise to such bait? It was not sufficient that I sit on his lap and let him play with my garters. Either he was the world's prize simpleton or he didn't, in truth, want anything from me. I decided to make a bolder effort.

"Indeed they are pleasant for me, Mr. Heely! I feel so comfortable with you. I like to sit on your lap this way. Sometimes . . . sometimes, though, I get feelings when I'm sitting on your lap that I don't understand myself . . ."

I felt him start slightly.

"What kind of feelings, my dear?"

"Oh, I don't know . . . they're hard to describe . . . kind of trembly, warm feelings that go all through me. Like just now, when you were rubbing my leg . . ."

"Are they pleasant feelings, dear?" he asked huskily.

"Oh, yes! Sometimes I think they are naughty feelings, and then again I think they can't be bad when they're so nice. Do you think they are bad feelings, Mr. Heely?" I continued, watching him covertly for his reactions.

"My dear child," he replied finally, taking one of my hands between his and squeezing it, "I hardly know how to answer you. Madame Lafronde told me, if I remember correctly, that you are fifteen years old. At that age the promptings of Nature are to be accepted as an entirely normal manifestation of a healthy body, I would imagine. I have, I must confess, often doubted the prudency of Madame Lafronde's course in bringing you into surroundings and influences which I fear will tend to corrupt your thoughts. I wish . . ." he continued sadly, "that it were possible for me to remove you from this questionable atmosphere, but if I were to suggest such a thing my motives would undoubtedly be questioned. So all I can do, my dear, is to offer you such counsel and advice as my more mature years may qualify me to give. I have never had any daughters of my own, and though I was once married, my wife was taken from me while we were both quite young. So now, in my old age, I have no one to hold on my knee but little Jessie."

"Why, you're not old at all, Mr. Heely!"

He raised my hand, which he was still holding, to his lips and kissed it. I was not so hardened as to be unmoved by his pathetic words, and I understood now for the first time with some degree of clarity, the exact situation.

Mr. Heely's interest in me was unselfish in that it was not actuated by the desire to play any fantastic sexual game, but rather by the promptings of the vague and unsatisfied longings of a man who has lived a repressed and virtuous life, and who, in the eventide of his days, realizing that something vital has been missed, gropes belatedly and blindly for that intangible sense of fulfillment which can only come through bodily and spiritual union with the opposite sex. Too late he had found a compliment which could have satisfied the longings he himself would probably have refused to recognize as merely physical; he must now warm the fibers of his being with the dying embers of a fire disguised as paternal. This he could do without suffering the loss of self-respect or the sacrifice of dignity.

If I chose to continue accepting his bounty indefinitely without thought of compensating him in any way other than by dressing to suit his fancy and playing maidenly innocence, I could do so. He would never make any sexual advances toward me except those of the mildest and most indirect nature.

But I was not without conscience, nor did I lack an elemental spirit of gratitude. The man had been both kind and generous to me, and without hesitating long I made up my mind to find ways to provide this gentle soul with an occasional moment of happiness flavored with just that degree of lubricity which would find an echo in his being, and leave him with a few soft memories with which to dispel the loneliness of his heart.

During the week which elapsed before his next visit I gave considerable thought to the subject, casting about in my mind for some formula which would fit the peculiar circumstances. Various ideas were entertained and discarded as unsuitable. But one afternoon there chanced to cross my thoughts the recollection of Mr. Peters, the watchmaker who had boarded with us when I was a child. In a vague way, Mr. Heely reminded me of Mr. Peters. He was far more cultured and refined, but there was a certain similarity of characters which might have been much more pronounced had their social and educational status been parallel.

Submerged in memories of the past which the thought evoked I saw myself again a child of eleven, slipping surreptitiously into Mr. Peters' room to be masturbated while I stood between his knees holding my little dress up. Again I saw his congested face and the tiny beads of perspiration which testified to the vibrant emotions he must have experienced vicariously through manual stimulation of my body. Had he not actually paid me to let him masturbate me and given other evidences of pleasure in realizing the act? And it had certainly caused me more pleasure than annoyance.

And mentally I began setting the stage for Mr. Heely's next visit.

So it came to pass that after the customary exchange of banalities had been effected, I set about immediately to warm the atmosphere preparatory to the course I had elected to follow with Mr. Heely.

"Mr. Heely," I began diffidently, "you never have seen all the pretty things you had Madame Lafronde buy for me. They're so pretty they make my heart beat faster every time I look at them, and then I think of you."

His face glowed with pleasure.

"I thought I'd seen all of them, my dear," he answered, fingering the hem of my dress. "I was just thinking today that perhaps you needed some new frocks. Madame Lafronde exercised very good taste in her selections and these black silk dresses become you wonderfully."

"I don't mean the dresses alone," I murmured, essaying a bit of bashful confusion. "There were other things, beautiful things; you've never seen them at all, Mr. Heely."

"Ah, you mean underthings, my dear. Quite true, I didn't see them, but if they pleased you that is all that is necessary."

"I never had such beautiful things in all my life, Mr. Heely. Some of them have got the prettiest lace trimming, it looks just like handwork. Hester, my friend, says it's machine-made lace, but I want to show you, Mr. Heely, and see if you don't think it's handmade."

Without waiting for his answer I slipped from his knees and went to my clothes chest, extracted from among the garments stored herein a pair of dainty cambric panties, around the legs of which were attached narrow bands of expensive lace. Thrusting the intimate garment into his hands, I continued to expiate on the quality and beauty of the material.

"Don't you think that's handmade lace, Mr. Heely?"

"Really, I'm hardly qualified to say, my dear," he replied, as he gingerly fingered the garment. "All I can say is that it seems to be well made, but whether by hand or machine I cannot say."

"The ones I've got on are even prettier, Mr. Heely. I don't mind if you see them on me. I want you to see how pretty they are and how well they fit me."

So saying, I raised my dress until a goodly portion of lace filigree and cambric panty leg, to say nothing of quite a bit of flesh, was revealed. Slowly I pivoted around on my toes so that Mr. Heely might judge both the dainty workmanship of the garment, and in addition such physical allurements as might catch his eye.

His face flushed slightly, and he half-averted his gaze, but his next words assured me that I had not missed the mark at which I had aimed.

"My child, it is your pretty limbs which lend beauty to the garment. I have never seen a more charming picture."

Visibly affected, he extended his arms and drew me again upon his lap. His arm prevented my dress from falling into place, and as I made no effort to adjust it I found myself seated across his knees with my legs exposed to the tops of my stockings and higher. I laid an arm over his shoulder and cuddled against him.

Soon I felt a hand lightly caressing my knee. It moved tenderly back and forth over the silken surface of my hose. I lay quietly with my head against his shoulder, my eyes half-closed. The hand moved higher and I sensed the tremor of its touch in a timid caress which dwelt a moment upon the bare flesh above the stocking. It receded downward to the knee, and after a brief hesitation again advanced until finally the palm lay cupped over the rounded curve of bare flesh. His other hand meanwhile passed under my arm, lay quietly and unobtrusively over one of my breasts.

Seated thus with nothing but the thin material of my panties and his own garments between the sensitive areas of our respective bodies I would have easily perceived anything in the nature of a muscular reaction to the erotic incitation to which Mr. Heely was now being subjected.

That there was none confirmed my suspicion that either through physical weakness or possibly a purely mental inhibition he was incapacitated sexually in the more material sense of the word. For him naught remained but such secondary exultations as might have their birth in psychic stimulation, the last dispensation of benevolent old Mother Nature who, tempering the wind to the shorn lamb, concedes that minor consolation, a measure of bliss in the mere presence of contemplation of pleasure through the awakening of an echo, or the touching of a responsive chord in our sensibilities.

Certain now of my ground, I advanced boldly.

Snuggling closer to him, and tightening my clasp about his shoulder, I murmured in a low voice:

"Mr. Heely, you have been so good to me, there is something I must tell you. I'm awfully ashamed to, but I think you should know, so you can tell me what to do. There is no one else I can ask, I just couldn't speak of it to anyone else but you . . ."

His hand clenched about the flesh of my leg.

"What is it, Jessie, dear? I can't imagine anything you could tell me which should cause you to feel ashamed. As you know, I want you to feel perfectly free to tell me anything that troubles you."

"Oh, Mr. Heely, when you know what it is, you may be terribly shocked, and not care for me anymore. I'm so ashamed to tell you I don't know whether I can get up the courage or not . . ."

I dabbed at my eyes with a tearful gesture.

"But, my little Jessie!" exclaimed the now quite perturbed Mr. Heely, "I assure you from the depths of my heart that there is nothing, absolutely nothing which would lessen my regard for you. It hurts me that you can even entertain such a thought!"

"Oh, Mr. Heely!" And here my sobs must have been quite convincing in their rendition. "You think I'm a nice girl, and I'm not! I have the most terrible longings when I'm with you, sometimes I can't sleep at all after you've gone, and other times I have dreams, oh, such dreams, they wake me up and I lie in the dark thinking, and it gets worse until, finally, well, I just have to . . . have to . . . !"

I paused, and after waiting a long moment for me to continue, Mr. Heely whispered tensely:

"Have to . . . have to what, dear?"

"Oh, don't make me say it! You must guess . . . without my putting it in words . . . I don't want to do it . . . they say it ruins a girl's health . . . but I just can't sleep until I make that feeling go away! Now, don't you hate me, Mr. Heely?"

The tension of his hand on my leg relaxed, and the hand moved gently back and forth over the flesh. I peeped at him through my eyelashes; his face was flushed.

"My dear little baby," he murmured in a strained voice, "and you thought telling me this would lessen my regard for you? Don't you remember that I told you the other night that certain emotions and impulses in healthy young bodies were quite natural? Of course, I never dreamed that I was unintentionally contributing to them, but I still don't think it serious enough to upset yourself about, except insofar as your rest and sleep is concerned. That . . ." he added in a troubled voice, "is something we'll have to think about."

"Then you don't think I'm bad for having those feelings, Mr. Heely?"

"Nonsense, child! Every normal person has gone through the same experience in the period of adolescence. But you must exercise self-control and not fall into habits which will undermine your health."

"But . . . but . . . Mr. Heely, if I don't do that, it happens anyway while I'm asleep! When I wake up, it's too late to stop it from happening!

"Oh, Mr. Heely there is something . . . I think . . . I know . . . would be good for me. It would smooth my nerves and take that feeling away . . . if only . . . but how can I ask you such a thing!"

"How can you continue to question my willingness to do anything in my power for you, my little Jessie?" the poor man insisted reproachfully. "If I am in any way to blame for a condition which can only be relieved by discontinuing my visits I'll have to make the sacrifice. Do you think it would be better for you if I didn't come?" he asked anxiously.

"Oh, no, no, Mr. Heely. That wouldn't keep me from thinking of you; it would only make things a hundred times worse!"

"What did you have in mind then, my dear?" he asked, vastly relieved. "Speak frankly; I'll not be offended!"

"Oh, Mr. Heely, it's something . . . it really happened in a dream once. I felt so much better that way than when I . . . you know what I mean . . . and the bad feeling didn't come back for a long time, but . . ." and I hid my face against his shoulder, "it's dreadful to ask you such a thing!"

"Let's consider that after we know what it is!" he urged tensely.

"If you . . . if you . . . oh, Mr. Heely . . . it sounds so terrible . . . but if you would . . . if you would just put your hand there where the feeling starts . . . if you would just put your hand there for a moment each night before you leave . . . I know the feelings would finish and go away and I wouldn't have to do that in the night!"

A tremor passed through his body, his arms gripped me convulsively, and though he spoke with forced calmness, I knew he was in exquisite torment.

"You think that would calm your nerves?" he asked in an unsteady voice.

"I feel sure it would . . . I know it would . . . if you wouldn't mind doing it!"

"Shall we try it tonight?"

"Yes, yes!" I whispered.

"Now?"

"Yes!"

So realistically had I enacted my self-imposed role of

ingenuous impudicity that, unconsciously, it had quite taken hold of my own imagination, and for the moment I was actually living the part I had assumed.

As I slipped from his lap I distinctly felt a tremor in my own knees, and the warm glow of sexual excitation was permeating my body. I had "acted" myself into a real heat.

With trembling fingers I undid my panties and without troubling to remove my dress lay down on my back upon the bed. Shielding my eyes with a forearm and in a fever of anticipation I awaited his approach.

He rose from his chair and sat down on the edge of the bed by my side. He hesitated uncertainly for a moment and then slowly inserted his hand up under my dress. Seeing that he had not the assurance or temerity to throw the dress back and expose my body, and having succeeded in working myself up to a degree in which my own organism was now imperatively demanding satisfaction, I reached down and pulled up the dress myself, revealing my cunny which just that morning had received fresh depilatory attentions.

Just as an electric current is transmitted from one metal object to another by contact so does that mysterious force called sexual exultation communicate itself from one body to another under favorable circumstances. I had deliberately induced an erotic tension in this man such as he probably had not experienced in years. I had been actuated by kindly rather than lewd motives for, as a matter of fact, I had never felt the slightest sexual inclination toward him. Now, having succeeded by my sacrifices in exciting his sterile passions to an exquisite pitch, I found myself caught in my own trap.

A moment or two after I pulled up my dress I felt his hand on my cunny. I separated my legs a bit wider, lay back, closed my eyes, and prepared to yield myself up to the pleasurable sacrifice. I sensed my clitoris, now excited and swollen, pulsing impatiently in anticipation. It wanted to be rubbed and rubbed vigorously. But as I waited expectantly there came no motion in the hand which lay firmly, but inactively pressed against it. I waited a long minute and then moved my hips suggestively once or twice. The hand still lay motionless over the pubic mound with the fingers, likewise motionless, resting lightly along the extension of the crevice below.

It was tantalizing. Didn't this man know anything at all? I wriggled my hips again, once, twice, several times. I squeezed my thighs together, compressing his fingers between them, and still that hand remained impassively quiet.

The tension in my nerves was now such as to render further delay unendurable. I seized his hand in mine and forcibly imparted a rubbing motion as I pressed it harder against my clitoris. Under this friction and pressure the current of erotic sensation began to generate swiftly.

Having set his hand on the proper frictional course I released it and lay back again to savour the ravishing caress until the mounting sensations attained their maximum and, like a bursting rocket, exploded and hurled their melting fires through my body.

Mr. Heely was all tenderness and solicitude as he hovered over me, nor was it difficult to assure him that I now felt immensely relieved and was certain of a peaceful sleep and rest.

Needless to say, the "treatments" were incorporated regularly as a preventative of further nocturnal disquiet, and thus, by the simple expedient of inducing the kindhearted man to think he was safeguarding my health and morals by masturbating me once a week, I found a way to warm the blood in his aged veins and recompense him in a small way for his generosity.

CHAPTER EIGHT

I had been with Madame Lafronde about three months when the patronage of Mr. Thomas, another well-to-do but also middle-aged gentleman was steered my way by the astute old lady.

Things had run along in a pleasant manner; I had gotten along very well with Madame Lafronde. She seemed to take a genuine interest in my welfare, and some of the girls who had at first treated me with a certain coolness, doubtless inspired by the fear that patrons might be tempted from them by my juvenile coquetteries, had been won over and were now cordial and friendly.

Mr. Thomas was too much a man of the world to be at all deceived on the matter of my alleged innocence, but beyond passing a few half-comical, half-cynical observations, he did not dwell on the subject.

Although this gentleman was fairly well along in years, he was hale and robust and had no physical deficiencies. My relations with Mr. Thomas were so entirely normal, or so purely ethical, if I may use the term, that there is little to tell which would be of interest.

Like Mr. Heely, he was a single man, but there the similarity ended. He had engaged my companionship for one quite specific purpose, and between times regaled me with piquant accounts of amorous adventures during his younger days in Ceylon. With apparently no qualms of conscience to disturb him, he told me of having fucked little native girls of eight, nine and ten years of age, of having two or three of them in bed with him at the same time, and of other salacious combinations.

I say he regaled me with these stories "between times" because it was his regular and unvarying procedure to do it to me twice on each of his visits. He was entitled, by virtue of an exorbitant fee paid for my companionship, to pass the entire night, but he never stayed after the termination of the second act. He arrived generally around ten o'clock, spent an hour amusing himself in the parlor, and then came upstairs, where I was waiting for him. He was always prepared for an immediate encounter with a hard-on which belied his years, the potency of which was probably contributed to by aphrodisiacal sights, conversations, and liquor in the parlor.

When the first episode was concluded an hour would be passed in conversation, stories and banter while I sat on his lap naked. As he talked, his hands roved over my body, caressing my legs, thighs, and breasts, and lingering on my hairless cunny where the tantalizing touches kindled fevers in my organism while his own recovered its original potency. When he was ready for the second round we repaired again to the bed and I lay on my back with legs clamped around his middle and wriggled my bottom until I coaxed his second spend from him, whereupon he was ready to cry quits, and I was free for the rest of the night.

This man frequently disconcerted me with some outlandish story, told so seriously that I never failed to be taken in. While in charge of a plantation he had taken a baby, left to the vicissitudes of life through orphanage, and with no facilities other than those available in isolated bachelor quarters, had endeavored to care for it and attend to its requirements.

What a kindhearted man, I thought, much impressed with the patience and benevolence the act implied, and passed some observation to this effect.

"She was a pretty little thing," he concluded, puffing meditatively at his cigar.

"Ah . . . it was a girl," I murmured.

"Yes. She had the most beautiful skin, a soft, olive tint. It was like silk to the touch. And her bubbies, not any bigger than orange halves, but as firm and . . ."

"How old was that baby?" I interrupted.

"Oh, she was eleven or twelve, I guess."

"It was indeed noble of you to have cared for her so tenderly, Mr. Thomas," I answered with heavy sarcasm. "I presume dressing and undressing her, bathing her and so on must have signified quite a sacrifice of time and labor for you. Possibly you even had to share your bed with her?"

"Unfortunately, there was only one bed in the place. And I couldn't let the poor little thing sleep on the floor, of course."

"Of course not!"

Next on the list came Mr. Castle. This gentleman had a complex for strange and unusual postures in sexual intercourse, and also an itch to experiment along lines somewhat contrary to the plans of Nature. Only the fact that he was both liberal and possessed of unfailing good humor made association with him supportable. Had it been possible to offend him, my angry reactions to some of his droll impudences would quickly have terminated our relationship.

No sooner was the door closed behind us on the occasion of his first bedroom visit than I was startled to find myself suddenly seized from behind and tumbled forward so that while the weight of my body fell upon my hands and wrists, my legs were caught and held under his arms.

In this undignified position, with my short skirts fluttering about my face and head, and with my bare bottom and all there was between my legs exposed, I struggled and protested angrily, but to no avail, for with imperturbable aplomb, while still imprisoning my kicking legs under his strong arms, he unfastened the front of his trousers and in an instant I felt his cock poking against my inverted cunny.

I tried to evade its thrusts as I sputtered angry protests, but he had me in such a position that I was quite helpless and in another moment I felt it going in, in this upside down fashion. The whole thing was finished and over almost before I was conscious of the pain which his cock, pressing against the side of my womb in this unnatural position, caused me.

He was what is termed in professional circles a "fast shooter," one of those men whose orgastic reaction is so rapid as to require but a few thrusts. In the midst of my kicking and squealing I felt the hot gushes followed by the wet, sticky trickle of semen down over my stomach. A second later he released me and sank down on the bed, shaking with laughter while I, after regaining my feet, stood before him, my face flushed with indignation, protesting such cavalier treatment.

"Excuse me, Sister," he gasped finally between gusts of laughter. "I'm sorry I was so rude. It's a weakness I have . . . I just can't resist temptation!"

"Well, why are you laughing about it, then?" I demanded, only half-appeased by the doubtful apology.

"Ha, ha, ha! If you only knew how funny you looked, standing on your head, with your cute little cunny upside down!"

"Oh!" I gasped, my indignation mounting anew, but before I could formulate a sufficiently withering retort, he continued:

"There was something . . . something . . . ah, yes; how is it your cunny hasn't any fur? I've seen them shaved off before, but they're like a man's chin, you can feel the bristles even after a close shave. Your pussy felt as smooth as silk. Let's take a peek at it Sister!"

I was still palpitating with anger, but under such ludicrous circumstances it could not last long and finally I smiled in spite of myself.

"You're a very abrupt person," I said. "Since you believe in caveman tactics, it's a wonder you bother about asking me to let you see it."

No sooner were the words out of my mouth than he acted on the suggestion. His hand closed over my wrist and I was jerked none too gently to the bed and tumbled over on my back. Again I raged helplessly while, shaking with irrepressible laughter, he adroitly subjected my wrists by holding them in one hand, and with the other pulled up my dress.

Apparently unfamiliar with the properties of depilatory agents, his visual and tactile examination seemed to convince him that the denuded condition was a natural one, which greatly intrigued his interest. While I continued to rage futilely, he felt and squeezed the naked lips and surrounding parts, and still not content, decided to have some more fun with me.

No one except a woman who has suffered the indignity can comprehend the conflict of emotions undergone in being jacked-off forcibly against her wishes. It is quite one thing to submit to the manipulation when it is desired, and another to be forced.

As the ball of the clown's finger rotated against my clitoris the treacherous little organ stiffened up in response, contrary to my wishes and despite all the mental influence I could bring to bear on it. When I breathed curses and demands for instant release it pulsed with increasing vigor under the friction, with the inevitable result that my resistance was suddenly stifled and my angry exclamations quite involuntarily changed into surprising moans.

The orgasm diminished my anger somewhat but I still felt resentful and complained bitterly of having been treated in such an outrageous manner.

"It was just the same as a rape!" I protested.

"Rape? Rape?" And again he burst into laughter. "That's a new one on me, Sister! I never knew before that a girl could be raped by a finger!"

"Well," I answered, my natural good humor beginning to assert itself, "it amounts to the same thing. When you make a girl do something against her wishes, it's rape, even if you do it with your finger!"

It was impossible to stay angry with this comical buffoon, and being further mollified by a gift of respectable denomination, I found myself looking forward to his next call, if not with longing, at least with curiosity.

The next eccentricity he manifested was a desire to try an inexhaustable number of unusual and strange positions. Because of the rapidity with which orgasm overtook him, the only way he could avoid ejaculation and prolong these experiments was to take his cock out of me after making a few quick movements. Naturally, this was very tantalizing, for it made me hot without satisfying me, but I had to stand it as best I could.

Obligingly following his instructions I stood on the floor, bent over, my hands resting on my knees, and let him do it to me from behind. I lay doubled up in a ball on the bed with my knees crooked forward against my chest while he knelt in front of me, I sat spiked on his lap in a rocking chair, I lay on my back on a table with my legs over his shoulders and went through other equally strained and arduous exercises wondering all the while why a man should want to take such roundabout and complicated roads to reach a place which was accessible by shorter and easier routes. All these strenuous gymnastics just to make a few drops of semen come out of his testicles, a result I could have attained for him in ten seconds if left to my own devices.

But it wasn't until a subsequent visit that I found I had more objectionable things still to contend with.

This time he had me on my hands and knees on the bed and was kneeling behind me. This is the position known as "dog fashion" in the social circles of prostitution, and inasmuch as it projects a woman's cunt out quite prominently, she has to be careful that the man does not injure her by too deep a penetration, especially if he has a large cock.

I felt his cock pushing against me, but it was aimed too high, and was prodding my bottom instead of my cunny. At first I thought that this was just an accident and putting my hand behind me I shoved it downward and got it headed in the right direction. But after two or three vague pushes, it slipped out and again I felt it punching against my bottom, this time in such a determined manner that it almost got its head inside.

Again I reached behind me to push it away, but he resisted the effort, and leaning over my back, whispered:

"Don't push it away. Let it go in for just a moment!"

"I will not!" I exclaimed, and jerked free from his embrace.

"There, there!" he answered, soothingly, "I was just teasing you, Sis! Come on and let's finish. I have to get away early tonight."

Rather reluctantly, and on the alert for a new attack on the unguarded spot, I again braced myself on my hands and knees, but this time he let Nature take her course in normal channels.

From this time on the man was unable to resist the temptation to try to do it to me in the bottom on every occasion which presented itself. Determinedly I resisted blandishments, coaxings, and even treacherous efforts to catch me unawares, but it got on my nerves and brought choleric protestations to my lips. In justice to Mr. Castle, I must say that he took my angry rebuffs and blunt refusals to gratify his unnatural whim in good spirit and unfailing pleasant humor.

It was then I intimated to Madame Lafronde that it would not hurt my feelings were his affections tactfully transferred to some other girl, but I was ashamed to tell her the exact reason.

"Why don't you want him?" she insisted.

"Well, I finally said, "he has crazy ideas. The first night I had an appointment with him he stood me on my head and did it to me upside down!"

"What!" she expostulated. "Is that the only reason you dislike him?"

Abashed, I made a clean breast.

"No, it isn't! If you must know, I'll tell you! He never gives me a moment's peace from wanting to do it to me in the bottom!"

I expected that this revelation would bring a decided expression of indignation from Madame Lafronde and that she would now be willing to concede that Mr. Castle was indeed a most objectionable client.

But, after gazing at me a moment, she began to laugh heartily.

"And is that all that is wrong with him?"

"Isn't that enough?" I responded stiffly.

"My word, girl," answered the old lady, "there is no pleasant road to success in anything, not even in whoring. You're going to meet men far more difficult to deal with than this Mr. Castle, so you must now learn how to get what you want from them and how to evade what you don't want by using diplomacy. They say the way to a man's heart is through his stomach. I don't know about that, I never did much cooking, but you can take my word for it that the way to his purse is through his cock. And his purse will stay open just as long as you keep his cock in a good humor and no longer!''

I was not too dense nor too stubborn to comprehend the wisdom of her philosophy and I did indeed learn eventually that more could be accomplished by cunning and diplomacy than by angry words.

''Sometime,'' I murmured to Mr. Castle one night as I deftly evaded a sly attempt on my bottom, ''sometime, I'm going to let you do that, just to see what it feels like . . . but not tonight!''

CHAPTER NINE

When Mr. Wainwright was added to my list of regulars I found need of all the philosophy I could muster. He was a suave, dapper little man, rather handsome in an effeminate way, but very nervous and emotional. He was not, I think, over twenty-eight or thirty.

There was nothing special in his appearance to suggest the possibility of any weird abnormality, yet here is what happened: As soon as we were alone in the seclusion of my room he went through a pantomine of courting me in the most exaggerated manner. Words of gallantry, adoration, and vows of eternal loyalty poured from his lips as he knelt before me, kissing first my hands, then my feet and legs.

In accordance with my usual custom when receiving new admirers for the first time, I was fully clothed, excepting one single garment which for convenience sake I left off, inasmuch as its absence would not be noted until the moment when its presence would be of no moment. Taken aback by this man's strange performance, and indeed not being sure that he wasn't simply trying to be funny, I remained silent.

Murmuring words of endearment and adoration his lips

gradually ascended to my knees, whereupon he turned his face upward and begged in supplicating words:

"Oh, my Fairy Princess! Give me your permission to raise the hem of this robe so that your slave may cool his burning lips on the sweet freshness of your divine limbs."

This was too much for me.

"Go ahead and cool them, Sweetie!" I giggled with a democratic sociability quite out of keeping with the regal estate he had delegated to me.

Ignoring the flippancy of my answer, he turned the edge of my dress up, not high enough to reveal the absence of the interior garment already referred to, but just high enough to expose two or three inches of bare flesh above the tops of my hose. Upon this isolated flesh he pressed more moist kisses clasping my knee meanwhile to his breast.

"Beautiful Princess!" he sighed estatically, and then in humble, imploring tones, "will Your Highness deign to repose upon the couch and let this faithful slave quench his thirst at the sweet spring of life?"

It was too ridiculous and I laughed hysterically, but supposing that he was now ready to "quench his thirst" in the customary manner, I let him lead me to the bed and lay down, still laughing.

Disregarding my risibility he slowly and with exaggerated deference, raised my dress and folded it back. He gazed for a long moment at my denuded cunny which was now in plain sight, and then, before I guessed his intention, leaned down and placed his mouth on it.

Whether this was just a little frisking preparatory to an orthodox fuck I had no means of knowing at the moment, but in any event it was a pleasant variation, and I was agreeably surprised. I have been "Frenched" on a few occasions even before entering Madame Lafronde's bordello, and sometimes Mr. Hayden would tickle my clitoris with the tip of his tongue for a few moments when Hester and I were with him. I was peculiarly sensitive to the caress and sometimes felt an inordinate longing for it, but with the exception of Mr. Hayden, none of my clients had ever taken the notion, and I, naturally, would never suggest it.

Consequently, when I felt this man's mouth on my cunny, and perceived the play of his tongue over the sensitive parts, I shivered delightedly, my clitoris stiffened up, and I relaxed my body to better enjoy the enervating caress.

It continued, actively, expertly. I felt my clitoris, now swollen and erected, clenched between his lips. A ravishing suction was being applied to it, and my sexual organism responded by throbbing excitedly with a mounting fever of lascivious ebullition. Heavens, it did feel good. If it were kept up a moment or two longer, something would surely happen.

I tensed my body, lifted myself up slightly on my elbows, and glanced downward to my companion. Unobserved by me he had opened the front of his trousers, and was frigging himself violently. I sank back with a groan. my ovaries yielded to the intoxicating incitation, and in a second I was suspiring in the ecstasy of orgasm.

No sooner had my sexual forces expended themselves than a feeling of revulsion came over me. I do not know to just what extent other women are similarly affected in this particular, but for several moments following ejaculation, the slightest touch upon my cunny causes me a disagreeable sensation. It passes quickly, but during those few moments I cannot stand even the softest touch or caress. As the last tremors of orgasm died away I put my hand on his head and gently but firmly pushed him away.

Yielding to the gesture, he released my clitoris from between his clenched lips. His face slid down a little and his lips attached themselves to the flesh on the inside of one of my thighs just below my cunny. This did not bother me, though I expected a discoloration would result from the strong suction he applied to the flesh as he continued meanwhile to masturbate himself vigorously.

The orgasm I had just experienced left me too languid to pay much attention to just what he was doing, though I was watching him through half-closed eyes. Suddenly, through his own lively handling, the jets of semen began streaking from his cock and flew all over my legs. And in the same moment, his teeth penetrated the flesh of my thigh where he had been sucking it.

Between pain and surprise I let out a shriek and sprang from the bed in a single bound. With mixed emotions of fright and anger I looked at him, uncertain as to whether I should fly from the room or demand an explanation of his brutality. He was lying on the bed, gasping and weltering in his own pollution, seemingly indifferent to my outraged feelings.

I raised my dress to examine the wound. It was less serious than I had first imagined, being quite superficial in character. He had bitten into a tiny fold of flesh, just deep enough to draw blood, which fact was attested to by several ruby drops which were slowly trickling down the inside of my thigh. When I saw that I was not wounded as badly as I had first supposed, anger dissipated fright, and I turned on him wrathfully.

"What kind of a crazy fool are you, biting me like that?"

He looked at me stupidly for a moment and then his gaze traveled downward to where the little red drops were visible between my legs. A look of contrition passed over his face. He flung himself at my feet, and clasping my knees to his breast, begged me piteously to forgive him. To my amazement his eyes were filled with tears.

"But why did you do that to me?" I insisted reproachfully.

"Sweet Princess," he moaned, "I did it unconsciously.

Strike me, beat me, kick me, do what you will with me in punishment, but do not be angry with your slave!"

What could one do with such a lunatic?

"Well," I said, finally, "I'll forgive you, but don't ever do that again!"

When he had departed I gazed wide-eyed at the material evidence of Madame Lafronde's sage philosophy, for without bothering to count them, he had flung upon my dresser a little sheaf of bank notes which totaled an amount in excess of anything I had previously received.

After I had counted the money, I examined again the tiny laceration in the white flesh of my thigh. It had stopped bleeding and no longer pained. Money can indeed cure many ails and ills. It was an obsession the man was prey to, but lured on by the irresistible magic of gold, I risked further mistreatment and got it, and today, on the inner surfaces of my thighs just below my cunny, are several tiny white scars, each punctuating a moment of insanity during which the teeth of a sadist bit into my flesh while with his own hand he lashed his sexual fury into its final torment of expression.

During the later period of my incarceration in the reformatory, and for over five months of the time I was on Madame Lafronde's staff, I had no word of my foster brother Rene. Letters sent to the last address he had given me in Canada came back unclaimed. His silence worried me greatly. I did not know but what some grave misfortune had overtaken him, but I suspected that, unable to send me any money, he was ashamed to write.

While thinking about him one day I recalled that in our old neighborhood dwelt a boyfriend to whom Rene was greatly attached, and it occurred to me to write this boy, or young man as he now was, if still alive, on the chance that he might have had some news of Rene.

I acted on this impulse, but the response, which came by return post was negative. He had not received any letters from Rene since the period which embraced that in which I had been in communication with him, and he likewise commented on the fact that a letter he had sent to the address last supplied him by Rene had come back to him unclaimed. Thus, my contentment and material success were marred by the preoccupation that something had happened to Rene, whose image was deeply impressed in my heart.

Accustomed to sleep until around midday or later, I was surprised one morning to be aroused from my slumbers by Madame Lafronde at the unusual hour of nine. When I was sufficiently awake to sit up in bed and ask what was wanted, she rather grumpily informed me that there was a visitor waiting for me in the parlor.

This was an unprecedented variation of the house regime, and I stared at her in surprise.

"Who is it?" I asked wonderingly.

"Don't sit there asking questions. Get up; comb your hair, put on a dressing gown and go downstairs."

Plainly, Madame was not in the best of humor at having been obliged to get out of bed at this hour. There was something ominously mysterious about this matter. In my mind I indeavored to find an explanation. With chilling apprehension there came across my thoughts the suspicion that it was in some way connected with the reformatory. Maybe they had discovered how I was living and had come to get me! My face paled and I glanced toward Madame Lafronde. Her expression told me nothing.

"Is there anything wrong?" I whispered.

"You'll think there's something wrong if you ever have anyone call here again at this hour!"

"But . . ." I protested, "I have never made any morning appointments with anyone!"

"Oh, it's nothing serious. Here, slip this on," she answered, holding my dressing gown for me. "Tidy yourself a bit and hurry up so I can get back to sleep."

Nervously, I tied my short curls with a ribbon, dabbed a little powder on my face and followed her downstairs where, after motioning toward the parlor, she left me and retired in the direction of her own sleeping quarters.

Still wondering who in the world could have had the temerity to upset the house traditions by calling at this hour, I pushed aside the curtains and entered the room.

Standing with his back toward me, looking out of the window, was the figure of a man I did not at first recognize. I approached hesitatingly, and as he heard my footsteps, he turned and faced me.

For a moment I stood paralyzed, unable to move or utter a word.

It was Rene.

The letter I had written to his friend with seemingly fruitless results had in the end been the instrument of our reunion, for through the address I had given in the letter Rene had been able to locate me without loss of time or difficulty.

He had come directly to the house, and Madame, on being informed that I was his sister, had consented to call me without delay.

In a flash we were in each other's arms, both talking at once. For an hour I sat on his lap, listening to the story of his adventures and misadventures. Shamefacedly, he confessed that, as I had divined, a long period of hardship, during which he had suffered many vicissitudes and disappointments, had been the cause of his silence.

"But, darling!" I interposed reproachfully, "I could have helped you so easily. I have lots of money saved, if I had only known how to reach you I could have sent you some!"

Our conversation was interrupted by the maid, who had come in to clean the parlor.

"Come on up to my room, darling, we can talk there, and I'll have the girl send us up some coffee and cakes!"

With his arm about my waist we ascended the carpeted and padded stairs. Within my room I hastily gathered up such pieces of clothing as were lying carelessly about and straightened out my disordered bed while Rene gazed about in evident wonderment.

"Gee, this is a regular palace you're in, Sis," he mused. "Just what kind of a place is it? That old dame wasn't going to let me see you until I told her you were my sister."

"Oh, Rene, don't you know what kind of a place it is?" I asked, in surprise.

"Well . . . I've got an idea. It's a kind of sporting house, isn't it?"

"Yes, it is, Rene."

"Gee, Sis, I'm sorry. I'll find some kind of work and get you out of it."

"But I don't want to get out! I'm getting along fine; its easy, and I don't mind it at all! Really, I don't! Madame Lafronde is awfully good to me, Rene, and you'll be surprised when you see how much money I've got!"

"It's supposed to be a tough life for a girl, but gee, Sis, you look absolutely topping. Word of honor," he added, standing in front of me and holding my arms, "you don't look a day older than you did when I went away. In fact . . ." he continued, eyeing me in a puzzled way, "you actually look younger!"

I laughed contentedly as he continued to look at me, perplexed.

"It's your hair, for one thing. Why did you cut it short? It's cute that way, but it makes you look like a kid!"

"That's what it's supposed to do," I replied, giggling. "Some of our most valued patrons are freaks that can't get a hard-on unless they think they're fucking an infant. Look . . ." I added, raising the short crepe-de-chine slip I had on under my dressing gown so that he could see my hairless cunny, "more of my disguise!"

"Gosh!" exclaimed Rene, breathing harder, "it gives me a funny feeling to see it like that, Sis! Reminds me of when it really was that way. But how did you get the hair off so smooth?" he continued, touching me gingerly with his fingers.

"It's some paste I put on it. It makes the hair come out clear down to the roots. Do you like it that way?" I asked, eyeing him mischievously. "You used to think one wasn't much good until it had hair on it."

"Gee, Sis, it looks good enough to eat! And your legs, why, Sis, you always did have pretty legs, but honest, they're perfect now; you're the best-looking girl I ever saw!"

What feminine heart wouldn't have thrilled at such sincere tribute as this?

"Oh, Rene, you old darling!" I murmured, half crying, half laughing as I put my arms around him and squeezed up to him. "I missed you so much! I never have had a fellow half as good as you! I've just lain awake nights remembering all the things we used to do! Sometimes when fellows were doing it to me I closed my eyes and made believe it was you, but nobody could ever make me feel the same as you did!"

Against my stomach as I clung to him I could feel the warm pressure of something hard and rigid which was pulsing with enough vigor to make its movements perceptible through our respective clothing. I slipped my hand down inside the waistband of his trousers and sought out the disturbing element. A shiver passed through me as my fingers closed around the turgid object and a vertigo of longing which demanded immediate satisfaction overwhelmed me.

"Oh, Rene, darling, it feels so good to have this in my hand again! I'll bet it's been up inside lots of girls since I had it last, though. Are those Canadian girls very pretty,

Rene?" I asked, the eternal feminine rising to the surface as in my imagination I pictured Rene with other girls.

"Some of them aren't so bad, but I never saw one that could hold a candle to you, Sis!" Rene replied uncomfortably.

"Come on, Rene!" I panted, "let's do it quick! Nobody is up yet, but as soon as the girls are awake, I'll have to introduce you to them!"

I flung myself on the bed, and in a jiffy the object for which I was palpitating with burning ardor was buried in my trembling flesh. With my arms entwined about Rene's neck I fluttered and moaned and received his thrusts in a regular frenzy of emotion. In it went, until I could feel his crisp hair pressed against my naked parts, and as if this penetration were not enough I hurled myself up against it and pressed with all my might so that it might reach the innermost depths of my being. Moaning, gasping, suspiring, and murmuring hysterical endearments, I clung to him, my arms clasped about his neck and my legs clenched over his strong back while my flanks quivered and strained to draw from his as quickly as possible the satisfying balm my body craved.

Hardly had I recovered from my first orgasm when there was a discreet knock at the door. While Rene hastily buttoned up his clothing I took from the maid a tray with coffee and toast. My hands were still trembling from the recent exhilaration, and my face was flushed and hot.

We lingered over our coffee for another hour, talking, laughing, reminding each other of little incidents which stood out prominently in our memories of the past.

"Do you remember when that little Marshall girl's mother caught you trying to do it with her in the coal shed?"

"I'll say I remember it! She gave me such a lacing with an old belt that I couldn't walk straight for a week. Do you remember how Mr. Peters used to send me out on fake errands so he could have you alone in the house and diddle you with his fingers?''

And so, immersed in reminiscences of the past, some laughable, some pathetic, some tragic, the time flew by, and the sound of movement and conversation elsewhere in the house reminded me that it was high noon.

''I'm going to call Hester to introduce you to her. She's the girl that was with me in that darned old reformatory. She's my best friend; if it hadn't been for her, I don't know what would have happened to me.''

I jumped up and went directly to Hester's room. Finding her awake and languidly engaged in combing her luxuriant hair I danced up to her.

''Oh, Hester, I've got the grandest surprise for you! Powder your nose and come quick to my room. There's somebody there waiting to see you! It's my brother Rene, come back from Canada! He came at nine o'clock this morning and Lafronde woke me up! I bet you'll fall in love with him when you see him; he's the handsomest fellow you ever saw!''

My excitement was contagious, and Hester rushed to make herself presentable. As soon as she was ready I led her to my room where Rene was waiting.

''This is Hester, my very dearest friend, Rene. Next to you, I love her more than anyone in the world!''

''Gee, I don't blame you for loving her, Sis!'' exclaimed Rene, as he jumped to his feet and admiringly appraised Hester's dark beauty. ''I could love her myself without half trying!''

''Well,'' I said, judiciously, ''she's the only girl in the world that would be good enough for you, and you're the only fellow in the world that would be good enough for her, so that leads to only one logical conclusion.''

Hester stayed with us until, despite my protestations to the contrary, she felt that we might wish to be alone, and with a promise to see Rene again before he left, she slipped out, closing the door behind her.

Rene wished to leave around one-thirty, and anxious to be as close to him as possible during the remainder of his visit, I again sat on his lap. Before long, new temptation began to assail me. Tentatively, I felt around inside his clothing with my hand until I found what I was searching for. It stiffened out magically under my fingers. For a few minutes I squeezed it, thrilling to the quick transformation and the significant throbbing which my touch had evoked.

"Once more . . . before you go?" I whispered, squeezing it tightly.

"Just what I was thinking myself!" he answered huskily.

"You lie underneath and let me get on top, like we used to do in the attic!" I suggested.

"Suits me, absolutely."

And this is how it happened that Hester, returning to bid Rene good-bye as she had promised, on opening the door was confronted by a most poetic sight.

I, for greater freedom of movement, had thrown off the dressing gown and, crouched over Rene with my bottom in the air, was working frantically up and down on the pivotal point which projected from his middle.

"T-a-a-h!" she gasped, ". . . I didn't think . . . excuse me . . . !" and she closed the door and fled precipitately.

"I forgot to lock the door!" I murmured, guiltily.

"Not the first time, Sis!" he retorted.

"Well, it doesn't make any difference here," I answered, resuming my efforts to attain the objective which had been uppermost in my mind up to the moment of interruption.

After Nature had taken her pleasant and satisfying course and the inward fires which consumed me had again been temporarily lulled with a copious shower of masculine sperm, Rene departed.

Hester had not returned, and so as soon as I had bidden him good-bye at the door, I returned to her room upstairs.

"Jessie!" she exclaimed, "you could have knocked me down with a feather!"

"Oh, that was nothing," I answered lightly, thinking she had reference to opening the door without knocking. "It didn't startle your modesty, did it?"

"But . . . but . . . your own brother!" she whispered, in low, shocked tones.

For a moment I failed to grasp the import of her words. When comprehension dawned on me, I burst into laughter.

"Didn't you know, ha! ha! ha! Didn't I tell you, Rene isn't my real brother, he isn't any blood relation to me at all, he's only a stepbrother!"

A look of relief passed over Hester's face.

"Jesse, no! You never told me that before! You used to talk about him in the reformatory, but you never said he wasn't your real brother. Gosh! I never was so surprised in all my life as when I opened that door and saw you on top of him, naked! I could hardly believe my eyes!"

"We were just renewing an old love affair that started when he was eight and I was six!" I answered, laughing. "What did you think of him?"

"Well," she replied, smiling, "let's go downstairs right now and tell Lafronde that we've just discovered we're lost sisters, so the next time he comes, he can be a brother to both of us!"

CHAPTER TEN

The days slipped into weeks, the weeks imperceptibly, into months, and almost before I realized it, a year had gone by. Barring the few disagreeable incidents of a minor nature such as those I have described, the time had been passed on the whole both pleasantly and profitably.

Miraculously, I had escaped all three of the afflictions whose menacing shadows are ever close at the heels of those who traffic with their sexual favors: syphilis, gonorrhea and pregnancy, the Three Horsemen of the Prostitute's Apocalypse.

My health was good, and I had gained in weight, having added several pounds of flesh which improved my figure even though at the cost of some of the juvenile slimness which in the beginning had been such a valuable asset. Nevertheless, I had for some time been observing a gradual change in my physical orgasm which was becoming more and more pronounced, and the condition was one which is not common in the walk of life I frequented.

I will speak plainly. Sexual sensibility, which is that capacity to respond easily and actively to erotic excitation, diminishes rapidly in the majority of professional prostitutes who are obliged to exercise their sexual functions with a frequency far in excess of the provisions of Nature. The sexual act becomes a mere routine in which pleasure or orgasm is only simulated to satisfy the customer's ego.

They moan and sigh and murmur passionate endearments, but if their minds could be read, the hollow mockery would be apparent, for one thought only occupies them: a wish to be finished and rid of the man as quickly as possible.

This is the rule which should have applied to me, but didn't.

Desires which should have been appeased by all too frequent gratification were quieted but for a moment, and almost at once flamed anew with increased insistence. And the tendency was growing. Strange as it may seem, sometimes after having had orgasm effected as many as half a dozen times in a single afternoon and evening, I was obliged to masturbate before being able to sleep. Pathologically and physically, I was oversexed, designed, seemingly, by Mother Nature herself, to be a whore.

Now in this propitious moment there entered into the horizon of my life, for the first time, a really sinister influence. And though in that influence I myself sensed a spirit of perversity, I was drawn toward it like a moth to the candle. Knowing that the destiny it signified was evil, I had no wish to resist it.

Montague Austin—what memories that name evokes. Memories of passion, cruelty, horror, blended with the cloying and intoxicating poison of a transcendental lust which knew no law other than that of gratifying its own frenzy.

I was supposed to have been infatuated with the man, but I never loved him, nor thought I did. No, I did not love him, but I did love the mad transports, the exquisite torment of lust which he, as no other man before or since, had the power to awaken in me. As an addict to the scented dreams of opium, so did I become an addict to

Montague Austin. He was to me a fatal drug which held me a willing victim in its embrace.

For the first time, in broaching the subject of a new patron to me, Madame Lafronde manifested a doubt as to the expediency of putting my youth and inexperience to the test which she clearly thought an alliance with Montague Austin would signify.

I had seen the man but once; he was not a regular habituate of Madame Lafronde's house, but her facilities for gathering information were such that within less than twenty-four hours his social position, resources, and such portions of his history as were available on such inquiry were known to her. All the information, excepting that which related to his economic situation, was unfavorable. She summed up her opinion in the one expressive word—rotter. But he had money, and money covers an otherwise inexcusable number of objectionable qualities. Possibly by the exercise of tact and vigilance I could handle him.

As for myself, I was the last person in the world to doubt my own capabilities, so Madame Lafronde finally and with patent misgivings, yielded to my complacent and optimistic self-assurance.

Now let us glance briefly at the man himself.

He was, at the time our paths crossed, thirty-four years of age. The younger son of a titled British aristocrat, he had inherited both money and social position. The social position had been forfeited by dissolute escapades, the money dissipated in part, but enough remained to qualify him still as a rich man. He was married, but according to rumor his profligate ways had brought about an irreconcilable estrangement with his consort.

At first glance one would have marked Montague Austin as an extremely good-looking man. But a less cursory observation would not have failed to disclose signs of a cynical and somewhat cruel character in his darkly handsome face and narrow mouth. A little above average height and signally favored with regard to other physical characteristics, he was in truth a figure to intrigue feminine imagination.

In my brocade jacket, high-heeled slippers, and with my grenadier's cap tilted at a jaunty angle I was going through my customary antics one night when I suddenly felt myself clasped from behind, and turning, looked into the cynically smiling face of a man I had not previously seen among our parlor guests. I paused, waiting for him to release me, but instead, he swung me around, dropped an arm under my hips, and hoisted me, cigarette tray and all, into the air.

"There is a tide in the affairs of men," he quoted, "which, taken at the flood, leads on to fortune. Baby, you're my tidal wave, the one I've been waiting for all my life!"

He got off this declaration with such well-simulated solemnity and impressiveness that all within hearing laughed, nor could I myself restrain a smile.

"I think you're the tidal wave," I retorted, "since I find myself quite swept off my feet. If you'll be so kind as to set me down, maybe I'll let you buy a packet of fags from me!"

"Lord love me!" he exclaimed tragically, "she peddles fags while Rome is burning! I perish for a kiss, and she offers nicotine!"

"Oh, all right!" I giggled, and kissed him lightly on the cheek. "Now be a nice man and let me down!"

He set me down on the floor, but still held me a prisoner with an arm under mine.

Yielding to his solicitation I unhooked the cigarette tray, placed it on a table, accompanied him to a secluded corner of the room, and let him take me upon his knee.

Dropping his bantering attitude he immediately became serious and asked for a room appointment. A shiver passed over me as his fingers boldly played with the nipples of my breasts. I glanced ito his eyes but hastily lowered my gaze as something of the lustful obsession which was later to dominate me came into being. Sensing the absurdity of telling this man any fairy stories, I explained frankly that I was not permitted to make any appointments except through the intervention of Madame Lafronde.

"Ah, I see," he answered, taking in the situation instantly, "you're a special attraction. So much the better, I'll see her immediately, and I suppose there's no use of taking up any of your time until I do."

"Any of the other girls can make room appointments." I proffered.

"Thanks for the information," he answered dryly, "but you've wrecked their chances. I couldn't even get a hard-on with any of them now."

"I've got a friend here," I murmured, looking around for Hester. "That's her over there by the door, the girl with the dark hair. She can give any man a hard-on. Shall I introduce you to her?"

"No thanks," he answered with but a brief glance in the direction I had indicated. "It's you or nobody now. When can I talk to your madame?"

"I'll tell her you want to speak to her, but I'm afraid it won't do any good."

"Possibly she can be persuaded. What's your name, baby?"

"Jessie," I replied.

"That's a nice name. Mine is Austin, Montague Austin, Monty to you. Skip along and tell the old lady I want to speak to her privately."

The result of his interview with Madame Lafronde I have already made known. Inasmuch as I had now become quite a parlor attraction, having in addition to my earlier accomplishments learned a number of naughty songs and suggestive dances, she was loathe to concede any of the earlier hours of the night, but an understanding was reached where Montague Austin, or Monty as I shall henceforth refer to him, was to enjoy exclusive prerogatives over my person one night each week after the hour of twelve.

A feeling of lascivious exhilaration was welling within me as I groomed myself for our first rendezvous. I had lately noticed that the craving for more frequently repeated orgasm was growing on me. It seemed that no matter how often I had it, the longing was never completely satisfied. Even the two or three patrons I had who were sexually potent now left me with the irritated feelings of a woman whose passions have been inflamed and then abandoned in a smoldering state.

The effeminate Wainwright, who still came regularly, caused me almost frantic torture with his licking, and sucking, and despite the preoccupation and the watchfulness I was obliged to observe to keep him from biting my legs, he left me in such a state that I nearly always masturbated as soon as he had gone.

It was a little after eleven-thirty. I had slipped out of the parlor, abandoning for the night my role of cigarette girl, and was making my toilette, preparatory to Mr. Austin's promised call.

"How nice it would be," I thought, as I fluffed violet talc over my body, "if this Austin would suck me French style and then fuck me about three times afterwards." My nerves tingled at the luscious vision thus evoked and a warm feeling crept through my body. The little scarlet tips of my bubbies swelled up and in the upper part of my cunny I could feel something else getting hard, too.

A few moments after twelve there was a discreet knock at my door and the maid appeared, inquiring whether I was ready to receive Mr. Austin. At this moment I was standing before the mirror considering the dress I had tentatively chosen for the occasion, having yielded to an impulse to use one of the short black silk frocks which Daddy Heeley had bought me. Just why it had occurred to me to put on this juvenile costume on the present occasion I could not say; some vague intuition probably, but as it turned out, a fortunate one as far as the effect on my new patron was concerned, though until the arrival of the maid I was still debating, undecided whether to wear it or change to something else more in keeping with the circumstances.

"All right, Maggie," I answered, "you may bring him up."

I tied my short curls back in a cluster with a band of ribbon, sprayed them lightly with my favorite perfume, and was just adding a final touch of powder to my face when footsteps at the door announced the presence of my caller.

The door opened to admit him, closed again, and the steps of the maid receded down the hallway.

Mr. Austin paused in evident surprise as he took in the scene which confronted him, then his face lit up approvingly.

"Are you the same girl I was talking to downstairs last night?"

"You mean that bold little hussy who runs around with a cigarette tray, showing her legs to everyone?" I answered jocularly. "No, I'm her twin sister. She's off tonight, and asked me to entertain you in her place."

"Well! I'm quite pleased with the substitution. You're much more attractive than your twin sister!"

"I'm glad you're not disappointed, Mr. Austin!"

"Not Mr. Austin; just Monty from now on, if you please!"

"Very well, Mr. Austin . . . I mean . . . Monty!" I agreed demurely.

After a brief exchange of pleasantries Mr. Austin proved again, as he had done previously, that he was a man who went promptly and without any unnecessary circumlocutions after whatever he wanted. With just the same directness as that employed to overcome Madame Lafronde's reluctance, he proceeded to take immediate advantage of the opportunity which was now his.

Abruptly he gathered me up in his arms and carried me to the bed. Seating himself on the edge he bent over me and his hand began to rummage under my clothing. With just the proper simulation of embarrassment I offered to undress.

"Not yet," he answered, "you're too pretty a picture just as you are." But a moment later his questing hand encountered panties which, if not exactly finger-proof, were at least something of an obstacle to easy exploration. He fumbled with them for a moment, then flipped my dress up and on his own initiative set about to unfasten and remove the panties.

I laughed nervously as he pulled them down over my legs. Already I was on fire. My sensibilities were reacting to the brutally frank sexual influence which the man exerted, and covertly I glanced toward his lap. The cloth down the inside of one of his trouser legs was distended over an elongated swelling. It looked enormous. As though drawn by some inner force I placed my hand upon it. It throbbed to my touch and I squeezed it through the clothing which concealed it.

Whether the thoughts that occupied my mind while I had been preparing for his visit were due to a premonition or mere coincidence I cannot say, but the wish I had expressed in thought was converted into a reality.

My dress was up, my cambric panties had been pulled down over my legs and cast aside.

Monty, on the side of the bed, leaning over my knees and supporting his weight on a hand which rested on the bed between my open legs had caught his first glimpse of my naked cunny. His eyes glistened and a faint flush crept over his cheeks. With one sudden movement his face was between my thighs and his mouth nuzzling my cunny. A warm, soft tongue penetrated it, tapping, touching, caressing, and then moved upward. The hot glow of the caress thrilled my senses and I relaxed in languorous abandon to the delicious ravishment.

His lips clenched my clitoris; it pulsed in response to the tugging incitation so vigorously that I was obliged to draw away to avoid orgasm then and there. I was torn between two impulses; I wanted to let it "come" and at the same time I wanted the delightful ecstasy to last as long as possible.

The problem was not resolved by me, however, but by Monty, who raised up, ripped his trousers open and sprang upon the bed between my trembling legs.

Hard, rigid and hot I could feel it in there, distending my flesh to the limit of endurance, inspiring me with a wild desire to work on it rapidly, violently, until it poured out the balm which the fever within me craved. For an interval he remained poised above me, motionless, looking down into my face. His body did not move but within me I could feel the muscular contractions of the turgid thing which penetrated me. They followed each other with regular precision and each time I perceived that tantalizing twitch my ovaries threatened to release their own flood of pleasure tears.

"Oh!" I moaned finally, and unable to resist the urge, moved my hips in pleading incitation. "You've got me in such a state! Please do something!"

"All right! Come on!"

And in a second that rigid shaft was plunging in and out in a mad dance of lust.

"Oh! Oh! Oh!" I gasped, and as though incited by my fervor, the turgid arm drove home in shorter, harder strokes.

Higher and higher mounted the swirling tides, lifting me upon their crest, no longer resisting, but an eager, willing sacrifice, panting to yield up the store of passion with which I was surcharged.

I perceived the approach of the crisis, that delicious

prelude in which one trembles on the brink of ecstasy, in which the senses seem to hesitate for one sweet moment before the breathless plunge.

And in that critical moment the throbbing weapon which was working such havoc within my body suddenly ceased its movement and was held in rigid inactivity.

Above me I saw a face which smiled sardonically down into mine and vaguely I comprehended that he had stopped his movements with the deliberate intention of forestalling my orgasm in the last moment. But he had stopped too late, the tide had risen too high to recede and with but a momentary hesitation, it swept onward and carried me, gasping, writhing and swooning in its embrace.

When the languid spell which always overcomes me after a hard orgasm had passed, I found him still crouched above me and his cock, as stiff and rigid as it had been at first, still inside me.

"Why did you stop just as I was coming?" I complained weakly. "You nearly made it go back on me!"

"That's what I was trying to do," he replied cynically, "but you put it over anyway. You know the old saying, baby, you can't eat your cake and have it, too. I like to enjoy the cake awhile before eating it."

"That's all very well," I rejoined, "but when there's plenty more cake in the pantry, there's no use being stingy with it."

"So!" he said, smiling, "there's plenty more in the pantry, is there? I'm glad to hear it. But tell me this, does the second piece ever taste as good as the first?"

"And how!" I exclaimed fervently. "The second piece tastes better than the first, and the third better than the second. The more I eat, the better I like it!"

He burst into laughter.

"You sound like you really mean it. I'd imagine that after a few months in a place like this you'd be so fed up on cake it would almost choke you. You're a cute youngster.

You're wasting your talents here. What's the story? Innocence and inexperience taken advantage of by some bounder, I suppose?'' he added quizically.

"I'm here for two reasons," I answered calmly. "The first one is to earn money and the second one is because I like to do what I have to do to earn it."

"Well, bless my soul!" he gasped. "What refreshing frankness! And you really weren't seduced by a villain?"

"Seduced, nothing! I was the one that did the seducing."

"Good for you! You're a girl after my own heart! You and I are going to get along famously, Tessie!"

"Not Tessie . . . Jessie!"

"Ah, yes; Jessie. Pardon me. Well, since you really like cake, how about another piece?"

"I'm ready whenever you are!"

"What do you say we get undressed, and really make a night of it? I didn't expect to stay all night, but I've changed my mind."

"That suits me, Mr. Austin. I'm yours . . . till tomorrow do us part!"

"Not Mr. Austin . . . Monty, if you please."

"All right . . . Monty!" I repeated, giggling.

Whereupon we untangled our respective anatomies, scrambled off the bed, and proceeded to disrobe.

That is, Monty stripped, but when I had gotten down to my hose and slippers he suggested that I retain these last articles of apparel for the moment. Odd, I thought, how so many men who get pleasure from the sight of a girl's otherwise naked body were so alike in preferring that she keep on the hose and slippers, and I murmured something to this effect to my new playmate.

"Very easily explained, my dear little girl," he replied. "Complete nudity may be as suggestive of cold chastity as obscenity, whereas, nudity supplemented by a pretty pair of silkclad legs and neat slippers is the perfectly balanced picture of esthetic lewdness."

"But suppose one's legs and feet are pretty enough to look good without stockings? Everybody says I have pretty legs!"

"It's not a question of beauty, but of eroticism. I'll make a clearer illustration. Suppose we take two girls, each equally pretty. One of them stands before us entirely naked. The other is dressed, but she raises her dress and holds it up so we can see her pussy. Which of the two is the most exciting sexually?"

"The one holding up her dress," I answered without hesitation.

"Right. And that's the answer to your question. You look naughtier with your hose and slippers than you would completely nude."

My attention was now distracted from the matter of my own nudity to that of my companion. His body was well formed and in admirable athletic trim. Smooth, round muscles rippled under the clear white skin, a pleasing contrast indeed to some of my other paunchy, flabby patrons. But most impressive of all was the rigid weapon which, during the conversation and undressing, continued to maintain its virile integrity, standing out straight and proud from his middle. I glaced at it admiringly.

"How did you ever get that big thing into me without hurting me?" I commented, as I considered its formidable proportions.

"It carries its own anaesthetic, baby."

"It looks strong enough to hold me up without bending."

"Baby, it's invincible. I could put you on it and whirl you around like a pinwheel."

"I'll take the starch out of it and make it melt down fast enough."

"That's a big order. You may lose a lot of starch yourself trying."

"Ha!" I scoffed, "I wager it will be curled up fast asleep in an hour's time."

A prediction which, as things transpired, turned out to be about one hundred percent wrong.

I returned to the bed and Monty, following me, placed himself on his knees between my outstretched legs. Gripping the cheeks of my bottom in his strong hands as he sank down upon me, he pushed home the lethal shaft.

Our previous encounter had hardly more than whetted my appetite, so, as soon as I felt his cock well inside, I raised my legs, hooked them over his back, and without loss of time began to work against him. Apparently satisfied with my initiative, he remained still and let me proceed unhindered.

Grinding my loins against him I could feel his pubic hair compressed against my cunny. Moving my bottom from side to side, then shifting into undulating, circular movements, I sought to capture a second installment of the cloying sweetness with which Mother Nature rewards the efforts of those who labor diligently in her garden.

The first warning of the approaching crisis was manifested by the muscular quivering of my thighs, and Monty, still squeezing the cheeks of my bottom, commenced to raise and lower himself upon me with slow, deliberate thrusts. Now the length of the hot thing was entirely buried within me, distending my flesh to the utmost; I could feel it pressing my womb. Now, it was coming out, slowly, slowly, out until naught but the very tip lay cuddled against the quivering lips of my cunny.

A pause, a teasing agony of expectation, and it was going in again, in, in, until the crisp hair at the base was again pressed against my clitoris. Orgasm was creeping upon me, I could feel it coming, and in a frenzy of impatience, I launched my hips upward to meet the thrusts, but, instead of continuing its trajectory, it remained poised midway in its course. My orgasm was trembling in the balance. In desperation I brought it to its fulfillment with a supreme effort and fell back, half fainting.

"What is that, Mister, a system?" I panted when I could speak. "You played that same trick on me the other time!"

An hour later the suspicion was beginning to dawn on me that, in the realms of erotic prowess, I had met my master. Two hours later, I knew it for a certainty. I had experienced nearly a dozen orgasms while my partner's cock was still stiff and rigid as it had been at the start. On each occasion he had succeeded in making me have an ejaculation without himself rendering any accounting to Nature. It lacked but a few minutes to three.

"You look a bit fagged, baby," he said smiling quizzically. "Think you can stand one more piece of cake?"

"Yes!" I replied valiantly, although in truth I was beginning to feel like a squeezed-out sponge. For once in my life I had about had my fill.

This time he rolled me over on my side and with his stomach against my back and his legs pressed against mine, he put it into me from behind, spoon fashion.

I thought to turn the tables on him and, by lying perfectly still, oblige him to work himself into a spending heat. But it was unnecessary. He was done playing with me and went right to work on his own accord. Before long the pressure of his arms tightened about me and I tensed by body against the harder plunges as a hot flood was loosed inside me with such force that I could distinguish each separate gush as it flung itself against my womb.

I held rigid for a moment in my determination not to let myself go, but the feel of that hot stuff spurting inside me worked havoc with my intentions and about the time the fourth or fifth jet hit me, the brake slipped and I was off again!

The aftermath of this last orgasm was a feeling of extreme lassitude and I was entirely agreeable when my companion, having apparently no further immediate de-

signs upon my person, suggested that we turn out the light
and sleep. I dragged myself from the bed, attended to the
customary hygienic requirements, divested myself of my
slippers, and hose, put on a silk shift, slipped back into
bed beside him, and in probably less than ten minutes was
deep in sleep.

CHAPTER ELEVEN

I slept profoundly, dreamlessly, but not for long.

Something was pressing against my face, brushing my lips, with an irritating persistence which defied my mechanical, sleep-drugged efforts to shake away. I endeavored to turn my face on the pillow away from it, and the knowledge that it was imprisoned so I could not turn it gradually crystalized in my mind.

As one coming out of a bad dream tries to dispel the lingering shadows, so did I try to free myself of something which seemed to be oppressing me, weighting me down, hindering my movements. I could not do it, and awoke to complete consciousness with a frightened start.

In the dim light which filtered through the curtains from the street illumination was revealed the fact that my erstwhile sleeping companion was now straddled over me, a knee on either side of my body. His hands were under my head, which he had raised slightly, and against my lips, punching, prodding, trying to effect an entrance, was that invincible cock.

I struggled to raise my arms to push him away, and at the same time tried to twist my head sidewise. I could do neither. My arms were pinioned down by his knees, and

131

his hands prevented me from moving my head. At my movements their pressure tightened, a sinister reminder of my helplessness.

Of course I realized what he was doing. He was trying to fuck me in the mouth, something I had never permitted any man to do.

In prostitution, just as in other circles of life, there are social distinctions. The cocksucker is at the low end of the scale and is looked down upon with considerable scorn by those of her sisters who have not yet descended to this level. If among the entertainers in a high-class bordello one is discovered to be guilty of accommodating patrons with her mouth she not only loses caste but stands convicted of "unfair" practice which makes it difficult for other girls to compete with her without also resorting to the same procedure.

This does not, of course, apply to those places known as French houses where cocksucking is the accepted practice, or to other places of a low and degenerate character wherein nothing is too debasing to be frowned upon.

These, together with the fact that I was both sleepy and exhausted sexually, were the considerations which inspired my efforts to escape the inverted caress which now threatened me rather than those of a strictly moral nature. The man appealed to me greatly in a physical way; I had reacted to his sexual advances with more passion and enjoyment than I had done before with any other patron. Had he endeavored earlier in the night to seduce me, with a little gallantry and coaxing, into sucking his cock, I might, under the influence of my exhalted passions, have yielded. But I have always been quick to resent anything smacking of impudence or effrontery and, as I have mentioned, I wanted at that moment but to be permitted to sleep undisturbed.

"I won't do that!" I hissed angrily, as I struggled to free myself from his embraces.

"Oh yes you will, baby!" was the confident and surprising rejoinder.

His legs pressed tighter against my sides, constricting my arms so that I could not move them. He lifted my head higher. The end of his cock, with the foreskin drawn back, was right against my mouth.

"You . . . you . . ." I gasped, inarticulate with rage, as I was forced to clench my teeth to keep out the invader.

"Open your mouth, baby!" he ordered coolly, and gave my head a shake to emphasize his words.

When I comprehended that my wishes were to be ignored and that my efforts to dislodge him were useless, full rage took possession of me. For a moment I was on the point of screaming, but sudden recollection of the penalty exacted of girls who permitted scandals or disturbances to arise in their rooms at night stifled the cry in its inception.

We were expected, and presumed to be qualified, to meet unusual situations and resolve them with tact and discretion. Nocturnal disorders were unpardonable calamities and justified by nothing short of attempted murder.

"Open your mouth, baby!" he repeated, and shook my head again, this time with more force.

"All right!" I hissed, "you asked for it!"

I opened my mouth. His cock pushed in immediately, and as it did so I sank my teeth into it. The intent was vicious enough, but the tough, resilient flesh resisted any actual laceration. Nevertheless, the pain inflicted by my small, sharp teeth must have been considerable.

He jerked it out of my mouth and simultaneously, withdrawing one of his hands from under my head, he dealt me a stinging blow on the side of the face with his open palm.

"Open your mouth, baby!" he repeated, undaunted, "and if you bite me again I'll knock you unconscious!"

The tears started to my eyes.

"Damn you . . . !" I choked. "I'll . . . I'll . . ."

The hands subjecting my head were again holding it in a

viselike grip. His thumbs were pressing into my cheeks, against the corners of my mouth, forcing it open.

There was nothing to do but yield or scream such an alarm as would arouse the entire household.

I chose the more discreet course and, though almost suffocated with rage, opened my mouth in surrender to the assault which was being launched upon it. The big, plum-shaped head slipped in, filling the cavity with its throbbing bulk.

For a moment I tried to keep my tongue away from it, but there was no space in which to hide. His cock was so big I had to open my jaws to their widest, and my lips were stretched in a round, tight ring.

Further resistance was futile and anymore biting would bring a swift retaliation. So, still boiling inwardly, I relaxed, and let him go ahead.

A faintly pungent taste filled my mouth; the head of his cock, from which I could not keep my tongue, was wet and slippery. Every few seconds it jerked convulsively, forcing my jaws further apart. Pretty soon he began to move it, a short in and out movement. The foreskin closed over it as it receded, leaving only the tip inside my mouth, allowing me to relax my distended jaws momentarily. As it went in, the foreskin slipped back and the naked head filled my mouth again, forcing my jaws apart.

This went on for several minutes, and all the time he held my head with his hands. His cock seemed to be getting wetter but whether from its own dew or the saliva of my mouth I did not know. I wanted to spit, but he would not release me and I was obliged to swallow the excess moisture.

Finally, with the head just inside my lips, he paused, and after holding it still for a few moments, shook my face and whispered:

"Come on, baby! What's the matter with you? Are you going to suck it, or do I have to get rough again?"

I knew nothing of the exact technique of this business, though of course the very title by which the art was known indicated that sucking was in order. Choking, gulping, I tried to suck as it advanced into my mouth. Taking cognizance of my awkward efforts he paused again, and as though for the first time taking into account the possibility that I was in truth a rank novice, queried:

"What's the matter with you? Haven't you really done this before?"

Mutely, I managed to convey a negative by shaking my head.

"Lord love me!" he ejaculated, and then in slightly apologetic tones, "I shouldn't have been so rough. I thought you were just stalling, my dear! However, it's something every young girl should know, and I'm glad to have the opportunity to be your teacher. Now listen: don't try to strangle yourself! You can't suck while the whole thing is inside! Wait . . ."

He withdrew it until just the head was encircled by my lips.

"Now suck while it's like that, and run your tongue over it!"

"Well," I thought in disgusted resignation "the sooner finished the better," and submissively I followed his indications. Vigorously, if not enthusiastically, I sucked the big round knob and rolled my tongue over its slippery surface.

"That's the way, baby!" he whispered tensely after a few moments. "That's great! Now . . . hold everything!"

And while I remained passive, he worked in and out in short, quick thrusts. Thus, alternating from one to the other, sucking one moment, submitting to having it rammed down my throat the next, my first lesson in cocksucking continued.

I was still filled with resentment, but the first fury of anger had spent itself, and my thoughts were now concentrated on bringing the ordeal to a conclusion as quickly as possible. To this end I now tried to make the caress as exciting and fulminating as I could. I sucked the throbbing glans, curled my tongue around it, licking, sucking coaxing . . . and the effect upon my companion was soon apparent. He groaned with ecstasy and from time to time jerked away from me so that the sensitive glans receded within the shelter of its elastic covering of flesh.

Perceiving that this maneuver was designed to delay an orgasm, I redoubled my efforts and when he again tried to withdraw I followed him by raising my head and with my lips firmly compressed around the neck of the palpitating knob, I sucked and licked without pausing.

The muscles of his thighs and legs, pressing against my sides, were quivering. Suddenly he withdrew his right hand from under my head and twisting sidewise reached behind him, groping with his fingers for my cunny. This was insult added to injury in my estimation and I tried to clench my legs against the invading hand. The effort was useless; he forced it between my legs and with the tips of his fore and index fingers he found my clitoris and began to titillate it.

Now began a new conflict. With every atom of mental influence I could bring to bear I tried to force that little nerve to ignore the incitation, to remain impassive to the friction which was being applied to it, to stay inert and lifeless.

I may as well have tried to stay the tides of the sea in their course. The traitorous, disloyal little thing cared not a whit for my humiliation and refused to heed the mental commands I was hurling at it. Despite the fact that it should have been as sleepy as I had been, it came almost instantly awake, hardened, and stood up stiffly.

He rubbed it in a peculiarly maddening way, a soft, twirling movement with the erected button lightly compressed between the tips of his two fingers. The little thrills began to generate, and communicated themselves to the surrounding area, up into my ovaries, down, seemingly into the very marrow of the bones in my thighs and legs.

Why say more? There was only one possible ending.

When the ultimate capacity of resistance was reached and passed, and in the very moment in which my organism was yielding to the diabolical incitation, my tormentor, waiting apparently for this precise moment, loosed within my mouth a flood of hot sperm. I choked, gurgling and gasping, as part of it gushed down my throat and the rest, escaping my lips, ran in hot, sticky rivulets down the sides of my cheeks, over my chin . . .

No sooner had the torrent subsided than he flung himself from me and lay panting on the bed by my side.

With the viscid stuff still dripping from my lips and its peculiar starchy flavor filling my mouth, I sprang from the bed and fled precipitately to the bathroom. First with water, then with tooth powder and brush and finally with repeated rinsings I endeavored to purify my mouth.

When this was accomplished I went back into the room, turned on the light, and flung myself into a chair where, for a few moments I sat silently glaring at my tormentor who, with drowsy indifference, contemplated me through half-closed eyes.

"Well," I said frigidly, breaking the silence. "Aren't you going to congratulate me on my graduation into the cocksucking class?"

He smiled dryly.

"Regular little powder magazine, aren't you, baby? Come on, kid, don't be a spoilsport. I'll admit I was a little rough, but that was a keen nip you gave me. I'll make things right with you. I like you, baby, you've shown me the best time I've had in a long while, and I'm not pulling your leg, either."

"A nice time you showed me," I observed bitterly, "trying to fuck me in the mouth while I was asleep and nearly choking me to death. You know girls aren't supposed to do that! Why don't you go to a French house?"

This plaint seemed to afford him considerable amusement. He sat up in bed, laughing.

"Don't rate me so low socially, baby! I'm a sort of high-class chap with estatic inclinations!"

"I see; a special honor conferred on me. Quite a distinction, I must say."

"Ha, ha, ha! Forgive me, baby. Word of honor, I'll behave quite properly in the future. Anyway, it wasn't so terrible, was it? Listen, I'll tell you a funny story. There was a young French girl just married and her mother was giving her some confidential advice. 'Daughter,' she said, 'the ultimate object of marriage is to have babies. Without the little dears no home is complete. However, the bearing and rearing of children is a confining task which imposes arduous and continuous obligations. It is my advise to you, daughter, that you do not have any babies during the first two or three years. You will then, in after life, not be deprived of the memories of a few years of happiness and freedom from care to which youth is justly entitled.' 'Ah, mother dear,' answered the blushing maiden, 'you need preoccupy yourself no further on that score, I shall never have any babies!' 'Never?' gasped the mother, 'why do you say that you will never have any babies, darling?' 'Oh, mother,' answered the girl, hiding her blushing face in the maternal bosom, 'I shall never have any babies because I simply can't force myself to swallow the horrid stuff! I always have to spit it out!' "

"And, so what?" I asked caustically, refusing to unbend at the ridiculous story.

"Don't you see, ha, ha, ha, don't you get the point? She didn't even know there was any other way of doing it. She thought she had to swallow the stuff to get a baby!"

Despite my efforts to remain haughty, my better humor was returning. I have always been like that, quick to

anger, quick to forget. There was something about this
man which was irresistible. Even his impudence had a saving
grace, an ingenuous, disarming quality. Only the memory
of the slap he had given me remained to irritate me. He sat
there in bed, smiling, a sheet draped carelessly about him,
half-concealing, half-revealing the smooth white muscles
of his torso. His hair in its ruffled disorder gave him a
boyish aspect, throwing a well-formed white forehead into
relief against the background of bluish-black curls.

After all, what harm had really been done? And, I
suddenly recalled, had he not earlier in the night given me
a most delightful ten minutes by putting his tongue in my
cunny? The service he had required of me was no less
intimate. I shivered involuntarily at the recollection of the
short but delicious episode. The last remnants of my resentment faded away. I began to feel slightly ashamed of
myself for having made such a commotion.

"Still peeved at me, baby?" he inquired quizzically.

"No," I answered, my lips twitching into a smile,
"only it was kind of . . . well, startling to be waked up
that way from a sound sleep. I suppose you don't believe
me, but I never did that before."

"Of course I believe you, baby," he interrupted, "it
was easy to see you hadn't any experience. Honestly, I
don't know what came over me. You gave me such a stand
tonight it came right back on me after I'd been asleep a
short time. I woke up, and lay there looking at your pretty
little mouth in the dim light, and the first thing I knew I got
into a fierce argument with myself about it."

"What on earth do you mean, an argument with yourself about my mouth?"

"Well, it was like this. At first I said to myself, it's too
small, and then I said, no, it might be a tight fit, but it
could be done. And the argument went on, until finally it
got so hot it had to be decided definitely one way or the
other, and so . . . and so . . ."

"And so I got fucked in the mouth to settle it. Very well, Your Highness, shall we retire now, or is there any other way I can serve you?"

"Well, if it's not putting too much of a strain on your hospitality, I'd greatly appreciate a shot of brandy!"

I rang for the maid. After a long wait, she shuffled to the door half-asleep, took the order, and was back again in five minutes with the liquor. When this was consumed, we turned out the light and again composed ourselves for sleep.

The tumultuous events of the night, abetted perhaps by the brandy of which I also partook, were reflected throughout the remaining hours in a regular phantasmagoria of distorted dreams. In all these dreams, I was sucking somebody's cock. Strangely enough, in them I felt no inhibitions, no reluctance. On the contrary, I seemed to be doing something quite natural, and which caused me the most delightful erotic reactions.

At first it was Rene as I had last seen him, but with an incongruous discrepancy in time which took us back to our old attic playroom days. "I'm going to do something nice to you," I whispered, and placing myself on my knees before him I unbuttoned his trousers and releasing his erected cock, took it in my mouth. "No, no, Sis!" he protested, but he made no effort to escape the seductive caress. The thrill of vicarious delight was trembling through me when I suddenly observed that Hester was standing nearby, looking at me reproachfully. I paused for a moment to tell her that it was all right, that Rene was only a foster brother, but even as I spoke, I saw that it was not Rene but Mr. Hayden to whom I was ministering. From this confusing tangle of composite personalities, I drifted into another ambience. The effeminate Wainwright was licking my cunny deliciously, and as he paused for a moment to masturbate, I twisted around and cried: "Wait! I'll show you a better way!" With my thighs across his face I took

his small but rigid member in my mouth and sucked it
until he had an emission.

When I finally awoke it was late noon and the echoes of
some of these lurid dreams were still reverberating through
my brain. I felt wet and sticky between the legs and my
clitoris was in erection. When I had gotten my confused
thoughts in order and separated the real from the unreal, I
sat up in bed and glanced at my companion.

He was sleeping soundly and quietly on his back, his
curly head high on the pillow, lips slightly parted over
white even teeth. He had thrown the blankets aside and
was covered only by a sheet. I glanced downward over the
recumbent form. Halfway down its length the sheet rose
sharply, projected upward in the form of a little tent. As I
fixed my eyes on this significant pinnaclelike projection, I
saw that it was jerking sharply at short intervals.

I lifted the sheet without disturbing him. That inde-
fatigable, tireless cock was standing upright, as firm and
rigid as a bar of iron. White and graceful the stout column
rose from the profusion of dark and tangled curls at its
base, its plum-colored head half-hidden, half-revealed under its natural envelope of satiny skin.

Still holding the sheet up, I looked at his face. It was in
the peaceful repose of sound sleep. I thought of my curious dreams and wondered if he too was experiencing rare
delights with some nebulous shadowland houri; maybe,
even he was dreaming of me!

The thought set me aquiver. Softly I drew the sheet
aside. I extended my hand, my fingers closed cautiously
around the pulsing column. For a moment I was content to
hold it thus, then, watching his face carefully for signs of
awakening, I moved my hand up and down, slowly, gently,
so that the silken foreskin closed over the scarlet head and
then, receding downward, revealed it in its stark-nakedness.

Twice, thrice, I moved it so, pausing after each movement to see whether it was going to awaken him. At the

fourth and fifth movement he stirred uneasily, murmuring some incoherent word. I waited, motionless, until his even breathing assured me that he was still deep in slumber, and began again.

"When he wakes up," I thought, "I'll make him tell me what he was dreaming about that made his thing hard this way."

My wrist slid downward, the white elastic skin descended, and again the scarlet head protruded nakedly. As I paused, holding it in this position, I saw a round, glistening drop of limpid transparency emerged slowly from the orfice at the tip.

As I observed this natural reaction to my manipulations a wave of lewdness swept over me, and in an instant I was in a state of passion bordering on nymphomania, dominated by but one thought, one driving desire, and that was to feel the rigid, pulsating thing plunging in my mouth, to suck it and lick it until the spurting essence brought relief to the frenzy which now possessed me.

I literally flung myself upon it, indifferent now as to whether he was awake or asleep, and engulfed the ruby head within the circle of my lips. In a regular fury of lust I sucked and licked and bobbed my head up and down to approximate the motions of ordinary fucking.

Of course, this violent disturbance aroused my companion instantly, but I was too engrossed in my own passion to be hardly more than aware that he was sitting up in bed, and that his hands were clasping my face as though to guide the movements of my bobbing head.

Indifferent to all else I sought only to force the living fountain between my lips to pour out its elixir as quickly as possible. Instinctively I knew that when it spurted fourth, my own organism would yield in harmony. It was trembling now in that delicious borederland of anticipation, and needed but the final inspiration to precipitate its own shower of lust.

Between my thrusting, encircled lips the muscular flesh seemed suddenly to grow more taut. It held so for a second, and then with mighty convulsions poured out its tribute, wave on wave of hot, pungent ambrosia. Gasping, choking with the deluge which threatened to strangle me, I writhed in the ecstasies of orgasm which came upon me in the same moment.

The reaction to this furious excess was a spell of enervating lassitude. As I came out of it and my chaotic thoughts took on a semblance of order, I was filled with amazement at the demoniacal frenzy which had taken possession of me. Next came the thought of what had become of the spurting jets that indomitable geyser had poured out. The odd, pungent taste was still in my mouth, but I recalled that I had almost choked with the quantity that had flooded it. When he had assaulted me the night before I had spit most of it out, though I had been forced to swallow some. I glanced at the bed to see if, unconsciously, I had ejected it. The bed was dry and clean. Seemingly, it had all gone down my throat.

I remembered the absurd story he had told me about the French girl.

"Well," I observed, "if it's true a girl can get a baby by swallowing that stuff, I guess I'm going to have one."

"Kid, that was great!" he exclaimed. "The first time in my life that I can recall that I really enjoyed being waked up."

"I don't know whatever possessed me," I murmured in some embarrassment. "It came on me all of a sudden. I woke up and saw your thing sticking up. I knew you were dreaming something nice, or it wouldn't be that way. I thought, I'd tease you by frigging it while you were asleep, and then, all of a sudden I just got a regular fit to do that and I couldn't stop myself!"

"It was wonderful, kid, wonderful! I always get a hard-on when I sleep late in the morning and there was something, oh, more than ordinarily thrilling in being waked up that way. I've had lots of women, but it never occurred to any of them to do that, I mean, while I was still asleep. It's something new to put in the book!"

"What book?" I asked.

"Oh, I was speaking figuratively. Something new to remember."

"Did you really enjoy it so much?"

"Well, rather! If the old pego could talk it would say: 'thank you, a thousand times, Miss!' "

"What were you dreaming about that was making it hard like that?"

"Well now, that's difficult to answer. Whatever it was it couldn't have been half as good as what really happened. I have funny dreams, but I can't seem to remember them clearly after I wake up. About all I ever recall is that there was a girl in them. I must have been dreaming about you this time. Do you have dreams . . . I mean, naughty ones?"

"I had some fierce ones last night," I confessed. "I guess they were mostly the cause of me doing that!"

"What were they about, baby?" he asked curiously.

"Oh, mostly about you," I lied, not wanting to say that I had dreamed of other men while sleeping at his side.

"Were they pleasant dreams?" he insinuated.

"Well, you saw what they made me do! I'll bet you think now for sure that I'm accustomed to doing that!"

"No, honestly, I don't, kid. I didn't give it a thought at first, but later I saw you weren't up to it. I felt kind of ashamed afterwards for having made you do it."

"Oh, I was mad at first, but I don't care now. It gave me a thrill, too. It's the truth, though, I'd never done it before. But I'll wager you've done it that way to plenty of other girls."

"You'd know I was lying if I denied it. And you

wouldn't like me any better, even if I hadn't ever done it before, would you?"

"No," I answered slowly, "I don't blame a man for having all the fun he can. If I were a man, I'd do everything there is that's naughty. I'd do that to girls, and the other way, too."

"What other way?"

"The way you did first last night . . . with your tongue."

"Oh, you like it that way, do you?"

"It just sets me crazy."

"Kid, I like your style. I made a deal with the old lady to have you once a week, but to tell you the truth I wasn't sure that I'd care about coming back even a second time. You couldn't shake me now if you tried. I like a girl who hasn't the silly idea of trying to fool a man with mock modesty."

"You're married . . . aren't you?" I inquired tentatively, though I knew he was.

"Yes, I am, unfortunately."

"Why unfortunately? Isn't she nice?"

"That's it, exactly. Too damned nice. She's the answer to why men like your kind of girl. She's an iceberg, a frigid monument to chastity in its most exaggerated conception. Everything related to sex is immoral. The only justification for a man getting into his wife's bed is when its for the purpose of creating offspring, and even then it's a nasty, degrading business."

In my mind's eye there formed a picture of a pious, dour-faced female, embittered perhaps through the lack of physical attractions, whose life was dedicated to the suppression of all those natural instincts and longings of the flesh which contribute to make living worthwhile. I had heard of such.

"Good heavens!" I gasped. "Why did you marry a woman like that?"

"Reasons of family," he replied gloomily.

Of a naturally credulous and ingenuous disposition, my heart immediately swelled with sympathy for my companion's misfortune. I had yet to learn that there are always two sides to every story, and that one must know both to properly judge their respective merits.

"I'm sorry to know of that," I said sincerely. "When you come here I'll try to make you forget your unhappiness. I'm not cold-blooded, but I guess you know that already!"

"You're a fine kid, and I won't forget you. Wish I could stay longer but I have an appointment at two o'clock and it's an important one. I'd better dress and toddle along before I weaken."

With further desultory conversation we dressed and Monty prepared to leave. He held me for a moment in his arms at the door, lingering just long enough to lift my dress, slide his hand inside my panties and give my bottom a few lascivious squeezes.

"I'll see you next Wednesday night without fail." And he was gone.

CHAPTER TWELVE

I stood for a moment thinking pensively of all that had transpired and then turned my eyes toward the dressing table upon which he had unobtrusively laid a bank note. It was for five pounds. I folded it up and tucked it in my stocking.

That afternoon I sat on Hester's bed, telling her about my new patron. She listened attentively, asked a few questions, and in a burst of confidence, I told her all that had happened.

"Oh, Jessie!" she exclaimed in genuine distress. "You shouldn't have done that! I had a presentiment against that man the first time I saw him talking to you. I just had a feeling that he'd get the best of you some way! Lafronde shouldn't have given him any appointments with you!"

"What's the harm?" I answered lightly. "He gave me five pounds!"

"What's the harm? There's plenty of harm! When a girl starts that, she's finished!"

"What do you mean . . . finished?" I rejoined skeptically.

"Why . . . why . . . it grows on you! You shouldn't have let him do that! You should have screamed!"

"Wouldn't that have made a hit with Lafronde, me

screaming at four o'clock in the morning that a man was trying to do it to me in the mouth!''

"I don't care whether it would have made a hit with her or not! You shouldn't have let him get away with it! And then you did it again in the morning, of your own accord? Oh, Jessie!''

"Yes, I did! It wasn't bad . . . I like him. Anyway, what are you talking about? You've done the same thing with Mr. Hayden. I've seen you!''

"Oh, Jessie, that's different. I never really did it with him. I just put it in my mouth for a moment to wet it. He never actually fucked me in the mouth and never wanted to. He's too much of a gentleman, and you know it!''

"Well, I don't see much difference.''

"Well, I see plenty, and I wish you had never met that man!''

"You're so funny, Hester. When I knew you in the reformatory I used to think there wasn't anything you were shy of. Now here you are preaching to me!''

"I'm not preaching, honey. It's just that I've had more experience than you, and I know what you have to watch out for!''

She smiled at me affectionately.

"Remember Heloise?'' I asked teasingly.

"Yes; she was an example of exactly what I mean now. Fooling with some perverted idea until it takes a hold on you, and the first thing you know, you're a regular slave to it !''

"You did something with her and you didn't get to be a slave to it!''

"I just let her out of deviltry and curiosity, and it disgusted me more than anything else. Just before you came here I had some more of that same stuff, too. Lafronde sent me out on a call from a woman.''

"You never told me that! Who was she?''

"Oh, some man-hating female with crazy ideas. I've

forgotten her name. She lived in a hotel. She telephoned here to have a girl sent to her rooms and Lafronde picked me. I needed some extra money or I wouldn't have gone.''

"What did she want?"

"She didn't want much of anything except to lick another woman's cunt. It was perfectly disgusting, but I lay down and let her do it. She called back twice after that, and then she told Lafronde not to send me anymore because I wasn't 'responsive' enough. Lafronde asked her if she could send a different girl and she said yes, if she had one with a little life in her. Imagine that! There was a cute little witch here named Yolanda, very shy and quiet, but she was supposed to be one of those kind that like other girls. Lafronde asked her if she wanted to go out on the call and she said yes. A few days after that, early one morning, she sneaked her things out without saying a word to anyone and disappeared. So everybody supposed she had gone with this woman. Poor kid, if she did, she's probably on the streets now. Those kind of women are more exacting and harder to get along with than a man. They get tired of a girl quick and want new ones all the time. You see, Jessie, I know all about these things, and that's why I'm not in danger from them as you would be. You're an innocent little fool, and you'll fall for anything anyone wants to put over on you.''

"Well thanks, you sweet old thing, for your compliments, and for being so concerned about me. If I was a man, I'd do something nice to you right now for being so good to me."

Hester laughed.

"I read in the papers that some doctor in Vienna has discovered how to change people's sex. If you'll let him change yours, I'll save my money to pay for it, and when you've got a nice cock we'll get married and live happily forever and afterwards!"

"O-o-o-h Hester!" I breathed in mock seriousness. "If

that doctor can make me have a six-inch cock and we get married, will you suck if for me every night?''

"You nasty little pervert!" she exploded, bursting into laughter. "You take a suck of this!" She pressed her hand between her kimona-covered legs and rubbed two or three times. "Since you've developed into a cocksucker you might as well suck cunts, too!"

"No, I won't suck your cunny, but I will suck your titties!" I exclaimed, and before she could defend herself I had tumbled her backward on the bed, pulled her kimona open, and gotten my mouth on the nipple of one of her bubbies.

"Stop! Stop! You're tickling me!" she cried, hysterical with laughter. "Jessie, stop! You're making me have goose flesh all over my body! Stop it, will you!"

Resisting her efforts to dislodge me for a few moments, I clung to her titty and then releasing it, raised up to look triumphantly into her flushed face. She was still shaking hysterically, both her plump, round breasts protruding from the disordered kimona.

"Let's see if we can fuck each other!" I whispered teasingly.

"You crazy little fool! Get off me!" she gasped. "Let me up! I can't breathe! You're pressing down on my stomach!"

"Come on . . . just for fun . . . to see if we can do it!" I persisted, now overcome with laughter myself at her comic, half-serious expostulations, and despite her efforts to stop me, I succeeded in pulling her kimona open entirely.

She had no panties on, but I, unfortunately did. To get them off, and prevent her from escaping while I was doing so would probably have been an impossibility. However, she suddenly relaxed.

"All right, you nasty little cocksucker! Let's see just how far you will go!"

This was a challenge which brooked no compromise,

and though it was all in fun, I wasn't going to be the one to back down.

Raising up on one arm, I slipped my panties down and wriggled my legs free of them. When I nestled down again, our bare breasts and stomachs were together, and against my cunny I could feel the soft pressure of Hester's silky pubic hair.

"Now do you still want to see how far I'll go?"

"Yes, I do!"

"Very well; when you've had enough, you can say so!"

Whereupon I slid down a bit and got my legs between hers. This maneuver brought our respective cunnies into still more intimate contact, and I rubbed mine against hers, pressing in as deeply as I could.

But I abruptly discovered that this was apt to be more devastating to me than to her because my clitoris and the sensitive parts of my cunny were exposed to the friction while hers were covered with hair. Furthermore, despite the fact that this had all started in fun, I was beginning to get hot.

Shifting away from her sufficiently to get my hand down to the source of the obstruction. I parted the soft hair with my fingers, separated the lips of her cunny, and then quickly pressed mine against the exposed membranes. She submitted to these manipulations without resistance, but flinched perceptibly as the moist flesh of our cunnies came together.

As for myself, I was almost instantly aware that this hot, moist contact of sensitive parts was capable of producing some erotic reactions I had not in the least suspected. I realized that they were not the normal ones which come through contact of opposite sexs in response to the laws of Nature, but rather the forced surrender of the senses to a purely mechanical stimulation, as in masturbation.

Nevertheless, a delicious sensation was the immediate result and it felt nicer than when I masturbated. I rubbed my cunny against hers as best I could. It was an awkward proceeding and her hair kept getting in the way, obliging me to stop repeatedly to draw it aside. Had hers been free of hair as mine was, the contact would have been much more satisfactory. Even so, I was soon trembling, and Hester was moaning audibly.

In an effort to maintain a comical aspect to what had now ceased to be a joke, I managed to gasp:

"Do you . . . still want to . . . see how far . . . I'll . . . go?"

Her arms tightened about my shoulders.

"Don't talk! Oh! You're making me . . . ah . . . ah . . . a-a-a-ah!"

"Oh! You're making me, too! Press . . . right there . . . o-o-o-oh!"

A few minutes later, flushed and disheveled, we were looking at each other in comical and guilty confusion.

Hester jerked her kimona over the glistening curls between her legs, and very red in the face, exclaimed:

"I never dreamed you'd have the nerve to really do that or I wouldn't have let you start it!"

"Oh, shut up, you darned preacher. You wanted it as much as I did!"

"If anyone had seen us, we'd never have heard the last of it," she murmured, glancing toward the door. "Yes! That door was unlatched! Anyone could have walked in!" she added in consternation.

I giggled, recalling other doors which had been left unlatched.

"Like you did when Rene and I were saying good-bye."

"Why don't you think of such things?" she asked reprovingly.

"Well, for heaven's sake! Am I the only one who's supposed to do any thinking? Anyway, nobody came in, so why worry about it now? And even if they did, this place isn't supposed to be a Sunday school exactly, you know!''

"Listen, you! Don't you ever dare tell anyone! It's something I never did before and I'm never going to do it again, either!''

"Don't be silly! You know I won't tell anyone!''

CHAPTER THIRTEEN

The week passed by and I was waiting for Monty's second visit. He had sent me a note, couched in affectionate terms, assuring me that he would be in without fail.

Of my earlier patrons but two continued to call on me with faithful regularity; Mr. Thomas, and the effeminate Wainwright. Poor Daddy Heely was in a hospital, a nervous breakdown, according to reports. I wondered guiltily whether maybe the excitation my antics caused him had something to do with his condition. I had become quite fascinated with the Miss Innocence role I had built up for his edification, and had gone to extremes in thinking up erotic situations which could be presented to him in the guise of "maidenly" confidences. He was physically unable to savor the more material delights of concupiscence, and I had supplanted the lack with artfully designed mental and visual extravaganzas. Probably I had overstepped the mark in my enthusiasm, and sent him into a psychopathic ward.

Mr. Castle had simply disappeared. In addition to Monty I had another new patron of several weeks standing and indifferent qualities who had so far not distinguished himself by any eccentricities worth mentioning except one: he required that I be fully dressed on the occasion of his visits, and that I permit him to undress me. With ceremonial dignity by me, he divested me of my garments one by one until I stood before him, a modern Eve sans fig leaf. Thereafter, what took place was of orthodox regularity, a proceeding sanctioned by custom dating back into the most remote of prehistoric times as far as I know. In other words, he did just what men have been doing to girls since the dawn of time.

Monty had asked me to have a substantial supply of liquor available on his future visits and I had complied with the request. On a little taboret near the bed was a quart bottle of Scotch whiskey of a mark he had indicated, together with a siphon of seltzer and glasses.

I hummed a song as I stood before the mirror for a last minute inspection to be sure that my hair was just right and that my face was properly powdered and my lips the correct shade of red. But my thoughts were not on the song, nor more than casually on the face that was reflected from the depths of the big mirror. I was thinking, with delicious little quivers of anticipation, of the several hours of unchastity which were in the immediate perspective. I was sure he would "French" me again, for had I not confessed to him my predilection for the delicate caress? And if he did, and if he were nice to me in other ways, well, maybe I would repay him by doing again what I had done when I woke him up.

Hester said that after a girl started she was finished, because it grew on her. Nonsense. That might be true in some instances, and not in others. Hester meant well, but she didn't know me as well as she thought she did. She had a room engagement herself tonight, but had slipped away for a few minutes to speak to me.

"You be careful with that man Austin, Jessie! He's not your type!"

Not my type, indeed! What kind of a man did she think

my type was? A senile old innocent like Daddy Heely, or a perverted fool like Mr. Castle whose one ambition in life was to do it to a girl in her bottom, or a semilunatic like Wainwright, who paid a girl to let him masturbate all over her legs?

From all of which it will be seen that I was pretty well convinced I knew better what I wanted than Hester did.

Reflected in the mirror, I saw the door opening gently and the face of the man I was thinking about appeared. I pretended not to have observed his entrance, and a second later he had clasped me from behind. With my knees hanging over his arm he lifted me into the air and buried his face in my bosom. I felt his hot breath on my breasts as he forced it through the texture of the scant garments which covered them.

"That's a nice way to come into a young lady's room, without even knocking," I scolded playfully. "Suppose I had been doing something I didn't want you to see?"

"In that case, I'd have shut my eyes!" he responded. "But what would you be doing that you wouldn't want me to see?"

"Sometimes girls play with themselves when they feel naughty, and they wouldn't want a man to see that!"

"Ha!" he laughed, as he set me back on my feet and drew off his gloves. "You're not confessing that you practice self-abuse, are you?"

"If I do, do you think I'd tell you?"

"Of course not! That's something no woman ever confesses to a man."

"Well, prepare for a shock them. I do it often."

"Amazing! I've known scores of girls and women and you're the only one that ever abused herself!"

"How do you know the others didn't?"

"Because I asked them and they said they didn't. Congratulations to you! Your score goes up another ten points!"

"Because I play with myself?"

"No! Because you admit it! Baby, you've given me an idea! I've . . . but wait . . . I'll speak of it later."

"Tell me now!"

"No; let's get comfortable and have a drink first. I've got lots of things I want to tell you."

"All right, but it's cruel to arouse a woman's curiosity and then make her wait."

"Let your curiosity suffer for a few minutes. I'll dispel it pretty soon."

"Well, then, let me hang up your things. Now sit down in this chair and make yourself comfortable. And here's that Scotch and seltzer you told me to get for you."

"It's for you, too. You like it, don't you?"

"Yes, but the trouble is, after I've had about three glasses I lose all my maidenly modesty."

"So much the better! Have three glasses right now!"

I laughed.

"Here goes number one. My modesty is now one third dissipated. What is it you've got to tell me first? I hope it's something nice."

"First, I want to tell you how absolutely topping you look. You're a good-looking girl no matter what you've got on, or haven't got on, of course, but those dresses, there's a sort of sophisticated childishness, about them that's irresistible. They're devilishly ingenious. Are they your own idea, or did somebody else think them up?"

The dress referred to, as you may have guessed, was another of the little-girl frocks Daddy Heely had paid for. I had worn one the previous week and as it seemed to have taken Monty's fancy, I had selected another on the present occasion. It was a single-piece frock of black silk with a white belt, and long, tight sleeves. The cuffs, neck and breasts were lined with pleated ruffles and underlaid with cream-colored lace.

To go with these dresses I had some dainty high-heeled Spanish slippers and black silk hose which I rolled just above my knees and fastened with elastic band garters. Except for one detail the costume was eminently respectable. That detail was the extreme shortness of the dress. It barely reached to my knees when I was standing, and when I sat in a normal posture there was no surplus material to be pulled down in a ladylike fashion. The dress was juvenile, but my legs were not. When I observed Daddy Heely's liking to sit on the floor at my feet I easily guessed the reason, and you can too.

Tonight, for certain optimistic reasons related to what Monty had first done on his previous visit, I had not put on any panties, and under the black silk frock was nothing except a diaphanous silk chemise, undervest, and brassiere.

I hesitated at this last question, not wanting to tell him the exact origin of the dresses, and as he did not press the query, I let it pass unanswered.

"What else have you to tell me?"

"Well, I must also tell you I've passed this whole blessed week positively thinking of nothing but you. I had such a ripping good time when I was here before that you've been on my mind ever since. The old pego has been in a continuous state of perturbation. Embarrassing at times, don't you know. Night before last I thought something really ought to be done about it. I tried the wife's door and it was unlocked, so I went in. She was asleep, or what I thought more likely, pretending to be asleep. The time is now, I thought, as I pulled the covers off her; the girl is here, and so is the place right there in the center of her bird's nest. If I hadn't been well soused, I'd have known better. This is what I got?"

And turning his face sidewise he indicated something I had not yet observed; three long, partially healed scratches down the length of his cheek.

"My heavens!" I exclaimed. "If she's like that, and you don't care for her, why do you want to do it with her?"

"Any port in a time of storm," he answered ruefully, shrugging his shoulders. "A man can't always make his cock behave."

"Well, I think that's strange! If I were a man and I didn't like a woman, I'm sure I wouldn't want to fuck her!"

"That's what you think, baby. When a man gets in a certain state, he has to do something. When I was in South Africa I even fucked kinky-headed Kaffir girls. A half a loaf, or even a black loaf, is better than none!"

"And so, you got your pretty face scratched. It served you right. Is that all you got?"

"To all intents and purposes, yes. There were quite a few commentaries and observations of an interesting nature thrown in for good measure."

I couldn't help laughing but at the same time, deep inside me, a little canker of jealousy that he should have wanted to do it with her began to form.

"Is your wife pretty?" I asked suddenly.

"About as pretty compared to you as a moth is in comparison to a beautiful, exotic butterfly."

His words relieved the vague foreboding which had come over me, and for the moment I forgot the matter.

"What else have you to tell me?"

"I want to ask you something. Suppose I should want to take you out some night to a show, a cabaret, a party, or maybe pass the night in a hotel, could you get away?"

"I guess so, I'd have to ask Madame Lafronde. She doesn't like to have the girls go out, but sometimes she lets them. I've never been away all night. I suppose if you gave her something extra you could get her to let me, maybe."

"All right; that's that. She can't hold you in captivity. If she gets rambunctious I'll take care of things. And now that the incidentals are disposed of, the momentous questions is: how shall we pass the night to get the most fun possible out of it!''

I leaned over close to him and, cupping my hands around my lips, slowly spelled out my recommendation, in his ear; "F-u-c-k-i-n-g!''

"Moved, seconded, and unanimously adopted! Let's start!''

"Shall I get undressed now?''

"No, I want to enjoy that dress awhile first, if you don't mind rumpling it. Let's lie down on the bed and just tease for a little while.''

"All right! But wait . . . you forgot something . . . you were going to tell me something else, you started to tell me and then you said you'd tell me later!''

"Ah, yes!'' he exclaimed, laughing, sinking back into his chair. "Before I mention that, I think you'd better take those other two drinks!''

"Oh! It's something that's going to put a strain on my modesty, is it?''

"Better not ask any questions until after you've had the drinks.''

"You're torturing me with curiosity! All right, here goes one . . . and . . . here goes the other. That makes three altogether. My modesty is now in a dormant state!''

"Well,'' he said, still laughing, "you put the idea in my head with your nonsense about playing with yourself. You made me think of something odd, a blank void in my life. I've been all over the world, I've lived with a dozen women more or less and enjoyed the transitory favors of hundreds of others. I've seen all kinds of naughty shows and exhibitions, and if anyone had asked me, I'd have sworn there wasn't a single act in the whole encyclopedia of sexual arts I hadn't witnessed. I've even seen actual rapes of young girls in show bagnios in Cairo. But while you were joking about abusing yourself it came over me that I never actually saw a girl masturbating herself. I mean, really by herself, just as though she were alone and nobody watching her.''

"Oh, heavens! I know what's coming! Give me another drink, quick! My modesty never lived through three before, but it's squirming and twitching now!"

"Listen, baby!" he exclaimed between convulsions of laughter, "I've had something squirming and twitching all week on account of you! I had it pretty well under control the last time, but it's ready to go off on the slightest provocation now, and I think I'd better not expose it to any direct heat, that is, if I want to keep it in a playful humor for a few hours!"

"What a lovely way of saying you want to keep a hard-on! All right, where do I fit into the picture?"

"Well, with the idea you put in my head, and having in mind your inexhaustible resources, I thought possibly you might be kind enough to stage a little entertainment, enjoy yourself voluptuously, and at the same time gratify my prurient curiosity. Kill two birds with one stone, as the saying goes!"

I could not, of course, restrain my laughter, but at the same time the erotic titillations which the lewd suggestion evoked were vibrating through me and my face felt like it was on fire.

"I guessed it. In plain words, you want to see me masturbate myself! Well, I've done it when there was no man around, but it will be the first time I ever did it with one right by me!"

"Then you'll be accommodating?"

"Excellency, I'm yours, body and soul, and your slightest wish is my command! How . . . how . . ." I exclaimed, again gasping with laughter, ". . . how am I supposed to do it?"

"Don't ask me! I don't know how girls do it! I'm not even supposed to be here! You're doing it just as though you were alone!"

"Very well! But I'd better take another drink to make sure my modesty stays unconscious. It was never put to such a test before! Well, first, oh, ha, ha, ha, do I have to tell you what I'm thinking about while I'm doing it, too?"

"That would add greatly to the realism!"

"Well, first, I'm all alone, like you said, and I'm thinking about something I did with a man I liked . . . I'm thinking about what you and I did when you were here before . . ."

"Just a moment! I'm not supposed to be here, but you oblige me to obtrude for a second. What you and I did when I was here before . . . we did a number of things. Be more specific in the interests of lucidity and realism!"

"Well, ha, ha, ha, I'm thnking of everything we did, and especially what you did to me first, while I was lying on the bed here, before I undressed!"

"Proceed. I'm withdrawn from the room again."

"I'm thinking about how you licked me down there, and it makes me feel hot. My little thing in the top of my cunny gets hard and I'm wishing you were here to do that again. And the more I think of it, the worse it gets, and pretty soon I think I'd better do something to relieve the feeling.

"I can't decide at first whether I will or not, and I walk over to my bureau and get these pictures and take this one out and look at it . . ."

"Excuse me for coming in again, let's see that picture . . . u-um!"

"As I was saying when I was interrupted by a phantom voice, I look at the picture. It's a very nice picture of a naked man and a naked woman, and the man has got his face down between the woman's legs and he's doing something to her with his mouth. I think to myself I wish that woman were me and the man Monty. But they aren't, so after I've looked at it awhile I put it back with the rest of the pictures and hide them under the clothes in my bureau.

"I think, what's the harm, I might as well do it, a little, anyway. So I come back to the bed and lie down on my back, like this, with my knees up and kind of apart, and pull my dress up out of the way.

"Then I put my hand down like this, with my two fingers, oh, ha, ha, ha, and shut my eyes, and, ha, ha, ha, rub this little hard thing, kind of slow and easy, with just the tips of my fingers, and it feels awful good, and the more I rub it . . ."

At this point the realism I had injected into the pantomime threatened to overcome me, and I paused, hysterical with laughter.

". . . and the more I rub . . . the more I rub . . ." I gasped . . . "the nicer it feels . . . until . . . until . . . the nice feeling . . . just seems to . . . burst inside me . . . OH! . . . like it's . . . DOING NOW!"

I wiped away the tears which hysterical laughter had brought to my eyes. My face was burning as I turned toward my companion. His face, too, was a dull red; his reaction to the lewd portrayal had not been much less than my own. He sprang toward me, and I knew what he intended to do.

"No, no!" I panted. "Not now! Wait for me a moment! I'm dead down there now! Let me go wash myself and then I'll be all right!"

On unsteady feet I went to the bathroom and laved myself with tepid, scented water. Before I had finished my vitality was returning and the warm glow of voluptuous desire was beginning to reestablish itself.

"Well, Excellency, is your naughty curiosity satisfied? Now you know a girl's last secret!"

"Baby!" he answered in a tense voice, "that affected me more than it did you, I think. I was so near going off I couldn't have held it another second! Look at this . . ."

Unbuttoning the front of his trousers he took his cock out and displayed it, turgid and throbbing, to my eyes; he slipped the foreskin down and the plum-colored head appeared, dripping with limpid moisture.

"Just sympathetic tears," he murmured, "I didn't come, but I was very close to it."

I went again to the bathroom and brought a small wet towel and wiped away the tears. "Careful! Careful!" he cautioned, as I fingered the palpitating column. "It won't take much to release the trigger! I'll have to let the fire die down a little before I put it in you, baby, and meanwhile . . ." he smiled understandingly, ". . . and meanwhile, you can lie down on the bed and take it easy while I pay you back for entertaining me in such a realistic way!"

"Shall I get undressed?"

"No, just lie down like you were a minute ago. You were really entrancing with your little dress up and the white of your bottom and thighs against the black background of dress and hose. That's it . . . just like you were before . . . with your knees up and your legs apart!"

He sat down on the edge of the bed, passed his fingers over the crevice between my legs in a lingering caress, and then his mouth descended on it.

What havoc an ardent, enthusiastic tongue can work in a girl's cunny! I tried to steel my nerves against it to prolong the exquisite sensation, but it was no use, I couldn't hold it back long and all too soon I was melting in his mouth. As the echoes died away, I pushed him from me to lie for a while in fainting languor.

It would take too long to relate all that transpired during those mad, sensuous hours, even if I could remember every act in all its lewd details. Suffice it to draw the curtain with the final scene wherein, hours later, intoxicated both with liquor and lust, I perceived that Monty's face was again between my thighs, his hot lips pressed against my cunny. My dress, now displaced and rumpled, partly hid his face as he sucked and licked the avid flesh.

He himself had long since disrobed and was completely naked.

As he crouched over me I could see his cock, still enticingly rigid, as it projected its muscular length outward.

"Turn this direction, Monty!" I whispered, "so we can do it the 69 way!"

He reversed his position and the next moment it was touching my lips in a moist kiss as he knelt over my face and again buried his own between my trembling thighs. My lips shaped themselves in a tight ring around its mouth and neck and took the visitor in.

The odd, indescribable savor again filled my mouth, breeding within me, not distaste or disgust, but a wild hunger to feel it spurting like a hot fountain in my mouth and throat. So imperious was the urge that I scarcely now heeded the penetrating tongue which but a moment before had evoked such exquisite torment. I thought of nothing but to drain the nectar from the living flesh about which my lips were pursed, to receive its hot gushes in my mouth.

It would give me an orgasm even quicker than having my clitoris sucked. I felt it, I knew it, the poison had entered my soul, this, this was the supreme act of voluptuous delight, and nothing hereafter would ever give me the same thrill. All else would be incidental, superficial, this was the ultimate caress by the side of which all others receded into nothingness.

CHAPTER FOURTEEN

When I awoke, it must have been around noon. My head was aching dully and in my mouth was a queer, pungent taste which puzzled me for a moment, and then I remembered. I sat up in bed. I was stark naked, and I was alone. On the little taboret near the bed was an empty whiskey bottle which accounted, in part at least, for the headache.

Draped carelessly over a chair were my clothes—dress, camisole, brassiere, and stockings. I had no recollection of having undressed nor did I know when or under what circumstances I had fallen asleep. Monty must have taken off my clothes and subsequently departed without awakening me. At what hour he had gone I had not the faintest idea.

Painfully I dragged myself from bed and went to my mirror. My hair was a tangle and there were violet shadows under my eyes. I shivered and pressed my hands to my throbbing temples. What a night! Monty had gone without awakening me. This reminded me of something, and I turned toward my dressing table. There were some bank notes there, weighted down with one of my perfume flasks, and under them a slip of paper with some penciled scribbling:

"The next time, don't have on any lipstick. You left red rings all around it.

See you next Wednesday night. Love and Kisses. Monty."

I rubbed my fingers over my lips and smiled involuntarily as I viewed the result. Then I tore the note into shreds and threw the pieces into the wastebasket.

I did not feel like dressing so I merely bathed my face, brushed out my hair, and went back to bed after ringing for the maid. She brought me some coffee and toast, and I asked her to tell Madame Lafronde that I had a headache and would not be down until later.

About three o'clock Madame Lafronde came up to see me.

"What's the matter, Jessie? Anything wrong?"

"No; my sleeper kept me awake all night, and I've a headache, that's all."

"You can rest up tonight. You needn't come downstairs if you don't feel like it. How are you getting on with Austin?"

"All right. He's not so bad, I like him. He gave me another five pounds."

"Well, be smart, and keep him in a giving humor. I was rather doubtful about him at first. He's got a bad reputation."

I stayed in my room the rest of the afternoon and evening, but along about ten o'clock I got restless, and hearing a great deal of laughter floating up from the parlor I decided to dress and go down.

Under the genial guidance of a gentleman who had just come from America, a game of "strip poker" was in hilarious progress. Five girls were seated around a small table, cards were dealt to them, and the penalty of a losing hand was the removal of one of the few pieces of apparel the loser wore. To keep up the morale of the players, a grand prize to the winner, and consolation prizes to the losers were being offered.

Already one of the girls was down to her panties, and another to panties, brassiere and one stocking. Even as I stood there trying to grasp the intricacies of the game, a shout went up, and the unfortunate in panties threw down her cards in disgust.

"Come on, Bobby! No welching! Take them off!"

Now it is one thing to take your panties off in the presence of a man in the privacy of a room, and quite another to take them off in front of a crowd of laughing people, and I smiled faintly as I watched the victim's flushed face.

But welching is an unforgivable sin in sporting circles, and she was game. Off came the little silk panties and the spectators, or the masculine element of them at least, had the pleasure of grazing on the patch of dark, twisted little curls that rose from the apex of her legs and spread fan-wise over her pubic mount.

"Now can I put my clothes on again?"

"No, no, no! Not until the game is finished!"

And so it continued, to the immense delight of the onlookers, until all but one of the scarlet-faced players were sitting around naked, some pretending a brazen insouciance, others trying to cover their cunnies and breasts with hands and arms.

"An insipid idea of fun," I thought to myself as I looked on indifferently. "Why are men so crazy to look at a girl's cunt? One would think it was the prettiest thing in the world. Whatever they find pretty about one must be in their imaginations. But . . ." I thought, continuing my moody philosophy, "if men didn't think they were pretty, it would be just too sad for us."

And an involuntary smile crossed my lips as there came to my mind the story about the orator for women's suf-frage who shouted from the platform: "After all, ladies and gentlemen, women are only slightly different from men . . ." Whereupon a voice from the gallery interrupted: "Hurrah for the slight difference!"

I lingered long enough to pick up some small silver in the form of a gratuity from a pleasantly inebriated gentleman who attached himself to me and could not be dislodged until I permitted him to put his hand down the front of my dress and feel my bubbies. He wanted very badly to go to a room with me, but I managed to divert his attentions to Hester and made my escape.

The next night was Wainwright's. He came punctually as always and went through his customary nonsense. Generally I extracted some amusement from my exalted status of Fairy Princess, and although I had always to be on the alert to keep him from biting me in the moment of ecstasy, there was something about the fantastic proceeding that left me in an excited condition.

He sucked me deliciously, but rarely continued it long enough to quench the fires the caress started. Before I could have an orgasm he would jerk away from me and masturbate.

This night I was in a particularly restless mood. The exhaustion following my orgy with Monty had passed away with a day and night of rest, and I was again charged with voluptuous longings.

Wainwright had concluded his preliminary gallantries and was crouched over his Fairy Princess on his knees, his head and shoulders inclined downward and his face between her open legs. His tongue had started its tantalizing maneuvers, and the first shivers of lewd excitation were beginning to generate.

With languorous, half-closed eyes, I observed his cock sticking out from his middle. It was small and slender, much smaller than the average, but it was turgidly erect. It was like a child's in comparison to Monty's.

This association of ideas put into my mind the thought

of how much easier I could manipulate so small a cock in my mouth. The thought took root and sent a hot glow through me, and in a moment it was no longer a thought, but a desire.

Without a word of explanation to the puzzled Wainwright I wriggled away from him, turned around on the bed, and got on top of him, straddling his face with my thighs. After a momentary hesitation, and with a clumsiness which betrayed his unfamiliarity with this classic position, his tongue again sought out my clitoris.

As soon as I perceived that its activities were in progress anew, I put my head down and took his little cock in my mouth. The mere fact that it contrasted so in size with the only other one I had dallied with in like manner inspired me with a sort of fascination, and I set to work on it with all my recently acquired skill.

But, alas, I suffered a deception which chilled and disgusted me. Like nectar turning to vinegar in the mouth, that erstwhile stiff little cock which I was so voluptuously sucking almost immediately began to wilt. From its former state of virile rigidity it degenerated into a flaccid, spineless, lifeless little worm, and the harder I tried to inspire it with a bit of manliness, the more fulminating was the disaster.

I released it from my mouth, disappointed, and emulating his own tactics, worked it patiently with my fingers in an effort to resuscitate it, but there was nothing substantial to grasp; it was like trying to make a piece of string stand up, so limp and flaccid had it become.

I could do nothing with it, and disgusted. I got up from the bed. Wainwright's abasement was pitiful to behold.

"Oh, Princess!" he moaned. "Beat me if you wish!"

He sounded as though he actually did want me to beat him. It came over me that if he left under humiliating circumstances he might not return again. He was too valuable a patron to lose. It had always been profitable to humor him; it might be wise to do so in this instance. As he groveled on the floor at my feet I came to a sudden decision.

"I will beat you, you vile creature!" I cried.

Glancing hastily around the room I spied his own belt partly visible under the clothing he had placed on a chair. Snatching loose the strip of pliant leather I flew at him and began to belabor him across the thighs and buttocks.

"Take that . . . and that . . . and that . . . !" I cried, "you evil, depraved beast! If you ever do that again I'll . . . I'll . . ." and I paused to think of a sufficiently ominous threat.

"Oh, Princess! Oh, Princess!" he moaned, and turned over on his back apparently indifferent as to whether the blows fell on his cock and testicles.

Careful not to strike him in these susceptible parts I continued to rain blows on him. He groveled, squirmed, and moaned, and suddenly to my great astonishment I saw that his cock was getting hard again. And there before my eyes was realized one of those strange, weird manifestations of sexual aberration such as delights the hearts of psychoanalysts and psychiatrists.

His hand descended to the reviving member which was now lifted upward in a half-erected state. His fingers closed around it, and while I continued to shower blows upon his naked body he masturbated himself to exhaustion.

A sight fit for a cabinet in Dante's Inferno would have been revealed had anyone unexpectedly intruded in those moments. The man, groveling naked upon the floor, furiously masturbating, while I, with nothing on but shoes and stockings, my hair disheveled, my face flushed, panting and crying imprecations, danced around him belaboring him frenziedly from all sides.

When it was all over and he was dressed and gone, I sank down on my bed. My heart was thumping and I felt half-suffocated. On the bed beside me was a heap of money. I figured it indifferently, and came to with a start.

The man had literally emptied his pockets! There were bank notes, shillings, pence and even pennies, a total in excess of anything he had given me before. Surely the man was a lunatic!

There came an insistent tapping at the door, and Hester entered. She looked at me in astonishment. I was still naked, my face flushed, my hair in disorder.

"Jessie! What's the matter! Did you have trouble with Wainwright?"

"No; no trouble."

"We heard you whipping him and I was uneasy. You never did that before!"

"Oh, the damned fool," I ejaculated, "I think he's crazy." And I related what had happened, omitting only the real cause of his having lost his erection. "He couldn't get a hard-on without my whipping him and I did . . . with his own belt!"

"Did he give you all that?" she gasped, observing the pile of money which still lay on the bed.

"Yes," I answered shortly.

"Gee! You have all the luck! I wish I had a regular who was crazy the way that fellow is! I'd even let him whip *me* for that much!"

"Well, he makes me dizzy. I'm still trembling."

"I see you are. You scared me when I first came in, you looked so . . . so strange!"

"What time is it, Hester?"

"It's about two o'clock."

"Are you going downstairs again?"

"No; there's nothing doing. I'm going to turn in."

"Listen, Hester, I'm nervous. Sleep in here with me tonight."

"All right, I'll get my . . . no! I won't either! I know what you're thinking about, you nasty little pervert!"

"Please, Hester!"

"I will not! Get the electric massage machine or jack yourself off if you're so hot!"

"Please, Hester!"

"What in the world is the matter with you, Jessie? Don't you ever get enough? You ought to have yourself castrated!"

"Please, Hester!"

"Oh, all right, all right, you disgusting little degenerate!"

CHAPTER FIFTEEN

Six weeks went by with Monty visiting me regularly, and week by week I found myself sinking deeper into the fatal fascination of the sexual perversion into which he had initiated me. I do not think he was responsible for the unnatural desire which was now dominating me, I think he was merely the casual and accidental medium through which existing but dormant instincts were aroused.

Like the Succubus of ancient Rome my sexual desires were now almost entirely concentrated in this one act. My inclinations for other forms of gratification were diminishing. Normal intercourse was only an aphrodisiacal irritant if it were not followed by cocksucking. I still masturbated to calm my nerves, but it was always with fellatio pictured in my mind as I realized the act.

In my hours of passion I felt an actual physical hunger for the spermatic nectar. It was as though it contained some vital, sustaining element necessary to my health and well-being, and the first taste as I perceived its saline presence in my mouth percipitated the wildest sexual frenzy. When it came pouring into my throat my own organism responded instantly, without mechanical stimulation of any kind. I no longer tried to spit it out as the hot waves laved my tongue; I drank it avidly, hungrily.

It is said that the cocksucking instinct is the heritage of children whose mothers, while in an advanced stage of pregnancy, and because of the discomfort or danger of normal intercourse while in this condition, have themselves resorted to fellatio, thereby afflicting the unborn child with the unnatural desire. Whether there is any scientific foundation for this theory, or whether it is mere superstition I do not know, but I feel certain, with respect to myself, that the instinct was inherent and not artificially created.

Without any special guidance, refinements and perfections of the art constitute in part its irresistible allure and enravish the masculine senses. Gently, softly and slowly realized, an orgasm effected in this manner sent the recipient, with few exceptions, into the seventh heaven of rapture. A soft, even suction, alternated with the teasing caress of an active tongue playing over the head and around the neck of the pulsing glans, supplemented with a slight up and down movement of the mouth soon had the object of these felicities groaning with erotic ecstasy.

If the subject was slow to reach orgasm, a more intense excitation could be induced by the use of the hand in addition. No normal man in a healthy sexual condition could long resist the luscious combination of gentle fingers and warm, wet, sucking lips.

As the untouched chords of a harp vibrate in harmony with those which are giving forth their tremulous melody, so did my own organism yield up its store of passion, an echo to the very paroxysm I provoked in another.

To Monty's manifest satisfaction the unique method of awakening him in the morning which I have previously related became a definite part of our erotic program. I looked forward to it with a pleasant glow of anticipation, and the thought, implanted in my mind, caused me to wake earlier than I would otherwise have done.

He was a man of unusual virile potency whose sexual vigor reestablished itself quickly, even after the most enervating exhaustion, and he always had an erection when I woke up. Slyly, cautiously, inspired with a prurient fancy to see how far I could get with it before he woke up, I bent my head over the succulent fruit. But in a few minutes my cautious, discreet restraint gave way to more energetic movements as my own passions took the ascendancy. And as soon as this happened, instead of a sleeping subject, I had one who was very much awake indeed.

Week by week I looked forward to Monty's visits with increasing impatience. My other patrons I simply tolerated. The lack of interest in them, which I could not entirely conceal, became apparent and before long I lost Mr. Thomas. Madame Lafronde commented on my petulant humor, and I told her I was tired of being merely an ornament and wanted as many men as I could get, like the other girls. Some of these, the more attractive, often had three or four different men in a single night. She was reluctant to change the existing order and evaded my request by telling me she would think it over.

I knew she felt that I was more valuable as an "inspirational" attraction, and that she feared the complications and ill-humor which would inevitably arise when my younger and fresher charms were used to lure the fish from less attractive bait. Maybe, too, she was aware of or suspected my recently developed cocksucking proclivities, for little escaped her shrewd old eyes and if so, no one better than she knew what this would do to the peace and tranquility of the house once the girls whose clientele I usurped discovered my technique.

In fairness to my sisters in vice, I will say that to most of them fellatio is abhorent and practiced only under duress or the pressure of necessity when fading physical attractions render them unfit to compete on an even basis with younger rivals. Sacrifices must be made to compensate for advancing years and shrunken breasts.

Girls who are alert, good-looking, and possessed of attractive bodies do not need to practice fellatio to hold a clientele. But men are quick to take advantage of any weakness and if the caress be obtained once, either by duress or persuasion or voluntary indulgence, it is extremely difficult to evade further demands.

Monty's confidence to me regarding his conjugal unhappiness and differences became more and more candid. Wrapped up in the lewd fascination which the man held for me I gave no thought to the fact that only a bounder and a cad would have made his wife the subject of such intimate confidence to a whore, regardless of what personal differences may have existed between them.

He had explained the origin and significance of some long scratches down the side of his face, administered by his wife's agile fingers when he had tried to force her. And subsequently, there was a big, blue lump on one of his shins, the result of a well-placed kick received while trying to impose unwanted attention on her.

"Wait till she's undressed next time," I commented viciously, "or did you have her like me, with just her shoes and stockings on?"

He laughed cynically.

"I'd have to chloroform her first to see her naked!"

Apparently, some disagreement of two or three years' standing had arisen between them and she had consistently and determinedly repulsed all amorous advances since then. Picturing her in my mind as I did, an embittered, shrewish woman, I could not for the life of me understand how he was able to feel any desire toward her. But men are contrary brutes, and to make them want something desperately you have only to prohibit it. She didn't want him to fuck her, and presto, the wish to do so was never out of his mind.

These confidences affected me in a peculiar way. I wasn't in love with Monty in the true sense of the word, but when he told me such things I felt twinges of jealousy. It annoyed me that he should perversely want to do it with her. So distorted can one's perspective become that his inordinate desire to fuck the unfortunate woman inspired me with a feeling of personal animosity against her.

At first he had seemed to accept the situation with good-natured indifference, but lately I had perceived an undercurrent of bitterness and vindictiveness.

"Have you ever read De Maupassant?" he asked one night, after having told me of some domestic disagreement.

"No," I answered, "I've heard of him, but I have never read his stories. Why?"

"Well, among them is one with an idea I'd like to apply to her, with certain variations."

"Tell me about it."

"The story is a long one to repeat, but the essence of it is this: A young French noblewoman discovers that her husband is unfaithful to her. She decides to revenge his disloyalty in a manner as startling as it is unique. She hires some ruffians to enter the house and bind and gag him securely. When this is done she has him placed behind some curtains in her boudoir where he will, perforce, be obliged to witness all that transpires within the room, but without being able to move or interfere.

"Then she calls an old servant who has served her all her life and gives her some instructions. Following these instructions the old woman, after wandering about the streets for a time, accosts a young man of genteel appearance, and getting his ear, asks him whether he would appreciate an amorous rendezvous with a young and beautiful woman of nobility sufficiently to bind himself to certain simple conditions, viz: that he permit himself to be blindfolded while being conducted to and from the assignation; that during the amorous engagement he lend himself unreservedly to all the delicate refinements of eroticism for which the French people are noted.

"The first condition being one of no great consideration, and the second one which could be easily complied with if the lady were as young and fair and lascivious as the servant claimed, the youth, who was of a naturally adventurous and romantic disposition, did not hesitate long in accepting the mysterious assignation.

"Whereupon the old woman signaled a hack, and when he was inside blindfolded him and conveyed him to the lady's boudoir. Here the blindfold was removed and the young gallant found himself in the presence of a vision of nude loveliness which far surpassed his expectations.

"For an hour the youthful pair disported themselves with voluptuous abandon, neglecting none of the more delicate and refined artifices in which mouth and tongue play an important part.

"When the cup of love was finally drained to the last drop, the lady sprang from the bed and jerking some curtains aside revealed to the horrified gaze of the youth the securely bound figure of a man who glared at him with baleful eyes.

"What transpired later when the outraged husband was liberated is left to the imagination."

"A very interesting story," I observed. "Get me the book so I can read it someday. But what has it to do with your wife? Do you want her to have you tied up and make you watch from behind a curtain while she Frenches with some fellow?"

"Heavens, no!" he exploded, "I'd tear her limb from limb if she were to play such a game on me. But there's no danger. She's too prudish. I was tickling my face with quite the reverse of the plot in the story, thinking what fun it would be to tie her up and then have some girl come in, you for instance, and do just what that French couple did, right before her eyes. Maybe strip her clothes off first, so she'd enjoy it more.''

"What a horrible idea!'' I gasped. "Why do you want to torment and aggravate her? Why don't you leave her alone?''

"She's tormented and aggravated me plenty,'' he growled vindictively. "I'll get even with her, though. Do you know what I'd like?''

"Yes, I do! It's not a bit hard to guess! You'd like to fuck her, and you won't rest until you do!''

"Wrong, you little spitfire. I'd like to find some way to make her so hot she'd go down on her knees and beg for it, and when she did, I'd tell her exactly where to go.''

"Feed her some Spanish fly then,'' I suggested dryly.

"By Jove! That's a dashed good idea! Wonder where one can get the bally stuff?''

"You'd better be careful. I heard a funny story once about a fellow who sneaked some into his wife's tea to make her passionate. He thought he'd better keep out of sight until it took effect so he went out and walked around the block a couple of times. When he came back he didn't see her around, so he looked in her bedroom. And there she was, on the bed, with her clothes up, and the butler on top of her. And the pantryman, the coachman and the gardener were all standing around holding their cocks, waiting their turn.''

"The moral being, that a chappie had better stick around after feeding his wife Spanish fly,'' he laughed. "I'll keep that in mind.''

"Well, come on, let's get started. I don't need any Spanish fly to make me passionate, I'm that way all the time.''

CHAPTER SIXTEEN

Through the damp London night a luxurious car sped swiftly and surely, the soft purr of its powerful motors hardly distinguishable above the swish, swish, swish of rubber-shod wheels upon the wet pavement as they flew onward toward their destinations.

Outside of the curtained windows a macabre fog eddied and drifted, at times dimming the street lights with its wispy, ghostly vapors. Within was snug comfort, warmth, life and color.

Had curious eyes been permitted to peek inside the glass and curtain-shielded tonneau, a scene of revelry, profanely at variance with the dismal exterior of the night, would have been revealed.

Outside, the interminable procession of half suffocated lights vainly trying to pierce the gray shroud which drew ever closer and closer about them; inside, the ribald levity of alcohol-inspired abandon, the sheen of silken hose on diaphanous garments fluttered in careless disarray above the silk-clad knees.

There were four occupants in the seclusion of the cozy, glassed-in, and softly lighted tonneau. Two of them were gentlemen, modishly attired in the habiliments dictated by

the fashions of the times for evening wear, and two of
them were young girls, whose apparel, if not exactly that
which would have been considered in the best of taste by
social arbiters, was at least beautiful and colorful. The
gentlemen, regardless of their half–inebriated condition,
were patently at home in the atmosphere of luxury which
both the car and their apparel suggested. The girls, had the
imaginary observer surveyed them with a critical eyes and
taken note of the extreme shortness of their dresses, the
rouge upon their cheeks, the exaggerated scarlet of their
lips and their indifference to the indiscreet disarray of their
clothing, would have been catalogued instantly as ladies of
that vast assembly politely described as "not nice!"

One of the gentlemen was Monty and one of the girls
myself. The second gentleman was another scion of aristocracy known only to me by the nickname Zippy, and his
companion was a young Spanish girl of saturnine but
piquantly beautiful features named Carlota.

This was not the first nocturnal outing I had participated
in. Yielding to the influence of the magic wand of gold
which Monty had waved before her eyes, Madame Lafronde
had consented to this departure from the accustomed routine.

"I don't want to stand in the way of your doing the best
you can for yourself, but watch your step, girl, watch your
step!" were her final words on the subject.

Tonight we were to be present at the clandestine showing of some naughty moving pictures which Zippy had
arranged for with an exhibitor at some obscure point far
over on the East Side of London. After the show we would
dine in the seclusion of a private room in a popular resort.

Zippy was a genial chap of very likable personality. He
was possessed of a humorous and witty disposition. His
droll witticisms and antics kept one constantly laughing,
and when he was half under the influence of liquor, he
kept those around him fairly convulsed.

Carlota, whom I had met a few hours before, constituted

something of an enigma. Her attitude toward me was perplexing; I had always been able to make friends easily, but my overtures to her left her unresponsive and I sensed some coldness, the reason for which I could not imagine. At times I found her looking at me covertly and imagined there was something baleful in the glint of her dark eyes.

Thinking that maybe she regarded my acquaintance with Zippy as a possible menace to the security of her domains in his affection, I was scrupulously careful not to presume upon the bon-homme spirit of the four-cornered friendship, and still this explanation did not seem to fit the circumstances exactly, for she seemed peculiarly tepid in her demonstrations of affection for the good-looking young aristocrat.

Tonight, however, she had apparently cast off her moody lack of animation and had entered into the festive spirit of the occasion. A silver-covered flask was being passed from hand to hand as the smoothly humming motor carried us onward toward our destination. Esconced in one corner of the luxuriously upholstered seat, Monty leaned back with me on his lap. At the other end of the seat, Zippy held Carlota in a similar fashion. A supple, beautiful arm was curved lightly about his neck, and a small, piquant face was snuggled against his.

In the pleasant spell of a mild alcoholic langour, I watched them dreamily. I felt happy, contented, and was looking forward to a night of joyous abandon with no premonition or presentiment of evil to mar my light-heartedness.

Carlota's skirts were up over her knees, revealing a brief extension of flesh which glinted ivorylike in the soft light and was accentuated by the black sheen of her silk-clad legs. The metallic clasps which engaged the tops of her hose, holding them smooth and tight about her legs by means of elastic garters which ascended upward and disappeared under filmy garments, sparkled like jewels as the movement of the car caused the light to vibrate against them.

An inquisitive hand, lured on, no doubt, by the seductive disarray of garments, fell upon her knee and began an insidious exploration upward, its movements contributing further to the disorder of her clothing and the revealment of more ivory thighs. Of the hand itself soon nothing was visible but portions of a white cuff, the rest of it being lost to sight among the filmy undergarments.

Carlota giggled nervously and pressed her legs together, by virtue of which maneuver the invading hand was firmly imprisoned between walls of warm, living flesh.

With my head resting on Monty's shoulder, I watched this lascivious play with half-closed eyes. What a pity, I thought, that Carlota was not always jolly and happy. When she was like this, she was really beautiful. What pretty legs she had, too, so slim and graceful and softly curved. When girls had legs like hers no wonder men admired them. Mine had been like that when I was younger, but during the last year or two they had filled out, become more solid, more suggestive of maturity.

I straightened my own legs out and contemplated them pensively.

"What are you doing, baby? Admiring your legs?" murmured Monty.

"No; I was admiring Carlota's, and comparing mine with them."

"Oh, envy! Thy name is Woman! Do you think Carlota's legs are prettier than yours?"

"Yes," I said, candidly. "I do. Mine are getting too matronly."

"Bosh," answered Monty, and he plunged his face between my breasts and set me to giggling by blowing hot, whiskey-scented breath through the cloth over my bubbies. "You're just fishing for compliments, and out of pure obstinacy, I refuse to bite."

"The only time to properly judge a lady's legs," expounded Zippy solemnly from his corner, "is when they're around your neck. I maintain that Carlota has the nicest legs in the world."

Monty and I burst out laughing and Carlota jerked upright in pretended indignation.

"Oh! What an insolent inference! I never had my legs around his neck in my life."

"In my dreams, my dear, in dreams! A man has a right to dream anything he wants to, hasn't he?"

"No! Not such defamatory dreams as that! If you want to dream about me, dream something decent! And . . . o-o-oh! . . . take your hand away from there! Stop! . . . stop! . . . you're going to make me wet my panties!"

The sudden slowing of the car, followed by two long and two short blasts of the siren warned us that we had reached our destination and Carlota, escaping from the fervid embrace, straightened out her clothing preparatory to leaving the car.

As it rolled to a stop, apparently in accordance with prearranged plans and in answer to the signals of the siren, the figure of a man materialized from the fog-enshrouded night to guide us to the rendezvous where the entertainment was to take place.

We were conducted to a room improvised to represent a theater in a crude way; a few chairs, a small platform elevated two or three feet above the floor, and back of this a white curtain. The projection machine and operator were hidden from our view in an adjacent room whence the pictures would be flashed through a small round hole cut in the intervening wall. There were no other spectators present as Zippy had arranged for an entirely private showing.

The exhibition lasted for about an hour and a half and consisted of several different films, some of them allegedly taken from real life among the apaches of Paris and which ran the gamut of every imaginable sexual indulgence and perversion. Another, based superficially on the question of whether or not it is a physical possibility for a man to be raped against his wishes, had as its theme the sequestering of a young man on his wedding day by a group of jolly, fun-loving friends.

Snatched from the side of his bride of a few minutes, he is carried away, stripped of his clothing, and chained against a wall in an upright position with his arms elevated and his legs separated.

Under these undignified circumstances he is turned over to the mercies of a bevy of girls who, with lewd acts, dances and other artifices, endeavor to make him have an erection. For a while this modern St. Anthony is able to subjugate any erotic reactions and successfully resists the wiles of the sirens. But alas, the flesh is weak, and despite his determination to withstand the impure temptations, Satan, in the guise of a beautiful young girl with nimble fingers, forces his cock to awaken from its lethargic slumber and raise its head in obeisance to the powers of Evil.

With this disaster, the battle is practically lost, for once a man's cock is turgidly erect not even the chaste determination of a Galahad can control its subsequent actions nor stay the course of lascivious Nature.

Raising her dress, the temptress turn around and stooping over, with her hands on her knees, backs her round, white bottom up against the rigid spike. Closer and closer she presses, until the treacherous obelisk, following the narrow road downward between the plump cheeks, reaches and penetrates the natural haven between her thighs, and naught remains to complete the victory of sin but the slow, weaving circular movement of her bottom.

By hand frigging, by sucking, and by other lascivious arts the unfortunate victim is subjected to further depletions of his sexual vitality as the sirens, one after another, drain him to exhaustion, until at last his cock is reduced to a state of unconsciousness and inertia from which no seductive feminine enticements on earth could arouse it, and when this is apparent, the luckless (?) groom is released and permitted to go on his honeymoon.

The entertainment terminated with a horrific exposition of a girl and a diminutive Shetland pony. It was incredible, unbelievable, but the evidence was there, clear, distinct and indisputable in the moving photographic reproduction upon the screen.

When the show was over we returned to the car and half an hour later were at a restaurant where a small private dining room had been reserved for us. We enjoyed a nice dinner, followed with exquisite wines, over which we lingered, joking, teasing, and otherwise enjoying ourselves. After the dinner, we would part company. Monty and I going our way and Zippy and Carlota another.

But it was very pleasant and comfortable in the little dining room. We were all in the roseate state of semi-intoxication in which everything is just right and everything that is said excruciatingly funny. So we dallied, telling naughty stories, rumpling each other's clothing, and indulging in all kinds of lascivious nonsense, while Monty and Zippy continued to drink until they had passed the half-way stage of intoxication.

"On an occasion of thish nashure," declaimed Zippy, taking advantage of a lull in the conversation, "ish an invariable, not to shay an inviolable cushtom for each guesh to relate in hish own crude way the chircumstances and detailsh of hish or her firsh sexual experiensh."

"What he meansh," interrupted Monty, condescendingly, "ish: everybody tell about their firsh fuck!"

"I believe I . . . hic . . . made myself clear without . . . hic . . . the necesshity . . . of an . . . interpreter!" protested Zippy with great dignity.

"You're half intoxshicated!"

"I resent that inshinuation! I insist that I'm not half

intoxshicated. On the contrary, I'm half sho . . . sho . . . sober!''

"Shut up, both of you! You're both intoxicated! If you start any arguments, Carlota and I are going to beat it!''

"What wosh thish argument about in the firsh playsh?'' interrogated Monty, scratching his head in perplexity.

"Oh, Zippy had an idea for each of us to tell about our first sex experience, and you interrupted him.''

"That wosh a good idea. I mosh humbly beg hish pardon for my intrushion. It would be mosh interestin' to learn under what unforshunate chircumstances you two young ladish losh your maidenheadsh. I nominate you to tell the firsh story.''

"Oh, no!'' I protested, laughing, "it happened so long ago I can hardly recall the circumstances. Let Carlota tell hers first. While she's telling hers, I'll try to remember mine! That is, if you two men will stop drinking. There's no fun telling stories to people who are too drunk to listen.''

"I shecond the movement,'' interposed Zippy solemnly. "Everybody lishen now, while Carlota tells ush about her firsh romansh.''

"Ah,'' murmured Carlota dreamily. "Until now I have kept the secret of my misfortune and the circumstances under which my ruin was accomplished locked in the innermost recesses of my heart, nor did I think ever to reveal them.''

She paused and remained pensively silent for a long time.

We waited expectantly.

"I was the only child of wealthy parents who showered upon me every care and blessing which loving hearts could devise,'' she began. "We lived on a beautiful estate in the country where the art and handiwork of man was supplemented by every beautiful and exotic creation of Nature. Close to our home was a charming wooded fairyland in which wild flowers abounded in bounteous profusion, and through which a little brook of clear, limpid water rippled on its way to the distant sea.

"From my earliest days I recall with what delight I wandered through this miniature forest, listening enraptured to the lilting songs of the birds which lived in its green boughs, gathering a scented flower here and there, watching the big black and gold bees as they skimmed the blossoms in their eternal quest . . ."

"Thersh too many birdsh and beesh and flowersh and not enough fucking in thish story . . ." growled Zippy discontentedly.

"Hush up, Zippy! Let her tell the story in her own way!"

"Up until the time I was fifteen years old," continued Carlota, unabashed by the interruption, "I was as pure and innocent as driven snow. My parents had carefully shielded me from every contaminating influence; I knew nothing; I was ignorant of all the true facts of life . . ."

"Terrible mishtake parentsh make," observed Zippy sadly.

"To that lack of knowledge, which I was old enough to rightfully possess, I ascribe the fact that my pure innocence was trampled in the mire of lust and my fresh young girlhood blighted forever," continued Carlota, her voice husky with emotion.

Monty wiped away a tear and Zippy turned his head to cough suspiciously.

"I shall never forget the day; it is burned into my soul with letters of fire. I had just passed my fifteenth birthday; I was a woman in body, but an innocent, unsuspecting child in all else. I thought that babies were brought by fairies who left them upon the doorstep in baskets woven from flowers and vines."

Monty was sniffling audibly. Zippy reached surreptitiously for a bottle and succeeded in pouring himself a stiff drink before I could wrest it from him.

"Got to have some kind of stimulation," he protested aggrievedly, "thish story ish breaking my heart."

"I had discovered a limpid pool among the rocks into which the water eddies so gently that the sandy bottom could be seen through the crystal-like depths. Several fish inhabited this little pool and it was my delight to lie on my stomach and watch them swimming lazily about, with the sunlight, which penetrated the translucent water, causing their irridescent scales to shine with all the colors of the rainbow.

"It was to this pool I hurried that fateful day, eager to see my little pets, each of which I had endowed with an affectionate name. I had brought some bread with me, and as I lay there watching them dart at the slowly sinking crumbs, I was startled to hear a voice close by me, 'Ah, little Miss Narcissus,' it said, 'does your pretty face enchant you so that you linger over its reflection in the water?'

"I looked up into the smiling countenance of a handsome young man who was standing there regarding me curiously. I was startled, but not frightened. I knew nothing to be frightened of. 'No, Sir,' I replied, 'I was looking at some fish that live in this pool. They are really very beautiful. Their scales shine like rubies and emeralds and sapphires in the sunlight.' 'So?' he answered, peering into the pool. 'You have to lie down and put your face close to the water to see them,' I explained.

"Whereupon the young man, who was an entire stranger to me, accommodated himself upon the rocks in a position similar to my own, and together we gazed into the limpid pool while I identified the various members of my adopted family.

"His interest in the fish waned quickly and he began asking me questions which I, candidly and ingenuously, answered without hesitation, thereby revealing to him by childish simplicity as well as my identity.

"I thought I had never seen so handsome a young man. He was much older than I, five or six years, at least. 'Do you come here often?' he asked. 'Every day,' I replied, 'unless it rains.' And then, my curiosity overcoming my diffidence, I asked: 'Who are you? You don't live near here, do you?' 'No,' he replied slowly, 'I come from a far-off city. It is a secret, but I will confide in you for I see you can be trusted. You must never tell anyone I listened with breathless interest. 'I am an emissary of the king. I am sent here to see that the animals and birds and flowers are not molested. When the little birds fall out of their nests I put them back, and when the chipmunks can't find enough acorns, I feed them.' 'Oh, how wonderful!' I breathed ecstatically. 'May I help you sometimes? Some wicked boys place traps to catch little bunnies, but whenever I find the traps I throw rocks on them and break them up!' 'Quite right, my dear little Carlota (he now knew my name), I will be very happy to have you assist me in my search for hungry chipmunks, and if we find any bunny traps we will assuredly destroy them. You may meet me here at this pool tomorrow, but remember, not a word to anyone, not even to your parents. The king would be very angry.'

"And thus, with a joyous secret clutched to my trusting heart, and in the happy anticipation of accompanying this wonderful young man in his search for little birds which had fallen from their nests, I ran home . . ."

"Mosh touchin' story I ever heard," mumbled Zippy, "but . . ."

"Hush up!" I hissed. "I want to hear the rest of this story without anymore interruptions!"

"Sure enough, he was there waiting for me the next day, and what a delightful time I had, wandering through the woods with him, exploring little glens and shady bosques where the vines and leaves were so thick I had never attempted to penetrate them alone. But it was easy with someone to hold the vines back, to lift you over fallen logs, and carry you across wet places where little green snakes might be hiding.

"There was a place where the brook spreads out, standing several inches deep in the lush water grass. Across this swampy terrain was a leafy hummock which I had seen from a distance but had never approached, not knowing how deep the bog might be around it. I pointed it out to my companion and without a word he picked me up in his strong arms and started across the intervening swamp.

"There was a strange, sweet sensation in being carried this way, one which I had never experienced before. It filled me with a soft, melting languor, impossible to describe. As he strode along, he shifted his hold to ease my weight and his hand, under my swinging knees, came in contact with bare flesh where disarranged clothing left it exposed.

"A gentle, tingling warmth began to generate there where his hand was supporting my legs, and an overpowering emotion gradually stole over me. I closed my eyes and abandoned myself to the unknown but delicious sensations, languishing, half-fainting, oblivious to everything else in the world.

"My subsequent recollection of what transpired was dim and vague. In a half-unconscious state I was dreamily aware that we had reached the hummock, and that he had laid me down on the soft grass and was doing something with my clothing. Indescribable ecstasies were being provoked by some mysterious caresses between my legs, right there where they came together, caresses productive of sensations so overpoweringly sweet that I neither questioned their propriety nor even wondered how they were being effected.

"Suddenly the delicious spell was broken by a short, quick stab of pain. An involuntary shriek of anguish escaped my lips, but the pain passed almost before the sound had died away, and again a flood of warm delight permeated my being and seemed now to be projected clear up inside my body. So intense were the sensations which we now being provoked that I fainted dead away.

"When I recovered consciousness with all that had occurred impressed on my memory only as a vague and indefinite, but delicious dream, I found myself in a peculiar situation. I was lying upon the grass with my head resting on my companion's folded coat. My dress was up and my panties had been removed. My companion was engaged in sponging my thighs with a handkerchief he had apparently moistened in the brook. As he squeezed the water from it, I perceived that it was stained with a dull red.

"I sat up and felt a twinge of pain and an odd, swollen sensation between my legs. I tried to stand up, but I was dizzy and weak. What had happened? Ah, my friends, there is no need to tell you what had happened. In that unguarded moment the heritage of purity had been snatched from an innocent trusting maiden; she had been robbed of that priceless jewel which once taken can never be replaced; her virginal chastity was gone forever."

Carlota choked, overcome with emotion.

"Dishpicable, unprinshapled scoundrel," groaned Zippy, "robbing a young girlsh pryshless jewel . . ."

"Misherable king's emishary ough to be imprishoned for life!" exclaimed Monty, bursting anew into tears.

I was the only one whose heart remained untouched. As the narrative seemed to have come to an end, I murmured:

"That was a beautiful story, Carlota. Now tell us the real one."

"The real one isn't nearly as beautiful as the one I told you," answered Carlota, who had now regained her composure.

"Wosh the idea?" growled Zippy, sitting up suddenly. "Imposhing on our shimpathies in such a . . . hic . . . inexcushable manner?"

"Thash what I shay!" echoed Monty, with an aggrieved expression on his face. "Wosh the idea?"

"Shut up, you two! We'll make her start all over again, and if she doesn't tell the truth this time, we'll do something to her!"

"Oh, well, if you insist on the truth you can have it, but I warn you, the circumstance was quite devoid of romantic interest. Fiction is always more interesting than truth!"

"Thash what we want, the truth," exclaimed Zippy with renewed enthusiasm.

"Never mind the romantic interesh!" recommended Monty.

"Well, let's see . . . I guess I was twelve, or very close to it. My Aunt Carmen and my little cousin Ferdinand were staying with us for the summer. One afternoon Mamma and Aunt Carmen went to the city, leaving Ferdinand in my care. It was just such an opportunity as I had been wishing for. A girl playmate had whispered some interesting facts to me confirming pretty well-defined suspicions I had already formed regarding certain phenomena of nature."

"I hope there ishn't going to be any birsh and beesh in thish story," murmured Zippy uneasily.

"Before Mamma and Aunt Carmen were out of sight I had made up my mind that I was going to find out all about it. Ferdinand was nine, just young enough to accept my leadership in everything, and just old enough to keep a secret when warned that its disclosure would bring parental vengence.

"He could be trusted, and so as soon as Mamma and Aunt Carmen were at a safe distance, I locked the doors, invited him to come with me to my bedroom, and under the pretext of teaching him a new game, got him to undress and did likewise. The game wasn't exactly a new one, but it was the first time either he or I had ever tried to play it, and we were a little awkward.

"By working his little dangle with my fingers, a process I had to repeat several times, for it persisted in going soft on me, I managed finally to get it stiff enough to fulfill its proper functions, and after a few erratic efforts, it suddenly slipped into the hole between my legs with an ease which rather surprised me.

"And this, dear friends, was the simple and unromantic circumstances under which I was fucked for the first time, though in truth it should be put the other way around, for it could more properly be said that I was the one who did the fucking. I hope you're satisfied. As a matter of fact, the first story I told you was also true, except in some minor details."

"What were those minor details, if I may ask?" I inquired politely.

"Well, in the first place, I wasn't entirely unaware of what was going to happen when he laid me down on the grass and took my panties off. In fact, I was rather hopefully anticipating it, for I had felt something hard rubbing against my thigh all the time he was carrying me. In the second place, I wasn't by any means unconscious while he was doing it to me, though I pretended to be. And in the third place, as I have just related, it wasn't my first fuck, or my second either for that matter, even though he did make me bleed a little because of his size."

Carlota tossed off a pony of brandy while Monty and Zippy remained pensively silent.

"Now," she observed, clasping her hands behind her head and leaning back in her chair, "let's hear yours!"

"Mine," I answered, "parallels yours . . . I mean your true one . . . so closely that I would only have to reverse the ages of the participants, for I was the younger, by several years. Which reminds me of something I intended to ask you in view of your experience . . . can you get any juice out of a nine-year-old cock?''

"Gosh, I don't know," confessed Carlota. "It always seemed to be wet when it came out, but whether it was boy-juice or girl-juice I don't know because I was twelve years old at the time, the hair was beginning to grow on my cunny, and the juice might have been all mine. But don't fool yourself, a kid nine years old can have an orgasm, whether he squirts anything or not.''

At that moment a waiter, after knocking discreetly, opened the door to murmur apologetically that it was well past closing time. A hasty glance at the timepiece on the wall showed that it was indeed two o'clock in the morning.

We gathered up our effects and prepared to depart. Both Monty and Zippy were tipsy. Carlota walked in the peculiar fashion of one who is not quite sure of the footing, and I myself found when I stood up that I was far from steady on my feet.

Monty's chauffeur, who was huddled up in his seat half-asleep, came to life, jumped out, opened the door for us, and stood patiently awaiting instructions.

For several minutes we stood there debating further exploits. For my part I was in favor of going directly to my room with Monty. My blood was heated and in my fevered, half-inebriated state I pictured several hours of delicious sexual abandon. But I was overruled by the others, who were still in an adventuresome mood. They wanted to go somewhere else to pass another hour or two before separating, and each had different ideas.

"Listen, everybody!" finally announced Monty with drunken determination. "We'll go to my housh! I've got a nish, comfortable room where everybody can relaxsh and enjoy themselves!"

"Oh, no, we can't do that!" I protested hastily. "Your wife will have us thrown out!"

I could not have voiced a more ill-advised objection. Monty instantly became stubbornly resolute.

"Lishen!" he said with injured dignity, "a mansh housh ish hish cashel! When he wansh to entertain dish in hish cashel thash hish . . . hic . . . ina . . . inalienable right!"

Nobody could offer a valid contradiction to this time-honored philoslphy, and though the chauffeur looked startled when he received his instructions, we were soon the way. Though even in my beclouded state I could not repress certain misgivings, I lulled them with the thought that his wife would undoubtedly be asleep at this hour, and I would think up some pretext to get them to leave as quickly as possible.

But, alas, under the effects of the silver flask and other stimulants which were drawn forth from hidden recesses in the car, the warning sense of caution diminished and before long I hardly remembered where we were going and by the time we got there I was nearly as drunk as the rest and but dimly aware of the surroundings.

The next thing I knew we were within the beautiful room which Monty had modestly described as "nish and comfortable." The feel of rich, thick carpets was underfoot, and about us every luxurious comfort and adornment which money could command. The soft nightlight which was burning gave way to a brighter illumination as crystal chandeliers burst into life. In an immense open chimney firewood was laid to light, and in an instant this stately, beautiful room became the scene of riotous revelry.

Carlota and I flung ourselves upon gorgeous divans while Money and Zippy divested themselves of their hats and top-coats and placed upon an inland table the several bottles, some full, some partially depleted, which they had carried up from the car.

A sleepy butler appeared unsolicited, and stood with gaping mouth in the doorway.

"Go 'way! Go on back to bed!" ordered Monty. "Thish ish a private party, we don't want any intrushions!"

The man retired hastily.

There was an interlude during which events remained only in my mind in a nebulous blur. Here and there were incidents which stood out in relief, surviving the chaos of the night. Of course, it was inevitable under the circumstances that Carlota and I should be wheedled into disrobing, for no drunken orgy is complete until the women have exhibited themselves naked, and when the cataclysmic hour struck, she was down to her slippers, hose and a short undervest, while I, more circumspect, had removed only my panties.

Across the room where the shaded glow of a rose-tinted light fell softly on her naked thighs and pointed, cone-shaped breasts, her head on Zippy's lap, Carlota lay, alternately shrieking hysterically and moaning as he realized some occult operation between her legs with his finger.

Upon the velvet cushions of another divan an equally exotic scene was revealed. Cuddled in Monty's arms I rested my head languidly on his shoulder while he fingered and played with one of my bubbies which he had succeeded in exposing by the simple expedient of tearing open the front of my dress.

My own fingers were clutched around something stiff and round and hot which projected upward from his unbuttoned trousers. I slid the satiny skin slowly up and down, and each time the rosy head emerged from its shelter of flesh the rigid column jerked like a live thing. I squeezed it tighter, gripping it with all the strength of my fist, and still the spasmodic throb was strong enough to break my grasp as the plum-colored head was forced through the tight ring formed by my thumb and index finger.

Each mighty convulsion awakened a corresponding throb in my own sexual organs, and an inordinate longing began to assail me. I wanted to feel that luscious, throbbing thing in my mouth, to run my tongue over its wet surface, to lick it and suck it until it burst.

What difference did it make that Carlota and Zippy were there? They were too immersed in their own pastimes to pay much attention to what I was doing. Very likely, too, they already knew I was a cocksucker, for Monty was very indiscreet with his talk when under the influence of liquor.

In another moment, doubtless, the luscious fruit for which I was panting would have been between my lips had it not been for an interruption.

That interruption was the quiet opening of the door which gave access to the beautiful but now disordered and bottle-strewn lounge. I was the only one directly facing the door and I was the first to perceive a new arrival.

I froze in rigid attention.

In the doorway, surveying us gravely and silently, stood a woman. Inasmuch as this woman was the direct opposite of the mental picture I had formed of Monty's wife I did not for a moment or two even consider the possibility that it was she. I simply wondered who she was.

The woman who stood there regarding us with a calm, almost expressionless face was young, not much older than I, probably. An embroidered robe of rich, wine-colored material was drawn about her and fastened with a loosely knotted, tasseled rope of silk. Under its lower hem, the lacy edge of a white garment, a nightgown, without doubt, peeked. She wore no hose, but on her feet were dainty, high-heeled bedroom sandals.

She was superbly, radiantly beautiful, a blonde of perfect type whose skin was suggestive of peaches and cream, and whose loosely coiled hair glinted in the light like spun gold.

So silent had been her entry and so quietly did she stand that for several moments no one but myself was aware of her presence. Monty, his attention finally attracted by my tense attitude, turned his eyes in the direction I was looking. Zippy in turn glanced casually toward the door, and started abruptly. Carlota, facing the opposite direction was still moaning and suspiring audibly. Zippy shook her significantly and murmured a warning"S-h-h-h!" She looked at him in surprise, and then turned her head to see what was holding his attention. When she saw, she sat up hastily, drawing her one diaphanous garment down over her hips as far as she could.

It must have been three-thirty or later. Monty was the first to break the silence.

"Wosh the idea of thish intrushion?" he demanded thickly.

For a long moment there was no answer from the immobile figure. She continued to regard us, coolly, unemotionally. Then:

"Take your disreptutable associates out of this house immediately."

The words were spoken in a quiet, dignified voice, low and musical, but firmly resolute.

By this time realization of the intruder's identity had dawned upon me and surprise gave way to a rapidly growing feeling of resentment and anger. In a confused, startled way, I comprehended that I had been cheated and imposed upon. So firmly roted was the conception I had formed of this woman, a conception in which she appeared as a flat-chested, sour-faced misanthrope, devoid of seductive feminine charms, that to find her in every respect the exact antithesis of all I had been led to believe, or permitted to believe, was at first a shock, and as this was assimilated, cause for rage which grew quickly to consuming proportions.

In some way, not yet clearly defined in my mind, I had been misled and hoodwinked. I had been permitted to assume that I had a rival unworthy of serious consideration, much less to be jealous of. Once, impelled by some vague uneasiness, I had asked Monty whether she was pretty. His answer leaped into my memory. "About as pretty, compared to you, as a moth is in comparison to a beautiful, exotic butterfly!" The recollection brought a new surge of anger, for it suggested that I had not only been deceived but likewise made the victim of my own ridiculous vanity. This woman was regal with a loveliness which made mine look like cheap tinsel, and I had the sense to realize it.

In the baffled, frustrated, angry grouping of my thoughts, I included her as well as Monty in my resentment. I had pitied her before, but I hated her now with all the bitter venom which jealousy can brew in the heart of a woman confronted by the superior and invincible charms of a rival. I could have sunk my fingernails in the soft bloom of her cheeks with vicious delight, I could have clawed the full, voluptuous breasts which swelled the dressing gown outward in twin globes with infinite satisfaction. I fairly suspired to hurl myself on her and disfigure every inch of her golden beauty.

Dimly, I was aware that Monty had lurched to his feet and was advancing toward her angrily.

"Lishen! Thesh ladiesh are my guesh! Wosh the idea of inshulting my guesh? Wosh the idea calling my guesh dish . . . dish . . . reputable?"

She stood her ground, receding not an inch before the menacing gesture of an upraised hand. No emotion was visible in her face except that of cool disdain.

"Remove these people from here instantly," she repeated. "I will not tolerate their presence here."

"Shay! Wosh housh ish thish? I refush to be embarrasshed in the presensh of my friensh!"

He made an unsteady lurch, and the sharp sound of a hand in contact with flesh was heard. He had slapped her in the face with considerable force.

A wave of cruel pleasure swept over me with the sound of the impact and the hot blood tingled in my cheeks.

Across one of hers a dappled, reddish outline appeared to mar the white purity of her skin. But she did not flinch. With outward calm and dignity she remained motionless. There was a moment of deadly silence, and the low voice spoke again.

"Take your degenerate friends with you and leave this house or I will go myself."

What followed can only be told in a summary fashion. My own emotions were so violent that I saw everything through a sort of red haze and the details were blended in a confused blur of movement and action.

Monty had seized her in his arms. They were tussling and swaying in the doorway, she trying to escape his grasp and he apparently intent on dragging her into the room. No words were spoken; there was no sound except the heavy breathing, the swish of garments, and the scuffle of moving feet deadened in part by the thick carpets.

The pallor of her face had given way to a vivid flush which burned in either cheek. One of her bronze slippers had been dislodged in the scuffle and she was panting audibly. With a violent effort she succeeded in wrestling an arm free from his clasp, and placing his palm of her hand against his chin she forced his head back. For a moment it seemed that she was about to free herself from his drunken embrace.

As she strained to loosen his grasp, the sound of ripping cloth was heard and the neck and upper part of her robe and nightgown were torn open. The folds sagged down over her shoulders and arms, and one white breast was exposed.

I can see it yet, that proud, round breast of alabaster whiteness protruding from the ravished garments, its rosy nipple standing out prominently.

The sudden yielding of the garment caused her to lose her balance and the temporary advantage she had gained. She tottered backward and before she could recover herself she was again helpless in his arms. But she did not cease to struggle as she was dragged toward the center of the room.

The blood was singing in my head. I felt choked, suffocated, and was breathing in short, dry gasps. Zippy and Carlota sat stiffly erect, watching with bulging eyes, but I gave them hardly a thought. Remembrance of his cynical admission of attempts to fuck her was simmering in my brain. Well, he would never lay hands on me again. Let him fuck her if he could, and let her claw him to shreds while he was doing it if she wanted to. That was what he had on his mind now. I knew he was going to try to fuck her right there in our presence.

The sound of more ripping cloth bore out the supposition and testified to his lust for the woman who had spurned him as he tried drunkenly to disrobe her. The kaleidoscopic, shifting blur of movement now revealed her half-nude as the entire front of her dressing gown was ripped open and the torn fragments of the nightgown underneath tangled about her legs.

I clenched my fists and bit my lips. My face was burning hot and my head felt light and dizzy.

As the torn fragments fluttered about her shapely limbs, he lifted her up. She managed to slip from his arms and regained her feet, but as she did so what remained of the garments was stripped upward and for a moment, not only her legs, but her bottom as well was left naked. As she twisted about the light shone full on the patch of little bronze ringlets of hair at the base of her stomach. Another violent movement and pieces of her torn garments again covered the exotic sight.

She was panting, choked, inarticulate, but as if aware of her half-naked condition she gathered herself for a supreme effort and placing both hands against his chest she shoved with desperate strength. Doubtless, divining what was in his mind, she put every ounce of her failing energies into a superhuman effort to escape the humiliation. She succeeded in pushing him from her. He clutched at her in an effort to regain his balance, tottered uncertainly for a moment, and fell backward. His head struck the edge of the iron grating in front of the fireplace. His body twisted once or twice, straightened out, and remained motionless.

There was a momentary silence, broken only by a faint, peculiar whistling sound from the lips of the fallen man, a sound which I, and probably both my companions, assumed to be more an indication of drunken stupor than anything more serious.

But the woman standing there panting beside him, looking down into his face, suddenly began to scream. It an instant the servants, who had probably been hovering around close at hand but loathe to interfere, rushed precipitately into the room.

"Call a physician! Call a physician! Call the police! Get these people out of here!" she screamed, repeating the words over and over.

While two servants lifted Monty from the floor to lay him upon a sofa, another scurried to telephone a doctor, and another addressed himself to us.

"I'd advise you to retire as quickly as possible. The Marster appears to be in a very bad condition. He's not responsible under the circumstances, and you'd better be off, seein' as the Mistress is quite 'isterical!"

It was a sober and quiet little procession that filed down the stairs and out into the night air. Monty's faithful chauffeur, aroused by the sudden movement and lights about the house, inquired anxiously:

"What's happened?"

"Oh, Monty staged a row with his wife. He fell down and hit his head on the fireplace grating," Zippy answered gloomily.

"Is he hurt?"

"I don't think so. Get us away from here as quickly as you can."

The uneasy chauffeur hesitated a moment but finally decided that the best course was to do as suggested. He put the motor into movement and the car slid off down the quiet street.

As my thoughts cleared I became aware that Carlota was putting on her clothes, and for the first time realized that she had left the house clad in nothing but a silken shift, though she had retained sufficient presence of mind to grab her clothes and bring them with her, which reminded me that my own panties were still decorating a chair back there in the house.

I was not tempted to return for them. The wild emotions of the past half-hour were passing and I felt weak and faint. A fit of trembling seized me and I began to cry.

Carlota turned suddenly on me and I was electrified to hear her hiss:

"Damn you! If it hadn't been for you this would never have happened!"

"What on earth do you mean?" I gasped, hardly able to believe my ears. "What did you have to do with it?"

The only answer was a string of curses and maledictions that left me petrified with astonishment.

Zippy tried in vain to quiet her. She began to shriek.

"Let me out!" she cried hysterically, "let me out!"

Thinking that the excitement and liquor had thrown her into some kind of a fit, I put my arms around her and tried to soothe her. She shoved me away with a violent gesture and screamed:

"Keep your hands off me, you damned little cocksucker, keep your hands off of me!"

The chauffeur, who of course could hear the clamor, slowed up the car, and opening the glass window at his back, peered in.

"Here! Here! What's going on?" he exclaimed anxiously.

"I want to get out! Let me out!" cried Carlota.

"Certainly, you can get out if you want to!" answered the man with alacrity, and he jumped from his seat to open the door for her.

Carlota literally hurled herself from the car, and sobbing brokenly, ran off and disappeared in the darkness.

"What . . . what in the world came over her?" I whispered dazedly, turning to Zippy. "What will happen to her, running around in the dark in a drunken fit?"

"Don't worry about her, Jessie. She can take care of herself."

"But . . . but why did she say such awful things to me? Why doesn't she like me? I've never offended her or done her any harm!"

"Don't you know, really?" he asked.

"No, I don't! Do you?"

"Why, she's jealous of you. That's what's the matter with her."

"Jealous of me? Why should she be jealous of me?"

"Well, you see, Jessie, she was Monty's girl before he met you."

"Why! I thought she was your girl!"

"No," he answered with a resigned gesture. "Monty shoved her off onto me to keep her pacified. I did the best I could, but I wasn't up to it."

"Oh!" I gasped weakly, "Oh!"

Zippy placed an arm over my shoulder and patted me sympathetically. "Monty is a good scout but he takes some wild chances. We all must have been crazy to let him take us to his house tonight."

"I didn't want to go; I tried to talk him out of it, but I'm glad now I went. I found out several things I didn't know before. I never want to see him again."

Unable to control my feelings, I began to cry again.

"Cheer up, kid. Don't let yourself get upset. You have

to take things as they come in this life, the bitter with the sweet!''

His arm tightened about me and unresisting I let him draw my head over against his shoulder where I continued to sob until I was able to restrain myself. This Zippy was a nice chap. I had always liked him but had never permitted myself to be more than discreetly friendly with him on Carlota's account. There was comfort and consolation in the sympathetic pressure of his arm, and soon I felt better.

"Will you come to see me sometime?" I murmured. "I'm not going to have anything more to do with Monty."

"Of course I will, if you want me. I couldn't ask you before because, well, it just isn't cricket to poach on another man's preserves."

"That's how I felt about Carlota. What a dummy I was! I knew from the way she acted there was something wrong, but I didn't have sense enough to suspect what it was. No wonder she didn't like me!"

The big automobile was rolling along smoothly and quietly and within another twenty-five minutes or so I would be back in my room.

Dawn was not far off, but it was still dark outside.

CHAPTER SEVENTEEN

So quickly does the heart respond to kindly words in moments of distress that already a tender feeling for Zippy was taking root. He was really nice and he was good-looking too. I put my feet up under me on the car seat, and cuddled down against him with my head resting on his lap. The soft vibration of the car was soothing to the nerves and soon I felt quite comfortable.

Under the pressure of my shoulders on his lap I became aware of a disturbing element which started a new train of thoughts. I moved my body so that I could lay my hand on the disturbance, even squeeze it softly. It immediately became more pronounced and grew into a small riot. For several minutes nothing was said.

The next thing I knew his trousers were unbuttoned, the cause of the agitation was out in the open and my head was being impelled down over it by hands which exerted a firm pressure.

I was surprised at such directness, but not displeased.

"The chauffeur?" I whispered questioningly.

For answer Zippy reached over me, manipulated a switch, and darkness equal to that outside descended upon the interior of the car.

Some fifteen or twenty minutes later two discreet notes of the siren advised us that my destination was near. When the car stopped and I stepped out, the sky was tinted in the east. The night was lifting. Dawn was at hand.

I ran up the steps, rang the bell, and after a long wait the door was opened by the night maid. Within less than ten minutes all told, I was in bed and sound asleep.

I slept for at least five hours, but I would have sworn that it was not over five minutes before I was dragged from my lethargic slumber by a violent shaking and insistent voices which continued relentlessly until I finally sat up to protest the commotion.

"Wake up, Jessie! Wake up!"

It was Hester who was repeating the disagreeable phrase and shaking me insistently, but as my vision cleared I saw Madame Lafronde standing nearby, and several girls besides.

There was something in their faces which dispelled the last vestige of sleep, and I now saw that Madame Lafronde was holding a newspaper.

"Wake up, Jessie! Wake up!" pleaded Hester. "Are you awake?"

"Yes! I'm awake! What's the matter?"

"Oh, Jessie, were you with Montague Austin last night? Something dreadful has happened!"

The blood drained from my face.

"What is it?" I whispered.

"He's dead, Jessie, he's dead! There was some kind of trouble in his home last night or early this morning; there were some girls there, the police are trying to find them! We thought . . . we were afraid . . . maybe you were mixed up in it! You were out with him last night, weren't you? The paper says there were two girls!"

"Let me see the paper!" I gasped, without answering her questions.

Silently, Madame Lafronde placed it in my hands.

Big black headlines screamed at me from across the top of a column on the front page:

MONTAGUE AUSTIN DIES UNDER MYSTERIOUS CIRCUMSTANCES.

I clutched the paper with trembling fingers and tried to read the smaller print, but my mind refused to concentrate upon the long drawn-out recital and only blazing fragments detached themselves here and there to impinge on my consciousness.

"Youngest son of late Sir Weatherford Austin died at an early hour this morning as the result of injuries sustained in his own home. Wife in hysterical collapse unable to give coherent account of tragedy . . . not known whether fall was accidental or whether he was knocked down . . . died without regaining consciousness . . . conflicting stories told by domestics suggestive of bacchanalian revelries motivate investigation by Scotland Yard . . . empty bottles and whiskey flasks . . . intimate garments left behind . . . half-naked girls flee with male companion . . . identity of man unknown . . . chauffeur to be interrogated today . . . victim has figured in many sensational escapades . . ."

"Now, Jessie," said Madame Lafronde not unkindly, seating herself on the edge of the bed, "for the good of all concerned, let's get the truth so we'll know what to do. Just answer my questions. Were you there?"

"Yes, I was! But I didn't . . . none of us . . . even dreamed he was badly hurt!"

"What happened exactly?"

"He was fighting with his wife. He was drunk and he slipped and fell and his head struck against the fireplace grating."

"What were you doing in his house while his wife was there?"

"Well, I . . . we were all of us half-drunk and he insisted on taking us there! I didn't want to go!"

"Who are these other people?"

"A girl, named Carlota, and a fellow, a friend of Monty's, everybody calls him Zippy . . . I don't know his right name."

"Who is this Carlota?"

"I don't know her full name, either. I'd met her two or three times before when I was out with Monty and Zippy. I didn't know it until last night, but she used to be Monty's sweetheart."

"Do either of these people know your name and where you live?"

"Zippy does. Carlota . . . I don't know. Monty might have told her."

"How did you get here this morning?"

"Zippy brought me . . . in Monty's car."

"In Monty's car? With his chauffeur?"

"Yes; you see the chauffeur . . . none of us . . . knew there was anything seriously wrong when we left."

"Then the chauffeur knows this address too?"

"I guess he does now, all right."

"All right, kid. If you step fast maybe you can be out of here before the doorbell starts ringing, and maybe you can't. There's no hard feelings, but you know how it is, I can't afford to have any of my girls mixed up in anything like this."

"I understand. I don't blame you," I answered dully, and got out of bed to dress.

"I'll have your money ready for you as soon as you're dressed and we'll slip you out the back way . . . just in case. I'll give you some address where you can get on easy if you want to get a new place, but use a different name and don't mention having worked here. If you do, there's a good chance you'll be picked up. The police are going to find out all they can about this affair, and if they get you, there's no telling what you'll have to go through.''

Hester went with me to carry some of my things and to help find a room where I would be safe from annoyance. We found one which appeared to be suitable, and though the landlady looked askance when she heard I was to occupy it alone, her misgivings were calmed by the sight of sufficient money to pay a month's rent in advance, and my assurance that I would be receiving no "visitors" other than Hester.

The room was cozy and comfortable, but after Hester had gone, such a feeling of loneliness and wretchedness welled up in my heart that I threw myself on the little bed and had a long cry.

The next afternoon Hester returned to tell me excitedly that within less than fifteen minutes after our departure the police, who had extracted the address from Monty's chauffeur just as Madame Lafronde had anticipated, were there looking for me, and in addition two barristers had called repeatedly in a vain effort to see me. I shuddered and from then on the little room seemed more like a haven of refuge than a lonely exile, for I entertained a profound horror of police and jails, the long months of deadly monotony in the reform school never having been forgotten.

"They found that girl Carlota, too. She used to be a dancer in a music hall. And who do you suppose your mysterious friend Zippy turned out to be?"

"I don't know," I answered. "Who?"

"No less a personage than that polo-playing Lord Beaverbrook! I've seen his picture in the papers lots of times. I think the whole thing will be hushed up soon. They know it was an accident and that nobody was much to blame but Austin himself."

True to Hester's prediction, references to the scandal disappeared quickly from the press and no great efforts were made to locate the missing witness. For a time I entertained the hope that Madame Lafronde would relent and call me back. But the hope was dissipated when Hester sadly informed me that it was futile. She herself had tried to pave the way for my return only to be told by Madame Lafronde that though she liked me, I was a "firebrand" and in the best interests of the business its doors must remain closed to me.

Hester came faithfully to visit me for an hour or two every afternoon.

"Did the papers ever hint what Austin and his wife were quarreling about?" I asked her.

"Yes; she objected to his having you and those other people drinking and carousing in the house. Wasn't that it?"

"Partly, but there was something else . . . something lots worse than that."

"What was it, Jessie?"

"He had her half-stripped. He was going to fuck her right there in front of all of us."

"Oh, Jessie! What did I tell you about that man? Why wouldn't you listen to me?"

She was on the point of tears again and I hastily endeavored to turn the conversation into a lighter vein.

"Don't worry so about me, you sweet old thing! I'll listen to your advice in the future. But it's fierce to be here all alone. Maybe I'll pay you to come and sleep with me some night. I've got lots of money. I'll telephone Lafronde and disguise my voice and ask for a girl, and you can volunteer."

"No! I won't sleep with you, you perverted little woman-fucker!"

"Not even if I pay you?"

"No! Not even if you pay me!"

"That's nice! You'd go to a hotel with some woman

you don't even know and do things with her, but you won't sleep with me!"

"Jessie, how can you even think of such things after what's happened?"

"Let's get undressed and lie down for a little while. You haven't anything to do this afternoon."

"Are you in your right senses?"

"Listen; if you'll stay, I'll do it like Heloise did . . . only nicer!"

"Oh! You're one of those, too, are you? Well, thanks, I don't want any today. When I do, I'll let you know. How much do you charge?"

"I'll bet I could make it last you a whole hour!"

"No!"

"Please, darling, sweet Hester! Think of me, locked up here alone in this room by myself day after day!"

"No! And if I did, you'd be sure to leave the door unfastened so anyone could open it and walk right in!"

"Look!" I exclaimed, and jumping up I twisted the key in the lock and held it up before her. "I'll even hang up a towel over the keyhole so nobody can peek at us!"

"Well, come on, then! I just want to see if you're really capable of doing that, too!"

I had paid a month's rent, but by the time two weeks had passed I found the loneliness and inactivity intolerable. Hester had brought a list with several addresses which Madame Lafronde had prepared, and feeling now that there was little likelihood of being bothered by the police, I set out one afternoon to see if I could find a place.

With one swift glance of appraisal the madam of the first house on the list invited me to a room, had me undress for a survey of my physical assets, and immediately began to ply me with flattering and enticing inducements to join her ménage. I was rather taken aback by such unexpected eagerness and the assurance of profitable earnings, but anxious to settle the matter of immediate occupation I accepted her offer without delving into promises which seemed somewhat exaggerated.

The bargain was struck. I was shown the room which would be at my disposition and introduced to several of the young ladies who would be my future companions. They were a slightly faded lot, considerably below Madame Lafronde's standards, and the depressing thought came over me that my entry into this second-rate bagnio signaled another step downward towards the abyss. But I shrugged the thought aside; I could always leave it if I didn't like it, and told the woman I would bring my effects in the morning.

Before opening the door for me to leave, she detained me a moment in the hall.

"Listen dearie," she murmured in low, wheedling tones, "I forgot to mention . . . I don't suppose it will make any difference . . . but I've got a special class of trade here . . . this isn't a French house exactly, but you know how it is . . most of my best paying regulars like it a little out of the ordinary . . . you understand. All the other girls here do it. You won't mind that, will you dearie?"

Ah! As I digested this bizarre announcement, which fully explained the cajolements and flattery and alluring promises, the woman watched my face anxiously, as though to read therein some sign which would tell her whether the bird was going to fly off affrighted or remain in the trap.

For a long moment I stood pensively silent. I knew from the dejected aspect of the place, the sallow-faced girls, the tarnished furniture, that the type of men who frequented it would be far, far different from those I was accustomed to dealing with. Up to the present, my cocksucking inclinations had been exercised voluntarily, to satisfy my own sexual cravings. Here, I would be obliged to do it, whether felt so inclined or not. I hesitated uncertainly, and then, with a gesture of indifference, replied:

"I'll give them what they want."

And thus, with six short words, did I seal my pact with hell, and bind myself henceforward to madden the brains of men and corrode their souls with the bittersweet poison of my sucking lips.

Madeleine

CHAPTER ONE

Why do I write these memoirs? Seated here in afternoon leisure in my luxurious boudoir at . . . Boulevard Haussmann, with my faithful Fleurette pouring me a petite *vere de l'absinthe,* a feeling of exuberant self-satisfaction so overwhelms me that I must find some expression for it other than sensual. Last night, in this very room, I entertained no less than a president. He was elderly and broken by many cares, and I enjoyed his conversation at dinner much more than his prowess in bed; yet I, who have scorned blood princes, stood— or rather lay—in awe of him.

But I am way ahead of my story. Just why do I write? Is it because I feel that in the account of my love-life lies the salvation of womankind? Is there any tocsin that I wish to sound to warn my sisters off any metaphorical rocks? No; scarcely that. Rather it is that I wish to record the experiences of my senses while their tinglings are yet echoing through my veins, and if any uncertainty of detail arises in

the course of my analyses, I can still reexper-
ience and reexamine those subjective states. To
depend on memory alone for other than the
mere external web of circumstances, as my
good friend Frank Harris does in his autobi-
ography, is a sad delusion. A slight gesture
from me and my cherry-lipped little Fleurette
yonder slips hither between my thighs, even
as I sit, pen in hand. Worshipfully she slips her
pretty head beneath my light silk peignoir, and
brushing aside the ribband of my chemise, with
her soft coral tongue stimulates in me such
warm delicious tremors as again assure me of
the worthiness of this, my project. And if there
are more vigorous amusements that I desire,
know, reader, that my Maison is the best in
all Paris—which is no mean boast—and I harbor beneath my hospitable roof, not only fourteen selected maidens of varying types and na-
tionalities, but also three handsome red-
cheeked boys and a great blond Finlandish
giant of massive proportions—thus qualifying
my household to administer every variety of
libidinous pleasure of whatsoever sex.

But I have digressed considerably—and before
I can well launch upon the story of my life,
there are certain justifications I wish to indicate, certain misunderstandings that I wish
to negate or correct.

First of all, I make no pretense about the
deathly secrecy of these memoirs—and there
would be no one more disappointed than my
ghost if ever I should peep down from over the
edge of a bed in heaven (or more conveniently
still, look up from a supine position in hell)
and see these notes cast into an ash can, or

used to start a fire, or perhaps hung up in the uncivilized backhouse of some illiterate to do vulgar service. I have never been so completely preoccupied with the study of the opposite sex that I have ignored the foibles of my own, and I would wager a season pass for the privileges of my establishment that there never was a woman who kept a diary of her love adventure who was not without hope that some day it would be discovered and exploited, that men far and wide might read and stand to her appeal, that women would read and be confounded with envy by the variety of her amorous exploits. True, women who marry, at least with the intention of permanency and not with the purpose of performing a Lucrezia Borgia, are known to destroy the diaries and letters of their youth; but so too does marriage entail the denouncement of all idealism and individualism, and this is a matter of mere expediency. Women contemplating the fatal step do not keep diaries. And so I am frank to admit that my purpose is to someday publish these memories for distribution to my friends and patrons. Not in the immediate future, of course, for I am still young—but 30 years of age—and though I am already turning overly plump, due to the lazy luxury of my present existence, and I can scarcely recognize these voluptuous breasts of mine when I remember what a sylph-like figure I once possessed—yet I feel certain that there is plenty more living ahead of me, and there will be correspondingly much to write about.

If then the present is not to be the last page why do I write now? It is because that handsome little doctor who comes to look in on us every now and then (and sometimes follows into the objects of his inspection himself) tells me that I have a slight aneurysm of the heart, and unless I slow down on the unendurable pleasures that are frequently mine, I may develop serious endocarditis. Admitting its possibility, I am yet but little troubled—for personally I suspect that *monsieur le docteur* tells me this that he may come to see me more often — and coming more frequently, collect more fees—and judging from the currency in which he collects his fees and the fact that the dear boy would never be *particeps criminis* to my death (though an unobjectionable manner of dying it would be), I need have no fear. And so someday, when I have long since retired gracefully from my last encounter and the girls carry on the show in my stead, I shall distribute copies of these memoirs to those who ignore me, and knowing my past, they will kneel admiringly before me even as the maidens flocked worshipfully about the chair of the Chevalier de Seingalt in his old age.

That consequently my private life may fall into the hands of the so-called morally minded, I know too, and for their eyes I wish to pen this challenge. Apart from some maladjustments in my adolescence, I have never for one moment had cause to regret the method of life I chose. The punishment for sexual promiscuity, to employ the terminology that is the best our puritanical forebears afford us, is mainly imaginary. I have had the advantage of attending an American medical school for two years and the reader may accept my assurance that if (and

I emphasize this *if*) conditions afforded legitimate medical attention, the avoidance of both veneral disease and unwelcome offspring could be insured beyond doubt. And I who have never permitted a rubber capot (i.e., condom) to be used upon me, say this. Far be it from my purpose to mislead some little miss into getting herself under double misfortune. There is no kind nature that takes care of such matters, as you who are more experienced no doubt ruefully know, and it is only because I must not insult the intelligence of the more enlightened, nor transform the character of these notes from a book of memoirs to a textbook on contraception and prophylaxis, that I refrain from giving to all who need it the meed of information that is mine.

I know how criminally misleading many books are on this point. Having adopted sex as my lifework from the moment of the full maturing of my reason I have pursued its science and lore into every cranny of literature. Thanks to the kind aid of my many patrons and admirers, and to some extent due to my personal efforts, I have gathered an unusually fine collection of erotic books to me. Hence I feel justified in making the observation that through some unfathomably perverted sense of propriety, writers will cover their pages with the most unmitigated licentiousness and yet fear to violate the law or convention against the spread of contraceptive and abortive information. It is bitterly amusing too, to note further, that the books that sin worst in this direction are those written by men. Torrents of the male ejaculate are poured into us, our thirsty wombs are supposed to suck it up, and yet our heroines invariably remain untouched by consequences. How preposterous this is, only those of my own sex can realize. The avoidance of impregnation and its dire physical and social consequences is the primary and major issue in every woman's life. It was in my case particularly. No woman can settle herself completely to enjoy the embraces of her lover—or even husband—no matter how overpoweringly delicious his rhythmic contacts may be, if in her mind there is any fear of this kind. And yet this is something that these women—created by brutal men who do in writing what they dare not do in fact—never tell. Other glaring disparities that many works delight in making continued use of are the insertion of fabulous ten-inch members, invariably compared to an ox's leg, into the virginal vagina of a 14-year-old girl. That such an effort would tear through the perineum of even a tried woman and inflict fatal internal injuries is never considered. I hope to be more sincere and accurate in my accounts, for the truth of my life has been sufficiently strange and interesting to discourage any use of fiction.

Another justification—though doubtless the reader is getting impatient—for I can't just dive into my tale until I have made my position clear. I chose the life of a prostitute. Worse than that, according to the moralist, I have become a panderess, proxinete, a "whorehouse mistress." There are many other ugly words that could be used, but so too there are more just and beautiful terms that have been applied to us in periods like the ancient Roman and Grecian, when our profession was regarded as on a vastly higher plane than many another—say that of the wife. Prostitution! Pray ask your moralist whether all men and women who work with their bodies do not prostitute themselves far more meanly than we, whose toil, if such it be, is of all forms the most lovable, seeing that it receives, even as it gives, pleasure. And those who are artists and sell the innermost thoughts of their souls, do they not prostitute themselves the basest of all? More pertinently still, take your smug married woman: her smugness comes only from the delusive safety—certainly not happiness—that comes with a compliance with her conventions. Basically, she is the worst prostitute of all—sexually, in her manual toil, in the shackling of her mind and will, in the degradation of living lies that are the very backbone of this institution. She knows well that if she had originally been honest with her husband—if she had given him what he was entitled to as lover—he would not have married her. But no, she has the questionable comfort of knowing that she used her sex, an intrinsically temporary appeal, to lure him into the marital trap.

As to the accusations that our relations are insincere, unnatural or too frequent, little reply is necessary. Nothing is more wearying than to crawl into the same familiar hole, night in and night out, knowing in advance every move, every gunt, of one's partner—and yet, just such a hypocrisy does the marital status breed. Wives must submit to their husbands out of duty or fear. Husbands serve their wives frequently with

225

no inclination at all other than duty or perhaps a jealous fear that she will seek outside relief if he does not assuage her. A wife is of frigid temperament and is brutally forced to submit, or a wife is of a more ardent turn and rides her husband to an early grave—for veritably it is no one man's task to quench an ardent woman. Both monandry and monogamy are sadly unworkable hypotheses. Though every spouse may think that his or hers is the only unfaithful union, yet icemen and bill collectors leave other than their commodities or receipts behind them in more cases than one may want to admit—and that cuckold husbands grow horns outside the uxorial bed that do not come in pairs and do not stay erect indefinitely, is proven by reference to the statistics of our profession.

Again, let what wife that will, deny that she does with her mouth what she cannot otherwise do at such phases of the moon as she is incapacitated below. We will not believe her. And how many married women are there—sans hemorrhoids—who have not had their pretty bottoms broken into from behind?—provided of course that their bottoms are charming enough to inspire that flattering toughness in their husbands that is essential to the execution of this difficult task!

Your so-called "saving sense of sin" can save you only from suspecting your neighbor of the things you do. Everyone believes that he or she is the only one that sinks to these secret doings, and it is well for this that the law protects to some exent the privacy of the marital chamber. I affirm again that there is more vice inside the married state than there is without. A vice with few or none of the thrilling recompenses that should normally go with them.

And what does a married woman get out of all this? A home and food, yes; but for this she pays with perpetual labors, household and otherwise, that would earn her untold luxuries if she were her own mistress. At this point one may object, indicating in refutation that the majority of my sisters and colleagues in the lightening of men's burdens never attain the riches and fortunes that I have. To this I reply that for them I have but scant sympathy. In most cases it is the fault of no one but themselves. True, it may be some comfort to consider that there are failures in all walks and professions of life. There are as many poor preachers as prostitutes—only the latter do not cite the former as evidencing the wages of righteousness. But I believe—and my own life will further demonstrate my belief considerably—that any woman who is at all equipped to give pleasure to man can climb to the level where she can command the worth of herself—that is to say at the very least a comfortable living. In our field as in no other is it our privilege to ourselves determine the price of our commodity. It is as easy to get a two thousand franc check from a man with one million a year as it is to get 20 francs from a poor dirty laborer—easier and more justifiable—for a stiff prick has neither conscience nor discretion, and the price may be raised at the same rate as the temperature of one's pursuer. The casual debauchee of tonight, haughtily turned away, becomes the ardent and generous admirer of tomorrow—and there is nothing that so whets the appetite as the illusion of unattainability. I do not say that all can achieve to the beds of dukes and princes—though judging from the amount of fucking these worthies do, there is room for a considerable number yet; but there are many intermediate stags, all preferable to the gutter or the bondage of marriage. Consider too that over 90 per cent of the world's wealth is in the hands of the aristocracy and the capitalists—and it is this leisure class who require amusement most—who, if they do not support more than three mistresses at a time, at least change them frequently—and it is not inconceivable that for a night or two, not of work but of pleasure, a shrewd dame may get enough to put her by comfortably for life. In this profession as in any other that is better recognized, there is plenty of opportunity for the employment of initiative and the projection of individual personalities. In all, I wish only to impress the reader into whose hands these memoirs may chance, that our profession is not inconsistent with the possession of intellect and refined sensibility of a sort. In evidence, I submit myself and these my writings in negation of the base generalizations that have been leveled against us. The day of the hetaera, with her esteemed position in society, is at hand again. The false morality that ousted her, that was necessary to the establishment of vicious ecclesiastical powers, that same religious degradation of woman is passing with the decline of the institutions that plotted it. A new and more beautiful paganism blossoms forth in the seats of our highest civilization. That the economic factor casts a shadow of aspersion on devotees of the art of pleasure is doubtless lamentable; but until the same reflection is removed from all the arts, pursuits and professions of our modern world, my audience who sits in judgment of me ought not to consider this in the evaluation of my life.

CHAPTER TWO

Disillusioning as it may be to those who have found an added lascivious fillip in my Parisienne name ("Madeleine!" How often have I heard it murmured as I gazed up into the face of some lover, flushed with ecstasy!) yet my real name is Louise—and I am not French at all. For I was born in the prosaic enough locale of Plattsburg, in the State of New York, U.S.A., in the year 1889.

My parents—and this too is commonplace—were stern, straight-laced people who subscribed to all the externalities of middle-class morality, and my early upbringing was of that dull, spirit-killing kind that is, alas, still typical of the average American home.

Whether fortunately or unfortunately, there were no boys in our family—only a sister, some twenty months older than I. I say fortunately, because my parents, disappointed at their lack of male offspring, had decided to give me an education that otherwise might have been limited to the technique of houeshold drudgery. Unfortunately, because my sister and I, deprived of the natural and free male companionship that only brothers can afford, were brought up in a peculiar ignorance of things sexual. Somehow the things we learned in later childhood from our companions possessed a vague impersonality that failed to relieve the drabness of our sexless lives. When the mysteries of creation were first explained to me by an older girl friend of mine, I refused to believe her. That my parents begot me by fucking was too inconceivable. After some days and nights of childishly morbid pondering, I dismissed the subject from my mind—and carefully avoided any supplementary discussion with her who had made this disagreeable disclosure.

All circumstances, as I review them hastily in my own mind—and it is needless to bore the reader with facts outside the pale of his interests—point to the fact that, my early life being so entirely sexless, my adolescence was abnormally delayed and it was not until my sixteenth year that I ever began to be a woman. Only one incident during this period do I wish to mention—and I leave its importance to the evaluation of the scientifically bent. It was when I was about nine years old. The dreariness of a rainy day had forbade even reading, my usual pastime, and I was rummaging through one of my mother's bureau drawers, unearthing silly old family tin-types and portraits, when I came upon an odd disk of brown rubber, much like a miniature automobile tire, only its internal area was covered with a thin membrane. My keen curiosity, coupled with my natural astuteness and precocity, served me but little in the assignment of some purpose or identity to this object. Climbing upon my parents' bed and spreading my dress about me, I proceeded to examine further, unrolling it only to become more mystified by its full cylindrical length, and inflating it with my breath as if it were a toy balloon. At this point, my mother, wondering about my long silence, came upstairs to see whether or not I was up to some mischief, and finding me with that article in my hands and at my lips, administered to me a beating the severity of which I could never forgive, and even now cannot reconcile with the offense. It must have been the hypocritical prudery of my parents, frightened in its apprehension even by one so innocent as I, for in those days the use of contraceptives was limited for the most part to the route classes. My mother's sense of sin was great. This contretemps served to sink me trebly deep in morbidity. I hated my parents bitterly for this punishment that I could not comprehend. And when some months later I learned the function of that criminal article, far from dissipating them, it but renewed all my hatreds. To this very day, despite all my intellectual emancipation, I cannot see or even think of a condom without a vague sensation of nervous nausea.

But to get on with my story—it is a beautiful warm June day—the kind that makes poets of us all. At her seat, gazing disconsolately out of the window of a classroom in the Plattsburg High School, sits a maturing girl of 17 with chestnut hair and a promising figure. A gorgeous day, she thinks. The girls are all going for a swim down at the lake after school. But a sticky oozy feeling high up between her thighs, that chafing elastic about her waist, and that soft bulky thing she is wearing, tells her that this time she cannot be one of the party. Disgusting . . . if only I were a man, she thinks bitterly. Or—as Mamie Smith says—there's one sure cure to stop these hemorrhages . . She shrugs away the silly thought and writhes uncomfortably on the hot bench as she feels the perspiration running down the small of her back. The afternoon is getting quite hot. The class has been reading *Ivanhoe*. A certain phrase keeps reiterating itself in her mind. "Front de Boeuf put the great key in the lock . . . and turned it." "—and turned it!" The words repeat themselves in her mind with an almost vicious rhythm. Biting her lips abstractedly, she chips tiny bits of wood off the edge of the desk with her sharp well-kept nails. Now the increasing discomfort of the heat seems merely to augment the unfathomable delight that she feels.

Then suddenly she relaxes into flaccid passivity and chides herself for her mad reverie; she squirms about again, and raising her hand weakly to the teacher at the front of the room, is excused with a nod.

As she enters the damp shadowy girls' lavatory in the basement, with its cool gratifying odor of blended disinfectants and urine, two girls' voices are suddenly hushed, and then she is recognized.

"Oh, hello Louise. Has teacher noticed our absence yet? You won't tell on us, will you?" It was Miriam Smith, hastily readjusting her

frilly lace drawers and trying to appear undisturbed.

"We were just talking about Ruthie—" put
in the other, Sylvia Watson, nervously rubbing
the fingers of her right hand in the palm of
her left. "You know—her mother's made her
leave home—because, did you hear?—she's in
trouble—and of course, the fellow that done it
is one of the military reserve men and can't
marry her."

Louise shrugs her shoulders and turns her
back to attend to some detail of personal hygiene. Another case, she thinks disgustedly. But
I wonder what it can be between Sylvia and
Miriam? Oh, it can't be! What could they do
to each other? She glances up briefly from her
occupation at one of the many pencilled legends
on the slate walls of the lavatory.

"Cock sure is a wonder
It makes a girl a fool:
It puts her in the family way
And gets her thrown out of school."

She smiles cynically and—her dress and petticoat held up at her waist by the pressure of
her elbows and her legs held somewhat apart
—she attaches a fresh pad of muslin, noting
with a rueful moue the two little red welts
high up on the soft flesh of her thighs that the
chafing had caused.

Sylvia and Miriam are lounging about, their
arms twined around each other's waists tenderly. She glances at them quizzically and returns
to the classroom, pondering. Little chills and
fevers alternately race up and down her spine.
An intermittent nervousness that is now delightful and now unbearable overcomes her. The

remaining minutes of school drag excruciatingly. Front de Boeuf put the great key in the lock —and? And turned it.

Such are the pains and fantasies of adolecence.

At last classes are over. Louise trundles out her bicycle from the shed behind the school. She has a hot dusty mile and a half to traverse before she is home. Wheeling wearily through the environs of the small town, she passes a detachment of soldiers from the nearby military encampment coming in from a hike. They gaze hungrily at the graceful girl-figure, at her shapely silk-clad limbs. Some respectfully, some insolently. "Hello, cunt!" one of the men leers at her as she passes closely on the narrow road. "Would you like to have something better 'n a bike between yer laigs now?" She hurries on, blushing furiously, hating. "Cunt! If they only knew what it is to . . . if they only had to . . " she blusters helplessly to herself and bursts into tears as soon as she is out of sight

A proper contempt for the rough mob of soldiery had been bred into her. The permanent military encampment was the bane of Plattsburg's respectable populace. Seductions were common. Rapes were not infrequent. Louise's own sister Mary was at present carrying on an affair with one of the lieutenants—and almost daily Louise had to listen to her mother's loud warnings and upbraidings. For all the constitutional guarantees, Plattsburg was at the time sadly under the nailed heel of militarism, and the maidenheads of the vicinity were no more respected than the pasture stiles when the men were a-march.

At the top of the hill and beyond the town limits, a cool breeze dries her tears and blows away her resentment. Now she yields to the exhilaration of speeding downhill. The rhythmic pedaling and the snug contact of the saddle are decidedly pleasant, while the passing clumps of bushes and the wooded, shady dells fill her with an exaltation that she would have found difficult to explain.

Arrived at home though, all brightness vanishes. A hundred yards away from the kitchen she can already hear mother's shrill hysterical tones berating Sister Mary who now and then tries in vain to answer in a tearful, crushed voice.

"That a child of mine should bring down such disgrace and sorrow on my head! Oh, how I curse the day when first you stirred in my womb! Why did the Lord see fit to test me with two accursed lazy daughters; that you should yield your honor to the first stranger. Didn't I warn you again and again? And now, as a living reminder to all the world of your sin, you are to have a child—a child without a name! And who is to suffer by all this but me?"

There was much more to this same effect— the whole punctuated by Mary's remorseful sobs. Frozen by the realization of what it meant, I crept away to the barn to be alone. Horror-stricken I was, and yet, I must admit that it was less sympathy for my sister that I felt than hatred of my mother's attitude.

Alone in the loft, I unearthed a novel that I had been reading, *McTeague* by Frank Norris as I remember, and in a few minutes the sufferings of the heroine Trina at the hands of the brutal Mac had me so enwrapped that my own troubles seemed remote and unreal.

The afternoon wore away until, from the rattle of dishes that came to me across the field from the house, I could judge that the family was at supper. But I remained on, reading till the very last rays of the setting sun had vanished, leaving my page a blurred uniform gray. As I could read no more, I lay back and shut my eyes to rest them. Before I had time to realize my tiredness, I was asleep and dreaming.

In my dream it seemed that I was imprisoned in a medieval castle dungeon. Sylvia and Miriam were there too; but while I was in a panic of fear, they seemed quite happy, petting each other in absurd ways that I could not understand, but which, even in my dream, reminded me of their conduct in the school lavatory. Wearing only lace drawers, they were embracing and kissing with increasing fervor. Sylvia was dark-haired and dark-skinned—also somewhat undeveloped about the bosom; but as if to compensate herself for her lack, she was caressing and molding the full young breasts with which the milky-white-skinned Miriam was generously blessed, as if she would like to wrest their soft yielding substance from her.

Seating themselves on a chaise lounge, completely oblivious to my presence, Sylvia slipped a seeking hand between the thighs of the other and inside her sole garment, titillating her with a strange effectiveness that soon had Miriam writhing in what seemed a very pleasurable agony. Murmuring endearing terms she threw

237

her arms about her friend's neck, gasping, "Faster! Faster! my darling Sylvia! You are but teasing me. Come!" And feverishly tearing from herself her last bit of clothing, she cast her beautiful nude body upon the couch, her thighs thrown with abandon wide apart—disclosing to my curious gaze the soft pink secret place where thighs become something else, and the tiny surmounting hillock covered with the most lovable light brown hair.

Sylvia, her face flushed with I-know-not-what urgent emotion, followed suit, impatiently ripping her pretty drawers to shreds when they failed to come open at her first attempt. Hers was a deep coral and black center of interest. Her loins were lithe and strong in a boyish way, but the cheeks of her buttocks seemed soft and well-shaped. There was a strikingly beautiful contrast of olive and snow-white flesh as she threw herself upon the prostrate form of her companion. What a tense tangling and gripping of thighs and legs, what mad writhings and spasmodic sobs ensued! In a wild frenzy they rubbed their soft bellies against each other, twining their legs so as to bring their silky mounts together. They filled the air with cries now of ecstasy and now of frustration, thrashing all their limbs about, assuming new positions, only to continue baffled.

And what of me? The mad fever that filled the place communicated itself to me, stifling me with its utter strangeness. My mouth became hot and dry. My body seemed racked by the same unbridled sensations and emotions that convulsed the two female combatants before me.

Suddenly there was a great knocking on the heavy iron-studded door.

"Who knocks there?" I felt compelled to say in archaic accents. "If thou be friend, enter. If thou be foe, I cannot prevent thee."

A key ground in the massive ancient lock, the door opened, and there entered a huge man, clad in breeches and doublet that were nearly bursting with his bulk. Instinctivly I knew he was the villainous Front de Boeuf. Fearfully I followed him with my eyes as he placed the key upon a sideboard; but passing me by with a sneer, he approached the pair struggling on the chaise and, stationing himself beside them with legs astride and arms akimbo, watched their procedures with monstrous glee. Then, suddenly wearying of this performance, he took up a long thin bundle of birch rods that had been hanging at his belt, and raising it high in the air, brought it down with a loud swish full upon the dark backside of Sylvia, who was then uppermost.

With a startled scream, still flushed and panting, she sprang to her feet and wheeled to face the intruder, her hand leaping with awakened modesty to hide her private spot. Smack came the rods across her fingers and the fortress was abandoned while her hand went to her mouth. Swish! went the birch again, and there was a cross-welt of bloody red across her pretty cherry cleft, while tiny black pubic hairs floated lazily off the rods. The monster roared triumphantly, and pinching the tender spot that had just suffered his inhuman onslaught, tore away another tuft of hair, which he laughingly blew from his fingers into the air.

But Sylvia, to my amazement, instead of fleeing her tormentor, with a look of insane adoration in her eyes threw her arms and legs about him, further irritating her lacerated cunny by rubbing it up and down against his buckler. Losing interest in this torture by reason of the evidence that it was not unwillingly received, he hurled her arms from him. But she continued to cling to him with her thighs about his waist and with a strength and temerity that only madness could beget.

Angrily he beat her off, slashing mercilessly at her neck and arms until she was forced to release her hold. Then, kicking her aside, he made for the corner where the frightened, weeping Miriam cowered—and his cruel eyes lighted up at the sight of this daintier morsel.

Dragging her to her feet, he admired for a moment the lily contours of her body, then, his savagery once more ascendant, he grasped in his large bestial paws her full maiden breasts —two of the choicest and most adorable little hills of flesh that ever gods had bestowed upon woman—and crushed them against each other till a tiny drop of blood appeared upon each of the rosette buds that crowned their soft elastic heights.

I could but bite my lips in despair as I witnessed this sight that would have made even the devil weep. Unappeased, however, our inquisitor carried her across the room, and placing her backside up upon the edge of the couch, summoned Sylvia also to the slaughter and placed her similarly. Then indeed did he employ those wicked birch rods to grievous purpose, for that double pair of beautiful buttocks—those of Sylvia comparable to a rosy dusk and those of Miriam light and dazzling as high noon— were soon streaked with sprays and sprigs of bloody welts, showing purple-brown on the lovely rachelle flesh of the one and brightest carmine on the white expanses of the other.

"Come hither, my darling Rebecca!" the villain addressed me, without abating his lashings. "All this is to whet my appetite for thy cold beauty!" I added my screams to those of my poor friends; but this only made him relish his task all the more fiendishly, and before long first one and then the other of his victims was blessed with the oblivion of unconsciousness.

Then Front de Boeuf turned upon me. Verily, his was the face of an ox. I tried to plead for mercy, though I knew nothing in heaven or earth would induce him to stay his hand; but my breath caught in my throat, my tongue cleaved to the roof of my mouth. What new torture awaited me?

For some endless moments he held me transfixed with his gaze. Then, as if tentatively, he rudely felt my breasts, my thighs, my buttocks. My clothes he took as a deliberate affront. A tiny crucifix caught on his brutal hand as he explored within my bodice caused him to become convulsed with blasphemous laughter. He tore it sharply from my neck and trod it under foot. Then, with one downward motion, he ripped my dress from my back, leaving me shivering in my shift. Once more he caressed me through the soft, thin linen of my underclothes—then that fell away too and I stood before him naked and unprotected.

Gathering me up in his brawny arms, he bore me to the wall, and pressing his beastly bulk against me, crushed me and crushed me till there was neither breath nor strength left in me. The while his hands sought out my very secret place, squeezing and pinching them until they were numb with pain. When he released me, I crumbled weakly to the floor.

Once more he took me up—this time depositing my fainting form upon a strange execution block shaped like a monstrous tooth, with the four prongs of a molar made of gold. Once more his cruel hand pried into my feverish slit, in, in, until it seemed entirely engulfed.

I gave myself up as lost. I would die certainly. But I could feel no more pain. And in this last moment of my life, I wanted, not to escape, but to savor fully in all its supreme agony the martyred ecstasy of conscious violence and death. He could tear me asunder now but I would feel only the maddest joy at the seeming indestructability of my super-carnal self.

Front de Boeuf, leaving me for a moment, returned with the great key lying across his two palms. It held a fearful fascination for me. It was the key that seemed to control all the mysteries of life and death. Over a foot long, its immensity was unimaginable. As he passed its full length close before my eyes, I gasped—for I knew, I knew!

Front de Boeuf, holding my thighs wide apart with his knees, plunged the great key into my throbbing center, insinuating it deeper and deeper. This was the end. I felt myself approaching the very climax of delirious dissolution. Front de Boeuf pushed the great key in to its hilt—and turned it!

I awoke. It was dark. For whole minutes I did not know where I was. My heart was beating with terrific rapidity. Gradually I reconstructed the present; it came to me that it was all an awful dream that I had just experienced, a garbling of my voracious reading. How relieved I felt. A peculiar congestion of my vagina seemed to have carried over from the dream; but on investigation it proved to be only my pad, which somehow had been wedged inward. My menses had ceased too, a day before its time.

Recollecting how I came to the loft, I was still unwilling to go home and face my parents. It was already night. The sibilant music of the crickets, the croaking of bullfrogs, and the cool damp night air calmed and reassured me. The distant sound of mother washing dishes at the sink told me too that though I had missed supper, it could not be very late.

I analyzed my dream and stored it away in my waking memory, deciding that nothing in real life could be so grotesque and cruel. Also, I thought up some excuse to give to mother that would permit me to go straight to bed without having any family conferences inflicted on me. I started to leave.

Just as I was feeling my way to the ladder that led down from the loft, however, I was frightened by a series of sounds. I held still. It was someone coming into the barn. There were whisperings.

"Oh, please! Bill"—I recognized my sister's agitated voice—"if father should catch you on the grounds, he would shoot you, sure!"

"Oh no, honey," came a masculine voice in reassurance, "I can take care of myself. Just let's not make any noise and everything will be all right."

"But won't you please go away! Haven't you put me into enough trouble already?"

"Oh, can that, baby! Didn't I offer you the money to have it fixed up? Who the hell asked you to go and tell your old man anyway? But come on now, let's be nice to each other. Just this once, and I'll go away and won't bother you anymore. Just this once." And he must have taken her in his arms, for her next words came as if smothered by an embrace and punctuated with his forcible kisses.

"But Bill—please—some other time then. The folks are watching me closely. I told them I was just going out for a moment to—"

There was a crunching sound as of two bodies falling to the piled hay. I peered anxiously down the loft-trap, but it was too dark to see a thing.

"Don't, Bill! Please let me go! They'll kill me if I stay out much longer." Sis sounded pitifully frightened, but the lieutenant's mutterings were not in response to her pleadings.

"For Chris' sake, Mary!" he was saying, "why the hell must you wear these goddam corsets? Open it for me. I don't know how the damned thing works."

"No, no, Bill. Not now, please! I'll do anything, but not now. They'll be out here looking for me any minute."

"Ouch! That blasted whalebone. Wait.
Where's that flashlight? Here we are. Now
we'll see what we can do."

An unsteady wavering beam of light partially illuminated the scene. I could see only the
prostrate form of my sister Mary, her skirts
thrown back to her bosom, her pretty thighs
bared and glistening pink above her stockings.
She was still protesting tearfully; but the lieutenant, laying down the light so as to throw
its rays on the field of operations and leave
his hand free, was cheerfully engaged in un-
hooking her stays. In another moment there
was laid bare to his delighted gaze the wide
expanse of her soft belly, and the dark full-
grown mossy hill shading the generous rosy
lips and even rosier chuck beneath.

I, up in my balcony vantage place, was growing tremendously excited. At first, in sympathy
for my poor sister, I had felt impelled to make
my presence known and thus to save her. But
now, my temperature and curiosity rising to a
furious pitch, I believe I would have sooner
helped in her subjugation rather than miss the
sight that was promised.

But the lieutenant needed no help. He was
now fumbling at his own clothes, in front,
where his trousers bulged menacingly. I could
scarcely wait. I had heard described but had
never actually before seen the magnificent male
instrument of female undoing that was uncovered.

I shall not lie and describe it in detail, for
closely as I was watching, I could discern only
that it was large and stiff and cylindrically
shaped, in a moment it was lost to my view as

he brought his body over that of my weeping sister. Spreading her unwilling thighs as she weakly resisted, he opened the lips, and planting his member between, pushed it steadily home.

Then triumphantly relishing his position, he folded back her clothes to her very neck and fondled and kissed her maturing titties. Mary's continued protests were taxing my patience.

"Oh, you brute!" she was saying, "don't you ever think of anything but this? Please! Let me go, Bill—and I'll meet you tomorrow night."

The lieutenant made no answer except to slip his hands securely under her soft buttocks, and raising himself at the waist a few inches, came down into her again with a short firm push. This motion he repeated at intervals while Mary squirmed as if to get away.

"Oh, Bill! You hurt me awfully! Please, please, please stop! Please go away! Oh! oh—you hurt me oh!—oh!—oh!—ah!"—her cries of irritation were becoming choked sobs of submission—even of pleasure.

"Oh—slowly Bill, slowly—no! faster, faster!" she gasped—and as if electrified into life, her buttocks began moving frantically up and down to meet his thrusts, now sideways and circularly, spurred on by some madness which seemed incomprehensible to me. Feverishly I watched, imagining myself so far as I could, in the position of my sister.

What a sight it was—there within the orb of the flashlight—the frantically moving buttocks, my sister's legs wrapped tightly about her partner's loins—and, as if in the spotlight of Fate, the impenetrable darkness around them, and there in the circle of light, blurred slightly by the dancing dust motes, the age-old symbol of life being enacted for my education.

On the calcimined wall of the barn, opposite the flashlight, could be seen a grotesque shadow-play of huge heaving thighs, now and again completely blotting out the circle of light. A symphony of ecstatic sighs from my sister accentuated each motion and put me in a veritable frenzy. Madly I rubbed my cunny against the end of the ladder where I lay. I would have forced it into me if I could.

"More—more—give me more, my lover!" Mary was gasping—and her lover, himself already beginning to breathe heavily, plunged fiercely back and forth into her.

"Now! Now!" she sobbed. "Love me now! oh—oh—o-o-oh—" and she subsided with a little scream and a low, long drawn-out moan—her buttocks quivering spasmodically and her movements becoming less and less until she was quiescent.

Scarcely a moment later, her lover, whose breathing had become hoarse and rasping, made one final master plunge as if to go through her, and crumpled up upon her, twitching in the last throes of some tremendous passion and murmuring, "Mary, Mary!"

There they lay, locked in each other's embrace for long minutes, while the flashlight burned dimmer and dimmer, and finally, the battery exhausted, went out altogether.

Instinctively I knew it was over—and at the same time my own emotional tension seemed to relax. I slipped back on a heap of straw. My cunny was swimming with a pleasant moisture and I thought that my period had resumed, but it was not that.

When I arose again, Sis and the lieutenant had gone. Back to the house I went, straightening my dress as if it were I who had a guilty conscience and cooling my still burning cheeks and forehead with a handful of fragrant damp elm leaves.

On each side of the lamp-lit living-room table sat father and mother, both asleep, the one over his Bible, the other over her knitting. Mother's eyelids were red from weeping; the harsh lines of her face were softened in repose. For a moment I allowed myself to pity her. But Sister's cautious steps overhead as she prepared for bed brought back before my mind's eye a mad picture of nude young flesh writhing in divine ecstasy, and my sympathies were solely with her.

I felt no inclination for food. I wanted only to be abed, reviewing the events of this eventful day. But first, I went to the bathhouse behind the kitchen, heated a boiler of water, and filled our old zinc tub for my bath.

Slowly I undressed, my mind full of vague dreams and longings. I admired the soft white contours of my body with a new appreciation as I let my petticoat slip down off my hips to settle about my feet on the floor. A more luxurious bathroom would have made a nicer setting; but well-to-do as my people were, they were more interested in saving money than in spending it— and, in their frugal severity, if they were alive today to see my gorgeous *"Chambre de bain"* in my Boulevard Haussmann home, done all in orchid and pearl tile, they would consider it worse than sinful.

Despite the surroundings, though, the warm water, as it received my white limbs and body, filled me with a soft luxurious feeling, kissing my lazy blood to the surface and turning my skin an adorable pale pink. Languidly I covered my form with the smooth, creamy lather of a perfumed soap, delighting to caress, through the enhancing slipperiness of the bubbly suds, my luscious young breasts and the indescribably soft yielding flesh of the inner thighs where they approached the center.

I lay back in the shallow, tepid water, looking down the outstretched expanse of my body: beyond the lush hills of my breasts, the undulating plain of my satiny belly, the tiny kissable depression of the coquettish navel and the slightly rising mount of Venus, its silky shrubbery lifted lazily back and forth on the surface of the caressing water. Beneath, the mossy little cavern of love and mystery—and beyond that the well-rounded promontories of my thighs, two lovely dimpled knees, a pair of shapely legs in perfect alignment, and then, far away, my little toes. I was just beginning to discover my body.

Long and languorously I fondled myself. With light, subtle touches that seemed to come instinctively to me, my hands glided everywhere, now pressing my glistening flanks, now lightly titillating the strawberry nipples that crowned the apex of my ivory-smooth breasts. Again I lightly twisted my fingers in the dark curly silk that marked the meeting place of my thighs, pulling gently upon it with a pleasing effect—and soaping the spot with thick, white, creamy lather.

During all this, I experienced a gathering impulse to steal within the pouting slit; but whether from vestigial modesty or from an unconscious appreciation of the part that suspense plays in the art of pleasure, I withheld my hand as long as I could. Finally, whether by accident or on purpose, I allowed my soapy hand to press firmly inside my cunny. The effect was electrifying. My already considerable nervous tension was instantly doubled and I felt more aroused than I had been at the wildest moment in the barn.

Coming hastily to a sitting position, and drawing up my knees, thus lowering the water level in the tub, I spread my thighs, and gently separating the fine, tangled hairs, parted the hot ruby lips with my two hands. For the very first time in my life I revealed to myself the fine, moist, velvety consistency of the soft crimson lining of my slit. So enticing was it that I would have kissed it if I could have reached it with my mouth; but as that was impossible, I stroked the now gaping scarlet lips with my fingers. Every touch brought me indescribable delight.

With bolder strokes now, I ventured deeper and lower down in my newly awakened organ; but this part was protected by a sensitive membrane as yet unfledged to the touch and I returned to the narrower upper region, where, just below the point at which the two clinging lips melted together, a tiny hard nodule made known its presence by rising to meet my passing fingers.

This was my first introduction to that marvelous electric key to woman's sensual illumination—the clitoris—and were anyone to ask me to indicate the most important event in my life, I would unhesitantly say it was the discovery of the existence and potentialities this wonderful little instrument, which now, joyancing at its rescue from oblivion, bounded up bravely again and again to consummate every contact, and seemingly raised up with it my whole pelvic parts, even my loins and belly, for this purpose.

That nature saw fit to bring together all the strings of nervous pleasure and tie them in a little knot tucked away in this warm and secret (but not inaccessible) place is, of all things, a blessing that womankind can never be too grateful for. A miracle indeed, this tiny *Multum in parvo* which, given the merest infinitesimal caress, can bestow over the whole body's area and to its innermost depths sensual ecstasies more intense and widespread than could a thousand artful hands fondling everywhere else simultaneously.

Up to now, my contacts with that supreme spot had been almost unwitting. By elimination, by trial and error, I had found it. But if I thought I was experiencing pleasure—ah, I had not felt the fraction of what lay in store for me.

Divine enough it would have been to continue on and on, bathed in the warm sensuous glow that spread through my veins and radiated through my flesh. But now, as I caressed the tiny knob with light, increasingly rapid strokes of my middle finger (How instinctively we learn!), I felt gathering in me a tremendous climax. Like an ascending rocket it shot suddenly, sizzling up through my veins and nerves towards my brain, a sensation so incomparably new and strange, a pleasure so immense as to be painful. It seemed to me certain that if I should continue and permit that fiery joy to reach my brain, I would faint away or else perish. I stopped in fright. Like the rocket returning to its point of origin; like the movie film of an explosion projected backwards, like a partially opened fan sharply closed, like a glimpse of heaven suddenly shut off, the ecstasy faded and was reabsorbed by the place of its beginning.

But now, though my body was at a feverish heat, I was shivering with desire—and the violence of the sensation, incomplete though it had been, had left me gasping breathlessly. My limbs and buttocks, no longer subject to my control, were writhing and twisting with mad intensity. How well now I understood the wild movements my sister had performed.

My hand still lay over, though not within, that magic center for which no name, whether amorous or scientific (cunny, cunt, vulva and vagina), could now suffice. But now, by no conscious effort of my will, my buttocks raised themselves upward of their own accord to press more closely against my curved fingers, moved themselves by their own motivation sideways to fumble for and find the stiff middle finger, writhed back and forth till my burning slit had swallowed it in—and continued moving in that selfsame manner.

More quickly now the temporarily-banked

fires blazed up, spreading through the tautened muscles of my belly, putting all chill to route before it, pouring down as far as the calves of my legs and up to my bosom a flood of warmth and tenseness.

My eyes shut, my head fell backwards, my breath came ever in shorter and quicker pants, my hips meanwhile lashing up and back with desperate lunges.

Electric thrills were mounting me at all points,—by my spine and down my sides, by a thousand distinct paths—rapidly now, as if seeking to complete the circuit in my brain and overpower me with unbearable voluptuousness. My cunny was swimming with soft sticky exudations. The local pleasure around my fervid clitty was being swallowed up by the more extreme general sensation. I felt approaching a terrible crescendo of rending pleasure. If my life had depended on it, I could not now have ceased, could not have stopped that fierce writhing of my thighs. Then suddenly with a last lunge of my hips, it came.

A scalding fire of ecstasy inundated me. My whole body stiffened to steely rigidity as the candescent waves swept through my every nerve fiber with a perceptible, palpable hiss as of molten metal poured into a mold. Flashes of color impinged upon my closed eyelids like sparkling pinwheels and flaring rushlights. Then, topping the crest of the supreme agony of gratification, I came tumbling as if through eons of time and illimitable worlds of soft fleecy substance, and I lay quivering and sobbing in the last paroxysms of pleasure, delicious warm tinglings in all my extremities.

Thus I lay as the delightful sensations faded slowly. As if to call them back, my finger again sought my clitty. A little spurt of after-pleasure shot through me, tickling my now extrasensitive nerves, contracting my tummy sharply and convulsing all my frame in a spasm so violent that I desisted, shivering with its unendurable sensual titillations, and gasping a long aspirated "ah!" that left me in weak, breathless collapse.

I was almost crying with joy at the new happiness I had discovered. How could I ever revert to my old gloomy moods again when there was this to live for? And to think that all this magic was literally at my fingertips!

The water in the tub was getting cold by the time I ceased dawdling and finished my bath. I dried myself lovingly. Where formerly I had hated my body with morbid perversity, I now pressed the moisture from my dear cunny with a new tenderness. I went to bed unnoticed and that night I slept with unwonted coziness and refreshment.

Friendly reader, I have given quite some space and time to the description of something that in actuality took much less temporal space, but you must consider how wonderful and important this fresh miracle was to me. And in retrospect I must say that though in later years the thrills I experienced may have attained greater heights of passion, yet in terms of pure sensual enjoyment they could not compare with this first orgasm, with its soul-shaking initiation into the violence of a carnal pleasure that has neither parallel nor precedent, with its utter newness and dazzling crisp sharpness as the current of lascivious sensation completes its first circuit in brain and body, blazing a new trail through nerves and muscles never alive before, and setting the pattern for all later libidinous reactions. Treasure well the memory of your "good-feeling," reader, for it was at that high moment that you became even like the gods.

CHAPTER THREE

In the weeks and months that followed, I found myself blessed with a new and delightful awareness of life. Where once I had been dully and almost entirely oblivious to my immediate surroundings, finding romance only in the distant periods and places described in books, I now discovered in myself and in nature undreamt of reciprocal responses.

There was love and sex everywhere. The birds, the farmyard beasts and fowls—even the flowers. My eyes were at last opened to the beauty of things. I felt a new sympathy for all living creatures. When our dog Swede rubbed himself affectionately against my legs, I caressed him with a new understanding—evoking yelps of joy.

I developed a new interest in animal life, in botany and in physiology, and completed my last year of high school in a flare of scholarly brilliance.

During this time, I did not abuse the wonderful power over my body that I had blundered upon. Introverted and self-directed as this pleasure was in its origins, yet, as I am trying to express, it resulted in a gradual outward turning or externalization of my feelings. From solitary self-worship orgies in bathtub or in bed, I turned, and utilized this thrilling manner of relief only at long intervals, in the woods, after long hours in the outdoors, when, filled to overflowing with the beauties that had poured into me through my senses, I felt compelled to relax my surcharged nerves by this method. It became as much a marvelous sensual communion with nature as any mere mode of self-gratification.

It was on one such occasion that something dreadfully important happened. I was lying back on a heap of dried grass in a deep woodland clearing, my skirts drawn back almost to my waist and my hand at my cunny. I was still quivering in the last throes of my self-induced pleasure, my eyes shut, my head rolling sideways ecstatically. As the wild fantasies of my concentrated imagination faded, I was made suddenly aware by a slight crackling of the underbrush that someone was standing nearby—perhaps watching me. It was a man—coming forward to me now! I screamed in fright and hastily attempted to readjust my dress.

It was all up with me now, I was certain. I had heard tales enough of wandering soldiers coming upon a girl alone in the woods, bestially working their separate wills upon her, and even murdering her to prevent complaint and identification. Why had I trusted myself thus, led on by the harmlessness of nature, when nature was presided over by brute men?

But it was only one man—and he was not a soldier. Instead, it was a very young and mild-appearing fellow, betraying by his clothes that he was from the city. He was blushing as confusedly and apologetically as I, as he approached, and my panic decreased considerably. Moreover, he was carrying a book, and to me that was a sign of refinement and a common meeting ground.

"Forgive me!" he exclaimed in a nicely modulated voice which, however, did not entirely conceal his own great perturbation. "I could not help but see you. I was lying just the other side of those bushes, immersed in my Thoreau, when I was startled by some noises. At first I thought it might be a bear. (I smiled) You do have bears in these woods, don't you? No? Well, anyway, when I mustered sufficient courage to investigate, I saw you. And you were in the midst of—well, anyway, I didn't want to disturb you. But I was too excited myself, and too fascinated to go away. You would have heard me anyhow if I had moved. So I waited—and here I am . . .

"No—don't be afraid of me. I shan't hurt you. I guessed from what you were doing that you are a good girl—a virgin—else you wouldn't be doing that. I wouldn't harm you for the world. I know how you felt. You looked so beautiful and innocently happy lying there, I almost fell in love with you. Only I did feel like a cad, standing there and intruding on your privacy. And now you must hate me. I would if I were you—and yet, please try not to be angry with me. . ."

His manner was boyishly impetuous and disarming—ardent even, as he looked down on me. He couldn't have been more than 19 years old. Then suddenly:

"Would you be frightened, miss, if I sat down beside you?" and as I did not reply, he dropped to the ground at my feet with awkward but charming friendliness. "My name's Bob. What is yours?"

I did not answer.

We were both silent for a time. He looked a bit feverish and was breathing with strange intensity. Then, though I had spoken no word to him, he unexpectedly seized my right hand and avidly kissed the tips of the very fingers I had just thrilled myself with.

"Oh, don't!" I exclaimed in dismay—not on my account, but on his. He dropped my hand and buried his head in my lap. I could feel his hot moist breath on my thigh, through the thin material of my dress—and something impelled me to caress his silky brown hair maternally. Somehow, by a sort of transference, I felt as if the orgasm I had enjoyed a minute before was due entirely to his efforts. I felt grateful—and at the same time I pitied him—for strangers though we were I knew enough about men to recognize that he desired me.

If he had proceeded then and there to force me, I would have considered it no less than justified, and would perhaps have even submitted passively. How much more thankful though was I when he continued lying there quietly by me—there in the peaceful woods, making no demand and taking no further liberties with my body other than to bury his face deeper in my lap till his breath caressed my cunny with its pleasing warmth.

When finally he raised his head, there was a wild, infinitely appealing look in his soft brown eyes. His hand made as if to raise my skirts—then restrained itself. A great battle seemed to be raging within his mind.

"Come here, Bob," I whispered. "You may lie here beside me." I was a little awed, a little afraid that if my dress were to be raised, it would be the end of my innocence for sure—and somehow I felt that I should like to consider more and be wooed more before I could yield my maidenhead to a man.

He slipped down beside me and lay facing me. If I put my arms about him, that would of course restrain his hands from the temptation of my skirts. I did so. He returned my embrace fiercely, pressing his body tightly against mine, his eyes narrowing in a way that frightened me not a little.

"Gods!" He broke the silence with a gasp. "What is there to prevent me from raping you here and now, if I so wish? We are alone—and God knows I want you!" He pressed me closer still. I could feel a hard steely bulge beneath his trousers, hurting my thighs as he held me. I struggled to get away, now frightened indeed. I didn't like him at all with that hateful determined look in his eyes. And that stiff metallic thing pressing against me—what painful havoc it would work with my now tender cunny if he were to put it in me as the lieutenant had done to sister. And then, if I were to have a baby—I struggled more desperately, kicking and writhing in his embrace. But he continued to hold me firmly, his hands restraining my buttocks as I heaved to get away.

"Stop! Stop struggling!" he suddenly whispered in a strange tone that was almost a whine. "I won't hurt you—only lie still a moment——oh——a moment——please" and he lunged against me two or three times more, his leg thrown over my thigh, his stiff trouser bulge rubbing against me. His glittering eyes shut, his body suddenly withdrew itself from me and he lay on his back in the grass, shuddering violently while a great streak of white became visible seeping through his blue serge trousers.

Thus he lay for some moments, until I became deeply alarmed, thinking perhaps he had taken sick with the excitement. But no. In another moment he opened his eyes, from which all violence had gone, and smiled to me, breathing a deep sigh, as if of relief.

"All over now," he said cheerfully, "and I'm sure glad I didn't do what I was going to. It was just as nice anyway. And now you're perfectly safe from me—at least for the time." And he plucked ruefully at his wet clothes.

I was still considerably bewildered, but his bubbling talk reassured me. "I'm sorry if I was beastly," he went on, "but a man is entirely irresponsible when aroused—and if you could only have seen what a maddening picture you made here before, you would forgive me for becoming a little the way I did. But now that we've weathered that storm, we'll be very proper and become really acquainted. Somehow I feel as if we just have to become friends."

And he went on to tell me all about himself. He lived in New York City, it seems, and was vacationing at nearby Port Kent on the lake, having just completed his first year at one of the metropolitan medical universities. Despite the fact that he persistently denied any real interest in medicine and confided that he hoped to go in for painting as soon as he came into his own, yet his speech bristled with anatomical terms and anecdotes of the dissecting room. I listened, fascinated—for, as I have said, my own interests had been of late tending in just this direction.

He professed a great disdain for "women," allowing of course for occasional, and insuperable weaknesses of the flesh (I blushed furiously at the unaccustomed freedom of his speech, but blamed only my own narrow rural upbringing) ; however, beneath his cynicism I could detect a decided sentimentality lurking. Even though he was my senior by perhaps two years and no doubt had considerably more contacts with life, I felt that my female intuitional sense made me competent to judge him and consider myself his equal. If this had not been so, we could not have become so sincerely friendly as we did—for I have never been quite the type of woman to sit worshipfully at the feet of any man, overawed by his superior accomplishments.

Perhaps too, the fact that he did all the

talking enabled me to judge more objectively, unclouded as my mind was by any effort to myself make an impression. His obvious boyish desire to dazzle his listener with a concentrated display of all of his knowledge and experience —a characteristic shared by all men, as I learned later in life—permitted me to feel just enough condescension to like him awfully and to benefit greatly by his friendship—but at the same time prevented me from falling in love. Similarly, I have never since been able, even if I had wished, to succumb to that form of physical, mental and emotional entanglement known as the aforementioned sentiment. Men to me have always remained either intellectual comrades or fellows in passionate amusement. Perhaps I have even employed them in the same manner that men are so notoriously supposed to use women, viz: as the highly desirable but not quite divine implements of sensual pleasure or material promotion. If this be treason, let's have more of it.

For fully three hours Bob poured into my attentive ears his views on poetry, marriage, the family, the state, and the hierarchy of heaven. Suffice it to say that when the downing sun and the bedtime chatter of myriad birds reminded me of the two miles I had between myself and home, we were deep friends—though he knew not even my name as yet.

The embarrassing circumstances of our meeting seemed happily forgotten. Moreover, he gave me repeated assurances of the platonicity of his affection—which was easy, considering that the joy of talking had overshadowed all earlier pleasures. Yet, as he left me at my

263

gate with a hearty handshake, his aspect suddenly changed and he made as if to caress my bosom. Perhaps it was the rosy-streaked skies that put him in mind of another rosy streak—but, coquettishly, I warded him off, quoting him teasingly to the effect that he would have innumerable other opportunities to study female anatomy in his school clinics.

Promising to meet him again "some day" at the same place in the woods, I bade him good-night and ran laughingly to the house, leaving him staring after me. His last gesture had redeemed my feminity from the impersonal tone of his harangue.

CHAPTER FOUR

How important to me this chance meeting was to become, I leave to the subsequent ages of these memoirs to unfold. Its immediate effect was to crystallize my heretofore vague intention of studying medicine—also it made me conclude that men were not such villainous intractible creatures after all.

That same evening at the supper table I broached the subject of my further education. Mother was dead set against it—and not without some reason, for it must be remembered that this was the year 1907, and there were then few precedents to overcome the conventional repugnance to the idea of women in the professions.

On the other hand, there was father's unsatisfied desire for a son to realize his own thwarted ambitions. And my prize-winning graduation from high school was a great factor in recommending me for the life academic. Mother countered to the effect that we could not afford the expenditure; but, of course, sister and I knew better—while father admitted that he could raise the money for my board and tuition by foreclosing one of his mortgages.

The battle raged to an unheard-of hour of the night, but though mother's consent could be neither wheedled nor wrested from her, the issue was substantially decided in my favor. I would attend school in New York City.

I lay awake in bed till nearly dawn, picturing my future life, devoted to the conquest of knowledge. A life of freedom, of books, of scientific investigation; what strange desires for a young girl at an age when most of the female of the species are forming their lives to the ideals of early marriage, babies and church membership! To this very day I often question the influences that made me thus. A complete list of all the books I absorbed in the course of my very eclectic and voracious reading would be the only explanation—and that is, perhaps fortunately, impossible.

To me, then as now, all of life was contained within the limitations of the body—and it was that latter, the physical organism, that embraced the infinity of the universe. External things, since they could be known only through ourselves, could be of interest only insofar as they affected us directly.

That people suffered continually from ignorance of their own workings—as for example in the case of my poor sister Mary—was obvious all around me. That I too should suffer similarly if I permitted myself to remain in darkness, followed without doubt. What then was more logical than that I should wish to go to the sources of physiological learning for my knowledge of life and the control of happiness?

I met Bob in the woods next day and told him of my determination. In the ensuing weeks we saw a great deal of each other—and yet the better we came to know each other, the less we indulged in physical liberties. I did not know at the time whether this was due to lack of inclination or to the added restraint of mutual respect; but somehow, when my as yet unpronounced sex desires came to mind, I felt as if I could sooner give myself to a stranger than to him.

Whether or not this schism between my sensuality and my more cultured intellectual responses was due to the ridiculous Victorian ideals unconsciously acquired from my reading, I do not know; but I can say that many women run to this division. It is either complete shameless licentiousness, untrammeled by any rag of respectability that we experience, or else our feeling of responsibility throttles any vestige of sensuality at its birth. Women are either very hot or very cold. True, both possibilities may coexist at any particular time—only a hair's breadth may divide the one from the other—a slight circumstance, a word, a caress, opportune or inept, may determine whether M'lady is to be the chaste Lucrece or the dissolate Lucrezia—but the violence of the contrast remains.

Romantic writers, when they admit sex in women at all, usually insist that her passions are tempered by loftier emotions. Only men would assert such stupidities—possibly because they attribute their own idealistic-amoral fusion to us; but every intelligent woman knows that her passions must put to route all "lofty emotions" or be doused by them. Don't dispense talk of the soul or of the superiority of mind over body to your lady love if you would have her more responsive than a recumbent cigar-store Indian. Fucking is fucking and politics is politics, as Lord K. once rebuked me. So talk cunt and prick to your daring baby, and don't be afraid to employ the words and things they stand for—and though she be a nun from an Icelandic convent, she may surprise you by figuratively bouncing your ass to the ceiling and shouting "Fuck me! Fuck me faster!" A strange mass of contradictions, Woman—but rarely a compromise. So permit us to be our close-to-nature, primitive selves, or else suffer the hollow celluloid dolls that your civilization would make us.

Bob and I were "intellectual"—and I managed to make him quite ashamed of himself whenever his mere manhood broke through for a moment. The only part his being male played in my thoughts was that I considered he might be marriageable some day. His intelligence would then be more important: he would be able to provide for me. The wealth of his family would be another important factor. His sex? Well, that was a requisite of the law in the case of a woman marrying— no more.

The idea of marriage, vague and unprepossessing as it was, yet sufficed to drag up with it all my acquired ideas of respectability, propriety and chastity. If, that first time we met in the woods, Bob had said to me, expressly or by implication, "Girl, I'm going to fuck you and make you like it. And if you won't lay now, I'll hang around till you will," our acquaintance would no doubt have resolved itself differently. But, no, his first words had been to the effect that I was a "good girl" and that he wouldn't "hurt me" for the world. Today I would consider that a deadly insult; but at that time I was aware, or thought that I was aware, that physical liberties were "hurts" and that girls who didn't bring such "hurts" upon themselves were "good girls"—consequently I had to accept it as flattery and pattern my conduct, consciously and unconsciously, to the ideal he had signaled for. When some minutes later he abandoned his platonic attitude, I might have yielded, had not this been utterly inconsistent with the concept of "good girl" he had set up for me.

Therefore, to the aspiring or would-be Don Juan, I tender this advice: don't commence a conquest by respecting the very conventions you hope to overcome. Don't remind a woman of self-control if self-abandonment is what you seek. Why praise her church activities if it's the swing of her hips that enchants you and that you wish to enlist for your pleasure? In brief, eschew hypocrisy and be yourself. My dear friend Frank Harris puts it more bluntly. "Place a stiff prick in her hand," he says, "and shed tears." The tears are, of course, rarely necessary. I would recommend instead that you go for her clitty, either actually and forcibly, or indirectly by proper word-picture stimulation. Of course, you may be slapped occasionally—but then again, you'll get a lot of fucking. And to say the least, either way you'll save lots of time and scores of futile erections.

Poor Bob! If he had only known! What incalculable suffering he would have spared himself! But he didn't know and I couldn't have told him—for my understanding was not so clearly defined then as now.

My little affair with him then, while it acted to free me in many ways, must be set down as drawing in a contrary direction so far as sexual emancipation was concerned. In fact, for a time, I became set in a damnable hypocritical prudishness—all due to his initial mistake, as I have just explained. Iron-clad virginity was to be my policy henceforth. Of course, if little concessions were to become necessary to keep his friendship, I might consider them; but meanwhile I was to hold them off as long as possible.

Thus, after we had been together some twenty times in as many days, he began making approaches to me anew—and as by now the wells of conversation had been pumped dry, I found increased difficulty in long diverting him from the goal of his intentions. On this particular occasion, he was begging permission to caress my bare bosom.

"Oh, why the devil doesn't he throw me down and do it without asking me!" I thought to myself in irritation. But since he insisted on placing the moral responsibility of the decision with me, and since I could imagine no especial benefit to myself to be derived from yielding, I refused him, indicating such a multiplicity of untenable reasons as makes me blush to think of them today, when I bestow my whole self so generously on many less worthy than he.

With elaborate logic, convincing enough, since my arguments of propriety had no leg to stand upon at the outset, and yet unavailing since my mind had been made up logic apart, he proceeded to prove to me just why there was no harm in his caressing my bubbies. I remained unmoved and untouched. He then quoted to me some lines from a poet, Walt Whitman, whom we had read at school, but which lines I did not recollect as being in the books, to the effect that all parts of the body are equal in beauty and unashamedness. This was convincing in another way—not by logic, but by flattery. It seemed like a poem written especially for the situation, and for me alone. I softened and gave him permission to touch my bosom, but only from the outside of my dress. He entered into possession of his new grant eagerly, but with an all too law-abiding respect for the specified conditions.

Tenderly, again and again, he fondled my young budding breasts through the thin fabric of my dress, nipping between his fingers in passing, with apologetic indirectness, the tiny sensitive nipples that marked their apex. How I wished that he would override my restrictions and caress me as if he really meant it! But no—there was the role of innocence I had to play up to.

Not to seem too miserly in the holding of

his new property however, he forsook it for a time, to wander with restrained impatience over the bare glowing skin of my neck, above my dress. I challenged even his harmless trespass—as a matter of disciplinary policy; but he claimed it was a common appurtenant to the lower freehold, so I gave way.

"To think," he was saying ruefully, as his fingers loitered jealously at the point where soft swells began only to hide away within the shelter of my bodice, "to think that I should be foiled by the imaginary deadline of your clothes—to think that I should be limited to such stingy privileges after all the time we've known each other! Why I've had more freedom than this with any number of girls the first time I met them . . . oh well, perhaps that's just the reason I like you so much better than those girls."

I proffered my lips in assuagement. In the midst of the kiss, he tried to introduce his tongue into my mouth. As if this were to violate my chastity, I resisted him, keeping my lips tightly compressed with a primness I did not feel.

Maddened by this one rebuff too many, he suddenly plunged his full hand deep inside the bosom of my dress. Over-shooting his mark in his impetuous eagerness, however, his fingers glided rapidly down the smooth valley between and came to rest beneath my titties on the soft plain of my belly, now wrinkled into velvety little folds by reason of my sitting position.

A shivery little thrill went through me, but on general principles this would never do. Should he be permitted to over-ride my authority once, there would be no limit to what he could do to me—and since I had set out to be obeyed, I must continue the enforcement of law and order without regard for my own transient weaknesses.

Imprisoning his hand between my dress and my warm flesh by expanding my diaphragm, I prevented him for the time from further marauding. Then, assuming my blackest and most threatening expression, I proceeded to beat him into submission—by sheer power of will as it were.

His assertiveness collapsed. He apologized plaintively. "Don't be angry with me, Louise," he pleaded, "I couldn't help it. I was just carried away. You are so wonderful—Your skin is like the softest, finest warm vellum, like—" and his fingers began groping again—for further similes no doubt.

"Don't you dare move your hand again—if you know what's good for you!" I pronounced with fearful ominousness—but still holding back my breath to allow him no leeway. "You may get rough with me once, but I'm not one of your hussies to stand for it again!" (What if he should reach down further and touch the hairs that were so dangerously close, I thought. That would be embarrassing. And compromising too.)

There was a silent deadlock for some moments. The combined heat of my body and the palm of his hand in such close contact was sending tiny spurts of fire inward to my very womb. I liked it. The slight perspiration resulting seemed to make us of one flesh. His thumb moved ever so imperceptibly to press into my belly button. I wiggled aside and spoke one word. "Don't!"

"Well, what am I to do?" Bob demanded, beginning to realize the advantage he held, and relishing in advance the knowledge that he would be able to remedy his first oversight on withdrawing his hand.

"You must take your hand out when I tell you to," I instructed him, "and you must do it quickly and mustn't touch my breasts at all." My self-consciousness and unpracticed pronunciation gave to the word "breasts" a pretty lisp. How unfortunate today that the word "prick" and "cunt" present no such opportunity for prettifying.

"Oh please, Louise," he begged me, "can't I feel the wonderful texture of your dear little breasts just this once? As long as I already have my hand there—and I promise not to do it again—can't I just caress their tiny cherry tips for a minute? I will stop at once if you don't like it."

I yielded his request in part. "All right, Bob, but you must only touch them for a second as you withdraw your hand. If you stop for more than a moment, I shall be very very angry with you."

"Here goes then!" he said, holding his breath with expectancy and gazing deep into my eyes with an intensity that made my eyelids flutter. I relaxed the tension against my dress, granting him the freedom of my bare flesh.

"Only for a moment?" he repeated. I nodded my head impatiently. Fearfully, lightly, and all too quickly, his hand passed up from where it had been resting on my belly, swept sideways up over the curve of my left breast and brushed past the hard, erect little nipple which veritably clamored for attention—but without pausing.

His hand emerged from my bosom. It was all over. Bob drew me close to him and started to kiss me passionately. I pushed him from me impatiently.

"What are you angry with me for now, Louise?" he pleaded. "Didn't I do it just as you said I should? Why, here I scarcely touched you at all and now you're angry at me!"

"That's just it!" I exclaimed furiously, "You scarcely touched me at all! Why you caressed me with as much passion as a—as a—as if I were the plague and you were afraid of me!" And I burst into tears.

"But Louise dear—didn't I want to really fondle you—and didn't you order me not to?"

"I don't care!" I sobbed. "I thought you loved me enough to disregard what I said. You should have known I wanted you to act more—more real than that."

Slowly it dawned upon him. Smiling now, almost condescendingly, he made as if to repair his late neglect of my titties; but the "moment psychologique" was irretrievably lost. I hated him now—and pushing him from me violently, left him sprawling on the grass while I hurried home alone.

CHAPTER FIVE

Life on the farm, contrary to the usual character of such things, was not entirely uninteresting that summer. Perhaps the fact that it was to be the last I should spend there, the fact that it no longer occupied the entire horizon of my future, help make it quite bearable.

I have already recorded how, my eyes opened to the division of nature into male and female, I found a new appreciation for life. From the rooster's fluttering momentary contact with the cloaca of the hen to the prolonged connection of a male and a female dog, intense pleasure seemed to be nature's main if not sole motivation.

What I could not understand, however, was why, if connection was so obviously pleasant, creatures were not more continually engaged in the delightful pastime. I was aware that the heat of animals was seasonal; yet I wondered at its short duration. It never occurred to me that there was such a thing as a limit to the capacity of the male.

With the vividness of an appropriate allegory, a little incident comes to mind. I have comforted many a male, chagrined by his inability to reach his determined score, with a recounting of just this tale.

It was early that same summer, if I remember correctly, and father had just purchased four beautiful sleek brown cows to add to the herd. At dinner table one day shortly after, there was some talk of borrowing from the Jordan's of the adjoining farm the fine pedigreed bull that they kept. Immediately I guessed that the bull's visit had something to do with the fresh young lady cows we had recently acquired. I had gathered on other occasions that old Jordan made quite a bit of money merely by hiring his bull out all around the county to sire the next year's crop of calves.

Wickedly I determined to see the process, and later in the afternoon when Mr. Jordan led his famous beast into the barnyard, I was ensconced comfortably up in the loft of the barn, that same academy of my earlier education.

No sooner did Mr. Bull spy the four cows than he snorted—I was about to say "like a bull"—and started for them. It was with difficulty that old Jordan, father and our two hired men prevented him from running into the fence by twisting his tether about a firm post—and with equal difficulty that the four frightened cows were rounded up again. Taking three of them out of sight behind the barn to spare their virgin sensibilities perhaps—the first lucky maiden, very attractive as cows go, was brought up and anchored within reach of His Masculine Majesty, who, as soon as he was released, made for her, roaring with delight.

Only for a moment did I catch sight of his royal sex parts. But what a sight! Not a whit less than a foot long, dear reader—and four inches in diameter would be but a conservative estimate. I gave thanks in my heart and in my cunny that, to the best of my knowledge and belief, the male of the human species was less terribly accoutred. And at the base of this apogee of virile members, overawing as it was in its stiff, reddish-brown dignity, clung a pair of to me then unknown organs, resembling in color, size, and apparent tautness and texture, nothing other than a pair of leather boxing gloves.

With scarce a howdy-do to his new playmate, the bull mounted with his forelegs upon her back, and with an infallible instinct, superior to all fumbling, plunged the part so intended into the corresponding but diametrical dissimilar part of the female, who now lowed with fear and pain at the assault upon her probably unaccustomed organs.

With fierce rapid thrusts the bull now proceeded to consummate his act, adroitly keeping close step behind the cow as she waltzed away from him the length of her tether—the slap of his belly against her flank resounding again and again like the vigorous beating of rugs.

Father and Mr. Jordan were watching this procedure with calm, impersonal approval. I, in my secret place, looked on with not a little trepidation, and even with sisterly sympathy for the cow, who seemed to be getting considerably the worst of the arrangement. Only father's two hired men below, great vulgar fellows with whom I had never any dealings, seemed to be having fine sport of the goings on, even to the point of cheering on their brother beast with lewd expressions which happily were drowned by the now earsplitting snorts and roars of the bull.

Then suddenly, just as the loud reverberations of their hooves upon the ground were beginning to make me fear for the very foundations of the barn, the lord of the herd let out one last unbelievable bellow that seemed to threaten the very skies. He had reached his crisis.

At this point he began slipping off the back of his amourette, but the two hired men rushed into the melee, and for reasons which became clear to me only afterwards, held the two beasts together as long as they could. Even as it was, when the bull's monstrous machine emerged from the place of its so recent and heated reception, it dripped a veritable puddle of white creamy fluid upon the ground— for all the world resembling the contents of an overturned milkpail. And from the cow bubbled more of the same pearly liquid, trickling generously down her hind legs.

But indeed the greatest miracle was yet in store for me. For that terrible engine, a moment ago comparable only to a long section of summer bologna, was now, before my very eyes, shrinking inward, both in length and in girth, to a mere three flabby inches by one that melted from view.

The recent bride was hustled off the scene, and heifer number two, a more comely beast still, if there be such things as standards of beauty in cow society, was brought on and hitched to the epithalamial post. But if I expected an immediate repetition of the earlier performance, I was doomed to disappointment, for the bull, instead of rushing in to partake of this daintier morsel, indifferently turned his back on her and walked away.

Mild consternation reigned among the *entremeteurs de marriage* in the barnyard. A pail of fresh water was brought, into which Mr. Jordan dropped a quantity of a white powder from a large cloth sack, and of this love-portion the groom was induced to partake; but no noticeable results ensued. Father then fetched a number of steaming hot towels which were applied to the lax genitals of the duty-shirking bull. This effort was crowned with some success, for the member emerged from its massage with some reasonable resemblance to stiffness and bulk. But yet, when he was led up to his bovine bride, who had been standing by meekly during this whole performance, blinking her brown eyes with coy expectancy, he did no more than sniff curiously at her charms, and no doubt deciding that she was not sufficiently different from his earlier experience to justify a repetition of those extraordinary exertions, he wheeled away from her once more, flicking her patient features contemptuously with his tail. Miss Bess—for that was her name—and surely she has by now earned sufficient of the reader's sympathy to be designated by her proper appellation—Miss Bess mooed disconsolately and to my indignation began following after her indifferent lord; but then, recalled, whether by her sense of ladylike dignity or by the limit of her tether, she returned to her station by the post and pretended to be absorbed in nibbling a bit of grass. I say pretended because the barnyard was utterly devoid of vegetation.

Meanwhile father and old Jordan had gone into heated consultation.

"I done warned ye—" old Jordan was drawling in his high-pitched voice, made even more unpleasant by passage between his toothless gums, "that thar' bull 'as 'ad a 'ard season of it. Now I ain't reckonin' thar' be no better sire in the state; but jes' yesterday we ad 'im over to Keesville to the Widder Jones's an' 'e served six 'ead o' cow afore sundown. Ahm afeared Charley ain't goin' ta be much good no more today. But ef you wants me ter fetch 'im over here agin tomorrer, why that'll jes' cost ye ten dollars more."

"Ten dollars, ay?" father was saying wrathfully. "Ten dollars a day, you say, Ebenezer for a bull that can hardly serve one heifer— and with calves bringing only eight dollars on the market. Why it ain't worth the time and labor to my cows and me."

While this dispute was going on, our two hired men, on their own initiative now, were still matching their none too sharp wits against the bull's tardy instincts. Leading the beast forcibly back into the vicinity of the female, the one of them took a handful of lard and, applying it to the bull's semierect member, proceeded to mold and rub it into a less pliable and more adventurous shape. At the same time the other made Bess approach, and introducing the bull's muzzle against her hindquarters, rubbed it against those areas whose perfumes should remind him of the sex thereof, and by association, of their true and proper usage.

It was indeed a humorous sight: the hired men vigorously rubbing and pulling on the bull's recalcitrant tool, and the bull himself being forced to nuzzle into the privates of the cow. The sum total of these efforts was, however, no more than this: that when at last the part had been restored to its previous majesty and the bull had mounted diffidently upon the back of the eagerly submissive Bess, that same part, displaying a temperament inexplicable to me at the time, began giving up in disgust—and Bess had to be dragged away perforce from the altar at which she had been so sadly disappointed.

I shall leave it to the reader to draw any of the obvious morals from this situation.

CHAPTER SIX

I have just mentioned our two hired men. One of them must enter into my memoirs for some further treatment in that he was another unwitting factor in my home education.

To describe either or both of them in any detail would be a task too distasteful to undertake. I have referred to them as vulgar. They were worse than that. Gross, hulking, leering brutes they were of a low order that—I must admit it with shame for my native land—can be found nowhere among the peasants or serfs of Europe, but only among the pseudo-republicans of America. I made it an unqualified rule to always keep as far away from them as possible, and I thanked my stars that father had not adopted the democratic practice of allowing them to eat with us at the same table. To merely pass within view of them was for me an ordeal.

One of them particularly betrayed by his features that he was of an especially sub-criminal or idiotic type. It gives me the shivers still when I picture him, puttering about the barnyard, always with a wisp of dirty straw between his teeth, and generally taking a cruel pleasure in setting the animals against each other. It was he who had manipulated the under part of the bull in such gross fashion that day.

I was wandering down through our orchard early one hot afternoon, immediately after the noonday meal, when, coming to the point where the orchard ended and our pasturage began, I spied him—Jock, I think he was called—partially hidden by the vine-grown fence, and behaving in a very strange manner.

The sun was stupefying hot; most everyone else was indoors. The loud droning of the bees in the clover must have drowned out the slight sound of my footsteps. Coming closer, with mixed curiosity and fear, I could see him, queerly enough, engaging in wrestling with our prize sheep Nan.

My first impulse was to run and fetch father —for I would not have put it beyond him to murder our cattle out of sheer malicious brutality. But the fact that he seemed to be employing no visible weapon, and might indeed be merely playing with her in plain exuberant idiocy, deterred me from the childish role of tale-bearer and led me instead to tiptoe up close to the fence, over which I could discover more particularly what in heaven's name he was doing.

What was my unspeakable disgust then, to find that, whatever the game, the beastly lout was playing it with his trousers down! His hand wrapped tightly in the thick wool of the sheep's back to steady himself, he was on his knees behind and somewhat under her, lunging back and forth against her viciously, his ugly hairy arse protruding in my direction at every rebound.

Already I had learned just enough about animals to have it slowly dawn on me that this male beast, no doubt unacceptable to any female of his own species, was imposing himself sexually upon a lower and more helpless order. Boiling with indignation at this outrage of nature's laws and man's rules of decency, I was about to pick up a rock with which to strike him unconscious—even as if I were executing the punishment of death by stoning prescribed by the Bible for such unnatural vices. I had in mind also to release our poor sheep from his abominable brutishness. But the sudden realization that I was wrong in attributing my angry sentiments to the sheep, made me pause in my impetuous resolve. For Nan was baa-ing in tones of unmistakable pleasure and was now and then wriggling her soft woolly bottom against the belly of her intruder. With that innate sympathy for all feminine-kind that I have referred to before, I abandoned all thought of violence, and soon my resentment vanished, even as against Jock, whom for the time I now regarded as a poor pitiable instrument of impulses more powerful than he.

Perhaps because of the very unnaturalness of his situation, it was a very long time before Jock attained his ultimate goal, orgasm. During this lengthy period Nan seemed to win no less than three complete climaxes—showing

285

her appreciation by quiverings and gestures almost human, and essaying to reach back and kiss her lover with her tongue.

Silently, except for an occasional grunt, or a growl of, "Hold still thar', sheep!" he worked tirelessly and desperately on.

At last he finished—and mine was the spectacle of a huge truncheon withdrawn, still fiery red and tumescent, glistening and actually steaming in the sun as the last gobs of the thick white fluid that seemed the inevitable concomitant of sexual satisfaction in the male, spread over its head and shaft, accentuating its dark crimson. It was the first human male engine I had ever witnessed at such close quarters—and in justice to all later ones I have experienced, I might have hoped that my first close-up should be of a less abnormally monstrous one. For indeed, so indistinguishable was this in size and bulk from the member of the bull I had so recently seen, that for years after I was repeatedly disappointed by the merely normal and therefore considerably smaller ones I met with. Of course, as the old adage has it, "short and thick will do the trick" and "long and thin goes further in"— and the matter of size is not nearly so important to a woman as is the deftness with which the tool is maneuvered. Yet it is but natural in us women to want a great deal of and to want to gorge ourselves with the things we like.

Pausing only to hastily wipe his dripping weapon upon the woolly back of the sheep— as handkerchiefs were then and probably are still unknown accessories in rural America—

Jock slunk away over the pasture without having discovered my presence.

I jumped over the intervening fence, and silly though it seems. I was bursting to put to Nan the one great question that to me was yet substantially unanswered: "How was it?" Of course she couldn't have told me—and so I had to content myself with a reading of the external manifestations of her body. Prompted by my burning curiosity, I made so bold as to examine her sex organs, and was surprised to find them, though still in a turmoil of red blood-gorged membrane and white sticky ejaculate, very similar in shape and structure to my own unfledged vagina.

I stepped around to her other end, and caressed her head as if I would read the secret in her eyes; but she switched herself around so as to bring her rear against me, and then disported her hindquarters in a manner that was plainly an invitation to repeat for her the good offices she had just sustained.

"Sorry, old Nan," I whispered, "I know you'd like more of it. But I can't do a thing for you. Perhaps I would if I could." And realizing that I had just admitted to a moral capacity for that selfsame heinous act that I had so recently censured, I left her, heartily ashamed of myself.

CHAPTER SEVEN

One day late in August Bob showed me a letter he had received from home, requiring his presence shortly and ending his vacation. With the cruel immutability of time, our last opportunity to be together arrived. I don't know how I ever obtained the permission of my parents—perhaps my own approaching departure helped—but we spent the earlier part of that last evening down to town as I remember.

It was a Saturday night, the big time in every small American town. The streets were crowded with farmers and their families, in from the outlying districts, and promenading with much noise and the frequent purchase of soda-pop. Groups of rowdy drunken soldiers also contributed to the general excitement. After the two-mile walk from home on the dark road, the many gas-lit shops were especially dazzling. Already I felt a presaging thrill of what metropolitan life would be like.

The town hall was the goal of most that evening. Plattsburg's first moving-picture performance was slated. I think it was called a bioscope exhibition then. I felt quite proud of Bob in his neat city clothes, and almost swooningly subservient when he bought the tickets from his well-filled wallet. It was my first experience of the power of money to purchase other than drab necessities. The ticket seller hadn't enough cash to make Bob's change and he had to bring it to him after we were seated inside and when more admissions had been paid for. I blushed with pleasure at the unctuous respect with which my escort was treated and unconsciously I became polarized to another new magnetic goal in life: money.

The show—my first—was a shoddy enough affair. First some cheap variety performances came on the stage and danced, sang and interrogated each other with insane catechisms that irritated me immeasurably in that all were laughing boisterously while I could find nothing to even smile about. Then, to my relief, the lights were turned out and Bob felt for my hand in the dark. There were loud snickers and cries of "Kiss me quick," "Let go of my leg!" and so on from the oafs in the audience, and on a large white sheet suspended on the platform, the newest marvel of the age flickered its jerky uneven shadow pictures. A disgustingly fat comedian sustained the usual clownish misfortunes of torn trousers, intercepted custard pies, etc. There were more film breaks, mechanical interruptions and failings of lights than the few minutes entertainment justified. And whenever the projection would seem to be really clicking smoothly, the film would suddenly end and a slide with the crude lettering "End of Reel One. Reel Two Will Follow Immediately" would be flashed on the screen. How different from the polished performance at any of the Boulevard cinemas today! I was glad enough when it was all over and we carefully wended our way out through the riotously overturned benches, the peanut shells, and the omnipresent pools of expectorated tobacco juice on the rough wooden floor. What memories for a lady of refined and luxurious sensibilities! But my memoirs none the less, dear reader, even if I am, alas, an ungrateful daughter to my native land to thus betray its culture.

It is the remembrance of the rest of that evening, though, that I indeed wish to treasure. We left the crude town behind us. Soon even the sound of the mechanical piano in Leary's Saloon at the railroad crossing ceased to march with us.

Nature alone was its own beautiful self. The cool refreshing night air was made fragrant by the odors of sweet newly-mown hay and fresh breathing grasses. I rank that perfume still as not inferior to my favorite Shalimar or 'L'Origon. And the sky—clear except for a few wispy ghosts of clouds scudding before a crescent quarter moon that was tipped up like a tiny silver cradle.

We walked slowly, Bob's arm about my waist—slowly, as if to make the two short miles last an eternity. There was a soft poignancy in my heart at his impending departure. True, I told myself, I did not love him; yet he was my dearest friend. He had opened new and brighter horizons to me. He had been a considerate companion. If I did not love him, it was no fault but my own. I ought to love him. And this night was meant for love.

About halfway home, he gently led me unresisting off the road. Unhurriedly, but with awakening pulse, we traversed a field of lush thick grasses that caressed our feet. We spoke no word; but we each knew that the road we had followed was a path of Heretofore, and that path we were leaving forever behind us.

A little incline suggested a halt. Silently Bob slipped off his coat, and spreading it for me, drew me to the ground. The earth was still warm from the day-long hot kiss of the sun. I lay back. The star-bejeweled sky seemed to come down to blanket us in a two-dimensional world. Bob did not touch me, and yet I could feel that he was shivering, despite the mildness of the temperature, in the throes of that same questioning: To fuck or not to fuck. For myself, I refused to confront the problems.

At last, as if to divert himself from that internal conflict, he broke the silence, speaking softly.

"The stars, Louise. Do you know their names?"

Timidly I pointed out the Great Dipper, the Milky Way. Supplementing my limited knowledge, he introduced me to Orion the Mighty Hunter, to Arcturus the Pole-star, to the bright flaming Sirius, the inseparable Castor and Pollux, to Betelgeuse and Cassiopeia and Aldeboran and the Pleiades.

Again we lapsed into silence—for a long time, during which his mind was again torn by following rough thorny paths of doubt—during which time I, lulled by singing crickets and the strange silver light of the moon, dreamt vague untenable, sensual dreams, which, when I tried to grasp them, vanished like magic moonbeams that we would imprison with our hands.

What worlds apart we seemed to be. Only the great expanse of the heavens held us in common. But suddenly I was recalled to him, hurtling through dark voids, past orbs of silvery sheen.

"Louise!"

How sweetly my name sounded on his lips. We turned to meet; our arms enfolded each other with one accord. His breath was hot and spasmodic on my neck; yet, beneath his silk shirt I could feel him shivering still. I pressed him closer, granting him the warmth of my body. His lips sought mine in a long kiss. My eyes shut. All the wide universe was wiped out, leaving only us two, and joined by that kiss we were but one.

For measureless minutes during which we both existed out at the juncture of our lips, we lay thus. Then, becoming again aware of the rest of my body that clung to him so hungrily, his hand wandered down my back to my buttocks, crushed me closer to him, till breathless I began passing into happy oblivion.

For a moment he drew back to admire my recumbent figure in the moonlight, then his hands sought my breasts, first through my clothes, and then, discovering the secret of the little clasps that held my dress together in front, he undid them gently, one by one, placing a hot moist kiss in turn upon each little area of my soft flesh as it was uncovered.

I made not the least resistance. What a different woman I now was from the haughty nay-saying Louise of the past. I was his now entirely, his to do with me as he would. I refused to poison the precious moments by words or thought or fears or scruples. I prayed only for his hands and his lips, and for the unbroken silence.

By now he had unhooked my dress to its limit, down to my very waist. I lay still, existing only for his pleasure, for his worship. He folded back the lappets of my dress, and baring both my breasts at last in their entirety, gasped with joy at their strange white beauty under the moon, broke down in tears of passion, and sobbing, buried his face in their soft warm expanse and passed his cheeks lovingly again and again over their yielding smoothness. Blindly his mouth kissed its seeking way to each of the tiny erect little nipples—and having found them, sucked and tongued these wondrous fountains, spreading thrills to my innermost being till my very bowels were knotted and contracted with intense pleasure.

His hands, hot organs of delicious contact, now ran down the sides of my body, found the edge of my dress and came up again over my silk stockinged knees to my bare thighs. Because of the heat, I was wearing no underwear. Hotly his hands fumbled for obstacles. Grateful he was to find none. Nestling his fingers between the soft warm flesh of my close-meeting thighs, he forced them gently apart. Up and on his hand slid, caressing the ineffably smooth skin, and as the distance to my secret parts decreased, that center of feeling came suddenly to life, tingling with suspense and anticipation.

Undeterred by me, and all the time kissing and biting my breasts with overwhelming passion, he at last reached the sacred juncture of my thighs, played about and around it, caressing the rich adjoining creases of flesh, smoothing my lower belly, combining with his fingers the tangled silky hairs of the luscious mount—withal working me up to such a pitch of desire that my cunny, burning with the teasing outer caresses, all but shouted for him to come within and work a consummation. From then on, adieu all fears of what he might do to me! Adieu, too, all modesty and restraint! Unashamedly I wriggled my cunny against his hand. At last his fingers parting the soft lips, entered, to my great relief—first the narrow upper part of the slit, and then lower down where it was swimming with the lubrications of pleasure. This delightful moisture he spread about to facilitate whatever operation he might be intending. Instinctively I threw my legs apart to aid him further, and my whole virgin fortress, with all its delicate warm membranes, lay fairly open to his mercy. Let him draw and attack now!

But no—his fingers continued to caress my burning part, found the sensitive clitty, and played upon it a gorgeous symphony of rhythmic sensuality. What unbearably pleasurable titillations! What waves of fire spreading through my veins! So this was the method he had chosen to thrill me; but I had no time to regret the substitute instrument he was employing: I knew only that it was incomparably divine.

Assured by my irregular breathing that he was working in the proper groove, he drew the lower part of his body close to me once more. Midway against my thighs (his head still at my bosom) I could feel through his trousers the hard pulsing bulge of himself. Yet despite this conclusive proof of his intense desire for me, he was not taking me for himself. It could only be because of his deep consideration for me, his unwillingness to hurt or endanger me or to take advantage of my obvious weakness, that he so restrained himself. His main care it seemed, was my happiness, my safety, my pleasure.

Realizing my selfishness suddenly, and in the full gratefulness of my passion, my hand crept to his middle, fumbled at his buttons, reached within, and with a boldness that only this moment could have begotten, disentangled his stiff throbbing part from his underclothes, grasped it in the soft perspiring palm of my hand and brought it forth. His breath caught with expectant excitement.

Never had I held in my hand such hot living flesh, that was yet not as any flesh I had known, in its paradoxical smoothness and hardness. Not nearly as large as I had expected was that cylinder of pulsing ivory, but its firm circumference filled my hand neatly, and the smooth velvety skin that sheathed it was pleasing to the touch.

Tenderly I drew back the soft fold of foreskin that rimmed it, caressed the sensitive spongy head, tickling the delicate groove of the underside with my fingertips, and squeezing the whole with my hand in a crushing agony of desire and pleasure.

With a tense back-and-forth movement of his hips, causing his blood-gorged member to slide in and out of my tightly clasping fist, he conveyed to me unconsciously the proper manner of handling the beloved organ. Learning quickly the dear lesson of love, I now stroked the whole length and surface of it with my full palm and fingers, in the same varying rhythm with which he was still stimulating my bursting clitty—now slowly and vigorously, now lightly and rapidly.

Suddenly Bob spoke his first words.

"Stop, Louise!" he gasped. "I want to come only when you do." Instinctively I understood his vague expression. Despite the handicap of a later start, he was approaching his climax more rapidly than I and he wished to wait for me. I complied, holding his tense quivering part still in my hand, resisting the impulse to caress it more actively again, while Bob continued to stroke my hot moist vulva with blind fury. Violently my whole body was now jerking back and forth to meet his caressing fingers.

The electrical sensations gathered. Rippling thrills of increasing warmth and intensity bubbled up from the wells of my being, filling me, overwhelming me with that incomparable ecstasy.

"Now!" I whispered, panting, as I felt the delicious limit of sensual endurance approaching—"Now!"—and again I added the stroking of his hot bar of flesh to my other movements, which, as the dams of my feelings broke, inundating me with delirious pleasure, became so irregular and spasmodic that it was essentially his own vigorous motion within my fist that brought his crisis up to join mine.

How infinitely was the sensuous joy of that approaching climax increased by the knowledge of his sharing it with me simultaneously! Every thought of his imminent pleasure redoubled mine. Every thought and evidence of my ecstasy must have doubled his. And so, on and on,—just as two facing mirrors will reflect each within the other indefinitely.

The two separate whirlpools of our sensations spread, spread out and met, met and melted together—together in one common overpowering frenzy of ecstasy. And just as the heavenly rending sensations passed their uttermost peak, contracting my womb within me and flooding my parts with my internal secretions, the same agony of pleasure in him was evidenced by a series of spurts of thick scalding fluid which shot against my quivering bare thighs and filled my hand as it still held and jerked his member in the last spasms of my own breathless joy.

For long minutes during the die-away afterpleasures, we lay in each other's arms, I sobbing and moaning with the immensity of my gratification and happiness, he still gasping with the violence of his enjoyment; both of us for the time oblivious to the general sticky liquid dripping between my fingers and down my thighs.

In the distance a dog barked, recalling us from our delicious dreaming. The moon shone again. All the world came into existence once more. A gentle breeze stirred the leaves of the trees behind us with a crisp, little rustling that whispered, "It is over. It is late!" It brushed lightly the surface of my bare breasts too and cooled the warm love-essence spread over my uncovered thighs.

Tenderly Bob placed two last kisses upon my bosom—in a little glow of passion cupped my young yielding breasts in his separate hands, then gently and slowly, with great reluctance, he drew together the front of my dress and re-hooked it clasp by clasp. Which, when he had painstakingly finished, and regretting his work, he suddenly made as if to undo again; but I dissuaded him with a few soft words.

Lovingly, with a large pocket handkerchief, he wiped from my thighs the prolific sacrifice of his passion, which in its peculiar lubricating quality, made even of this procedure a delightful caress.

"It was as wonderful as if I had possessed you altogether," he said, "and better too, because now that I must go away, I can do so without any burden on my conscience." He began pulling down my dress; but raised it further instead to sink his face in my belly in a long kiss just above the mount of my grateful cunny. Embarrassed, I pushed him gently from me.

A freshening wind with a suggestion of rain on its breath hastened us homeward. For the last time he left me at the gate, promising to write to me and to meet me soon in New York. For the last time he took me in his arms and kissed me—and, his desires reawakening, begged me to stay awhile longer. But there was a light on in the house, someone would still be up. I reminded him that it was very late and that he had a number of miles to walk to Port Kent. Another kiss, a whispered farewell, and he vanished into the dark.

Mother was waiting up for me in the kitchen. Angrily she pointed to the Dutch clock which read 2 A.M. and demanded to know what mischief I had been up to and whether I was following in my sister's footsteps to complete the undoing of the family.

"Would you like me to show you my maidenhead, mother?" I said simply if a bit sarcastically, confident in my completeness.

"You insolent girl! Go right to bed!" mother exclaimed, exasperated beyond words for once. I obeyed, anxious to be abed with myself. Undressed, I found a fine smooth coating as of enamel on the soft flesh on my thighs, where Bob had thrilled. I did not wash away this patina of love, but slept amid delicious sensuous dreams, my body curled up in self-caress, my hands buried between my thighs.

CHAPTER EIGHT

New York! Mecca toward which every country girl in America turns her face or her heart! City of fabulous wealth and untold poverty. City of exquisite refinements and gross depravities, of churches and bawdyhouses, of wide streets and narrow souls. In brief, a city of contrasts and contradictions. Anyway, this was the year 1907—a long time ago. Perhaps things have changed since then.

My sister Mary and I emerged from the old New York Central Station into a strange, noisy, bustling world. Electric tramcars clanged by at breakneck speed. Carriages, cabs, and many of the awkward automobiles of that period crowded the curbs. Heavy wagons and drays clattered and rattled over the cobblestones of the wide streets, while underfoot could be heard the deep rumblings of passing subway trains. Every other building seemed to be a theater, café, or other place of amusement. Gigantic posters hung across the streets announced a play with Clyde Fitch in the star role, another with Trixie Friganza and Jefferson de Angelis.

And people—thousands of them, everywhere. The women, heartbreakingly beautiful in their large picture hats, modishly corseted figures and long trailing skirts. The men, neat and debonair, with their brown bowler hats and fancy vests. And the policemen, impressive and handsome in their tall gray helmets.

Mrs. Murray, an old friend of the family, formerly of Plattsburg and now of Brooklyn, to whose care we had been consigned, met us at the station. She was a buxom, good-natured, typically Irish woman of about forty with whom I felt we would have little difficulty getting along. She seemed not at all scandalized by sister's interesting condition, and even tried to put us at ease with some remarks to the effect that pregnancies among unmarried women were quite the fashionable thing in the metropolis just then. Ordinarily I would have resented her vulgar familiarity, but I was so relieved to be spared the embarrassment of the usual sanctimonious small-town attitude that I was deeply grateful.

From the station we rode in a fine two-horse hackney downtown as far as the Brooklyn Bridge, Mrs. Murray proudly pointing out many of the points of interest intervening but, urged by reasons of economy, she dismissed the carriage at the bridge and bundled us onto a three-cent trolley car that carried us the rest of our journey in short order.

Mary had been rather weepy all day on the train, her errand to the city being a more serious one than mine. Truth to tell, the pre-

301

scribed term of her embarrassement drawing
near, and none of those misfeasances of nature prayed for by mother and father having
occurred, the folks had in effect disowned her,
sending her off to bear her child among
strangers. Again and again I had advised her
to do something to avoid the impending disgrace; abortionists would no doubt be plenti-
ful in the city. But with a damned perversity
that exasperated me on more than one occasion, she insisted on going through with it. I
have often wondered how much effect the accident of her name, Mary, had in the development of this Madonna complex.

Sure enough, to anticipate a bit in point of
time, two months after our arrival in New
York, she brought forth, under the beneficent
care of the Sisters of Mercy, the fruit of her
love: a lusty little brat with hair as blond as
its mother's and with noisy desires as pronounced as its father's. The lieutenant, inci-
dentally, had been sustaining her with infrequent letters containing the stereotyped promises, lies and excuses that all men can generally stew up under such circumstances; but
after her successful accouchement—and perhaps because of its very success—his letters
ceased, and Mary, tiring of her role of neither
maid, wife nor widow, lost interest in her offspring and, recovering from her earlier sentimentality with a rapidity for which I could
credit only the atmosphere of the city, turned
the child over to the orphan asylum of the
same kind Sisters of Mercy and went out to
meet life afresh. The further development of
my dear sister is a matter even more astound-

ing than any aspect of my own history; but this I shall sketch briefly in due time and on later pages.

After we were duly settled at Mrs. Murray's, my first act was to register for the October opening of the Medical School of — University. No entrance examinations were required, my high school references being considered sufficient for matriculation. True, the dean of the medical department, in a long, helpful conference in his office, tested the strength of my determination by trying to dissuade me from undertaking that subject, pointing out its many difficulties and hardships; but when once he realized that my purpose was no mere feminine whim, he was just as emphatic in his encouragement.

I next wrote to Bob, in care of the college club address he had given me, and he responded with gratifying promptness by calling upon me in a luxurious motor car on the very evening which he received my note.

In the few remaining weeks before school commenced, Bob was of untold service to me, taking me to see most of the interesting sights of the city and introducing me to scores of his well-to-do friends, many of whom would be attending the same college as I, though in higher classes, and might be of great aid to me. And modesty must not restrain me from recording that I made a most favorable impression upon them, as was evidenced by the profusion of offers I received from them to attend parties, theaters and other functions. Bob, of course, was tireless in warning me that

I must not allow social engagements to interfere with my scholastic work, else I would not
last through the semester. Perhaps he was
jealous. But anyway, I proceeded at once to
augment and urbanize my slim wardrobe from
the extra allowance that father sent me secretly every week.

On many of these pleasant fall evenings Bob
would drive with me far out of the city on
the Westchester road. Here, under the same
stars, and amid surroundings reminiscent of
that beautiful Saturday night, we would stop
the car and sit talking for hours. Or perhaps
we would walk from the road to lie upon the
grass—on which occasions serious problems
would arise. Now that he and I were reunited,
my problem was to keep his affection simmering without allowing it to boil away. But
there could be no question of going backward:
the privileges he had so far attained were substantial conquests that could neither be ex-
punged nor denied.

And so on many of these evenings, despite
my weak resistances, his hands would follow
in the paths of their earlier explorations and
discoveries and seek out my breasts, my thighs
and my secret charms, destroying all vestige
of my personal privacy. No matter how many
petticoats I wore, he would lift them all. No
matter how involved the combination of my
silk drawers and garter belt, he would find his
way through. If they were loose, he would
insinuate his hand up my thighs and under
them. If they were tight, he would pull them
down and off altogether. And it seemed I was
always repairing torn shoulder straps and

ripped silken brassieres after an evening alone with him.

Of course, it was all very nice and exciting for the most part, and with practice Bob became even more expert and satisfying in the subtlety of his titillations—in the way he was able to slowly work up my clitty, charging me with the delicious forepleasure almost but just short of the limit, then slowing down to avoid that consummation which is alas also an ending—then recharging me with the electrical sensations anew—and finally bringing it on with a breathtaking suddenness that set ajar for me the radiant gates of ecstasy and left me quivering meek and vanquished in that indescribable afterglow of pleasure.

Naturally, I would not shirk my part of it. I would grope for his rampant member in the dark; sometimes he would already have it out for me, and then, no matter how moonless the night, I could recognize it by its lovely white luminosity—and grasping the dear warm flesh, I would reciprocate delights in the same measure as he had bestowed upon me or was then simultaneously bestowing. Sometimes I would envy him what I mistakenly concluded was the greater violence of his enjoyment from the more prolific love sacrifice that always accompanied the height of his pleasure. I did not long labor under this fallacy. The only fluids necessary in a woman are those for lubrication: hence its lesser generosity. But so far as actual enjoyment is concerned, the woman's organism being more sensitive than that of the man, the probabilities are that she is, if anything, more extremely affected by the pleasurable reactions. And since whatever substances within her cause the ecstatic climax are not ejaculated but remain, her delicious feelings must continue for a longer time. I have observed this again and again in actuality. My male partners in love may come more quickly than I, but then their good feeling is over almost immediately, while I, more slowly stirred to the crisis, enjoy ecstasies that linger for a considerable time after.

Delightful, however, as these interludes were for the both of us, there was sometimes a serious qualification, and one that I would find it hard to explain. My inhibitions were not yet then so completely annihilated that I could yield myself even partially on every occasion. Somehow it seemed that to permit a man to thrill me, even if only with his hand, to reduce me to a quivering frantic bit of feminity, was a form of subjugation that required justifications other than that of mere pleasure. Perhaps it was the age-old expectation of woman to be worthy of a price, to demand marriage, to be compensated for her submission to man, that so cropped up in me. Anyway, I do recollect that on such evenings as Bob brought me a gift of flowers or of some trinket, I experienced no such compunction or reluctance, and on the contrary, gave myself up wholeheartedly to his dominance. The primitive bargaining old prostitute in Woman! And yet this subconscious requirement of a consideration did not oust the sincerity of my participation when once I yielded, nor did it negate the coexistence of my finer feelings. It merely added an additional gratification, as of the creative satis-faction of a man who has worked well and has something to show for it.

That I was not a conscious bargainer, how-ever, was proven by the fact that no matter how indisposed I was myself, I never refused Bob his pleasurable relief when the circum-stances called for it. Naturally, it was not so psychically satisfying to him when I forbade him to fondle my cunny specifically and did for him alone; but I daresay, for him to lie back while an attractive young lady stroked and molded his sensitive joy-stick with her satiny palms and dexterous fingers, and finally coaxed it to a not-reluctant gush of the tears of happiness, was not exactly the most unpleasant thing in the world.

On one such occasion, Bob insisted on telling me a rather off-color story. It was about a circus midget who applied for a marriage li-cense. "You—want to get married?" asked the astounded clerk. "Sure—I'm twenty-nine years old," answered the mite. "Who do you want to marry then?" pursued the clerk. "Here she is," replied the applicant, indicating an even tinier person of the opposite sex, who had been till now completely hidden by the desk. "But she's no bigger than your fist!" exclaimed the clerk in surprise. "Yes, no bigger—but much better," explained the midget.

I did not admit at the time how much I enjoyed this story—nor could I pretend not to understand it. But I did playfully strike his lips with my fingers in reprimand—and pro-ceeded to question myself whether or not this story might have been prompted by an incipient discontent with that instrument, "the fist," than which there was avowedly something "much better."

Surely enough, only two days later, when we were alone on a dark country road, sitting in the broad tonneau of his car, and I had just reached for his John Thomas in order to forestall what threatened to be a dangerous attack of amorousness, he took my hand away and spoke in a troubled voice:

"You know, Louise, what I'm going to tell you will sound awfully ungrateful, but I must say it just the same. I think you've been just as nice as nice could be; but—that way you satisfy me—oh, I'm not denying that it's the most wonderful thing I've ever experienced in my life— but somehow it doesn't satisfy me, you know, internally. I don't like to sit back while you bring on my orgasm without any aid from me. It's not like a man to take his pleasures passively. And then perhaps it's because what you do is so much like—mechanically at least—what every boy can do for himself. Forgive me, honey, for seeming to minimize your kindness; but it's only natural for me to want something more distinct, something more peculiarly personal of you—something that would completely transcend myself in every way."

I was deeply troubled.

"But Bob," I said, "what would you have me do? It's not at all clear in my mind that I could yet bring myself to follow the unconventional way of life that you've so often spoken of. And it would be altogether unfair to urge me to something that could never be undone. Why, I'm scarcely grown up enough to realize what it all means. I give you my word, Bob, that if I were considering anything like that, you would be the one person in the world whom I would think of. But I'm not. At least, not yet. Why can't we be happy just as we are? If you only knew how my conscience troubles me, even for the things we do do. How wrong it all is! And now you are asking—oh no, Bob, it just can't be. Now be a good boy and let's not talk about that anymore. And if you won't think about it, you won't want it. So there!"

"If only it could be dismissed as easily as that, Louise! But perhaps you misunderstand me. I still don't wish to do you any harm. It's nothing like what you think—nothing irreparable. What I want is just to be a bit closer to you, to be able to delude myself that I am possessing you altogether—but not really. How can I explain it? I got the idea from reading Petronius—*inter femores* between the thighs—I haven't been able to sleep for nights, revolving the thought in my mind. Why not?" He was speaking passionately. "You no longer shrink from touching me—so why not between your soft lily thighs? I would not impair your virginity—wouldn't even come near your dear cunny—there wouldn't be the least danger. All I beg is that you trust me—"

For once he was astute enough to accept my silence as assent. Stretching me across the wide, luxuriously upholstered back seat of the car, his hands ran quickly, like lambent flames, up my stockings, over the little stretch

of bare flesh and over the soft expanse of my
silk drawers, to my waist. Here his fingers
engaged the yielding elastic band that held
up my underthings, and drew it down over my
hips, raising my buttocks with both his hands
to give clearance to the dainty bit of silk protection he was stripping me of. The widest
part passed, it was but a moment before he
had whisked it down over my knees and off
my legs altogether, burying his face in its
perfumed silk intimacy.

Only for a moment. Again his hands returned
to my body, this time in a reverse direction
to pull up my remaining clothes, my dress
and my petticoat, upward above my buttocks,
and upward still, past the wide plain of my
belly, and past the full tight swell of my
bosom, till I was entirely nude, except for my
stockinged legs and the clothes rolled and
crumpled up under my chin.

Falling upon me, his lips proceeded to reassure my flesh with a thousand kisses, dis-
tributed everywhere, from the peeks of my
breasts and the valley between to the deep
dimple that marked the center of my white
belly, to the jeweled meetings of my thighs—
bringing to the places of his visitation the hot
flush of my blood as well as of his fevered
lips.

Once even his hungry mouth sought through
the soft tendrils of my mount of love to the
very entrance of my tender cleft and his teeth
bit savagely, though restrainedly, into the juncture of the fleshy lips, compressing my clitty
within till it stiffened in rigid self-defense. A
tremor of trepidation racked my whole frame

at this deep worship. I shivered in an agony of desire—of despair too, when I realized that I must not yield myself entirely to the complete possession of pleasure. How nearly abject and forlorn I felt when his teeth forsook that central point. I blushed to admit it to myself. Now his lips resumed their generous distribution of warm caresses; but alas, a kiss in each spot is a neglect of every other part, whereas that momentary abandon in which he bit me so deliciously was a homage felt in my every nerve and organ.

Now he produced his own dear part, which I saw, in the moment before I shut my eyes tightly, was more upstanding than ever before —not at a mere right angle to his body, but up, almost touching his waist.

Gently he lowered himself upon me, already panting with the violence of his passion. As he nestled his stiff burning member between my soft fleshy thighs, which, hot as they were, must have seemed cold in contrast with his own excessive heat, I would have thrown my legs wide apart and wrapped them tightly about his waist, to allow him to enter, to break in and take all. It was at moments like this that I regretted the burden of my virginity and prayed fiercely for its abatement. But, perhaps for the best, it suited my lover's present purpose to himself keep my thighs between his, thus to have his part more closely gripped between my soft generous flesh, close-meeting enough as it was. Now he commenced that movement in regular cadence which is the rhythm of love, his smooth organ slipping between my close-pressed thighs in the pleasant groove formed by their well-rounded plumpness. Like velvet on velvet it was—yet there was just that sufficient clinging difficulty of motion to spur on his desire and pleasure. Dangerously close to my fervid cunny he came on his inward thrusts, the padded head of his steely bar pounding against my pubis like a battering ram, as if to force admittance, its master willy-nilly.

Soon from the hot frictioning member came a few drops of albuminous fluid that is nature's *avant courier* and love-lubricant, though but the merest sample of the full generous sweets to come. The back-and-forth thrusting of his now fully-oiled member between my thighs became so deliciously slippery, so wonderfully and insidiously caressing, that I could scarcely refrain from screaming out to have that magic piston operate within and not without my burning slit—which was by now prepared to furnish a lubrication all its own. And now the miracle! Unanticipating as I had been of any pleasure for myself in the arrangement I had conceded, the gods rewarded my generosity. "Give and thou shalt receive." Even as I was supplementing his pleasurable movements by wrigglings and rebounds of my own in response to some inner urge, that strange-familiar ecstasy heralded itself within me. For the forcible contact of mount against mount and part against part, external to my hungry grotto though it was, yet sufficed to create a friction of a sort within that center of all my senses. And my clitty, avid and raring for every caress, strained itself to snatch the benefit of every touch and pressure. This same straining anxiety and uncertainty only increased my intensity and susceptibility to pleasure.

Each time that he came down upon me, I heaved up to meet him, grinding my part against his with a fury that would have inflicted pain under ordinary circumstances but now gave me agonies only of delirious delight. I lost all restraint, moving my bottom madly up and down or sideways to prolong a rubbing contact, with fully as much vigor as he. Soon I was stirred to a keen pleasure, violent beyond bearing. What if he should finish now and leave me thus? The critical ecstasy seemed to have reached in me an unendurable height; but, due no doubt to the indirectness of those needed contacts, it seemed to be arrested, paralyzed, neither subsiding nor passing on to the melting flow of relief. Wildly I lashed my body about as if it were a matter of life and death. And indeed, so killingly extreme was that static state of being spitted on the peak of pleasure that I thought I would die if it did not subside.

Bob's breath was coming short and fast. It was for me now or never! My sighs and moans were overheating my lover in a manner that threatened the imminent end of this indescribably wonderful combat. My motions were becoming mad as to displace his tantalizing engine altogether for whole precious moments!

But oh! Just as I would have expired from excess of pleasure, I caught and held him in a crushing part-to-part embrace that ground my turgid clitty downward and wrested from it its till now supreme dominance.

With what exquisite dissolving joys did I pass that fearful height of ecstasy—and none too soon, for my lover, breathing with the raucous ardor of a forge, suddenly withdrew his member a safe distance from my gasping cunny and with that one final plunge upward along the groove of my hot thighs that announces the beginning of that oh-so-delightful end, spurted a copious flood of the thick warm liquor of love with such impetuous violence that it struck first high on my belly just beneath my breasts, with a perceptible little thud, and then in ever shortening jets left warm streaks across my navel, in the thick silk of my bush, and along my thighs.

Only a few moments separated our respective effusions of pleasure. But we were reunited in the final agonies of delight and we shared the melting floods of bliss together, lips enlocked. When we came to, Bob slipped from me and lay nearby, inert, panting softly, exhausted by his dear labors. As for me, when my hysterical sobbing had subsided, I realized that I had learned what I deem the most important lesson in love: that the greater the difficulties and obstacles to be overcome, the more insane and impossible the manner of loving and the more prolonged and violent the effort necessary to bring on the consummation, just in that ratio will the ineffable joys be increased to soul-wracking ecstasies. To have a facile and quickly rendered finale is to enjoy, yes; but not to experience. One must strive and strain in order to live life to the extremest limitations of our wonderful bodies.

CHAPTER NINE

The medical school opened early in October.
I was on hand, keen with ambition, at last
about to grapple with the many-tentacled octo-
pus of science. I was disappointed at the outset; but my disappointment did partake somewhat of the nature of a postponement of my
expectations. Instead of diving forthwith into
obstetrics and learning all about sex-connection,
pregnancy and its avoidance, and abortion—
things which, naturally enough, would interest
a member of my sex above all other subjects—
we were launched upon the drab mathematical
affinities of chemistry and the remote embry-
ology of the pig. Instead of the ghastly thrill
of exploring human corpses that I had steeled
myself for, we diddled at the minute dissection of bugs, frogs and rats. In brief, I found
the knowledge I yearned for was still exactly
a year ahead of me in the second term of
college.

My being the only female in the medical
department was, at first, a source of consider-

able embarrassment to me. My classmates, all strangers to me as yet, ranging from beardless youths to bearded oldsters, treated me with every degree of respect, shameless admiration or contempt, according to their personal idiosyncrasies and respective ages. And many of the instructors, too, unaccustomed to the distraction or pleasure, as it might be, of having an attractive young lady in their classes, added to my discomfort by playing up to me with foolish simpering compliments in the course of their lectures.

All in all, though, after a few weeks I became accustomed to my conspicuous position and soon learned even to enjoy it, allowing myself to be spurred on to extra scholastic effort by the mere fact of my being the lone representative of my sex. During those earlier trying times, however, it was a great relief, at the end of the day, to be joined by Bob and to go to some quiet dining place where he would spend most of the time consoling and reassuring me. I don't know whether I'd have had the courage to go on if it had not been for him.

And then the long evenings of study in my room or at the college library, pouring over the pages of an atlas of anatomy, memorizing the location of the red lines that were arteries, the blue ones that were veins. and the miscellaneous shadings that represented muscles, glands and what-nots. Soon, to my mind's eye, every person appeared as a skeleton *bon-chart* or a figure from which the skin is lifted to show the organs and blood vessels. When Bob caressed me, I would find myself unconsciously rehearsing the names of the bones of hand, wrist, arm, shoulder, leg or thigh, as he traversed them.

The effect of this temporary dehumanization was to make me the encyclopedic heroine of the class. "Miss ——," the seedy anatomy teacher once said to me, taking my arm and looking at me just a wee bit lickerish, "you may yet make history as the first great woman anatomist." Of course, I thanked him, but to myself I thought that I would much prefer to be Cleopatra or Catherine of Russia or Lucrezia Borgia. Women will always go down in history, just as they go down in bed, as women, and not as the tillers of some arid, joyless field of learning.

Nevertheless, during the whole of my first year at school, with but one or two deviations, as this record will bear out, I attended strictly to my work, and again and again turned down the most attractive social proposals of my acquaintances and classmates. But during November of that year came a catastrophic event —utterly unexpected and demoralizing.

Bob, my main refuge and support, was torn from my life. His father, of German birth, who had amassed a fortune in America, had, in view of the current financial panic, suddenly decided to wind up his affairs and remove with his family to Berlin. And now, in less than a week from the time he advised me of the fact, Bob would be gone.

Not at all strangely, Bob's regret at leaving me was tempered with decided satisfaction at the interruption of his medical studies and his pending proximation to Europe, the goal of his dreams. As for me, I was cast to the depths of despondency and it took all of his power to cheer me up even a little. Thus it is always when one person allows his or her happiness to become dependent on the presence of another.

It was during that same week of leave-taking that sister went to the hospital—fortunately enough, because on Bob's strong urging, we two were able to take advantage of the opportunity to spend a whole delicious night together . . . at a small quiet hotel with uninquisitive management. Unused as I was to such escapades, it was with a great deal of nervousness that I announced to Mrs. Murray that I was going to spend the night at the hospital at Mary's bedside, and with even more fearfulness that I watched Bob sign as Mr. and Mrs. something-or-other in the hotel register.

My first night abed with a man! What a historic occasion over which to rhapsodize—I, who have since, all in all, spent more nights of my life with men than without.

Oh, that blushing virginal trepidation, that shivering delight of first undressing in full light before a worshipful lover, who, hastening to have you nude, yet hinders and delays each step with his impetuous kisses and greedy caresses! With what ardor did he toy with my provoking breasts, now widespread as I stood before him, with their pert little nipples pointing in nearly opposite directions. But even these soft contours could not for long bribe his hands from wandering farther in search of my various other charms: my full curving buttocks, my shapely close-meeting thighs.

318

At last however he forsook the patting and squeezing of my yielding womanly flesh enough to slip hastily out of his own encumbering clothes—which he did with scarcely less modesty than I.

Then followed that supreme delight of delights, to seek refuge from the chill of the November-cooled room and find it between the warm clean sheets of a bed, against the hot glowing flesh of a lover. Oh, that breathtaking ecstasy of bare flesh against bare flesh! We glued ourselves together in every fold we could make the parts of our bodies meet in—the only obstacle to our coalescence being that stiff bar of flesh that stood out in front on him—but this he tucked away for the time being between my quivering thighs. Then, resuming, he caressed me with a mad passion, a passion as mad as if he feared that some part of me might go uncaressed and unpressed, and being thus unclaimed by his hands, so be forfeited by him.

Once more he assured me that he would do me no harm and begged only that I trust myself to him entirely and implicitly. Thrilling with fear and desire, I whispered my assent, giving him carte blanche for the night.

In satisfaction of a strange whimsy, he left off his hot dallying, and slipping to a superior position in the bed, caressed the soft cherry-tipped hillocks of my bosom, not with his hand, as he had done so many countless times before, but with the satiny head of his pulsing member. Each ruby nipple in turn vibrated and came to erect quivering attention at this deliciously intimate salute.

319

Then, turning me about on my sides, he slipped that warm bulky instrument of his, of whose fine smooth texture any woman might be proud, beneath my armpits from behind me. Lodging here for a time to relish the delightful tropical humidity of this silk-begrown station, he next plunged further the bulging head of his member till it emerged from my armpit just beneath my shoulder, beside the full, soft, yielding luxury of my breast.

At this point—forgive me reader—I could not resist the impluse to lower my lips to that so conveniently near part and place upon its beaming crimson countenance a full, moist, luscious kiss. But so instantaneously with the caress of my mouth did that ever wondrous organ swell to double what had already seemed its maximum size and thickness, so violently and suddenly did it throw back its shoulder as it were and expand in length and girth, that I desisted, afraid lest I really cause it to burst through its skin. And Bob, dear Bob, did not dare to allay my fear, did not venture to ask for a continuance of that oral caress which since then I have learned is the supreme refinement of pleasure for both men and women.

For a time he tarried in this high perch between my arm and ripe white breasts, then, bethinking himself of me perhaps, and how my own organs of delight lay further south, he removed his tool from the warm nest, now perspiring with the addition of heat to heat, and directed himself to an even warmer clime.

Lying in my latitude now, and upon me, he lodged his stiff, now madly rampant part between my soft hot thighs, just below my own equatorial region, which I so designate not in mere figure-making, but because that area, in close sympathy and intimate connection with my titties, as in every sensitive woman, was so extremely excited by the titillation of my nipples (those analogues of the clitty) that it was indeed a torrid zone.

With uncanny instinct now his bursting penis so determined its every motion as to bring it closer to the goal intended by nature, and soon it was full up against the entire length of the outer gates, our mounts pressed together, their respective foliage intertwining and veritably crackling with the electric currents of positive and negative polar magnetism, and the valley of love itself almost steaming with the excess of heat and already exuding thick, nearly simmering fluids for lubrication of the ultimate connection.

Then were the frontiers of my virginity extended, though not annihilated, in a most delicious and satisfactory manner. Bringing his hands from behind me, where they had been pressing and molding the cheeks of my buttocks and holding my whole form passionately close to him, his fingers found their way to the moist lips of my cunny, and separating them over their full length (ah, Gods! What suspense!), he introduced his member, not heading inward to rend and destroy me, but downward, to lie in the full tight groove formed by the soft fleshy lips of my vagina. With a muscular action independent of the contraction of my thighs, these lips closed hungrily about the dear organ that distended them and gripped it tensely. Nevertheless, as a guarantee that he had no designs of blood and pain upon my maidenhead, my lover instructed me to bring my legs together and keep them thus, though my urge as always was to throw them wide apart.

So delightfully and cozily settled at last, he commenced now those divine up-and-down motions of love that spring from the deepest-rooted rhythmic impulses in man. As for me, already I was writhing breathlessly about, to bring in closer, to hug in its entirety that wonderful morsel—and, oh joy of joys, as the dear piston rose and fell, traversing for the first time the well-oiled groove, a full sweeping stroke fell generously to the shore of my anxious clitty. My heart sang with happiness within me, as by my own instinctively-timed movements I kept the vital little projection in the longest possible contact with the broad back of his organ, meeting his every stroke with mine and sending those sparks and tongues of pleasurable flame through me.

With those vigorous frictions of voluptuousness, even more directly upon the essential spot than in the normal manner of intercourse I have learned, how long could nature hold out? One, two, three, four divine welding strokes and already I felt coming on that ecstasy to which no description can do justice. Five. Six. Each plunge, as I raised my hips to meet it squarely, catapulted me in great arcs to higher levels of pleasure. Seven! My eyes rolled back, beyond voluntary control. I wanted to wait for my lover's corresponding ecstasy, but oh the eighth! His quick down movement hurtled me sharply to the high point which I knew was just short of the supreme crisis of delight! It was too late to withhold. I gave myself—and as his stiff part drew upward once more, more slowly, like the bow of a master musician drawn firmly to crescendo over the strings of the instrument of pleasure, sounding almost simultaneously the deepest vibrating chords as well as the highest trills in the register, the great orgasm rushed, burst upon all my sense with a long singing "mmmmmm." I gasped and moaned with delight in unison with the sweeping music within me, as I came tumbling softly through the various orbs of the lesser degrees of pleasure.

All this took place in the time that may be but a fractional moment in the outer world and yet a divine eternity within the senses. And Bob, like the musician who has played his concerto well but has not yet completed his program and therefore plunges too soon into his next selection, unaware that his audience would like some time first in which to savor and relish the delightful tunes still echoing in their ears, came down upon me once more with fully tautened bow. I screamed—actually screamed out—at the unendurable agony of a new stimulation upon the not yet subsided one. He stopped and hushed my little cries with hot, imperious kisses.

Then, again, but now very slowly, he commenced his movement, and this time the delight was not so agonizing. Instead, his gentle motion seemed merely to wring out of my innermost nerves the final little spurts and drippings of the effusions of pleasure just past. And soon my clitty, recovering from its recent frenzy of extrasensitivity, remembering how nice it all was, nobly rose again as if to say, "I don't mind if I have another."

Gradually, as he noted that I no longer winced at his contacts, Bob increased the speed and length of his thrusts, until he was fucking me vigorously once more. And from passivity I soon passed to active participation. Now we were writhing and heaving with full steam ahead, his member slipping with almost too great a facility in my now fully-flooded parts. The first eddyings of ecstasy again began within me; but my companion was now panting with the intensity of a railroad engine taking off—and the violence and speed of his panting increased so rapidly that soon I knew the locomotive of love was in danger of shooting off its cylinder head.

And sure enough, a moment later, his separate gasps came so close together as to pass for one explosive exhalation. At the same time, his turgid part, exalting at the climax of its labors at last at hand, took a last tense plunge through the hot clinging lips of my cunny, ending up of necessity, however, not within me, as that way was by nature still effectively closed, but with its swelling head emerging below and beneath the vital parts and wedged into the alternate intimate crack formed by the close-pressed cheeks of my buttocks. Here, with a last violent pulsation of its own, it ejaculated an almost continuous stream of thick, hot love-liquor that lasted for nearly half a minute and flooded the full groove of my underside with its soothing warmth.

For a time he remained there motionless, resisting the impulse to continue moving back and forth lest he thereby bring some of the generous life-saving but danger-dealing fluid within my vulva whence it might be sucked up by my avid vagina and womb. Eventually my own excitement died down somewhat and I accepted my disappointment in good grace, considering my earlier gratification and my shameless but delicious precipitancy in coming before my lover.

When at last he withdrew, he was careful to have me spread my thighs first and move away from his still dripping organ. Then, with a soft hand towel, he gently wiped and blotted away the vital sticky moisture that covered my anus and buttocks.

Turning my back to him now, not in anger by any chance, be it understood, but only to better snuggle the fullest curves of my body into the corresponding parts of the front of his body, we rested, while his hands, encircling me from behind, toyed lazily with my soft breasts and his knee crept between my thighs to better relish their smooth texture. Thus intertwined, in scarcely a moment it seemed, and unintentionally perhaps, we were both fast asleep, no doubt overcome by the delicious languor that so aptly follows the arduous ardors of love.

When I awakened some hours later, it was to find that Bob, still behind me, had slipped his organ, which I could feel was entirely recuperated from its late efforts, up between the full soft hemispheres of my buttocks, in the deep cozy valley so nicely formed by their contiguity. He was gently rubbing it back and forth with restrained bodily movements. For a time I did not disclose that I was awake, relishing the little breathless anxiety I felt as to just what he intended executing now that he thought me unconscious and at his mercy. Perhaps his purpose was to break into my pretty, tightly puckered little bum-hole—in which case (I confess to a strong curiosity at the time as to whether or not it could be done) I would let him essay it just so long as he didn't hurt me too badly. At the stimulation of this nefarious thought, my dormant clitty suddenly awoke and perked up. But just as earlier in the evening he had eschewed any direction that led inward to my secret vitals, so again, his part, ordained by nature for perpendicular usage, traveled merely horizontally to and parallel with the surface of my body, brushing over again and again, but not accepting the challenge to enter the strong-muscled little love-alternate beneath.

Tiring finally of my implausible role of sleeper, I announced my consciousness—and approval —by adding my own motions in cooperation. Noting with joy that I was awake and not unwilling, his member, moving up and down through the full luxurious groove of my behind, slipped lower down to the tangled silk of my grotto. Now his deft fingers sought and easily found the narrow love-cleft, still moist from its recent sacrifice. Parting the ruby lips, his middle finger entered and met the tip of my erect clitty, and by that light contact I was brought into complete communion with him and made to share his own delicious titillations as by his vigorous movements he simultaneously stroked both his own essential part against me and my essential spot with his finger.

Picture our delicious attitude, dear reader, and require no assurances that it was indescribably wonderful. And knowing that one may tire of descriptions (though never of the magic specific), I shall not weary you with further exposition of the "same thing" for this night—except to remark that it was not at all the "same thing." The second time that we came—and we came together to the moment —the sensual climax was a thrill of a deeper and keener sort, by very reason of it being a second and greater call upon our nervous forces.

Bob ejaculated with even greater intensity than before, though somewhat less generously, and his love substance, as it sprang from his blood-gorged member couched between the soft swelling mounds of my buttocks, shot so forcibly as to streak all the way up my back, between my shoulder blades and almost to the nape of my neck.

And then, later, as the dawn crept into our chamber and we were aroused to snatch a last joy from love before parting, we tenderly manipulated each other to a final ecstatic climax, lying face to face, our hands crossing to the other's pleasure zone. And when at last we came, our lips and tongues interlocked, the thrill was of such sharp and burning violence that our transports were indeed the tremors and twitchings of hysteria rather than the mere quivering of passion. That the greatness of the apex of pleasure bore, if at all, only an inverse relationship to the freshness and fullness of the instruments of pleasure, was proven by the fact that though Bob (me too, for that matter) was writhing in the delirium of his most supreme ecstasy, yet his turgid penis gave forth this third time the merest exudation of a few thin drops of crystalline moisture. If in the general single-rounded love act the volume of ejaculation represents an intensity of pleasure, it is only in the degree that it drains the participant to capacity for the time. How triply then, how infinitely, were we experiencing the agonies of unendurable pleasure by thus bravely draining dry life's cup of joy!

I slept late, as I was not to attend classes that day. When I awoke, it was past ten o'clock of a bright sunny autumn morning. Bob was gone. On his pillow was a tender note, telling me that he could not bear to awaken me, could not sustain the torture of a personal farewell, and begged me to see him off at 3 p.m. on the Cunard pier. I dressed sadly, yet convinced that it was best he left me thus. Perhaps his sense of remorse, that slightly puritanical characteristic I could not quite fathom, made him afraid to confront me after what he might consider the abandoned orgy of the night. I too might have found it difficult to keep from blushing.

I left the hotel in a daze that screened me from embarrassment. The rest of the morning I spent shopping for some things for sister and for a number of well-chosen books for Bob. I was on time at the pier, but our farewell, apart from our interchange of significant glances, was the merest formality, for there were more than a score of his friends and relations about.

Thus heartbreakingly came to a close one of the major episodes of my life.

CHAPTER TEN

Enter Charley. Close upon the heels of the receding Bob he came, and how refreshingly did he breeze into my life.

The gangplank had been withdrawn and the great liner that carried my lover away from me was just moving out from its Hoboken dock when a bright, handsome young man whom I had noticed among the sending-off party, accosted me.

"Hello! Do I know you?" he queried with an impertinence that was entirely becoming to his lively eyes and light golden hair. Gracefully, I made a quarter turn away from him, anxious to make some fractional concession to the requirements of conventional respectability and at the same time not to appear too offended. Though my back was thus turned upon him, I rejoiced that my profile—and a not unbeautiful one it is, dear reader, let me admit in all due modesty—was yet visible to him. And I was glad that the brisk autumn wind was so prettily whisking my skirts about my ankles, and piquantly disclosing the form (if not the substance, as in the modes of Paris today) of my calves and thighs. So too, the ringlets of my chestnut hair, bursting from under my hat, played about my ears and cheeks, lending to them an additional lively charm.

My stranger did not allow me to remain long in doubt, if in doubt I had been, as to the cumulative effectiveness of these attractions, for he emitted a long whistle of the most awed and ardent admiration.

"What a beaut!" he exclaimed most audibly, stepping around to confront me face to face. To hide my happy blushes now, if for no other reason, I once more turned my back to him.

"Lady," he spoke close behind me, "I'm not denying that your back is pretty enough to look at all day. But even at the risk of being handed over to a policeman for mashing, I'm going to make your acquaintance."

Once more he stood in front of me. I raised my head haughtily, but the icy look I would have assumed was melted almost instantly under the warmth of his earnest, handsome countenance and I burst into rippling laughter.

"That's better," he pronounced in relief.

From that point onward, we proceeded rapidly to weld a fast friendship. Standing beside him on the windy deck of the ferry that carried us back across the Hudson, I had my first opportunity of really examining my new acquaintance. Charley was without doubt the most handsome man I had ever met. Bob, for all of his sufficiency of maleness, had possessed an indefinable sensitivity that was essentially effeminate—and I could think of him only as a bright boy whose emotional and intellectual intensity far outweighted any consideration of physical attractiveness. I might indeed say that in the case of Bob, I was flattered into love by his superior cultural attainments—his conquest being completed by my own sensuousness and susceptibility rather than by any compelling power of his own.

Charley, however, was my first honest-to-goodness, flesh-and-blood man. Handsome, I have already said. Of medium height and a bit stockily built, he radiated a frank, blunt, unqualified masculinity that made me shiver internally with soft fears whenever I pictured to myself what it would be like to have his full male weight upon my tender body.

It would sound awfully silly—perhaps uncomplimentary too—if I were to say that somehow he seemed to bring to mind vividly that bull scene I have earlier described. But I must repeat to the reader that what impressed me in that barnyard incident was not its bestiality, or even its obvious humor, but only the majestic sex symbolism presented. And so I do not mean to infer that dear Charley was at all comparable to a bull, except that just as the bull is the most masculine of the members of the animal kingdom, so was Charley one of the finest representatives of his own race and sex.

I would need only to exhibit to the reader a contemporary photograph of him to correct any misunderstanding caused by my excessive verbosity. With the head and gracious locks of the Apollo Belvedere himself, he had a high forehead that proclaimed a long line of noble ancestors, a narrow-bridged faultlessly carven Grecian nose, and a determined chin like that of the later American movie idol, Bert Lytell. His eyes—alas, I have no recollection of their color—and though it would be the simplest thing in the world to fill in at random either brown or blue, I shall not thus depart from the complete veracity of my account even for so harmless and indifferent a matter.

His shoulders were broad, even massive; his hands, with their wide palms, expressive of great generosity. In his whole bearing there was that pleasant threat which seemed to say to me, "I would fuck you and hurt you—but I would make you like it!"

There was a similar directness in his general attitude that I feared, but which at the same time delighted me. Though we were not yet friends of half-an-hour, already he was addressing me only with the most audacious double entendres. Up to a certain point, I did not mind the excision of conventional hypocrisies. I even told myself that I would not object to having him for a lover—his physical attractiveness was indisputable. From his aristocratic dress I rightly concluded that he was of the wealthy. (I later learned indeed that his father was president of one of the great American railway systems.) But when, in unmistakable terms, he proceeded to paint himself as a most prodigious roué, commenting on a famous actress, "Oh, she snores," of another, "she has a weak bladder and gives me insomnia," I determined to be on guard against him. Not for me the role of Easy Conquest Number

6495! Not for me to become just another of his clever anecdotes or epigrams, to flatter his enormous vanity, be he no matter how handsome, by serving as his mistress for a fleeting day!

And yet I was immensely fond of him notwithstanding. At least, in between the times when he said such nasty things as, "If there's a virgin over sixteen in this whole damned city, I'd like to have it proved to me. And there's only one way, I suppose you know, to establish a girl's virginity and that's to destroy it." At such times I hated him. Such statements made me ashamed of him and of myself. Anyway, if I was still a virgin, it was through no fault of mine.

Something else he said filled me with conflicting sentiments. He had seen me in the company of Bob a number of times in the past few weeks, and had been much smitten by me; but, he went on to explain, his code forbade him to "cut in on his friend's piece." A very creditable sentiment, but his use of the colloquial "piece," taking for granted as it did that I had been Bob's mistress and hence a sure thing for him, made me wonder whether Bob had told or whether it was just Charley's natural evil-mindedness. I dismissed the first hypothesis as inconceivable. As for the second, I was glad that I still had it in my power to prove that he was wrong. "Prove?" No, not his kind of proof!

It was already night when we reached Manhattan. Charley insisted that I have an early dinner with him at Delmonico's that very evening. I tried to beg off on the plea that I was not properly dressed for the occasion, but he countered by saying that he would get a private dining room, and to this, of course, I could say nothing.

What a thrill I experienced as we entered this world-famous dining place! The manager himself came forward to greet my companion; he seemed to know him well. But my enthusiasm was just a trifle dampened when he suggested to Charley, with an apprasing glance toward me, "Will you have the Orchid Room, as usual?" So I was not the first he had taken to a private room.

And sure enough, the elaborate appointments of the isolated upstairs chamber we were led to betokened possible uses other than that of dining. For, beside the gorgeous white napery and dazzling silver accouterments of eating, there was a sumptuously cushioned divan that bespoke too much the seraglio to have any legitimate business there.

After a sense-stimulating meal that included caviar, lobster and champagne, our waiter cleared the table and discreetly withdrew, leaving us alone. Already both of us were a trifle flushed, if not tipsy, and Charley, leading me to the luxurious sofa, continued to ply me with more of the bubbly alcohol.

Contrary to the accepted belief that such indulgences deprive a girl of all moral judgment and make her unfit to defend her virtue, I found that though the champagne made me feel exuberant and more sensuously alive, yet my mind and will seemed equally sharpened. No doubt if I had been at all so-minded originally, the liquor would have helped

335

my surrender. But as it is, any little wench who assigns the loss of her cherry exclusively to the grape is concealing the fact that she was anxious to be seduced at the outset and seized upon her partial intoxication as the fine pretext to release her from moral responsibility.

Comfortably settled by my side on the divan, Charley proceeded with breathtaking rapidity to become more thoroughly and tangibly acquainted with me. Accompanying his manual exploration with delightful little kisses on my cheeks and neck and the lobes of my ears, his hands took possession of my soft bosom with deliberate and practiced artistry. I protested—but verbally only; in truth, I was most anxious to have him progress to the climax I had planned.

Deftly he caressed the upstanding strawberry heights of my breasts. One of the clasps that held to my form my low-necked dress burst apart. Instantly, to avoid a further repetition of this disaster, his fingers undid the rest of the hooks. Then, slipping down from off my bared shoulders the ribbons that supported my flimsy brassiere, he laid to light the full expanding treasures of my bosom.

I continued to protest in the time-honored formula: "Stop, Charley—I'm not that kind of a girl." But I took care that my meekness belied my words. Now he is placing hot kisses on every inch of the ivory surface of my breasts, now he seizes with his mouth one of the ruby nipples, sucking it in passionately until his lips encompass all its surrounding delightfully puckered aureole. He slipped to his knees on the floor to bring himself opposite these inflaming charms—and now his eager hands sought my ankles, crept up under the hem of my skirt and stole lightly over my silk-stockinged calves to my knees. A bit further and the silk of my hose gave way to the warm satin of my bare thighs. This he could not pass over so lightly—for his hot hands gripped and fondled the yielding polished flesh as a miser his gold—only with more passionate desire.

Now he encounters and avoids successfully the slight obstacle that my tangled hose-suspensory and silk chemise present by allowing his hands to detour my buttocks. Then, brushing under the silk edge of that most intimate piece of my underthings, his burning fingers slip—all too skillfully—up and around to the place high between my thighs whose texture is the finest to caress, where it converges toward that central point which requires no mariner's compass to be found.

As the Mecca of his pilgrimage approaches, he finds it necessary to stifle my objections with overruling kisses. I lock my thighs close together, but his strong hands force them apart. Already his fingers are attacking the moss-grown gates of the sanctuary of love, demanding admittance.

"No! no! no! You mustn't. You will hurt me, Charley!" I manage to cry between his kisses. More gently, he goes. His fingers feel for and find the outer groove, stroking it up and down to part the tangled silky hairs before entering. Now my blushes become more expressive of desire than modesty. But a woman's vanity, if anything, is greater than her desire. I could afford to wait. The moment of my triumph approached. If only nothing went wrong—

His impatient fingers enter between the lips of the cloven spot—despite my protestations. A moment he caresses the familiar zone of my clitty, eliciting from me little gasps of pleasure, which, however, I disguised as cries of pain. But now his fingers venture lower and deeper, to a territory heretofore untouched even by himself. Here the membranes were softer and fuller and more generously inundated in rich moisture. But so unfledged and sensitive were they to his avid touch, that I uttered a loud cry of now genuine pain at his first contact.

He pauses—moves his finger again. I scream. He stops in astonishment—demands to know what sort of fraud I'm trying to work on him by thus pretending to be so easily hurt.

"I don't have to commit rape, you know," he says angrily. "There are plenty of women who don't find me so unattractive. You're not sick, are you?"

"No, Charley," I succeeded in stammering tearfully, "I'm not sick. I've just never had this done to me. I—I'm a virgin—"

"Virgin?" he laughed incredulously. "So's the mother of Christ!" and brutally proceeding to plunge his finger inward, inflicted upon me such cruel torture that I nearly choked genuinely enough now. What carried more weight than my shrieks, however, in bringing him to a stop, was the decided obstacle of a strong, though sensitive membrane that closely guarded the entrance to the inner temple and effectually blocked his further progress.

Perplexed, and even somewhat awed, he desists from his painful probing, though he cannot resist the temptation to once more, but very gently, run the tip of his finger from the top of the delicate groove down to its very bottom—as if to reassure himself of something whose existence he did not yet believe in. Everywhere it was sealed over. At no point could he penetrate more than a scanty inch, and this depth was made possible by the full outward plumpness of my cunny's lips.

Charley's whole demeanor, which a moment ago had frightened me so dreadfully that I had contemplated making a rush for the bell-rope to summon aid, now changed almost miraculously. Removing his marauding hand, he respectfully helped me to readjust my clothing, and sitting beside me, wiped away my tears, begging me to forgive him.

"You poor child!" he was saying remorsefully. "What an injustice I've done you! But hell! Who'd guess that a beautiful piece like you could last long in this damned city? I admit I was wrong. You're the first virgin I've ever run across—and probably the last.

"As for me—well, I've done a lot of rounding in my day—but no seductions. Not that I wouldn't like to—in this particular case." His arm tightened about me almost threateningly. "But I realize that her maidenhead may be a girl's sole stock in trade—and there's too much stuff around that can be legitimately acquired for me to stoop to robbery.

"Well, you delicious piece," he concluded

after an awkward silence, "we'd better be going while I'm still feeling so virtuous. The best of us may change our minds if we wait around long enough. I'll wager I'll regret plenty this passing you up. But let's go. There's still time for me to meet one of my professional girl friends and take it out on her—and I don't mind telling you."

"Oh, don't, Charley!" I spoke with deep sincerity. "I'm so sorry for you—so sorry this had to happen. Can't we be just good friends anyway?"

"Why certainly, baby," he said with an assumed jauntiness that was now pitifully transparent. "I'll stick around till a less squeamish friend of yours does the trick and then I'll step in for the seconds I've always had to be satisfied with."

"Oh, Charley!" was all that I could exclaim in pity and despair. My hands were anxiously and vainly engaged in the task of trying to remedy the gap in my bodice where the torn clasp permitted the all too enchanting swell of one of my breasts to show through. For a moment he watched me with an impatient cynical smile that flustered me so completely that a second clasp came open under my nervous fingers. He blanched, swallowed hard, then overcome, gathered me into his arms and buried his mouth and face on the bared luscious swell of my elastic bosom.

"Christ, you are wonderful!" he gasped intensely, looking up. "Why, I'd give a thousand —two thousand dollars for a night with you. I'd murder my best friend . . . but what's the use!" he went on, calming himself with an effort, "I can see that you're the kind that can't be bought. And I wouldn't know how to go about getting you any other way. You see—ever since I've been scarcely thirteen years old, women have always made a play for me —for my money, I guess. It's only now that I begin to see how meaningless all that is."

He sat twirling his watch chain and looking dismally at the floor. Suddenly he brightened.

"Say Louise—you may think I'm crazy; but will you marry me? Now? At once?" His eyes sparkled with earnestness.

I laughed heartily. This high flattery and the fact that I once more controlled the situation made me feel quite exuberant and gave me back my poise.

"Oh, you great big silly, Charley," I said, mussing his hair playfully. "You are a dear. I'm almost in love with you right now. But you shouldn't propose to strange women, else, God knows, one of them is likely to take you up. You are a temptation. Now if I were a woof-woof adventuress, I'd march you right down to City Hall, and at the point of a gun, force the night watchman to make you mine. But I have other ambitious plans for myself, and a rich husband might make me lazy.

"I will say this though," I continued, rising and reaching for my wraps, "I'm just a poor girl, subject to the whim of her parents, and if ever I'm hard up for money and your earlier offer is still open, you may have first option on my—my sole stock-in-trade, as you called it."

Poor Charley was dumb-struck at this sudden transformation of the weeping girl begging for mercy to the laughing woman puppeteer. He sprang up and strode toward me.

"Why not now?" he whispered fiercely, grasping me by both my shoulders and breathing hotly on my cheek, "Yes, five thousand dollars is nothing for a magnificent woman like you! Make it now!"

"Oh no, Charley. That wouldn't be fair to either of us. I have no particular use for five thousand right now. The very sound of it frightens me. And then again, you'd better think it over. After taking it out, as you put it, on perhaps the five dollar kind, you may conclude that I'm not worth the difference. At any rate, I'll be glad to have you call for me anytime after hours at the medical school—that is, if you promise to be good."

Charley was waiting for me outside the college portico the very next afternoon. He hadn't changed his mind. Nor had I.

CHAPTER ELEVEN

Another month speeds by. Sister, home from the hospital with her bouncing buster, is already chafing under the burdens of motherhood. Charley is still my most ardent admirer and accepts his enforced platonicity good-naturedly but not finally. I give him no further opportunity alone, however, in which to really match the strength of his purpose against mine. Whenever we go out, oddly enough, it is always with a number of his male acquaintances—and soon I am considered one of the "gang." Perhaps he has in mind to overwhelm my stubborn virginity and exclusive femininity by a combined front of maleness. Or perhaps he still hopes that, since I would not fall for him, I might still succomb to one of his many handsome friends, in which case he would get his come-in as I made the communal rounds. At any rate, I was wholly skeptical of his ability to really love in the conventional monogamous way.

What talk-fests our group would have together of a late afternoon or evening at some rathskeller or private club! At times my differing sex was forgotten, and mine was the privilege of sharing their complete confidences and partaking of uncensored masculine conversations. What a lot I learned about men—and women too, of course—on such occasions. Even my vocabulary was gradually broadened, and the stock of erotic stories that I acquired from them would have enabled me to match talents with a cardinal.

Through all this, I preserved myself intact. And for those who may doubt the logic of this, may I interpose a little theory? An erotic picture, kept in one's mind, will no doubt be arousing. So too, such a picture acquired from another's account may result likewise. But the very act of expressing an erotic thought or vision is a form of vicarious relief which leaves the raconteur far less amorous than if he had held silent. Conversely, the listeners must be stimulated, especially if their reception is of a fresh or unfamiliar erotic scene; but so long as they are stimulated only to "tell another," there will be very little of the original emotional or sensual content left to their memory: consequenty they are not apt to commit rape as a result.

Only Charley was becoming less and less talkative. He would sit, silently watching the effect of all this frankness on me. Later, at my doorstep, he would naively flash his checkbook, and with eyes glittering ask, "How about it, baby? How about it?" And I, who had engaged in the refreshing talk and felt no less than purged and aerated thereby, would kiss his nose blythely and say, "Not tonight, Charleykins, not tonight."

New Year's Eve Charley and a number of the boys were going on what they designated a "slumming cruise" and I was invited to come along. As the party contemplated touching on some rather rough places, and the company of a woman might cause embarrassment, it was devised that I should masquerade as a man. Each had some bit of masculine haberdashery to contribute.

All in all, I made up rather successfully as an attractive, though slightly hothouse-grown young man. The greatest problem was the disposal of my long, thick hair, which I thought I could conceal but temporarily beneath a soft checkered cap. I was assured, however, that at the places we were going to visit, gentlemen did not remove their hats—or rather, there would be no gentlemen.

I even spent some time practicing to speak in a lower register. My voice being naturally somewhat strong, this was not difficult. Yet at times I struck tones that were much too musical to pass for other than those of a Priscilla or a "pansy."

That evening was a haze of tobacco smoke and alcoholic fumes, a succession of fancy and cheap cabarets, with their corresponding demimondaine habitués, a medley of shouts, songs and tooting horns, with sex stories presenting a continual obligato.

At about 1 A.M. we were encamped in a somewhat quieter type of rendezvous, where the great number of unescorted ladies—and more particularly their boudoir costumes—made it obvious that drinks and music were not the only commodities for sale here.

No sooner were we all seated at a large corner table than a number of these ladies gathered about us. I was surprised to note that many of them were astonishingly good-looking and all had some considerable fund of bodily charm. The slight contempt that I had had for men who patronized prostitutes vanished immediately. Somehow I had always felt that only those women who were insufficiently attractive to ensnare permanent mates ever resorted to this profession. But now, with this proof positive before me, it seemed more likely that only those whose charms were too slight to insure numerous successive admirers would steer for the safe harbor of marriage with its stagnant waters. True, some of them seemed rather hard, vulgar specimens. But marriage is more likely to contain great numbers of viragos than this profession whose purpose is to please—and I was beginning to learn that there are degrees of refinement even among the votaries of Venus Pandemos.

One of their number, the youngest by appearance, singled me out for her especial attention. My embarrassment could be better imagined than described—particularly, when my companions, realizing the humor of the situation, urged her on to overcome my "bashfulness."

The lady in question was a delightful young thing of about my age and size, with titian-red hair and eyes of a strange dark blue that bordered on green. Beneath the diaphanous black silk combination, that was all that she wore, could be discerned the pink-white prominences of her pretty form, the firm tract of her belly, and a pair of pert, luscious breasts that seemed so deliciously edible that even I, who should have felt a minimum of response to such charms, experienced a deep impulse to bite into them—just to feel those tiny cherry nipples upon the back of my tongue with the surrounding ivory flesh caressing my lips. Her thighs and legs, though they demanded less attention by very reason of the fact that they were entirely bare except for the uppermost segments, were as shapely as any I had seen. A string of jade beads and a pair of tiny scarlet slippers completed her clothed protection—and little enough it was.

Sitting beside me on the wall-seat, she made herself agreeable to me in what I supposed was the conventional manner.

"You are a very handsome boy," she said, with a slight accent that I immediately surmised as French, running her fingertips in a peculiarly subtle manner up my thighs. "You would make a very pretty girl." I winced, but smiled to her in lieu of the words I dared not speak.

"But I like you," she went on. "Do you wish to kiss me?" I shook my head. "No? You're afraid of me? Come now, I won't bite you. Give me your arm. Now—put it around my waist, so. And your hand—here. Like that? Nice, isn't it? Make you feel like doing anything? No? Then your other hand." She pursed her pretty red lips patiently. "Put it here on my thigh, so. You like that? Nice

and warm, isn't it? Well, *do* something!"
This time with a tiny trace of exasperation.
"I'm not your maiden aunt. You can move
your hands a little bit. I won't slap you."

Complying, I closed one hand over the firm
little hillock of one of her bosoms, while with
the fingers of the other hand that lay in her
lap, I felt timidly about, sensing, through the
silk of her combination, the crisp tiny clump
of pubic hairs that rustled at my touch. Simultaneously, her deft, naughty little hand crept
up my trousered thigh again to my corresponding part, feeling about for the expected result
in vain. Of necessity, the phenomenon she desired was impossible; but little did she suspect
that the strangeness of the situation was arousing me more than her caresses alone could
affect any mere man. And if a penis had been
the indicator of my suppressed excitement, I
am certain it would have burst every last button
on those borrowed trousers I wore.

But finding no index to my state, and therefore, reasonably deeming it a mark of her in-
sufficiency, Nanette (for that was her name)
pushed my hands from her, much to my regret,
and spoke petulantly.

"You don't like me! I am too ugly for you
perhaps. You want me to leave you and send
one of the other girls?"

"No, no! I like you," I ventured to say in
low tones that were fortunately made hoarse
by my sensual commotion. Whether the as-
sumption of male clothes had worked a sexual
transformation within me and my feelings were
those of a man for a woman, or whether I had
brought to light a heretofore concealed homo-

sexual tendency or not, I cannot say. A simpler explanation would be that the presence of anything associated with sexual pleasure—and lord knows this creature's every curve and fold spoke only of the extremest sensual ecstasies —would stimulate male or female alike, by being interpreted associatively either actively or passively, as the case might be. "I would like to fuck her" or "I would like to be her when she gets fucked" is the idea.

Whatsoever the reason though—and too much reasoning is inimical to joy, I must remind myself again and again—I was anxious lest I lose the company of this luscious girlie, and forgetting myself completely, threw my arms about her neck and placed on her mouth a fierce, salacious kiss. I was pleased to find that her ripe moist lips were fresh and sweet, with that vague ambrosial perfume that women can give but cannot receive in kissing a man—and I was not averse when she prolonged the delicious contact by introducing the scarlet tip of her tiny tongue into my mouth. I am not idly employing metaphors when I write that during those few fervid moments my very heart sprang to my lips.

It was only after this compromising admission that I became aware that my companions, though they had been occupying only the periphery of my consciousness, had focused on me at least half their entire attention. They were nudging each other and laughing delightedly at my performance, not for a moment dreaming that it had not been entirely unwilling.

"Would you like to come upstairs with me,

dearie?" Nanette whispered when she noted how discomfited I was by the onlookers. I shook my head negatively.

"Would you like to take me home with you then?" I shook my head again.

"Then we can spend the night together at a hotel. I will be so very nice to you. Everything. Yes?"

Again I shook my head. By this time the boys gathered from my repeated "no's" the way the land lay, and considering it a rare joke, boisterously gave aid to her cause, urging me to go upstairs with her.

"Go ahead, Lou. She'll make a man of you!" Such were the jibes cast at me. At last, to put a stop to this roistering, which already was attracting the attention of all present, and to spare the little lady the public insult that my continued refusal would now be, I nodded my head in assent. She took my hand happily and led me away; but not without my turning back to give my blackest look to my companions for subjecting me to this unspeakable embarrassment.

At a sort of office in the rear, Nanette was thrown a towel and a key—much like the procedure of renting a bathouse at our beaches —and I was handed, imagine, a rubber sheath. Instantly falling out of role, I threw the condom back and continued on. My petulance drew only a polite smile from the madame and an "As you will, sir."

On the stairs, I decided it was time to disclose my real sex and bring to a close this comedy of errors. I tapped Nanette on the shoulder and stopped halfway up; but some-

how, the words I would have spoken did not
come. Perhaps the strange excitement, or fear
of an emotional outbreak on her part, or perhaps curiosity as to the outcome, inhibited me.
She merely took me by the hand once more
and dragged me on, saying, "Don't be afraid,
child. It'll do you a lot of good. And you'll be
glad you came. I like it too. For my sake you
will do it; because you are a very nice boy
and already I love you."

We entered a brightly lit but plainly furnished room and the key was turned in the
lock. Against the wall was a large heavy bed
with fresh white linens. Over the lowermost
part of the sheets, however, was spread a strip
of dark blanketing—probably as a footrest for
those who didn't stay long enough to remove
their shoes.

"Now we are alone, honey," Nanette addressed me as I continued to stand near the
door. She approached, embraced me tightly,
and rolling her waist and hips against my middle with a tense, slow movement that once
more made me regret that I possessed no more
projectible antenna with which to savor this
contact, she placed a long hot kiss upon my
mouth. I returned it with sudden, abandoned
fervor.

She stepped away from me. A slight shake
of her body, and the flimsy black silk under-
garment that had been her sole costume slipped
down from off her shoulders till only the upstanding heights of her breasts sustained it; another motion, and it slipped down to the station of her full wide hips; another, and the
cloud of silk glided shyly down her thighs and

settled slowly about her tiny slippered feet.

There she stood before me, nude—an apparition of beauty that not even Chrysis of old could have surpassed when she disrobed for some burning, handsome lover in the moonlit groves behind the temple of Aphrodite.

What devine flesh! How lovely a form! I would have envied her inconsolably, had not the thought flashed upon me that I could not have loved that gorgeous body one half so passionately, so desirously, if it had been my own. From her gracious neck to her swelling, rounded young breasts my gaze went to the snowy valley between that widened downward to the broad delicious plain of her belly; the dimpled navel; the well-shaded triangular patch, overspread with curling silken hair of the richest sable—beneath which began a scarcely discernible rift that shaded modestly down and inward to seek shelter between two plump fleshy thighs of just that proportion which is not too much for grace and yet enough for love's luscious demands.

A moment she stood for my admiration, then turning away, presented to my intoxicated view less consciously, another side that put me in deep quandary as to which, front or back, was the more beautiful. The rear of her thighs, more curved, more fleshy, more lascivious than the front, where, in close conjunction they plumped out in a pair of the most delicious white buttocks conceivable, would have stricken dead with desire any sodomist worshiper of Venus Callipyge.

Briskly, and to reassure the fearful young man that I still was to her, she bent over a sort of *bidet pour abolutions intimes,* and with an apologetic smile to me, proceeded to quickly soap and wash her private parts. Grotesque as this action may have been in reality, yet it in no way interrupted or dispelled the tense atmosphere of desire that enwrapped me. On the contrary, if I had been a man with all that belongs to a man, so inflamed by her suggestive squatting position would I have been, that I would have rushed upon her and impaled her soap and all, then and there!

Humming a little tune and watching me intently, she gently dried herself with the towel, leaving her pubic hairs more silky, more curly and delightfully tousled than ever. Then, throwing herself on her back across the bed, she drew up her legs, spread wide her thighs and awaited me.

Irresistibly I was drawn near. The fascination of the vista spread before me held me breathless with a strange wild pleasure. Through the dark silky curls of her mount of Venus could be seen, like the setting sun through foliage, the merest suggestion of vermilion. And beneath that, the veritable red-centered velvety cleft of flesh itself, with its soft lovely little lips, shading gradually inward from palest pink through intermediate delicate tones of red to deepest carmine—expressing a harmony of line and color, of softness and vividness, that Renoir at his best has never attained.

But alas! I could do no more than gaze upon it. Nature had sadly failed to bless me with the wherewithall to give that darling cunny that which it pouted for.

For a while the adorable creature continued in her expectant attitude. At last, seeing that not only had I not made proper application of the essential specific, but had not yet even disclosed it, she sat up on the edge of the bed and sighed patiently.

"Still bashful, eh? Well, come sit beside me. Either you've had too much of women or none at all. Which is it? Are you a virgin?"

I nodded affirmatively. All too truly.

"Well, well. I should feel honored. You are my first beginner. But I thought nature would take care of herself and tell you what to do. Come closer. Put your arms around me. Now play with me while I get you ready."

She bit her lower lip, and with a pretty little frown of earnestness, began studiously to attack the front buttons of my trousers. I was mortified beyond words. What could I say, after leading her on so far? I could only await the inevitable.

The last button was opened. Her pretty little hand insinuated itself into the gap with becoming awkwardness, felt about with increasing anxiety for the stiff bar of flesh, the male *ne plus ultra*, that should have sprung to her grasp, but was not there.

Instead she encountered only the soft silk of the feminine underthings I had retained despite my disguise. Grope as she might, there was not even the meagerest suspicion of the affirmative instrument she was no doubt sufficiently acquainted with to certify the absence of.

"Mother of God!" she exclaimed in horror, rapidly making the sign of the cross over her nude bosom. "What kind of man are you? Have you been castrated? Were you born this way? And those silk underclothes—Ugh!"

I could only hang my head in shame.

"Why don't you answer me?" she went on. "Are you deaf and dumb too? Why do you come here to waste a poor girl's time, you—you dirty catamite!" And she slapped me sharply across the cheek.

Still I could not articulate a sound. Bursting into tears of discomfiture and shame, my head still hung low, I pulled off the cap that till now I had kept jealously on my head. The loosely piled up tresses of my hair tumbled about my face and bosom like a shower of autumn leaves.

"Good Jesus, help me!" exclaimed the pious Nanette in amazement at this denouement. "A woman! Or can it be a further deception of the devil?"

"No—a woman." I spoke for the first time. Still skeptical, the good Nanette, with native directness, whipped down my already fully opened trousers, and searched through the tangle of my silk chemise till she found the conclusive proof of my statement.

Laughing delightfully now, with relief and appreciation for the jest, she placed a kiss on the bare smooth skin of my thigh, a quick little kiss that set us both blushing furiously.

"And a very pretty woman, too. My faith—but you surely fooled me." She was looking me up and down, her eyes ever glistening and dancing with interest. "But I don't care. I'd rather you were a woman anyway. I don't like men. They're just my business. But you—

there was something about you that I liked from the beginning"

Her bright smile was irresistible. "You too, Nanette; there was something about you that made me really almost fall in love with you. Even now I wish I were a man."

For the first time in that whole hectic evening I felt happy and released from the strain of carrying on my pretense. Kicking the trousers off from my ankles, I lay back upon the soft bed.

"Why don't you take those stiff ugly clothes off, dearie?" Nanette suggested. "You've only been up here a few minutes. Your friends are probably busy with the other women and have forgotten all about you."

I complied, while she considerately helped me off with the now hateful coat, vest, shirt and heavy shoes. In a moment I was lying comfortably on the bed with nothing on but a pale green silk chemise.

"You are built beautifully," Nanette said in low, admiring tones. I returned a similar compliment, but she ignored it, engrossed only in me.

"Your breasts are so full and rounded," she went on. "How did you ever keep them out of sight without a corset? They must be much softer and more compressible than mine. Mine are hard and firm. Feel." And she led my hand to one of her globes of ivory, which may have been firm, but hard, never.

"Do you care if I touch yours?" she asked now, rather anxiously. I assented.

To complete her comparison, she gently slipped my chemise down off my bosom to my very hips—and then, suddenly abandoning the pretext of polite conversation, she threw herself upon me, fondling, kissing and biting my breasts with the fierce ardor of a lover and murmuring, "I love you! I love you!"

The strange, perhaps abnormal, emotion, the merest suggestions of which I had felt before, now flamed forth in an overwhelming fever that must have out-temperatured Nanette's hot lips at every point where they met my flesh. My will melted away. I lay, grateful and passive to her caresses. Vaguely, I wondered at the forceful affirmativeness of her passion; as for myself, I still felt only deliciously feminine —although in my consciousness a gathering undertone insisted on mad, wild pleasures, the more forbidden, the more perverted, the more blasphemous to codes of man or God, the better!

My Nanette was leaning over my outstretched form at right angles to it, thus giving herself access to every part of me. Using her hands no more than if she had had none, she continued covering me with hot kisses. Now she leaves off sucking my nipples to tongue the tiny ticklish depression of my navel, leaving a path of deliciously wet kisses in her wake.

On every exposed part of my body her lips worship. Now she is venturing lower to my hips. At this extrasensitive zone her kisses cause my abdomen to contract sharply, spasmodically, again and again.

All over my belly again and down toward my thighs her kisses trail delightfully, setting off little titillating explosions of sensation through my whole body. As she goes lower, and lower still, she pushes before her with her head the loose silk chemise that lies lightly in her path—still not deigning to use her hands. I aid her by slightly raising my hips and buttocks from the bed, and thus she drives this last flimsy garment down before her with her kisses, down every fought-for inch to my thighs, and to my very knees.

Now up my thighs, and as deeply between them as she can reach, her lips and tongue run their delicious way. Gradually, I allow her to force my legs apart. Unceasingly she kisses and bites the inviting soft white flesh of my between-thighs, closer, closer to my awakening center.

Panting with passion, she arrives at the edge of the very spot; then, exhausted by her continual kissing, she rests, burying her face deep in that strategic area where thighs at their most luscious meet belly and mossy mound and velvety cunt.

Full upon the sensitive seat of all my sensations her hot breath comes, in panting blasts like the scalding draft of a blacksmith's bellows. Up from my vulva to my very womb the heat spreads, firing further my already burning senses to a white unendurable heat, bringing down generous vaginal secretions and lubricants that are but oil to the flames. Uncontrollable as a nervous tic, my cunny is shaken by little spasms, and my hips begin writhing about in upward spirals. I cannot long endure her inaction. I am a soul in torment.

At last my exquisite female lover resumes. Boldly her mouth seizes upon the lips of my tender cunny and places full upon it a long luscious kiss. My clitty is galvanized into quivering erectness, and I almost scream with delight. Now I know my torment is past, that this way lies ecstasy and relief—that Nanette is not simply engaging in fruitless caresses and abortive titillations.

But no. Her dear mouth abandons the vital spot that so deeply craves her attention, and goes awandering again. Heavens! Why does she torture me so? Has she found that part distasteful? Or is she merely teasing my senses with prolonged suspense?

Happily it is the latter—else surely I would have died from that excessive, stinging desire.

Her pretty ruby lips once more make the circuit of my body, everywhere stirring up nervous reactions and reflexes that I had never before so much as dreamt of.

I open my eyes, which till now have been closed, to more fully concentrate upon the universe of sensual delights within and upon the surface of my body. Nanette too, it appears, is sustaining the full lash of desire. Her whole form, though flushed with internal heat, is shivering and vibrating with a strange nervousness.

Up till now her attention is all to me. But now, as her lips once more steal downward to the home base, she brings her whole perfect nude body around and upon me, in a reverse position, not for one moment abandoning the stimulating, titillating aggravation of her mouth.

The wondrous treasure of her glowing form is now suspended over me as she supports herself, her hands on each side of my thighs, her knees bestraddling my head. For a moment I glimpse down the vista made by the quickly narrowing space between our parallel naked forms–above my quivering abdomen. And overhead, her plump white thighs, crowned at their juncture with her now widespread pouting cunny, ripe, luscious and scarlet as a freshly severed pomegranate, and padded for protection of its delicate membranes with soft, curly hairs.

Our bodies at last in contact, flesh to flesh, our breathing now becomes synchronized with the rise and fall of breasts against diaphragm and diaphragm against breasts. Nor do her lips relinquish their activity for one moment during this transaction.

Her arms now slip under and embrace my thighs to bring my middle the closer to her. A moment she reaches down to whisk my chemise from off its last post on my lower legs, and now I am free to throw my limbs wide apart. Awhile longer she circles my anxious center with a barrage of kisses. Now her face burrows deep between my fleshy thighs, and then–good God, what ecstatic relief–her mouth seeks and finds unerringly my palpitating cunny!

A sucking kiss upon the very clitty itself makes me nearly swoon with joy. Now her tongue softly but firmly plows down through the whole groove of my cunt, gently parting the adhering lips and laying open new sensitive zones, new nerve cells, for her ineffably wonderful lingual caresses. What an exquisite feeling pervades all my senses! Oh, gods and men, how I pity you for not having such a deep membranous organ as a cunt with which to experience this superheavenly exquisite delight. For no prick, be it ever so large and sensitive, can have that quantity of mucous nerve-netted surface that a woman's cunt is blessed with, and that makes possible such subtle sensations as the sacred ritual of the cunnilingus alone can give! Oh gods and men, I exclaim again, I would not have accepted all the wealth of ancient Carthage in exchange for that one first lapping stroke of joy-giving tongue in my cunt!

Up to this moment, though Nanette's exquisite little quim was directly overhead, the inertia of modesty had restrained me from making any overtures comparable to hers, and I had kept my head slightly averted. But now, as more rapidly her agile tongue stirs up my boiling passions below, I, in gratefulness and in plain unadulterated lasciviousness, reach up with my arms, encircle her buttocks so conveniently near, and draw her quivering coral cunt down, down toward my face, to my panting mouth, to my waiting, lolling tongue. Her soft velvety thighs settle close about my cheeks. Immediately before my eyes are the lovely swelling prominences of her buttocks, the skin, even at this close range, whiter and more flawless than I had deemed possible. Between them, her pretty little bum, puckered delightfully, of a sepia tinge that faded to pink, to white, as its harmonious ridges melted into the gracious snowdrifts of her bottom. Below, separated from it only by a narrow little partition of pink flesh, the mystic grotto of love itself, leading in, inward, to woman's most vital organs and the wondrous womb of life; but more immediately showing a perfect ellipse of the most luscious vermilion that gaped invitingly at its widest, and melted together, just the other side of a small but inescapable projection, the clitty, in a little rift that lost itself in the abundant silky shrubbery of the Hill of Venus.

I raised my mouth to this delightful valley of love. If ever I had imagined qualms or compunctions about what I was on the verge of doing, they vanished instantly. Was it Juvenal, that old smart-acre, who insinuated, "The breath of pederasts is foul; but what of those who lick the vulva?" If so, it is because his country was bathless and his women unwashed. No doubt his own mouth, unacquainted with the toothbrush, was nothing to write odes about. But in this modern day, a woman's personal hygiene is an accepted fact, and the vaginal cavity may be as clean or cleaner than the oral.

Nanette's delicious quim possessed only the faint wholesome, personal odor of a young and healthy woman. This was subtly blended with the artificial perfume of her adjoining parts, and the whole gave a delicate local aroma that was stimulating and indescribably pleasing to my senses. Avidly I breathed it in, as I plunged my tongue into the exquisite crimson cavern. The warm, moist membranes, ineffably smooth and soft, gave as much caress to my lips and mouth as I in turn gave them.

In the meantime, my beloved Nanette is by no means idle. Now deftly and rhythmically, now with the uncontrolled fury of passion, her tongue weaves in and out among the folds of my inner cunt, now straight up and down through the full length of the tender cleft, now across, now in zigzags that run from end to end, now in little circles that concentrate on my clitty and put me wholly out of my mind with unendurable pleasure, now in sweeping ovals that stir up wide rippling waves of divine ecstasy, waves that somehow spread, not in circles, but in ever-widening ellipses that take in more of my entire being.

Unconsciously, at the other end, I adopt the rhythm and actions that she employs—and all that I describe as one doing was done and felt by each and both of us. In tense pleasure, she tightens her thighs against my cheeks. Instinctively I draw up my knees from the supine position and wrap my thighs tightly about her head, thus enabling me to bring her whole beloved face in closer to my tender parts.

Now dear Nanette is moving her whole body to the rhythm of lapping tongue, rising and falling to meet every caressing stroke. Soon I am adopting the same tempo, my hips and ass writhing madly up and down to follow the fullest presence and pressure of her tongue.

Demonically inspired by passion, my teeth seize fiercely, though restrainedly, the erect palpitating little bulb of her clitoris and press firmly into it. Nanette gasps with the extremity of her pleasure; as I gently nibble the sensitive projection, I can hear her murmur in a muffled manner:

"Ah! Mon Dieu! Que je t'aime!" In her excitement she lapses into her native language.

363

The sound waves, spoken directly into my cunny, send peculiar vibrations through all my bone structure.

Recovering, Nanette reciprocates in even finer measure. Opening wide her hungry mouth to encompass the whole, she sucks in with her lips and breath all the succulent folds of my cunt. Already blood-gorged and sensitive to the utmost, this action overcharges the blood vessels and nerve cells almost to the bursting point. At the same time, the vacuum made by her delicious sucking suddenly causes my whole vagina and womb to contract with a strange tingling that wrenches and cramps my entire being in an agony of delight and brings down an inundation of the sweet secretions of love as if this were already my climax. I would have screamed if I could, but Nanette's dear part hushes me with its luscious caress.

For long, deliciously agonizing moments she holds that strange mouth-suction, during which I am in no less than a state of suspended animation. Then, having wrought in that part the maximum of hypersensitivity possible, she suddenly releases her magic oral grip and proceeds as if to devour me with mouth, lips, tongue and teeth. A series of deep tremors shake me, so surcharged is my whole nervous system with all these kissings and teasings and bitings and suckings.

But relief is at hand: dear, desirable, delicious relief from those tortures of love, which are no sooner ended when we wish only to renew them again and again. She now ceases her hungry random attack, and with scarcely an interval, takes up with her tongue a hand to hand duel with my bounding clitoris. And with what magnificent swordmanship! Back and forth with light but firm and ever-quickening little strokes, the sensitive tip of her tongue does battle with the even more sensitive little sentinel of my Palace of Pleasure. Not the fraction of a moment's respite does she give him. Scarcely has he rebounded, much less recovered, from one stroke than another and another and another falls to his share.

Doughty little clitty, who often enough in more common battles can vanquish and outstand in fight many a strong penis five hundred times his size—we cannot hold you to blame for your quick surrender! For what prick or clitoris, be it ever so stubborn, could long withstand that steady rain of caresses given by the moist tip of Nanette's deft, subtle tongue?

More and more rapidly the little strokes come, till the electrifying sensations that follow each come so close together as to blend into one continuous, ever-increasing, candescent ecstasy that wafts me softly skyward, as if on the magic rug of an Arabian Night's tale.

Try as I will, my own unpracticed tongue cannot meet the pace she sets. And now, as the dear climax heralds its approach in my deep, violent gasps, my tongue strikes blindly, jerkily, missing strokes with every panting exhalation that is torn in sharp blasts from my writhing body. Only dear Nanette continues steadily and unflinchingly, though she too proclaims by the desperately irregular wrigglings of her buttocks that her dissolution is near.

Together now! Oh, to come together! To weld our ecstasies into one! My tongue and lips and teeth lap and kiss and bite wildly with every current of delicious pleasure that shoots through me! With difficulty I hold her madly writhing cunt to my mouth. All our universe becomes a tangle of dripping tongues and soft, warm cunt-flesh, of legs and thighs and buttocks—the whole mad scene illuminated by more and more frequent flashes of red-glowing sensation.

Suddenly, in this welter of pleasure, already superlative beyond conception, comes that infinitely superior, super-superlative of the climax!

Oh! What mortal pen can describe those divine orgasmic transports for which kingdom, life and honor are well lost? Only from the violent external manifestations can the inner turmoil be surmised. My whole body twitches in the supreme agonizing pleasure—and as the apex is reached, my thighs close so stiffly and tensely about my dear Nanette's head that I would have hurt her sadly, had not her face been cushioned by my own well-padded cunt and soft parts. As is, I crush her mouth inward to me and hold her as in a vise to put a stop to those unendurable titillations—for already my orgasm has sufficient momentum to finish of itself. But she manages to continue the fierce motion of her tongue. I am completely out of my mind! My alarmed senses scream out and struggle to retain consciousness in this turmoil of stimulations and new sensations; but despite all this, there is one obsession—to continue my own active part and to drag my companion down after me into this maelstrom of intense pleasure, to drown with me in all these swirling joys.

Madly my tongue continues lashing away, while I grip her form to me in every part. As one being now, we writhe in our embrace. Another moment, and I can tell from the sudden stiffening of her body and the sharp contraction of her cunt that she is with me! Then, and not till then, do I feel that the real apex of my own crisis is at hand.

Two long low moans go up from our tensely tangled form. First blinded, then entirely overcome, by the tremendous conflagration of sensations, I faint dead away—for long sublime moments of which, alas, I can give no report.

My joy-clouded brain begins to clear. We lie quivering and twitching in each other's arms like persons mortally stricken; but in truth we are still swimming in head-over seas of bliss. We have survived the delicious danger, and the delirium and tumult of our senses subside.

For a time we lie thus, breathless and happy, more languorously savoring the delightful afterpleasures of love. Our bodies relax, my thighs fall away from her head; Nanette's white naked form now rests upon me softly, her belly upon my breasts, a welcome blanket of gently palpitating flesh. Her cunt still lies upon my lips, but my tongue is withdrawn. As I open my eyes, till now closed in ecstasy, I can see that its folds are glowing with a more flaming vermilion than ever; but its so recently irritated membranes are now bathed

367

and soothed by a generous flood of fine mucous. Through the vista of her still-widespread thighs and buttocks, I see the gas chandelier on the ceiling burning with what seems a dimmer flame. It is not my passion that is dimmer, however, for my mind is yet full of memories and desires for what is so recent; it is only that my eyes, their pupils contracting with languor, present the outer world thus dully in contrast to the brightness of sensation within. Oh, to lie with her forever! To sleep perhaps awhile, and then to awake to renewals of this subtle ecstasy!

Nanette is the first to stir. Much to my regret she removes her beloved body from over me and automatically resumes her dress of shoes and black silk chemise. I proceed to follow suit, but she halts my progress, covering my breasts with a round of tender kisses.

Then, full upon my mouth, still full of the dear moisture of her cunny, she places a luscious kiss. Alternately we suck each other's lips and tongues, exchanging the sweet secretions of our mouths. As for myself, I find a deliciously wicked erotic stimulant in the thought that I am thus drinking from her lips the joint lubrications of our secret parts.

Reluctantly she begins to help me on with my clothes. Then suddenly, in a little flurry of passion, she falls to her knees as I sit on the edge of the bed and parting my thighs, she places upon the lips of my cunny what is meant as a grateful farewell kiss. Then, noting that it is still very wet, she compresses the lips together with her fingers, and leaning over it again, sucks away the moisture that she thus squeezes from it. Next, regretting the early completion of this pleasing task, she impulsively undoes her work by inserting her tongue and kissing it more moistly than ever.

Still unable to tear herself away from this most delicious part of me, she lingers on, saying good-bye again and again, fondling, kissing, admiring it, on her knees before me.

"A pure sweet virgin cunt! How long it is since I've seen one of those! To think—it has never been touched by man. That dear velvety maiden membrane—let me run my tongue once more across its delicious smooth surface —while it's still there! And those unfledged, unstretched lips, how nicely they kiss me back! And your lovely little joy-button, so small and sensitive and undeveloped. Oh, I must nibble it off!"

She suits the action to the word. It does not take a great deal of such delightful toying to reawaken my desires. My clitty stands up when spoken of with so much flattery. Nor does the gentle nibbling of her small regular teeth tend to lessen its self-consciousness. Little ripples of pleasure begin spreading from my cunny to my spine—But why worry the patient reader with a new recounting of what has just gone before? Only the delicious act itself bears repetition, and not with my inadequate words of attempted description. Suffice it to say that whether she had originally so intended or not, she accepts my gentle invitation to continue when I place my hands about the back of her pretty head and hold her more snugly to my reawakened cunt.

Scarcely a minute after she has begun, I come deliciously. But this climax I recognize as being just a part of my first thrill—a sort of warm wringing out of the remains of the earlier bacchanalia of pleasure—and so with continued importunities of my writhing hips, I wrap my thighs about her neck and shoulders and imprison her to a continuation of this delightful stimulation. Not at all unwilling, darling Nanette goes on, centering her dear labors of love exclusively upon my spongy little clitty for efficiency. I lie back on the bed and experience again her divine gamahuching. This time it takes a longer time for me to come—perhaps all of ten minutes—but oh, dear reader, so delightful is the process of going to that "come" that I am almost sorry when I arrive and it is all over. No—I lie. That third thrilling orgasm, though thinner, as it were, and less pervading (perhaps because of the familiarity with the paths over which the sensation has so recently blazed its way) was even sharper and more violently enjoyable than both those that went before. It left me sobbing and moaning in an overwhelming agony of bliss that—well, I am glad that I promised not to describe it, so completely would it defy my pen.

As I dressed, we exchanged our full names and became better acquainted in the more usual sense of the words. Also, we agreed to meet again in the early future.

Downstairs, I found that my marvelous adventure had occupied scarcely half-an-hour by the clock. Charley was sitting about disconsolately, consuming scores of cigarettes, alone except for a woman of the house who was wooing him in vain. All the other boys had retired with their respective choices and had not yet come down.

His eyes brightened when he spied me; but he was gloomy and sullen again when I sat down beside him.

"What kept you up there so long? A joke's a joke; but not when it's carried too far. One would think you were really up to something. What were you doing?"

"Oh—just chatting, to waste time. I didn't want to be the killjoy of the party and keep you from getting yourself a woman."

"But don't you see, Louise?" he said earnestly, covering my hand with his and looking at me intensely with his handsome, pleading eyes, now seemingly shadowed by deep anguish, "don't you see that I want no woman but you? I'm waiting for you. And damn it, I've been faithful to you for more than this half-hour that you've been gone."

I blushed violently. My conscience was not clear.

"Charley," I said, "I'm afraid I'm scarcely worthy of this, your deep affection and unshaken faithfulness."

He must have thought that he detected a note of sarcasm in my words, for he said roughly:

"Never mind, baby. I'm waiting."

CHAPTER TWELVE

Months passed. Charley waited, becoming almost haggard with thwarted desire. What grand passion was this that my spoiled rich boy had developed for me? None whatever, dear reader. I did not delude myself even then. Mine was the first refusal that an excessively kind fortune had ever served up to him. He was stubborn—it was a hard dish for him to swallow. Immediately, all his complacent mistresses, who I dare say may have been at least as attractive as I, became worthless and unappetizing to him. He wanted only the poor little country girl whom he had so nearly possessed, and who dared to refuse him.

"Believe me or not, Louise," he said bitterly to me once, "but you've driven me to masturbation—something I've never had occasion to practice before. Someday I'll do it before your very face, just to show you what a worm you've made of me."

If I had loved him, if he had really loved

me, I would not have allowed him to suffer so long. And perhaps if it had not been for my happy meeting with Nanette and my initiation into the harmless joys of the lesbian rite, I might not have been able to hold out against him as long as I did.

As it was, if ever his desire communicated itself to me, I had only to send a little note to Nanette and we would arrange to spend a Saturday or Sunday afternoon together—which could be done without arousing the least suspicion, since we were both of the same sex. Delicious hours we would thus spend together, experiencing again and again those divine titillations and delirious panting orgasms that defy all descriptions. Sometimes we would read to each other from an erotic book, *Gamiani*, that Nanette presented to me and which I treasure to this very day. Then, our imaginations and senses fired by the lustful tribadistic scenes between the Countess and Gamiani, we would duplicate in every manner possible the mad caresses and rubbings and tonguings described in that priceless volume.

Once, during a lull in our exquisite orgy, Nanette gave me a detailed account of her earliest sex experiences and defloration. More interesting a story even than mine it was, and I would recount it here were it not for the undue prolongation of these memoirs it would require, and the fact that I deem it an illegitimate device to put a story within a story and so annex the glamour of another. So far as she affected my own destiny however, I must record that, born in *la belle* France nineteen years ago, she had been only four years in this country. Nanette explained to me, displaying a delicacy of sentiment that is rare indeed, that though she disliked men heartily for their sexual selfishness and inadequacy, and rarely got the deep satisfaction from a fuck that love in the lesbian manner afforded her, she had nevertheless insisted on entering her mother's profession for no other reason than to keep her mother, a successful madam, from ever having to consider herself on a level lower than her daughter.

From her, I caught my first visions of the country which soon I was to adopt as my own: France—with its mellow, easygoing civilization. More particularly it was she who first turned my heart toward Paris, world's metropolis of pleasure.

In our hours together, she helped me to perfect my poor high-school French—while I reciprocated by aiding her with her already creditable English. Confusion of tongues, it will now appear, is a doubly significant expression in describing our entrancing tête-à-têtes—or *tete-a-pieds* if the reader has our delicious "sixty-nines" in mind.

All in all, no one will marvel at my Spartan restraint and ascetic conduct toward Charley, now that I have explained my enchanting relationship with Nanette. It was an unfortunate mischance, for which he paid heavily, that he had himself connived in our initial meeting. As it was, I felt quite self-sufficient in my femaleness, and taking Nanette's word for it that there was nothing nicer than what we did, I experienced only a tolerable curiosity toward what lay beneath Charley's ever-bulging trouser front.

If his state of affairs had continued much longer, who knows but that I might have become permanently and irrevocably homosexual. The sex or pleasure instinct is plastic up to a certain point only, and during that time we may sexually relate to any or all things, male, female or neuter, that give us delight. It may be one or more members of the same or opposite sex; it may be some other species of the animal kingdom; it may be a favorite fruit —banana or orange, as your sex may be. But after a while the thin strands of association become the chains and cables of habit—and then we have the so-called abnormal types, whom scientists attempt to explain by their ridiculous theories of heredity. There would be no such creatures as perverts if, at the first definite sexual awakening, the youth of both sexes could have normal assuagement for their normal desires. There would be no incurable masturbators. There would be no buggery with beasts if poor country swains could have access to some passable public woman. But again I digress. No such fate was in store for me. My senses were to remain eclectic—open to all further kinds of stimulation

Here is how it was. April or May was at hand. Sister Mary had outgrown her madonna-complex with the first pangs of childbirth. Nursing babies was not nearly the fun of making them. Scarcely two months after it nosed its way out of the spot where, nine months before, something else had nosed its way in, her child was consigned to one of those charitable institutions that make a speciality of bringing up little Jesuses, and mother proceeded to recapture her freedom. Already she was spending her time with a most dubious set of young men and women. One day, on returning home unexpectedly, I found her coming out of her bedroom in a singularly ruffled condition with an insolent young man who looked at me as if he'd like to take me in next. Soon after she began to remain away for whole nights—and before long she announced to me that she had obtained a job in the chorus of a cheap burlesque theater on Fourteenth Street. No doubt she had fucked her way to the manager, and through him to the job. But that was her affair, not mine.

Once I consented to go to the theater and watch her performance from the wings. I did not mind the vulgarity and suggestiveness of the comedians, nor the virtual undress and lascivious dancing of the girls; but what angered me was the free promiscuousness reigning backstage, by which every dirty scene-shifter considered it his privilege to make a grab for any breasts or posteriors that passed his way. Between numbers, the "straight" man nuzzled sister, the newest member of the chorus, up against a heap of scenery and proceeded, before my very eyes, to administer what I later learned is designated a "dry fuck." And later some fat, detestable individual in shirt sleeves, puffing a great cigar, actually had the temerity to accost me and put his arm about my waist. I slapped him peremptorily and he left me. At the first opportunity I asked Mary who he was.

"Oh—that greasy, cock-sucking, whore-mongering, hermaphrodite bastard there—excuse my pointing—he's the stage manager."

What a difference a little environment makes! I left sister to her tender influences and took no further interest in her theatrical career.

But events have their far-sounding echoes. Within the next few weeks, a yokel from our home town comes to the Big City. Naturally, he gravitates to Fourteenth Street. And he would have to see that very burlesque show, recognize sister from a front seat, and carry the great news to the eager inhabitants of Plattsburg.

Soon an indignant father comes to investigate. "Your sister is dead to us," he tells me in the classic manner of fathers, "but there is still a chance for you. But you must leave this wicked place, abandon your studies and come home with me immediately. Otherwise, I disown you and wash my hands of all responsibility." I refused unconditionally. He left in a great huff. I pitied him and hoped that he didn't mean his threat. But my next remittance day came without a word or a check from father. Sister packed up her chemises and left me to take up her abode in some theatrical boarding house or bawdyhouse. I was stranded on my own.

For days I made no mention of my predicament to Charley, but went on with my college work more diligently than ever. When I had been so rashly dropped by father, I had in mind, not so much Charley's standing offer as a confidence in my general ability to get along. If necessary, I thought I would fuck my way through college. But now that I was really confronted with the necessity for some action, it was not so easy.

Before long, however, Charley came out of his own engrossing misery long enough to note my serious preoccupation. He questioned me. I confessed everything. His face lit up.

"I don't want to be gloating over your misfortune, Louise," he said, "but this looks pretty much as though, in the words of the villain of the melodrama, my time has come."

"Oh, not yet, smarty!" I retorted, reassured to find his interest unabated. "I still have about fifty dollars, and with a little economizing I can make it last about ten more weeks, to the end of the term."

"Oh no you won't!" he broke in, grasping my shoulder desperately. "You're meant for better things than starving on five dollars a week. I'll put you up in the finest apartment that money can buy—and there's the five thousand that I promised you. Where's all your former broad-mindedness? I'll kill you if you say no after keeping me waiting so long!"

To prevent tragedy, I had to yield in the end. With magical rapidity, my wonderful Alladin obtained a sumptuous ready-furnished apartment facing Central Park West within 24 hours of my decision. It gave me food for thought: the happy anxiety with which he put the last touches of luxury to his love-nest, the lengths to which man will go for a little physical privilege that I would have given away gratis and without thought, if my vanity had not been brushed the wrong way. But that is just the mysterious thing about sex: it is worth to man whatever woman demands, everything or nothing. Because it is so completely unmeasurable by monetary standards, it is the one commodity that a clever woman can deal in profitably. I was learning my most important lesson—inconceivable though the whole situation still was to me whenever I considered the small significance of those few membranes that formed what Charley sought so ardently in me, my unpracticed cunt.

I had little expectation of physical pleasure— what with the example of Nanette—and awaited the fatal hour with some trepidation. My valise was packed with a supply of toilet articles, the most prominent among them being a douching syringe and some antiseptic fluid. I was going to take no unnecessary chances.

Charley calls for me in a cab. His attitude is tense to the point of cracking.

"Wait till I fuck you!" he exclaims huskily while his eyes gleam with combined love and murderousness and his hands clench and unclench. "I'll take all my months of suffering out of it at once!" But his smile allays the threat.

There is little opportunity for caresses in the carriage, though the drive is interminably long. Sometimes he slips a hand to my knee or grasps my thigh convulsively, but that is all. The afternoon is still too young to admit of more.

As we are driving up Fifth Avenue, the alignment of expensive shops reminds him of something. He reaches for his wallet and fans out ten crisp $500 bills upon my lap.

"After you've spent that," he says, "there's

plenty more. I needn't hurt your conscience. I lose that much sometimes in a day at the races."

I burst suddenly into tears.

"What is it now, Louise?" he asks anxiously.

"Oh, nothing!" I sob. "Bought and paid for—just like that! Do you think I'm a common prostitute to accept your money? I'd sooner die. Take it back. I won't accept a penny of it. Take it back at once or I'll get out at the next street! The idea of your thinking you can buy me, even with all the money in the world! If ever I give myself to a man, it will be because he loves me—not because he's rich. Have this cab stopped at once. I'm going home!"

"But Louise!" he expostulates earnestly, "dear, darling, sweet Louise! What have I done? You yourself accepted my proposition when I made it in my first enthusiasm. Do you think I would have waited so long and have lived only for this approaching moment—and now you go back on your word. Oh, believe me, Louise! I want you more than I've ever wanted anything on earth. It must be love. Yes—I love you! I love you! Now will you come with me?" And daring all the passing traffic, he takes me in his arms and comforts me with kisses. This is more like what a woman wants. I consent to go with him, I only insist that he return the money to his pocket and make no further mention of it. I could trust more to his generosity as protector than as purchaser.

At last we arrive at the gorgeous apartment-hotel that is to witness the next great adventure of my life. As we enter our own suite, breathtaking in the luxuriousness of its appointments, he says, "It is all yours Louise, for as long as you like."

Then, as the page retires, discreetly transferring the key from the outside to the inside of the door, Charley crushes me in his arms whispering hotly, "At last we are alone!"

So many times since that memorable moment have I heard this same formula pronounced by men, dear reader, that it has ceased to arouse any trepidation on my part. But that occasion was substantially my first. Charley was quite a brute of a fellow, and there was that dangerous gleam in his eyes. I was filled with terror.

What he did next did not serve in any way to allay my girlish fears, for sweeping me off my feet, he carries me in his strong arms through two intervening rooms to a richly furnished boudoir where, without ceremony, he drops me over the edge of a huge silk-counterpaned bed, where he leaves me lying.

Then, without so much as pausing to remove my cloak or shoes or any apparel of his own, he impatiently throws my skirts and petticoat up toward my face, uncovering my stockinged legs, bare thighs, and the lace edged white satin drawers which I had put on especially for this occasion. I would have demurred, but his passion-flushed countenance, the veins of his forehead standing out as if to burst, advocated nonresistance. Perhaps I had gone a bit too far in keeping him waiting so long.

No much-needed wooing does he employ to reassure me, but fumbling impatiently at my dainty close-fitting panties, he suddenly, without the least regard for the fact that they are my best pair, rips them off my waist. The frail material gives and my most intimate charms lie at his mercy.

Only for the briefest moment do his eyes light up in recognition of their beauty. Then, resuming in the fierce impatience of his desire, he proceeds at once to unstable his own part. In a flash, as if of their own accord, his trouser buttons are open. Another moment and I can see, through the tempting disorder of my clothes, his overstrained, blood-gorged bar of flesh. This burning object he rests for a moment against the soft cool flesh of my thighs, just above my garter, and still brooking no delay, he forces my legs apart, raises them about his waist, and placing my thighs about his hips, proceeds to an immediate assault.

Scarcely troubling to part the tangled silky down that protects the outposts of my unprepared cunny, he forces apart the tender lips of the cleft with the throbbing head of his fierce engine, and presses inward to the very quick. Trembling, I shut my eyes and clench my teeth, bracing myself for the rending impact to come. But no. Whether because in his lustful haste he has badly directed his battering ram, or whether because of the unusual toughness and slipperiness of my maiden membrane—certainly not because of any lack of strength, size or thickness on his part—his engine skids down through the groove and out behind me.

With a panting oath he retrieves and redirects his blind tool. Again it slides through the moist resilient lips of my part, more easily even than the first time. Perhaps this whole position, efficient enough for use on a practiced woman, would not suffice for a defloration. A third and a fourth time he repeats this unsuccessful maneuver, each time more and more confused with passion, each time more futilely.

Then suddenly, just as he entrenches for a fifth attack, ungovernable nature gets the best of him, boils over, and he reaches the ultimate fitful period of his lust. Great spurts of his scalding thick love balsam are projected into my cunny, but finding shallow reception there, splash and splatter and overflow from my vulva, leaving streaks of pearly albumen shot through my dark pubic bush, and giving most of the benefit of that generous effusion to my thighs and petticoat, which are left drenched, wet and sticky. But I am still a virgin.

Laughing almost idiotically with the extremity of his relief and pleasure, as well as at the humor of his contretemps, he releases my thighs, and falling to the bed beside me, embraces me happily.

"Serves me right for being such an impetuous beast. But you can't expect a starving man to use his best table manners, can you? Well, I'm glad it didn't work. Now I still have it before me to do." He dries his still dripping member on a silk pocket handkerchief. Out of the corner of my eye I watch fearfully, and I can see that it is still stiff and upstanding—only its excessive redness has vanished with the partial subsidence of his blood, and now its column is white as polished ivory—only the full rounded head retaining its ruby sensitive shade.

Reaching for a fine soft linen towel, he next

gently mops up from my thighs the vital liquid that is still purling in little rills down to the valley of my buttocks.

Then, immediate urgency postponed by his so recent little snack, he leisurely does the many little things he had before in his desperate haste omitted.

Temporarily sacrificing the view of my bare thighs and center, he helps me to my feet and removes my street-cloak. On his knees, he reaches up beneath my perfumed petticoat, and disentangling my garters from my silk stockings, draws the latter slowly downward, relishing with his hands each inch of my smooth bare skin as it is uncovered.

I seat myself on the edge of the bed while he embraces my legs and places repeated kisses upon my satiny dimpled knees. For its added piquancy, he decides to let me retain a short enchanting white silk slip that I wear next to my body; but this is little protection for me or impediment to him: his hands take added delight in violating its territory, now reaching up under it to judge of the texture of my thighs, now forcing a hand down its bosom to weigh or admire a full blooming luscious breast. Withal though, he is now so kind and tender to me that I would needs be inhuman to long withhold forgiveness of his earlier flattering brutality.

Having me thus undressed to the precise extent of his taste, he forsakes me a moment to remove his own clothes, which he does with that quick expectant impatience which only the win' of love can lend. He returns, entirely nude, and I forget myself in admiration of his glowing manly form.

Imagine, all you my female readers, a handsome broad-shouldered Apollo, his whole body of that healthy suntanned hue which proclaims that boudoir sports are not the only pastimes he engages in. A magnificent chest, rippling with little muscles here and there, its wide expanse rescued from monotony by two delightful little pink-brown paps of which our own too generous breasts, though beloved of the opposite sex, are but a travesty. Then the strong downward sweep of his spare, well-exercised manly abdomen, this in turn relieved by the depression of the navel: below which trails a path of fine tendrils, leading the eye irresistibly downward to that meeting place of his strong athletic thighs where a thick growth of light golden pubic hairs marks the root of that important male equipment which I must now take another breath to describe.

Rising proudly from its cozy nest, a relentless column of what might just as well be bone as flesh, so hard and unbending does it appear, is that terrible engine for my undoing, the male reaper that is soon to crop my maiden flower, balanced at its base by a full tightly puckered bag, which I know is the reservoir of those liquid sweets he will soon pour into me. The ruby knob that crowns its outstanding length curves slightly upward, as if in additional assurance of its undrooping power, and as its stiff majesty vibrates with excitement, it seems to shake its head fiercely toward me as if to say, "Let me at her!"

He approaches and clears the ground for ac-

tion by stripping the luxurious bed of all super-
fluous covering, leaving only the sheets and
pillows. He throws himself beside me, and
trusses my silk slip up to my very chin; but
before he can take me in his arms, he must
needs tuck away that insolent bar that wards
me off by levering it up with sheer force and
laying it between my soft belly and his, where,
by its heavy pressure, it keeps me continually
reminded of the sore operation awaiting me.
Now he diverts me, like a dentist who will
say, "That tooth doesn't need extraction. Let
me see it," and before you know it, he ex-
hibits your molar between the forceps that
he has concealed in his sleeve with that intention all the time; only Charley employs for
that purpose the blandishment of hot tonguing
kisses, first on my mouth, then on my breasts.

Now his burning hands wander afield, over
my sensitive back and posteriors and velvety
thighs. He massages my mount with a vigorous caress of his hot palm, his fingers comb
through the silky hairs and set up a funny little
tingling in that area. He is restraining his impatience admirably—and impatient he is, as is
evidenced by the throbbing of his member
against my abdomen. At last his fingers gravitate to my Arcadian valley, find the little
hairy spot, and dance upon it a delightful
rhythm that instantly electrifies all my senses.
It is characteristic of the omnipotence of this
little thing that rules woman's desiny that
soon my terrors are mixed with soft desires—
and as my desires increase, my fears become
less acute and soon I pant for food more solid

386

than his fingers. I throw my legs apart, inviting him to do his worst.

He does not delay, but coming between my thighs and spreading them wider, immediately applies the point of his instrument to the narrow slit, parting the lips with one hand, and guiding his bar with the other into the rosy chink. Then, with unrestrained vigor, he employs the entire weight of his body to hammer up his entering wedge. But again stubborn nature—or faulty technique—intervenes. He slips. His baffled engine flies up from my cunny and lays panting with exertion on my heaving belly.

A moment he considers, his face, already flushed with passion, turning a deeper red with shame for his repeated failures. Apparently this is a case calling for a surgeon or an engineer, not for an impetuous lover.

The next time he proceeds more carefully. Placing a pillow beneath me to obtain an elevation more favorable than the natural plumpness of my buttocks afford, he once more brings his weapon to bear upon the target. Now he opens the pouting lips of my moist slit, still lubricated by his recent emission as well as by involuntary secretions of its own. He plants the head of his ram within, looks, feels, is not yet satisfied with my position, has me draw up my thighs higher, retrenches lower down in the softest, moistest part of my fortress, and then, lunges fiercely inward.

For a tense, fearful moment, the membrane of my brave maidenhead strains and tautens, but holds him back. Then suddenly it gives beneath the furious pressure of that bone-hard

gristle, collapsing, tearing, rending the heretofore lifelong faithful closure of those parts,
and causing me, like many another bride, to
cram my upturned silk slip into my mouth to
keep from screaming out with the sharp, unendurable agony.

All thoughts of pleasure flee my mind, all
vestiges of it leave my body. I am just a poor
miserable mistreated little girl. I wish I had
never met a man. Would that I were home with
mother. My eyes fill with anguished tears.

The cruel torture is not yet over. He has
gained only the partial insertion of his thick
member. Scarcely the whole of its throbbing
head is within the wound. But Charley is too
far gone, too inflamed with passion and with
his partial triumph, to have regard for my
tearful entreaties to desist. There is nothing to
do but stifle my sobs and set myself to endure more.

With glistening eyes and determined mien,
he scarcely troubles to conceal his exaltation,
but resumes the onslaught, following up his
advantage with another ferocious stroke. Inch
by inch, thrust by thrust, he forcibly deepens
the gap which till now has never seen light of
day or part of man. Every bit of the way is
blocked by the close adherence of the sides of
the soft passage—while his member, stubbornly or with excessive pride, only seems to swell
thicker and harder at the proximity of the
close tight membranes, thus increasing even
further the difficulty of progress.

My dear murderer—what could I expect—is
blind to my sufferings and deaf to my prayers.
If he pauses now, it is to relish the warm

constriction that closely grasps the half of his weapon, and not to alleviate my unbearable pain.

Then suddenly, lashed on by passion to end all dallying and strike to the root of things, he throws his whole force into one tremendous shove. The last chaste resistance of those parts is overcome, and as the final union of those membranes is split apart, his hard thick instrument crashes home to the hilt and I faint dead away.

When I come to a moment later, he is moving back and forth within me—more easily now, for though the sheath is still tight and painful, my kind womb has welcomed the bulky intruder with a gush of soft mucous fluid that oils and smooths the tender passage and enables him to slip in and out without inflicting further injury. I sigh with relief that the worst is past, that the "gem for which men dig but to destroy" is no longer mine to excite their envy and assaults. Like a patient recovering from serious surgery, I do not mind the minor after-pains—as now, oh how I wince as he pushes his point vigorously homeward till his very pubic bone presses against the so recently taken gates of my tender citadel. Thank God—he now lets up that forceful pressure to draw out again. But oh—how empty and forlorn I feel inside, as that substantial cylinder of flesh leaves me—and how glad I am now when he returns and fills that aching void within me!

In terms of such successive contradictions do my thoughts run as he continues his teasing game of come and go. A strange warm tingling begins at those places and at such times as his part is in contact with me. Soon I find myself unconsciously raising my hips to meet his thrusts, or following up to baffle his withdrawals, my cunt clinging to him to prolong the increasingly pleasant meeting.

Suddenly my clitty, till now prostrate, springs into action—and what my vagina loses temporarily, he makes certain to get. So this is nature's divine plan, this delicious rhythmic alternation of happy sensations till they coalesce or blend together in one overpowering ecstasy.

With this goal in mind, I wrap my legs tightly about his loins and exert all my powers to speed up the tempo of this ineffable in-and-out motion—to make of the kiss of the vagina and the kiss of the clitoris one melting gorgeous experience. I learn quickly. Charley's eyes dilate with unspeakable love and gratefulness for my quick responsiveness.

Now we work together in delightful unison, my heave meeting his every thrust, each sweet cadenced collision being marked by the deep sharp exhalations of our breath as if by a metronome. But soon our divine transports become too violent to observe any such measured order, and now, sobbing and moaning, I writhe about in all directions, madly wishing only to retain within me that dear object which could not now be too large for my taste or endurance were it to fill every orifice and cavity in my body simultaneously.

With desperate fury Charley continues his plunging motion howsoever he can, grasping my buttocks with his hands and straining me closer to steady me, to restrain me—but in vain. I sob, I cry, "Oh! Oh! I can't stand this! Oh! Stop! No—keep on! Faster—or I die!" I throw my hands wildly about, now fitfully brushing my hair back from my fevered face, now futilely trying to push him away from me, now drawing him madly closer. I am utterly beside myself with the unbearable fires running through my veins, with the stinging spur of pleasure, when suddenly, Charley, who has himself been falling considerably out of step with his own exertions and bed-quaking gasps of approaching dissolution, drives forcibly up my burning quivering cunt with a final dispatching thrust as if he would wedge his whole dear body up into me, or as if it were necessary to pass entirely through that way to gain access to that kingdom of heaven which is now about to be his.

At the same time, torrents of his warm elixir pour into me with such explosive hydraulic violence as to cause him to recoil. My so recently ravished membranes are bathed and flooded, soothed and titillated by this tremendous inspersion of hot ejaculate as it pours into me. Convulsively my cunny closes about its soul-stirring visitor and bids him stay, while with frenzied anxious thrusts of my own upon the beloved bar that impales me, I hurry on to that dear crucial joy, that excess of pleasure which was delayed in me by the earlier excess of pain. A moment later I add my delicious return to his. All my body and soul, melted into a fluidescent state by all these insupportable firings and frictionings, pours down to that one vital part which of all of me alone remains. My eyes roll back in ecstasy. I pass away into that delirious momentary death caused by unendurable agonies of supreme pleasure, by floods of unbearable bliss.

In rapturous transports of indescribable delight I writhe and cry hysterically. I must have fainted away with the violent joy, for the next thing I remember is Charley, withdrawn from my body, comforting me and hushing my little sobs with kind assurances, with a look of unutterable love in his eyes. I move my still involuntarily quivering form just to prove to myself that I have lived through the delightful danger, then fall into the delicious languor that follows the honest exertions of love.

When at last I arose and examined myself, I found my part, the gash that never heals, glowing a deeper red than ever it had been. As I stood, a tiny stream of thick pearly drops trickled down the inner side of my thighs, streaked here and there, like opals, with the pink of my virgin blood. I had indeed lost forever the jewel that cannot be lost twice.

Excusing myself, I went off to the bathroom adjoining, to tend to a little personal need as well as to wash away the various marks of the fray. The fittings of this place exceeded in luxury and sumptuousness my most colored imaginings, and I would have been willing to live the rest of my life in that room alone. Carefully I douched my newly accessible vagina with the chemical solution I had brought—in order to plasmolyze any of the semen left within me and render harmless the millions of reproductive germs with which it was teeming. For the benefit of the curious let me report that although this method of avoiding conception is not a hundred percent certain, and if relied on solely over a great number of intercourses may fail in time, as the avid womb frequently sucks up the warm streaming love balsam immediately as it is injected—yet, as time showed, I was not "caught." Later, I exercised the additional precaution of employing a so-called French pessary, a little soft rubber cap which blocks the tiny mouth of the womb and altogether avoids the possible mishap I have just referred to. However, since girls and women who have never given birth to offspring possess very minute openings into the womb, the douche alone is substantially efficacious.

After attending to this essential detail of protective hygiene, and feeling greatly refreshed thereby, I decided to take a hurried bath in the luxurious inlaid bathtub—if only to linger in this delightful place awhile longer. Anyway, as I discovered on peeping through the door, Charley, in dressing gown, was engaged in delivering a complicated dinner order to a liveried attendant whom he had rung for.

I had scarcely filled the tub with water from the silvered faucets and stepped into its soothing warmth, when Charley, impatient of my return, violates all conventional rights to privacy and comes in after me. And noting what I am engaged in, he suddenly becomes interested and laughingly offers to wash my back.

Of course, I ordered him out; but my indignation was not great—although, indeed, my male readers may not believe me when I say that I still retained a considerable vestige

393

of modesty, even after what had taken place. I had worn a slip, you will remember, in the bedroom. And anyway, a woman will do things and overlook things during the moments of passion that she will shrink from and deny at all other times.

He washed my back. And, though I really blushed to let him do it, he washed my front too, soaping and fondling my breasts till the tiny rosebuds that crowned them sprang into erectness—and declaring that portion of me the divinest part of the divinest woman he had ever seen. Then, suddenly deciding that he would like to be closer to me, he throws off his dressing gown and slips into the capacious bath beside me.

Oh, what rapture was ours in that double warmth of ourselves and of the hot water—as we rubbed our generously lathered bodies together and experienced that dreamy, creamy contact of skin against skin. With gentle compulsion he leads my hand to his center part, now, of course, fine and upstanding with the excitement of our singular embraces. I can just barely make my fingers meet about its thick majestic column. And to think that had just been in me! A delightful little shiver of wonder and awe goes up my spine.

From here, to complete my acquaintance with that manly equipment which is to figure so largely in these memoirs, he directs my fearful fingers lower. Here I cannot help but find the capacious treasure-bag that is the source of love's generous liquid sweets. Its skin is flexible and tender as fine chamois—and within there play about two firm but elusive balls, each the size of a small egg, that evade all but the lightest pressure from without. These are the parts that correspond to the ovaries in woman. The scrotum or bag is merely analogous to a womb turned inside out.

With boyish pride, Charley parts the hairs from the root of his instrument to display its full unhidden length. This he makes me measure by spanning with my outstretched hand—then he asks me to mark off the equivalent distance up from my cunny, to show how far into me he must get. A span and a half, if you must know, dear reader—and that reached so high between my breasts, that I must warn you that all this was inaccurate anatomy, in that no internal curves are taken into consideration.

It is only a short step from exhibition to demonstration, dear reader. What with our mutual toyings and dallyings and fondlings, what with his insistence that I soap his standing staff and see how easily it slides through my clenched fist—and what with his own little investigations into my personal topography, it was not long before we were confronted with the necessity for choosing between the hard bathtub or the soft bed again. It was with difficulty that I was able to postpone him enough to make it the latter. With my own hurried impatience scarcely less than his now, we dry ourselves quickly. Then, still in a boasting mood, Charley, stopping only to anoint his part with some sweet smelling pomade, crouches a moment before me as I stand, and bringing the head of his glistening member to the lips of my cunny, sends it home with a single continuous motion as he raises himself. Then, clasping me tightly in his arms, and instructing me to wrap my legs about his waist, he bears me triumphantly thus spitted upon his cock, into the bedroom and lays me down upon the couch of our recent consummation without losing his advantage for a moment.

Then follows a reengagement in that sweet conflict which of all battles men fear the least and women soon come to love the most. For such a delicious eternity is he this time able to keep up in the divine duel, that I come twice to his once, putting myself thus irrevocably in his indebtedness. Oh how I worshiped his strong maleness, when, as I recovered from the exquisite spasms of my first thrill, I found him still moving vigorously within me, slowing down his firm piston-plunging only for a moment, as during the height of the crisis the muscles of my cunny tightened about him with steely deathlike rigidity—and then picking up speed till my cries of protest against the unendurability of these supreme titillations changed to delighted moans for more!

And then, what an incomparable experience when, as finally I could judge by his irregular breathing, his own time was approaching, I tensed and strained my nerves and senses and employed every instinctive subtlety of movement to keep up with him! The rippling of our respective sensations spread and gathered force, spread and overlapped till we both were sucked into the resulting whirlpool of frenzied pleasure.

"Do you love me, Louise?" he gasped with his last slow, subsiding thrust. Did I love him? When my whole body was quivering and my womb melting in helpless abject adoration for him? I told him so—in a small tremulous voice. He hushed my last moans of pleasure with a deep soul-imbibing kiss.

"Oh, that was great!" he tells me, still breathless, as he removes his tongue from my mouth, but not his wagon-tongue from my lower mouth. "I could go on loving you forever. Over and over again, and nothing else. Again, Louise darling, may I?" My wide adoring eyes granted him permission. I was his, I could refuse him nothing. And I was not averse even to dying if from an excess of this blissful godlike communion.

He begins again; but now I am witness to a phenomenon since then more familiar to me. His rampant stalwart soldier, even as he moves and spurs him on to action, begins shrinking within me, my whole dripping vagina collapsing upon it with the removal of its distention. He pushes desperately inward. It curls up in quiet rebellion. He pulls back for another charge. His man tumbles out of the trench altogether.

Shamefacedly he pinches and prods and massages his infantryman to wake him to a realization of his duty. He shoulders him toward the scene of battle and concentrates all the weight of his forces to shove him on. But he crumples underfoot, and much as Charley sweats and grinds against him, there is nothing tangible between us. The once valiant, blood-gorged part is now a soft shriveled little bud--"a cold, bloodless worm," as Charley perhaps too unkindly calls it.

I laughed and laughed at Charley's humorou:
chagrin. "Da! da! da!" I said to his shrink
ing coward, supporting him on the palm of one
hand and striking him lightly across the face
with the forefinger of my other hand. In dul
resentment, it started up from its lethargy a1
this taunt by a lady. Fitfully, and pulsating
with the reawakened beat of his blood it thick-
ened and rose to a still somewhat drooping
state of semierection. Playfully I pressed open
its red little mouth. "It's sick," I said. "Don't
you see, it's tongue is white"—for sure enough,
it was dribbling a bit of whitish fluid. But at
this insult—or perhaps because of my naive
handling, it suddenly springs to full attention,
as if to belie my words.

"There you are!" Charley exclaims exultant-
ly, "I didn't think he'd lay down on the job
so soon—especially after waiting so long for a
peck at you. Come, Louise."

But his triumph is short-lived. No sooner do
I withdraw my supporting hand than the subject under discussion doubles up and retires
once more.

"He's all tired out," I say softly. "Let him
rest awhile—and perhaps later—"

Yes, later, dear reader. After a refreshing,
not to say stimulating meal, served to us in
our room, we retired together for the night.
Not to sleep however, until twice more we had
successfully wooed and won the delights of
Eros.

When I awoke next day, it was nearly noon.
Charley had gone out to buy me some clothes.

On my pillow was pinned a sweet little note,
advising me that he would return soon. I lay

abed lazily, deliciously reviewing the ecstasies of the preceding night, not at all regretting the new estate of real womanhood that was at last mine.

A knock on the boudoir door, and a pretty, neat young mulatto maid entered with a dainty breakfast tray for me. She had been engaged for Madame's personal service, she told me in a refined, sweet voice. Soon we were acquainted. As she helped me out of bed for my morning bath, she noticed some bloodstains on the sheets. I blushed at these telltale traces; but Clementine immediately burst into tears. It reminded her of her own similar downfall, she confessed, sobbing. And I wondered whether I would shed tears at the recollection of the loss of this much wept-for virginity. To date, not yet, dear reader.

CHAPTER THIRTEEN

Time passed. Apart from school hours, when I still affected simplicity, I became a grand lady. As I guessed, Charley made a generous protector. His resources were unlimited. And being sprung from a father who has gone down in history not only as a financier but also as a woman fancier, he had little need to hide me away or relegate our meetings to back rooms. In fact, our liaison took on as much of a social as a personal aspect, and many a theater party, cotillion and society hunt did we attend together. Of course, I was not accepted without some qualifications. Most of the young women missed no opportunity to display their dislike for me in their usual catty manner—flattering me, as it were, by considering me a dangerous rival for the possession, legal or illegal, of the highly desirable Charley. Needless to say, however, I was immensely popular with the opposite and less prejudiced sex.

Charley showed very little jealousy. On the

contrary, he seemed to take a definite pleasure in having me dress as attractively and suggestively as possible, thus arousing the admiration and envy of his friends. Then, my value reenhanced by such factors and a new luster cast upon me by the gleaming eyes of other men, he would rush me home to our apartment and love me with an ardor renewed to better than new. This is the only way I can explain the phenomenon of our affair enduring as long as it did. Permanence of love is the one thing I disbelieve in most. If Cleopatra herself had given her love unstintedly to Marc Antony for from two to five times a night—and that, almost every night of the week—even she, queen among women as she was, would soon have been tired of him. The certainty that, should he drop me, I could now succeed him with almost any male out of his circle—for even his dad, a naughty widower whom I met, would have gladly taken his son's place by my side—must have put him doubly on his mettle.

I finished my first year of college successfully, but not on the merit of any work I had done in these last six weeks or so. The summer vacation luckily intervened to relieve me for a time of the increasing burden of my double life.

I resided at the apartment all alone, except for my maid Clementine, and except for the evenings or nights that Charley spent with me. Yes—"spent" with me. A number of times I received visits during the day from my darling Nanette, and that relieved me of any strain it might have been to live continently till the evening brought Charley and more solid satisfaction. What with visits to modistes and milliners, what with the reading of exotic literature which already had captured my interest, my days passed pleasantly enough. Already I was savoring the life of the deluxe courtesan—days spent leisurely preparing and priming oneself for the night's more delirious joys.

The month of August, which is far hotter in New York than here in Paris, Charley and I spent at Newport, an exclusive summer rendezvous of wealthy society. That month was one endless, breathless round of pleasure: fetes and functions, boat races and yacht parties. During this time I added continually to my poise and sophistication, learned to drink exhilarating liquors like a lady, and made many valuable friends that I was to profit from later on in life.

Nor were the more tender joys omitted. The bracing salt sea air was a continual aphrodisiac. Also, a change of background for one's fucking is almost as piquant as a change of partner—and Charley was refreshingly original in picking various unusual places to indulge our desires in. Besides the privacy of his or my hotel room—we engaged two just for appearances—besides a few times in the woods and once in a canoe, he had the daring once to tousle me deliciously while we lay under a blanket in two adjacent deck chairs one moonlit night at a friend's yacht party, for all that there were scores of other couples seated around, singing, playing string instruments, and mildly fondling each other. The danger of discovery, the utter unprecedented madness and wickedness of it, made this one of the keenest, most poignant and thrilling sex experiences I have ever had. The people around merely served to accentuate our sense of aloneness together, while at the same time our sense of propriety lashed us on to a more furious and concentrated consummation by reminding us of the actual risk. How fortunate that the sweet romantic accompaniment of the music burst into louder tones in time to disguise Charley's gasp and my own little moans, which, clench my teeth as I would, I could not entirely stifle.

Another similarly precarious and delicious adventure took place one time at a fancy dress ball when he asked me to sit through a dance with him out on the lawn. Here in a little garden bower, with guests promenading not ten feet away, he raised my skirts and had me sit upon his lap while he entered my vagina from behind. Another couple, in search of privacy, perhaps for the same purpose, came upon us without warning; but our attitudes seemed harmless enough, my dress was down in front, and kind shadows concealed any incriminating detail. They went away apologizing. Bending forward a trifle to bring my clitoris in closer contact with his part we finished off together, to the tune of a delicious, dreamy waltz that was wafted to us from the house.

To all you readers who cannot understand the exquisite joy of such things, I can only say, "try it." The summertime is the time for all lovers, amateur or professional, to come out of their stuffy, cowardly little bedrooms and make for nature's open places. Sensual love and nature's beauties are too closely related to be kept apart. In the winter, your dwelling and your fireplace attempt to duplicate the summer; but when that blessed season comes, why continue with your outseasoned makeshift? To the wood and the fields and the parks, I say, all you lovers! The police? Oh, fuck the police!

Our maddest lark of all however, was one afternoon when, while bathing in the sea at low tide, Charley suddenly developed the desire to possess me then and there, underwater. He confessed that all his life he had been curious to find whether it could be done, but heretofore had not met a girl with spirit enough to attempt it with him. I was not loathe. My own tastes were becoming more and more exotic, more and more strongly developed. I was always ready for it—and unlike men, always able. Furthermore, my own natural desire for knowledge, if not experience, made me wonder too what it would be like. Drawing off some distance from the rest of the bathers, and standing in water up to our armpits, he untied the string that upheld the lower part of my bathing suit, in order to put himself to me. Some difficulty was encountered in that the water, though not actually cold, was yet too cool to allow of his retaining full stiffness easily. By rubbing it between my thighs for a moment however he soon restored its full stature for long enough to hasten it into a warmer place. On being spread open, my vagina immediately filled with water, the displaced air breaking to the surface in little bubbles. His member looked humorously fat and distorted as seen through the intervening water, seeming to bend in one crazy angle, now in another, with the slight wash of the waves and the consequent refraction of light. Its entry into me was not easily accomplished, for the water washed away the more external lubricants of my cunt and shrank the flesh of the outer lips. Then again, there was the water within that part that had to be gently displaced. I must confess, it felt rather cold and clammy at first and a chill that was not quite pleasant went through my innards. But soon the addition of his bodily heat to mine thawed out that area and with arms clasped about each other's waists we proceeded to a vigorous execution of the requisite movements that soon made things warmer still.

It seems that I had the best of the arrangement, for my own sexual organs being most internal, and only indirectly affected by the water, it was not long before I came. A sharp, rather brief thrill it was—very nice, but mostly localized. Charley however, his love reservoir being entirely exposed, was considerably retarded. When after over half an hour's exhausting work, he told me his own climax was coming, I had had no less than three separate little shooting thrills. I tensed myself to join him at the end—both of us writhing so vigorously as to churn the water about us into froth. As it was, I reached my orgasm just a moment before him and he, coming at last, collapsed with the delicious relief, lost his footing and slipped out of me into the water. Laughingly I dragged him up to the surface, else he might casually have drowned in all that prostrating pleasure. His thick love-juices, plentified by their lengthy generation, shot into the water and rose to the surface in a sort of coagulated mass that resembled, must I say it, a great sprawling sea-nettle. It took an hour of rest on the sunny sand beach before Charley was at all recovered, and he ruefully complained of a stiff back for days after. All in all, it was one of those experiences, nice enough while it lasted, and certainly worth trying once; but more pleasant and stimulating in retrospect than in the actuality.

With such disporting and broadening experiences, the summer flew by. "Did all this dissipation affect my health?" the anxious reader asks. Yes, dear friends, most favorably. I gained weight. The last slight angularities of adolescence passed away. I blossomed forth with increased vigor of mind and body. From an attractive girl I became a beautiful woman.

And I never said no to Charley—just as I have said no so very few times to men since him. Realizing that the relations between the sex organs and the mind or nervous center can awaken the sex parts, I acknowledged no period of necessary quiescence. I knew that just around the corner from the most indifferent lassitude and satiation lay awaiting the unceasing possibilities for more body-rousing, nerve-electrifying, and soul-stirring delights. The fact that I feel sex-surfeited at any particular moment does not dictate how I will feel after a few kisses and fondlings, a caress of my clitty, or the slow invasion of my cunny by some staunch masculine charmer. "All right then, we'll try it once more." Now surely I have had enough. But now I am turning the pages of my *Perfumed Garden* or my *Horn*

Book, and here is a new position we have never tried. I wonder how it works out, what it feels like. I try to visualize it. My clitty becomes interested, concerned, anxious. We take to the bed and go down for another round! In this manner is life lived to the fullest. There is only one life—and there is no joy comparable to the delights of love. For those women who are not so fortunate as I in being sensually matured at so early an age, I can only say that even if it takes years, awakening will come quickest with persistent utilization of the sexual faculties. And in the meanwhile, a comforting thought—if such extra compensation should be necessary—would be these words that I quote from the letters of Mlle. Gaussen, a French actress: "It costs us so little, and gives so much pleasure to men . . . "

I repeat: I never said no to Charley. Strangely perhaps, though he was a lion for varying postures to exercise the age-old connecting passion, his grammar of love was limited to the conjugation of "cock" and "cunt." If he had asked for more, I am sure I would not have refused him. The requirement for some degree of modesty alone restrained me from myself suggesting other innovations that occurred to me once in awhile.

Even during my monthly disabilities, I did not discourage his advances. Taking only added care in my personal cleanliness, I allowed him to love me even in that slight blood which he had deigned himself to draw on that night he took my virgin flower. I enjoyed intercourse as much at such times as at any. Even more so—because of the added sensitivity of my feminine organs; and by removing the major conventional disability of my periods, I eliminated that depressed sexless feeling which all women feel during their monthlies because their parts are all packed away and *hors de combat*. When fucking is so delicious, can any woman afford to throw away one-sixth of her life by respecting a useless outgrown taboo? And if she loves a man and wants his faithfulness, can she reasonably hope to check his hot ungovernable desires for four or five full days and nights of every month? Most certainly not.

But to get on with my account. In September school reopened. Of course, my tuition was taken care of—Charley insisting on opening a small bank account to my credit—and I got down to the serious work of the second term. Human dissection, much as I had looked forward to it, turned out to be a form of butchery that I could go through with only with the greatest difficulty. We are all accustomed to seeing, and perhaps handling or eating the dead bodies of rabbits, fish and fowl. But when it came to maiming and slicing the remains of my own humankind, it was quite different. The hand of even a corpse is a human hand—associated with the hands of living persons—and I just couldn't develop the impersonal attitude necessary for the pursuit of this work. It was beyond my comprehension how my careless classmates could snatch up a half-mangled corpse and do a lightsome jig with it around the laboratory. And the attendant who had charge of the "stiffs," a peculiar pasty-faced young fellow of about 28 who appeared to have himself absorbed all the characteristics of a corpse except immobility, guessing my squeamishness, seemed to take especial grim pains to arrange revolting tableaux for my benefit—placing the stiff in the most horrible and grotesque attitudes, or nosing through a scrap bucket to find some revolting gross specimen to display. And then, when at the end of a long day's work I went home, I found myself so completely pervaded by the pungent odor of the formaldehyde that the stiffs were preserved in that three successive baths and a complete change of lingerie would not get rid of it and I had to resort to the most arrant perfumery.

October—November—December—I gritted my teeth and held on. Once or twice Charley was compelled to suggest to me, gently of course, that I was not so loving to him as I had been, that my morbid work was killing my spirit and that I ought to drop medicine and accept womanhood as a sufficient career in itself. I was sorely tempted; his argument was unanswerable, but my pride would not allow me to quit so easily.

Early one evening during the Christmas adjournment, I received a message from the medical school hospital. During the year thus far, though I had been anxious to get a female stiff to dissect, only male subjects had been available. I had, however, put in a standing application for the purchase of a female, whenever obtainable, and had forgotten all about it. Now, it seems, they had for me the body of a young female nullipara (one who had never given birth to a child) who had died the day before in the free ward from self-administered poisoning. It had been sent down to our dissecting room prior to autopsy, awaiting my inspection.

Knowing how careless the authorities were in such matters and anxious to arrange at once for the proper embalmment of the subject, I excused myself from an unimportant theater date with Charley, telling him what turned up and advising that I would probably have to spend the whole evening supervising the preservation of the cadaver. He shrugged his shoulders disgustedly.

"You're beginning to give me the willies, Louise," he said. "If you don't cut out that graveyard work soon and resign, I'll just have to see your dean and have you expelled for some cause or another—say immoral conduct."

I hastened to the school. Except for a few charwomen cleaning the main hallway, the building was deserted. Down to the basement dissecting rooms I went, feeling little shivers of fear that somehow reminded me of the similar nocturnal excursion of the heroine in Mark Twain's *The Gilded Age*. Luckily, there were some dim lights on in all the corridors and the janitor or watchman, I thought, ought to be around someplace. Surely enough, there was a light on at the end of the hallway in our laboratory. But all was deathly silent, except for the low humming of some dynamos in the cellar.

It was all so eerie—this same building which during class hours was so bustling and noisy. I approached the doorway and peered in. Thank God, there was someone in there. Only it was the detestable caretaker. I held back.

There was a stiff on my dissecting table and he was in the act of removing the canvas sheet that enwrapped it. Something stealthy in his manner compelled me to slip behind the door that stood ajar to see what he was about. The powerful droplight that hung over the table illuminated everything in vivid detail.

The figure was entirely uncovered. It was that of a girl of about twenty, beautifully proportioned as a Phidias statue of Venus, and of a stark whiteness, accentuated by the glare of the light, which alone belied her aliveness. Immediately all thought of the horror of death left me. There was a peace and repose in that form that sleep alone could never give to one who labored still in life's fitful fever. Only her hair contradicted the perfection of this impression, for, uncut and in the original disarray of her recent death, it hung loosely about her cheeks and shoulders and lay scattered behind her like that of a nymph captured and dragged forcibly through the woods by a satyr on rapine bent.

Even the crude caretaker stands for a moment in awe of this cold, beautiful spectacle; then, to my deep surprise, he passes his hands caressingly down her flanks and thighs, leans over and kisses her breasts! But a far more violent shock is in store for me. He draws down the lower half of the unresisting figure till her thighs project over the edge of the table, then, forcibly separates her legs, rigid in her demise. Even at this point I could not believe that he was really intending that which he was then about. Perhaps only a morbid curiosity led him to examine the anatomy of this statuesque corpse—legitimate enough, since I myself attended school for just that purpose But a moment later, with a nervous, furtive glance about him, he whips out his sex organ and applies it to the cold insensate slit . . .

I was frozen with horror. Surely this was some mad hallucination I was suffering from; certainly, no such vile desecration could find expression anywhere other than in my imagination! He had forced his ingress—and now as he shoved violently in and out in his demonic possession, the white body vibrated with a grotesque mechanical stiffness. I turned and fled.

"Ghoul! Corpse violator!" I wanted to scream at him—but one who would commit such a revolting crime as I had witnessed would not stop at the murder of his discoverer. Breathlessly I ran up the stairs and out of the building. The pervading smell of formaldehyde that was always present in the laboratory and that in the past months I had been getting slowly accustomed to, now seemed to pursue me into the street with a renewed nauseating vividness. For two blocks I continued running to get away from it, filling my lungs again and again with the crisp, frosty night air to revive myself. Only when I regained control of my nerves and felt assured that I would not be seized with a vomiting spell did I venture to take a cab back to the apartment.

"Misfortunes never come singly," is an old saw that I would much like to see retired from the body of man's platitudinous knowledge. They're twice as likely to come singly as doubly. However, it is true to a certain extent that sustaining one stroke of ill fortune makes one extra susceptible to the recognition of a second which otherwise might have been overlooked entirely. But wait . . .

Riding home in the cab, I revolved the horrors of the past few minutes in my mind. I was sick to death of the whole ill-smelling graveyard of medical science. I had wanted to learn life, but not from corpses. Rather would I pry with my bare hands in the bowels of a living sensate person, and hurt and pity, then touch my scalpel to the empty mockery of a dead person's shell. One thing was now certain: I could not go back to that dissecting room, to that table, and work under that same cruel leering light, perhaps on the same dead girl.

Wearily I climbed up the stairs to our apartment, unwilling to be seen even by the elevator boy in my present disturbed condition. I had to rest my head against the doorpost to collect sufficient strength and steadiness to insert my key in the lock. I entered the sitting room. There was no one there. The lights were out. I was just about to call Clementine to help me off with my things when her voice, coming from my boudoir, arrested me.

"No—please sir—not here—not now! Mistress may return at any moment and catch us. Won't you wait and come around in the afternoon sometime again when mistress is at school? It would mean my discharge if she found us here."

"Discharge, hell! Who do you think pays the bills around here?" I blanched. Was this another hallucination? It was Charley's voice.

He went on. "Come on kid. Let's knock it

413

off now. Your mistress won't be back for hours yet. Here, have some champagne. Now, to the bed with you, and do your stuff!"

I could not believe my ears. If Charley had been lying to me every time he told me so earnestly that I was the only woman on earth that he wanted, I would simply—well, I would simply lose all faith in men.

Silently I trod over the heavily-rugged floors and approached my room, to verify, to disclose myself and sever all relations with him immediately. With no intention of eavesdropping, I stood boldly in the open doorway; but unable to master any words to express my indignation, I merely remained stationed there, waiting for them to see me. Clementine was on her back on the bed—my bed—her eyes closed and her hips wriggling expectantly, or perhaps in prelininary practice. Charley had his back toward me, and was so busy uncovering the mulatto wench that even if he had been facing my way he would not have seen me. Up went her white apronette and skirt, disclosing her lithe but substantial thighs, encased in black silk stockings up to the garter, and above that bare flesh that would easily pass for white.

Not satisfied with unveiling her to the waist (the little hussy wore no underwear) he rolls up her dress to her very chin. Reluctantly, I had to admit to myself that her figure was not bad. Her breasts, if anything, appeared firmer and more outstanding than mine, more conical than round, coming to two sharp pointed peaks that betokened unusually good pectoral muscles and lent a sort of fetching impertinence. Except for the region around her nipples, which was of a typically Negroid shade, her skin was only a trifle more tanned than that of the average white woman. Her pubic hair too, seemed thicker and darker and less silky than that of a Caucasian.

But my faithful Charley does not give me much time for either reflection or observation. Drawing his weapon forthwith, not wasting time for fondling or kissing (somewhat to my relief), he takes up his position at the breach. Then, with a tremendous shove, as if thinking perhaps of the difficulty he had with my maidenhead, he charges fiercely inward. But if he flattered himself that there were obstacles to overcome, he must have been sadly disappointed—for he falls in as suddenly and completely. as if he had stepped into a bear pit. Generous as was the size of his engine, yet it was not comparable to those that the members of her own race are credited to possess—and it was no doubt with huskier and more gigantic engines that her cavern had been explored and exploited—and now he is floundering helplessly about inside her, seeking no doubt in vain to reach bottom or touch sides.

To offset this overspaciousness however, Clementine launches upon a campaign of concentrated movement that I watch with growing envy. Wrapping her legs tightly about his back, and throwing her arms wildly about his neck —a familiarity which I hoped he would resent with a "Here now! This fuck is off!" but which brought no such interruption—she thus suspends herself entirely from his body. When, with his knees and hands upon the bed, he raises himself for another dive into the abyss, she comes up clinging to him, much like an agile ape hanging to the bottom of a strong bough. With her whole underside thus unimpeded by pressure upon the bed, she proceeds to perform a series of furious gyrations with her buttocks and the hollow vaginal cylinder that surrounds her visitor's piston, which actually set me dizzy. With quick circular and spiral motions, she manages to keep all sides of her mortar in rapid successive contact with his pestle, thus compensating with artful vaginal counterfeits for what she lacks in snugness and tightness and overcoming the disparity of size and spaciousness.

I could not imagine a woman of our own less-primitive race performing the love act with such unabashed eagerness and furious affirmative activity as she. At best, we can be responsive or abandoned—rarely so aggressive in movement. But that we might well emulate, witness the effect on Charley, who is soon gasping in admiration, "God! But you can do it!" His own attempts at movement are ridiculously futile alongside the mad grinding and pumping of the female wildcat hanging to him.

Now, the climax of her efforts approaching, she suddenly changes from her rotating centrifugal tactics to a quick direct up-and-down motion, rubbing her joy-button upon his member with a frank directness that must have exceeded in effectiveness anything that man's blundering motion could do in dispensing pleasure.

"Fuck me hot!" she pants in ecstatic elation, but Charley's ensuing efforts are an insignificant sideshow compared with the magnificent main. circus of rapid acrobatics that she performs.

Soon she brings on for him that divine discharge which without her active help he could not have engineered for himself in less than an hour. Gasping with the supreme paroxysm of pleasure, he collapses upon her, and as he shoots his white man's sperm into her hybrid body, betraying his racial duty, he murmurs, perhaps from habit, perhaps irresistibly, "I love you!"

Since that dark moment, dear reader, I have heard these words spoken on so many frivolous occasions that they have become meaningless to me. What a man or a woman says at the moment of sexual orgasm is no more to be held against him or her than what is said when one is doubly drunk. I have had men gasp to me at such times everything from "God!" "Mother!" "My sister!" "My wife!" to "Oh! You darling bitch!" or "I will love you forever!" or "I could rip you apart!" every form of endearment, the wildest promises, the most murderous threats—all to be forgotten immediately. Perhaps Charley had his eyes closed and was thinking of me at the time. Who knows? But at that moment, his words added insult to injury. Blind with rage, I wanted to rush upon him and strike him with my fists, to break furniture and mirrors, to denounce him and tell him I had seen all. But suddenly it occurred to me that to do so would be to admit that I had been eavesdropping. I backed away from the open door. I was stifling with hate and anger, with the heat of the lustful scene I had just witnessed, with the still lingering malodor of my earlier miserable experience. I must get into the air and think! I left the apartment quietly.

It was after ten o'clock. I sat on a bench in the nearby park and tried to straighten out the tangle of my thoughts and emotions. I was not jealous. If I had been in love with Charley, no doubt I would now have been bent on murder; but I had looked too objectively upon him—upon all of life, for that matter. Faithfulness? Well, he had never made concealment of the fact that there had been many women before me. I could scarcely read an agreement for chastity into our relations. Vanity? Yes, that was it. Hurt pride. That he should resort to a little nigger wench, so far beneath him in every way, when I was available to him. That my favors should be of insufficient strength to bind him to me, if not forever, at least for the duration of our affair. The piquancy that a man finds in a change of cunt was a principle that I would not recognize. I knew only that, in all modesty, I was more attractive than that nigger, and a better piece all around. Consequently his action was an insult that merited punishment or vengeance.

Revenge—to throw myself into the arms of the first man that came along! That would be the only way to even accounts. It did not occur to me at the time that Charley had paid generously for my virginity and chastity, not I for his. I was just a woman whose vanity had been hurt. Too much reason could not be expected of me under the circumstances. Yet, even as I revolved my plan for vengeance in my mind, I decided that it might be best, after all, to postpone action for a while. I was in no mood for men anyway, what with the two examples of the indiscriminate nature of their lust that had just been presented to me.

I walked down to Broadway and found a public telephone, called Nanette and asked her to meet me downtown at midnight, called Charley and told him hurriedly that I would work late and he needn't wait for me. I did not return to the apartment at all that evening. Nanette and I spent a delicious solacing night together at a hotel for women only. I told her everything. We agreed that men were detestable.

When I saw Charley next day, I gave him no inkling that I knew of his escapade, and of course, he volunteered no information. There was, however, in his appearance, or at least so it seemed to my knowing eye, something remorseful and chastened. He even seemed a bit ashamed of himself, as if to make amends, treated me more tenderly, impersonally; but as a woman I could not quite forgive him. When in the evening he took me to bed earlier than was his practice, I could not help but feel that he did this deliberately to avert suspicion of his recent infidelity. When he had entered me, I cooperated with him to bring on his own ecstasy; but I held myself back entirely. I might lend him my body, but I could not give myself to him.

There was a deep reproach in his eyes as he finished alone. This had never happened before. It hurt his male vanity. Not to wound him too deeply however, I took up my movement anew for the sole purpose of bringing on my own discharge. He remained stiff within me. Like the Grecian women of old, who would spit themselves on the artificial phallus of a statue of Iachus their satyr god, I worked myself up and down with an economical maximum of movement and thus brought on my own critical orgasm. He didn't like my impersonality. It flattered him so little. And it wasn't much fun for him, having me wriggling on his sensitive penis just after he had come and when a little intermission is generally necessary before a man can enjoy further friction.

With such little subtleties did I vent my woman's wrath upon him—indirectly, without committing myself. Our affair, which till recently had filled me only with a conviction of its permanence, now seemed a thing drawing to a close. Charley was pained. He guessed that some intuition had made me vaguely wise to his little African interlude. He tried to bribe my forgiveness with prodigious gifts of clothes and jewels. I did not discourage him. Jewels had an easy money value. Looming in the offing was the time when I would be on my own again. With the vanishment of love, a woman becomes as shrewd and calculating as before she has been generously naive and sincere.

"I don't think I'll go back to school this year," I told him offhandedly toward the end of the holiday recess. "I just don't feel like it." He was surprised, but pleased. Perhaps with the burden of my work lifted, we could once more become the blithesome companions we had been.

I tendered my resignation and went for a round of visits to my instructors to bid them farewell. My favorite was the young professor of psychiatry. I had been most promising in his subject. He called me into his private office and asked me to tell him frankly why I was quitting. I confessed my deep aversion for dissection. Very few men liked it, he told me —hence the small number that go in for surgery after graduation. But it was a necessary part of the curriculum.

He led me on. In a burst of confidence, but stumblingly and with halting words, I told him of that horrible laboratory scene that had been to me the last straw. He laughed reassuredly. Abnormalities were, of course, his "pie."

"Necrophilia, eh? Not exactly to my tastes, but not against my conscience. I know about that attendant Jones. I've made a study of him. This is not his first offense. However, so very few female cadavers pass through the school laboratories that we didn't deem it urgent to discharge or prosecute him. He has an interesting history. At the age of twenty-three, normal and healthy, he married a sickly girl somewhat older than he. On the very nuptial night, as he was about to consummate his marriage, his bride was taken with a heart attack in bed. As he confessed to me, he knew at the time that he should call a doctor; but unwilling to further postpone his possession of her, he went ahead. She died in the midst of the love act and he, though horror-stricken, was yet unwilling to leave his long-desired mate. He remained beside her all night, having connection again and again before he called in aid. Since then he has been slightly deranged. The sight of a dead female can arouse him—

and when it does, his passion is more the compulsion of horror than that of desire. You must pity all creatures, Miss Louise, and condemn none. Of course, I will have that female cadaver removed from his custody. And let me say again how sorry I am that you are leaving us."

The ensuing days were idle days. And the devil finds work for idle hands to do. There was a handsome little page boy of about fifteen who was employed by the house to render odd services to the occupants. He was from upstate, just as I, and his fresh, rosy-cheeked brightness reminded me of the days preceeding my own loss of innocence. Lots of times I would call him to get me some postage stamps or some toilet article from the drugstore, and he would gaze at me with that open worshipful admiration that so eloquently proved that women were to him a still unfathomed mystery. It was just this clean, wide-eyed innocence that captured my interest. Sometimes I would send for him on some pretext, just to see how prettily he blushed when I complimented him on his light golden hair, his perfect complexion, or his graceful gentlemanly bearing.

On one such idle afternoon, I was lying about in a negligee, reading a copy of *The Memoirs of Fanny Hill* which a bookseller had just picked up for me at rather a preposterous price. Charley was at the races. It was Clementine's afternoon off. It was indeed an inflaming situation. I, a young lady of healthy erotic tastes—alone—with the greatest pornographic masterpiece of all time—and my imagination. Soon I found myself writhing about voluptuously as the vividly drawn erotic pictures writhed before my mind. My hand unconsciously caressed my body and came to rest in that sensitive slough whither most things gravitate in a woman's life. I would have thrilled myself with my hand, something I hadn't had occasion to do in ever so long a time, had not the passionate scene I was following come suddenly to an end—as such things will.

Hurriedly I read on, anxious to join in on the very next arousing passage. Fanny comes home one day unexpectedly to find her worthy master betraying her with a slovenly servant wench—the similarity between her and my own recent misfortune—and I suppose something like this happens in every woman's life, whether she discovers it or not—awoke all my former resentment. I read on. Yes, Fanny seeks revenge—as what woman would not? She seduces a handsome young boy who is in her master's service. What could be more logical? Except for that tremendous oversized penis the page, despite his youth, possesses, and that is merely part of the author's dramatic scheme of making every prick she encounters larger than the one before (and even the first one is the largest of all when she meets it again toward the end of her career). My own adventures showed no such perfect architectural design. But I am ahead of myself. My amorous state, my aroused resentment against Charley, and most of all the utterly delicious wickedness of seducing a spotless virginal boy, of giving him first glimpse of heaven and his first knowledge of the wonder of woman—all this appealed to some deep submerged desire within and set my pulse beating wildly.

The book fell from my lap—its insidious work done. The young page Tommy was just the thing. Desire alone would never have brought me to what I was about—nor would revenge alone; but the two motives together were irresistible.

I rang for the page. He was not long in making his appearance. I received him as I was, in my intoxicating dishabille, lying on the bed.

"Tommy," I said, "come closer. You see, your friend is ill."

"You look fine to me, ma'am."

"Oh ho! What a cavalier! Come here. What do you know about women?"

"Nothing much, ma'am—except you are the prettiest woman I've ever seen."

"Thank you, Tommy. Already I feel better. I was going to send you for some headache powders; but perhaps if you keep me company a bit, I'll get well without. Here, sit by me on the bed." And in settling him beside me, I made as if carelessly to give him a little glimpse of my luscious breasts. His eyes were riveted upon my bosom and he was blushing furiously. I took his hands. "Oh, how nice and cool your hands are, Tommy. Do you mind if I put them to my forehead?" He was as in a trance still gazing at my bosom, where the flimsy half-transparent lace and silk of my negligee drooped down to allow a tantalizing view of part of two round, swelling globes, with a soft valley between leading the eye and the imagination down and down.

"What are you staring at so?" I went on. "Don't you know what these are?" and I led his hands to the soft-contoured objects of his inspection. "Don't be afraid. Your mama had these, did she not? And your sister? Now tell me, are mine as nice?"

Timidly and still childishly he handled the exquisite flesh of my breasts; but at every attempt to speak he choked in his throat, so overcome was he. The innocence of his touch served only to inflame me doubly. Was I experiencing the incestuous desire of a mother to take her child into her and so perpetuate herself by the seed of her own body? Or was it just a lasciviousness to which innocence lent a stirring fillip? I only knew that my own countenance was beginning to burn as hotly as the boy's.

I drew his face down to my scented bosom. His soft hot lips kissed me there. "Do you like to play with me, Tommy?" I murmured. "Then go and lock that door." He sprang up, turned the key and came back at once. While he was away, I quickly opened my negligee a little in front, leaving uncovered all of my legs and part of my thighs. He was by my side, now torn between the two sets of views open to him. "Will you remove my slippers, Tommy, please?" I asked, extending my bare legs.

He hastened to obey—gently removed them—and kissed the arches of my feet with uncontrolled ardor. Encouragingly, I played with his hair, then, reaching for one of his hands, placed it high up on my bare thigh.

"Oh, how nice and smooth you are!" he gasped, "and so beautiful!" His fingers moved tremulously back and forth above my knee.

"Am I smooth all over?" I asked, my voice a little cracked by the intensity and diabolical lasciviousness of my feelings. He looked into my eyes worshipfully, questioning. I nodded my head.

"I don't mind a bit, Tommy—you're such a dear boy. Go ahead."

More boldly his hands now weave their caressing way around and upward. The suspense becomes unendurable as he approaches my burning center spot, and to bring the moment of contact nearer, I wriggle my whole body downward to meet his blundering childish hand. At last his fingers reach the tangled silky outposts; but startled, he quickly glides over the hill of love and caresses my lower abdomen, looking extremely abashed. I sighed with disappointment; but, to say the least, I could easily forgive this further proof of the innocence of which I so relished the destruction.

"Tommy," I said softly, "am I so hideous that you refuse to look at me?"

"Oh no!" he expostulated, and guardedly, he let his hand run down my body to that mysteriously shaded meeting place that, when all is said, remained the region of greatest fascination for him.

"If you're afraid to look at it," I laughed, "you might hide it with your hand." With a combination of anxiety and hesitancy he did so—finally mustering enough courage to insert a finger in the slit as I slowly edged my thighs apart to aid him.

I drew him up beside me on the bed, and with my lips slightly parted, invited his awkward but ardent kisses. Then, opening my negligee all the way down the front, I brought him in close to my naked, glowing form. As his hands caressed blindly about my bosm and belly, my own fingers went softly to his trousers, where a bulge, not too phenomenal but yet interesting, merited my investigation. Undetected by him, I opened all his buttons —then softly inserted a finger. He sprung back in affright, then, seeing that my entire front was nude, he buried his face for shame between my breasts.

I laughed delightedly at this youthful compliment. "Have you ever had a woman before?" I asked. He did not seem to comprehend. "Have you ever played this way with a girl or a woman before?"

"Oh no!" he reassured me earnestly, blushing anew.

"Well, then, since you are in love with me, Tommy, and since I'm very fond of you, we're going to do something very nice—" I was beginning to breathe heavily with the weight of gathering desire, "and you mustn't fear anything I do."

With these words, unable to brook further delay, I reached into his trousers and brought out his part. It was scarcely half as large as Charley's, dear reader, but when will people abandon the fallacy that size is the only criterion of pleasure? It was only about four inches long and an inch thick—all that could be expected of the untried and unused plaything of a boy; but it was stiff—and that is what counts most to a woman.

His eyes closed in grateful pleasure as I gently stroked his white pulsating part. Hugging him close to me, I slowly turned onto my back, bringing him over me. Then, with our bodies in the proper position relative to each other, I spread wide my thighs, and myself coupled his throbbing pego to my anxious, hungry cunt. His utter awkwardness made this process not an easy one; but at the same time it delighted and keened me, for it was yet further evidence of his innocence. With the little muscle that guards the entrance to my cunny, I clasped the head of his penis, then giving him the motion by the rhythmic rise and fall of my hips, I asked him to emulate. Fitfully and irregularly he did so, but on his first really vigorous move, his member was torn from my cunny's grasp.

Once more I placed it in position, this time, however, bringing my thighs together and clasping his penis tightly between the lips of my vulva, which, moist and overflowing with the exudations of my own unbearable excitement, gave him sufficient play without danger of losing him again.

So tensed was I for pleasure, so maddening was this wicked situation, and so delicious his irregular, unexpected little motions within me, that my climax came on almost immediately. As I began writhing and moaning in the extremity of my ecstasy, Tommy suddenly stopped and asked solicitously, "Do I hurt you, ma'am?"

"Oh no, dear boy!" I gasped, crushing him closer to me. "Keep on! I love it! Only faster!"

He complied. At once I was bathed in bliss. He kept on with his delightful pressures and frictionings of my clitoris and vulva. I had expected him to go off almost immediately, and here he was outlasting me.

"Do you like it, Tommy?" I asked, as with my motions I now regulated the rhythm which mother nature was teaching him quickly enough. His speechlessness was the most eloquent possible answer. His pretty blue eyes were clouding over, dim and misty with pleasure. For a moment I felt like a goddess bestowing beneficences; but then my rearoused clitty demanded my attention and cooperation. As if my life depended on it, I squirmed and strained to get the utmost from every contact, to myself join in the boy's approaching orgasm. My efforts, as all such dear attempts, were crowned with success. Just as he collapsed upon my soft generous body, quivering and pouring a remarkable torrent of hot, stinging sperm into my vulva, I brought myself up to him with a last thrust, sending down my corresponding internal secretions and causing my drenched cunt to twitch spasmodically around his organ.

Voluptuously we lay thus for a time, then, drying and replacing his part, I pledged him to secrecy, promising to let him come and see me again. So overwhelmingly grateful was he to me for his initiation into the secret rites of Venus that I had difficulty wresting his arms from about my neck and sending him away.

Charley, of course, suspected nothing that evening when he entered into possession of what he still deemed his exclusive private territory.

"Ah," I thought to myself as he fucked me, "if you think that yours alone is the delight of possessing many, of comparing partners, the satisfaction of concealing a wicked secret, you are wrong." And stimulated by such thoughts, I enjoyed the connection much more than I would show.

In the following weeks, I saw increasingly more of Nanette. Freezing out Charley as I was, yielding but not often giving myself, I had need of some reliable satisfaction, and there is nothing so dependable in this respect as a delicious mouth to cunt *soxiante-neuf*. As for Tommy, I lost interest as quickly as he lost his innocence. Handsome as he was, his unsophisticated mentality could not long bear me company. I was very kind to him and tipped him generously at every opportunity; but as for the rest, I told him that what we had done was very wicked and could not be repeated. Imagine! Nanette, on the other hand, was always ready with some intriguing story of the goings-on at her place, and with such stimulations our practices were made ever more enjoyable.

More important still was the data I was avidly gathering from her on Paris—for, dear reader, with the waning of the last bond that held me to crude Yankee-land, my intention of moving to France became definitely crystalized. I confided my intentions to her. Though sorry to lose me, she was glad for my sake. Perhaps she would be able to join me there some day soon. Meanwhile, she aided me with information of every conceivable sort, with concentrated lessons in her language, and with numerous references and addresses of friends.

Before long, I felt as if I could find my way about Paris blindfolded.

Secretly, I made reservations for a future trip to Europe. In those days, a first-class passage on the Cunard liners was only about eighty dollars—and of course, this amount was an insignificant part of the few thousand I was able to realize on my jewels. Unknown to any but Nanette, too, I bought a trunk which I filled with such of my gowns and possessions as I wished to take with me, and stored it at the steamship company's piers. There remained only to affect a satisfactory final break with my protector—and that was not difficult.

As the springtime approached, with its renewal of sexual urges in mankind, I made no effort to come up to Charley's requirements. I never told him nay—and yet at the same time I managed things so that he rarely asked for another. Soon he made no attempt to conceal his dissatisfaction, though unwilling to give me up he was still.

After starving him as much as possible, I set the stage for my finale. To Clementine, from whose attitude I gathered there had been resumption of engagements, I made a gift of a number of my dresses, stockings and unmentionables, insisting that she appear at all times clothed only in the most alluring manner. From the standpoint of flaunting, outright provocativeness, she soon had me far outdistanced.

At length my day arrived. Charley was spending the afternoon with me. I kept Clementine much in evidence. My clothes and her natural attractiveness did the rest. Soon most of his glances were for her alone. He watched the lascivious motions of her hips in a manner that I would have resented ordinarily, but which now made me quite glad.

When I felt sufficiently assured of his interest in her, I pretended suddenly to remember that I had some important shopping to do. Charley made no effort to dissuade me. In fact, he could scarcely conceal his eagerness to have me go.

"How long will you be gone?" he asked.

"Oh, for quite a long time," I said.

I left; but went only as far as the street, then, timing before my mind's eye the precedure for overcoming the chaste objections of even the most bashful maid, of leading her to the bedroom and maneuvering her unwilling fall—allowing even time for engineering the entrance into the tightest conceivable cunt—I returned to the apartment, admitting myself quietly.

"Fuck me hot!" were the first, now familiar words that met my ears. I presumed that things were nearing the proper crisis. Humming aloud, I walked ostentatiously into the boudoir. This time Charley was at the bottom of the amorous heap, lying on his back, his trousers down. Upon him, her clothes high above her hips, uncovering her splendid thighs and buttocks, rode Clementine, with a fury equaled only by the charioteers in the days of Ben Hur.

He saw me enter and made as if to rise. But Clementine in the complete savagery of her lust would not let him up, but glancing around for a moment, continued her passionate pumping contortions. Hers was the right idea after all. As long as she was caught, she might as well get the full benefit of her misdemeanor.

"Don't mind me"—I made my speech clearly, indifferently—"and don't stop on my account by any means. I have merely returned for my traveling bag and some clothes. I am sailing for Europe this very evening. Now, children, just go ahead and have a nice time while I get my things." And playfully, I slapped Clementine's heaving posterior.

By the time I had hurriedly thrown my remaining possessions into my valise, Charley stood before me, nervously readjusting his trousers. Whether he had finished or not, I did not know.

"What does this mean, Louise?" he demanded piteously.

"A fine question for you to ask me, indeed —while you stand there buttoning yourself! It means merely that I have known all along what you two were doing. I don't blame you a bit. But you can't expect me to enjoy it. I have my pride, you know—and rather than wait till you cast me out into the gutter, I am leaving you. My ship sails tonight, and all my arrangements have been made. No ill feelings, I want you to understand. Just good common sense. I'm grateful for everything you've done for me, Charley—and if ever you think of me in the future, you will concede that you have had your money's worth. Now let's shake hands and part as good friends as we met."

Tears came to his eyes. He fell to his knees abjectly, kissing my hand again and again. In a broken voice he succeeded in murmuring,

"I've acted like a cad, Louise. I deserve the worst, I know. But won't you give me another chance?"

My heart went out to him. Our delicious months of intimacy could not pass, surely, without leaving some residue, no matter how small, of genuine affection. For a moment I was tempted to abandon all my plans and stay. But a greater wisdom reminded me of the futility of trying to revive dying embers. The end must come sooner or later.

Gently I released myself from his embrace. "Good-bye, Charley," I whispered. "Best of luck to you! I'll write you from Paris." And then, ashamed of the utter sentimentality of this tearful leave-taking, I allowed my beastly cynicism to come to the fore.

"Oh, by the way, Clementine," I addressed the cowering mulatto, as I made my exit, "your master needs cheering badly. So be sure to fuck him hot."

THE END

CARROLL & GRAF

GREAT EROTIC FICTION FROM CARROLL & GRAF

VICTORIAN CLASSICS (MASS MARKET)

❏ Anonymous / Carnal Knowledge	7.95
❏ Anonymous / Autobiography of a Flea & Other Tart Tales	5.95
❏ Anonymous / The Best of the Erotic Reader	7.95
❏ Anonymous / The Best of the Erotic Reader II	7.95
❏ Anonymous / The Best of the Erotic Reader III	7.95
❏ Anonymous / Carnal Knowledge	7.95
❏ Anonymous / Confessions of an English Maid & Other Delights	7.95
❏ Anonymous / The Cunning Linguist	7.95
❏ Anonymous / Eroticon	4.95
❏ Anonymous / Eroticon II	4.95
❏ Anonymous / Eroticon III	4.50
❏ Anonymous / Fallen Woman	4.50
❏ Anonymous / Getting it Good	7.95
❏ Anonymous / Intimate Memoirs	7.95
❏ Anonymous / A Man with a Maid & Other Entertainments	7.95
❏ Anonymous / More Black Magic	7.95
❏ Anonymous / Pagan Delights	7.95
❏ Anonymous / Pure No More	6.95
❏ Anonymous / Romance of Lust	7.95
❏ Anonymous / Secrets & Scents	6.95
❏ Anonymous / Tropic of Lust	4.50
❏ Anonymous / Victorian Fancies	4.50
❏ Anonymous / Wet Dreams	6.95
❏ Cordell, Cleo / The Flesh Constrained	6.95
❏ Cordell, Cleo /Temptation and Torment	5.95
❏ van Heller, Marcus / Seduced	6.95
❏ van Heller, Marcus / Sweet Friction	7.95
❏ van Heller, Marcus / Venus in Lace	3.95

❏ Villefranche, Anne-Marie / Confessions d' Amour	6.95
❏ Villefranche, Anne-Marie / Passion d'Amour	7.95
❏ von Falkensee, Margarete / Blue Angel Confessions	6.95
❏ "Walter" / My Secret Life	7.95

Trade Paper
Jakubowski, Maxim (ed.) /

❏ The Mammoth Book of Erotica	10.95
❏ The Mammoth Book of Historical Erotica	10.95
❏ The Mammoth Book of International Erotica	10.95
❏ The Mammoth Book of New Erotica	10.95
❏ Lloyd, Joan / Black Satin	8.95
❏ Lloyd, Joan / The Love Flower	10.95
❏ Lloyd, Joan / Slow Dancing	9.95
❏ Scott, G.C. / His Mistress's Voice	9.95
❏ Scott, G.C. / Their Master's Voice	10.95
❏ Schimel, Lawrence /	
The Mammoth Book of Gay Erotica	10.95

Available from fine bookstores everywhere or use this coupon for ordering.

Mail order to: Publishers Group West, attention: Order Dept., 1700 Fourth Street, Berkeley, CA 94710, or fax to (510) 528-3444.

Please send me the books I have checked above. I am enclosing $_____ (please add $4.00 shipping & handling charges for the first book, $.75 for each addtional book. International shipping & handling $5 for first book, $1 for each additional book.* rates in effect at time of publication; subject to change.

❏ Check ❏ Money Order (US dollars only. No COD orders accepted)

Credit Card #_____ Exp. Date:_____

❏ MasterCard   ❏ VISA   ❏ American Express

Signature_____
   (if paying with credit card you must sign this form)
Mr. / Mrs. / Ms._____

Address:_____

City:_____ State / Zip:_____

Please allow four to six weeks for delivery. All orders ship via 4th class mail.